SHELTER FROM THE STORMS

LINDA CAGGIANO

I

SHELTER FROM THE STORMS

This Journal belongs to: *Sara Anastasia Johnson,*
Address: *At the present time I have no address*
I am somewhere, a long, a very long way away from home.
Currently riding around in the back of a military re-
location vehicle.
Date: *8ᵗʰ October-2197.*

We, meaning the entire human race – have been hijacked, dragged into this horrendous situation like innocent lambs to the slaughter. The official reports say that over an undetermined number of years, an exclusive group of academically gifted Science Graduates, young men and women, have been hand-picked for their outstanding aptitude in one area and one area only: Geo-engineering - Master of Applied Sciences Climate Modification and Adaptation research. Or ASCMA. The candidates were relocated to various nameless establishments – owned and operated by Sphere Research Laboratories. Of the fifteen laboratories owned by Sphere Research, three were traced to remote areas in different zones (Locations undisclosed at this time) All three facilities are co-owned and operated by eminent scientists, however their involvement in these clandestine activities have only very recently come to light.

These covert laboratories performed experiments eschewed by mainstream science. Three extremely secretive research laboratories, dedicated to studying, reviewing data and meticulously revising the intricate multidimensional complexities, and intricately convoluted behavioural patterns within the ranges of Normal: Heavy: Severe: Tropical: and Catastrophic weather patterns and conditions across the globe.

Sphere Research Laboratories felt confident that the timing was right. They considered the three teams to be more than capable, they were prepared, after all, they had twenty-one of the very finest brains in the scientific world who'd joined forces dedicating themselves exclusively to this unique project, and what's more, they believed they were better equipped at that point in time than ever before. They'd assured themselves they possessed the technology vital to the success of the experiment. Disregarding the immutable fact that their technology was still very much in the experimental stage. Their technology at that point was untried, untested and *unproven* outside of the strictest laboratory conditions. Yet somehow, they had convinced themselves *and* their superiors, that their information, their calculations and the statistics were all 100% accurate. But above all else, they were supremely confident that with their abilities combined, they were ready to take complete control of the weather.

However, we – being the entire Human race - now know that their research was hopelessly flawed, somewhere along the line something, or someone, had miscalculated, they were wrong, so very, very wrong – *on-every-single-count.*

And now *we* are paying the price for their arrogance. We are paying with our lives.

Mother Nature is ever vigilant, she'd been watching… and waiting. She's been fully aware of every supersonic, ultrasonic and subsonic-charge being directed into the void of space, and deeply troubled by the unstable, irregular and uneven pulsations having far-reaching, highly undesirable effects on the rhythms within her universe. The scientists believed they understood why, in the most recent series of laboratory tests the results achieved hadn't quite been what they'd anticipated. Denying even to themselves that they actually weren't anywhere near as prepared as they'd believed, and being unwilling to delay further, they ultimately agreed that they'd erred with the settings, they were too low. After discussions that lasted for days on end, they reasoned that by delivering significantly more clout to the load, a resounding success along with global recognition would be their reward.

It was the day we now know they not only failed utterly and absolutely, but they'd succeeded only to rape and violate every law of Nature, and in doing so, surrendered planet Earth to its doom...

For long, terrifying months nature's been retaliating, demonstrating the immensity of her powers, she's refused to relinquish control and is giving the planet Earth a very arduous lesson. It will be a lesson that no one will ever forget... that is *if anyone can survive* such relentless ferocity.

This evening the sunset seemed to be such a long, drawn-out process. Almost as though the daylight was making the utmost of its time, and prolonging a day that for all of us, has been so unpredictable, so fraught with menace, panic, with dread, and many times, stark terror. Today has been beyond terrifying and I'm positive that I wasn't the only one who was convinced that every man woman and child, every animal and every bird crowded together in this convoy of trucks, was about to die.

I am not, nor have I ever been, a particularly religious person, but I'll readily admit that after the knuckle-biting experiences we have, by some quirk of fate, managed to survive today, I feel blessed, truly blessed, to still be alive and to, well, to still be able to appreciate this incredible, really awe-inspiring display of pure beauty, especially after witnessing so much devastation, and so much unimaginable savagery on such a cataclysmic scale. The only real comparison was made by one of the boys, who at one point cried "I think we're stuck inside a horror movie and can't get out" and that kind of sums up our situation.

But right at this moment – this quiet, calm, even serene evening, belies the rampant ferocity we've somehow lived through today. At long last the brutal, eyeball searing force of the sun has been gradually decreasing, as it fades away the stifling air temperature is easing off to a more manageable level than it was a few hours ago, but even so it's still far hotter at night in what is actually mid-winter, than at noon on a mid-summer day in a heatwave. By rights, at this time of year we should be waist deep in snow. A little boy, he's probably about three years old, came to stand with me. He told me his name's Patrick, but his mummy let's everyone call him Paddy. When I asked him how old he was, he looked up and holding up five wiggling fat fingers, told me proudly, that he's fwee years old! "I had a birfday party with fwee red balloons, a cake, and I got a bag of sweeties!"

He was standing close, holding onto my hand and pointing up at the wonderful, though somewhat peculiar colour waves in the sky saying "look at the priffy sky uppy dere" oh, he's such a little cutie, he really is!

We were both watching the fantastic colours changing with the setting sun; a lingering, shimmering light, was giving us a truly magnificent fantasy display of luminous golden oranges, brilliant greens misted into yellows and all the colours were bleeding into an intense, fiery red that had been gently swept through with delicate wisps of purple. Those incredible colours glowed through the entire length of silvery wraithlike clouds that hung motionless, filling the heavens. The exquisite blending of colours has set tonight's picture-perfect horizon ablaze, it was like looking through a magical kaleidoscope.

While we stood there marvelling at this enchanting spectacle, slowly, but surely, I became all too aware of my tired aching arms, my weak knees and shaking legs, the tender neck muscles; and oh my, my poor battered and bruised spine feels as though it's still trying to crack right through the top of my pulsating scull. My hands, knees and feet are all equally as sore, torn and bleeding where the flesh has been gouged out –pretty painfully too in some places, from scraping along the old dried out and damaged wooden flooring that is full of long splinters, and from sliding over and over again across the really rough old wooden bench seats, that for self-preservation, we've all been forced to hang onto for dear life. I couldn't help skidding around all over the place, even though I tried desperately hard not to, but more than a few dozen times it was impossible to keep a decent grip. Why? You might well ask … Well, it's because whoever was driving this old rattle trap truck thinks he's an exceptionally brilliant, highly skilled, racing car driver. He's not.

Yes, I do know, and *yes, I do understand* that they need to cover as much territory as is humanly possible in the shortest possible time, even though it's to a completely unknown destination – and that's only *if* there is somewhere left for us to go to, but… as far as the people inside, well we were all left feeling that we're just so much cargo! Well… hello there Mr *driver*, we've got a news flash for you. We're all actual living, breathing, *people* here in the back, we're *not* crates of *cargo*! Oh, and as if all the bouncing and sliding around wasn't difficult enough, the next minute he'd change down into a lower gear to thundering over, across, or through, the countless deep potholes in the roads. Seriously? It felt like he was trying to force yesterday's breakfast back out through our ears. And he's darn near succeeded, quite a few times! Surely, he could have at least *tried* to miss *some* of those craters!! I'm beginning to think he deliberately finds the biggest, widest, and deepest ones in some sort of crazy contest he's got going on with the other truck drivers, probably to see who can be the first to catapult a passenger out through the roof - because they're all driving these antiquated trucks the same stupid way.

I'm young, and I'm fairly fit and strong, but I have to say, I have one heck of a lot of trouble hanging on, so I feel really bad for the two older ladies in this truck, because the poor things are quite literally, being tossed around like they're in a giant popcorn machine!

Unfortunately for those poor ladies, they'll be covered in painful black and blue bruises from their heads all the way down to their toes by tomorrow morning, and *that* will make travelling so much more unpleasant for them. I have the feeling it'll probably be an even longer, and more miserable day for those poor ladies than it will be for the rest of us, and believe me, *that's* really saying something.

I closed my eyes for a few moments trying to clear my mind of all thoughts, and just for those moments I surrendered myself to the soothing sensation of being cloaked in complete serenity, savouring the simple pleasure of being able to stand upright and motionless, in spite of the too warm gluey mud that's oozed up between my bare toes and is creeping towards my knees. In that one single, magical moment, I found some peace in this twilight silence, and even if this's only going to be a brief respite from all the jiggle and bounce – it's so very welcome.

When I opened my eyes again l was surprised to find that complete darkness had claimed victory over the sun, and has -hopefully- brought this dreadful, day, to a close.

Looking up, the night sky was awash with brilliant pinpoints of light resembling trillions of tiny diamonds scattered across a black velvet cloth.

Standing outside, and away from the closed-in confines of the truck, breathing is so much easier. For a short while we've been allowed to climb down and take whatever pleasures this somewhat cooler night air has to offer. After breathing in the sour, hellishly overheated thick air we've struggled with all day; the night air's a soothing balm to our dried-up throats.

So many bodies are crowded into such an itty-bitty space, each person is squished up against or wedged between complete strangers, everyone's irritable and short-tempered because we struggle for every breath, and choke on the stale super-heated dry air that reeks of old dust, we're jammed so tight inside trucks that are roasting under the blistering sun. To add to the list of pleasantries, everyone, myself included, is sweating profusely, as much from fear, as from the punishing heat. I heard someone from another truck say they feel as though they've been entombed or buried alive! I'm pretty certain that every person in this truck, and in all likelihood everyone in every other truck in this convoy has been left feeling exactly the same way too. It's been such a long, intense and emotionally demanding day, another immensely difficult day for everyone. Even while we're all complaining we know full well that we're actually fortunate to be under the thick canvas, yes, it's suffocating and yes, it's hotter than hell, but it's shielding and protecting us from exposure to the sheer brutality and savage intensity of the sun, without it none of us would survive more than a few hours. *If* one could even survive those few hours because this incredible heat sucks every drop of moisture out of a body in no time at all, leaving only a desiccated husk behind. At least we've been spared that horror.

My heart really goes out to all these little kids though, I'd assumed that they were either friends, related somehow, or at the very least that they knew each other, but a few minutes ago I was told that that's simply not true at all. In fact, the greater majority of these children are actually displaced! They've originally come from so many different districts, the younger ones don't even know exactly where they lived prior to being loaded into these vehicles, and tonight they're understandably *very* distressed. They're scared, upset by all the strangers, and by the weirdness of absolutely *everything*. It's no wonder they're so irritable. And in this situation, who could blame them? I think it's a normal reaction, because, well naturally they want to be with *their own* families, but no-one knows *where* those families are now, if it comes to that, we don't know where *we are* or where we're *going* either, so no-one can truthfully say whether or not we might meet up with them again at some point. What's also making things so much harder for them, is that there's *nothing* for them to do inside the trucks, nothing to keep them occupied, so they're not only scared, they're bored silly as well, and that's making them even rattier. Now they're arguing, and under these, what can only be described as the most frustrating conditions, I reckon that's only to be expected; these kids are hot, they're tired, thirsty, and really hungry, they're scared because they probably think they've been abandoned, and that alone is enough to make each and every one of them terribly, dreadfully, frightened, and sick at heart.

The truck I've been traveling in today is different from the one I was in yesterday, and it's more than likely that I'll be in a different one again tomorrow. Some of us in this convoy have grown up together, so we know and get along with each other extremely well, but instead of keeping us all together -as any logical person would expect, nope, not a chance, instead we've been shuffled around, and put in with complete strangers, some are from the much larger, High Ridge towns - and to be perfectly honest, one of those groups is, for whatever reason, being truly hostile and hateful toward the rest of us, even though we were all practically neighbours! These people are from the cattle breeding community that sits high up on the ridge, and directly above my little home village, Shady Haven.

There is no first-class seating in this convoy, it's *all* cattle class, and I think that is their major objection! They don't want to mix with the riff raff... While I know a couple of these ladies by sight, I don't know any of them personally, and even though two of those ladies are invariably pleasant, polite and kindly toward everyone, their husbands are the exact opposite. Those men are proving themselves to be *the* rudest, most selfish, and downright nastiest people to have as unavoidable travelling companions, and believe me, they're real thorns in our already sore backsides.

The Marine Sergeant - we were informed that *Master Gunnery Sergeant Tyler,* is his full title, or would it be his rank? I'm not sure. Well, whatever it is, he seems to think that seeing as though we're all traveling together, we should become *familiar,* and get to know each other! Huh as if that's ever likely to happen! Does he actually believe that we consider this to be some sort of a fun holiday excursion, perhaps a delightful overland cruise or what? (If it is – I'll take that refund now please!)

Exactly *how* we're supposed to get all warm and fuzzy with each other when we're shut up inside of a dark, overcrowded, overheated, extremely claustrophobic, noisy and horribly smelly canvas box, a box that rocks and bounces us all over the place incessantly, often heaving us around like loose bowling balls, is beyond me. Unless of course he considers having our heads knocked together, getting an elbow in the face or bouncing into, onto, or across each other, on these wooden seats, getting our hands, legs, feet, and our backsides full of splinters, or landing –usually face first- in some strangers' lap, or else falling down and landing at their feet – to be getting familiar. Really? He's gotta be kidding! I'd like *him* to spend just one twenty-four-hour period riding in the back (I'd gladly give his comfortable seat up front to one of the older ladies) and we'll see how *familiar* or *friendly he* feels by the end of the day. I reckon he'd be changing his mind pretty damned quick, most likely within the first fifteen minutes!

We've come such a long, long, way away from homes, but the world outside isn't even vaguely recognisable as being a part of our planet anymore. We're surrounded, in every direction, and at every turn, by death and unimaginable devastation, it's everywhere.

Every single person here has been uprooted and taken away from everyone, everything and everywhere, familiar. As things are now, we have nothing left, our homes, our jobs, the children's schools, and for so many in this big mixed-up group, myself included, our families and closest friends, have all been lost to us too. There's no way of knowing how long it will be until we see them again, or if we'll *ever* see any of them again. Can anyone even begin to imagine how that feels, the emptiness, the hopelessness of it all, and what it does to you inside? Or the way it messes with your head?

The very last news broadcast I saw was, I can't remember *when* exactly but it was weeks ago, anyhow, we learned that the president, her entire family, all of her many aids, the top military chiefs, and our Zone States' military, aeronautical, commercial and financial personnel, along with the current and historical medical records -in their entirety- have been relocated to the survival bunkers. In addition to those most fortunate people, there have been many Horticulturists relocated to the bunkers as well, complete with countless numbers of seed varieties taken from preservation vaults, and many live specimens ready to be transplanted for their food supply. They have the DNA of every species of plant be they: fruit, vegetable, flower, grass, bush or tree, on planet earth. There is also said to be a large assembly of Specialised Zoologists' who have the DNA and specimens of every animal, bird, insect, fish, any, and all, known ocean vegetation and inhabitant, each specimen has been logged with accompanying scientific data. It was also being reported that there was a two-mile-long convoy of InterCity coaches transporting the most brilliant, musically and academically gifted young people. Those lists were restricted to only the most exceptional, most intelligent, truly incredible children and teens. There are dozens of medical research teams, surgical and nursing personnel taken from every sector of the medical field. The DNA profile of every person who has ever been registered in the Main Zone State has been documented, verified and stored. Each of the selected personnel have been transferred to one of the numerous survival bunkers. The layouts and furnishing of the living quarters within the bunkers have been reported as being rather extravagant too. Each of the vast survival shelters was constructed and specifically designed, to meet the requirements and comfort essential for the new occupants. Each underground shelter contains separate, individual living pods to accommodate the new community comfortably.

The multi-level survival bunkers are many hundreds of feet down, deep inside the earth, they have been built beneath the mountains, with each bunker connected to the others via a vast network of subterranean road tunnels. The commentator said that these high-tech survival bunkers were located in *each* Major Zone, *plus* they are (apparently) able to comfortably sustain each of the thousands of inhabitants, plus their descendants, for at least one hundred years - or permanently- should it prove necessary. As the bulletin ended so did the power supply, and any future information.

There have been fantastical rumours doing the rounds for years, telling of complete underground cities being built in case of another Global War, and even though I didn't believe one word of it then -I sure do now- and I imagine Mother Nature's Retribution would fall under the banner of warfare quite well.

In that last ever news bulletin, the commentator delivered a real hammer blow when he reported that *countless millions* of people in Major Zones, minor settlements, and even whole islands, have vanished to no-one knows where.

Am I the only one who finds it impossible to get their head around a report that tells me countless people, entire communities, even whole islands and their populations have been completely wiped from the face of the earth?

There doesn't seem to be a definitive, or a fixed point of origin to all this devastation either since all weather patterns *–globally–* just went completely berserk, quite literally overnight. It's just too far beyond anything my poor simple brain can even begin to grasp. I suppose that being out on the coast, where I've lived my whole life, and being so far removed from the concerns of any large city or industrial zones, where the populations number in multiple millions, I highly doubt we'd even have a hundred people living in Shady Haven, so we've always considered ourselves to be isolated, private, carefree, unimportant and untouchable. Peaceful, quiet, Shady Haven was nearly unknown to the outside world and therefore, in our minds, unchanging and everlasting. And that was certainly true as far as anything concerning the major centres or the larger, very densely populated areas were concerned anyway. Yeah, well not any more my friend, because as it's turned out even being tucked away in our tiny, close-knit coastal community, we weren't immune to the terrifying changes either, quite the contrary really, what we'd long considered to be security in isolation, was merely an illusion. We were warned –oh, it was ages ago now, that living right on the coast, we would be first in line for a whole lot of truly deadly, absolutely ferocious storm conditions too. For the first time in my *life*, I heard back-to-back Tsunami warnings. 'Tectonic plates are shifting at a rate never before recorded, there are catastrophic off the scale earthquakes ripping the earth apart, mountain ranges are collapsing, rivers and lakes are disappearing, multiple enormous sink holes are appearing, they're swallowing up people, herds of livestock, vehicles and machinery, multiple building multiplexes are being swallowed whole, leaving deadly, seemingly bottomless holes in the heavily populated coastlines hundreds and hundreds of miles long' and according to one news report 'more than thirty miles wide, are breaking away and crumbling into the sea.' The announcers' dreadful words continued 'There have been rolling volcanic eruptions both on land and deep beneath the seabed, swallowing small and large islands alike. Volcanos long believed to be extinct have been erupting, they're generating Tsunami's that've wiped out millions of people in far off zones, there are dense layers of ash clouds being spread even further by the storm winds, blanketing the ground in some places, burying whole areas in others, but effectively blocking the sunlight and turning day into everlasting night for thousands of miles around. The polar icecaps are almost completely melted now and raising the sea level, it's unprecedented in all earth's history, recorded or otherwise.' the broadcaster was shouting, it sounded like he was practically frothing at the mouth, and his agitation came through the speakers and curled around the dread that's already taken root in your gut ' There are wildfires raging out of control in every zone where the incredibly intense heat has sucked the moisture out of the forests turning them tinder dry.' Maybe I don't know much about what goes on in other zones, but one thing I *do* know for certain – this amazing earth of ours is in serious, deadly trouble.

They wouldn't, or I suppose with all the turmoil and ~~widespread~~ wholesale destruction, perhaps they can't really give us any accurate information about the storms. A while ago we asked *why* the frequency was escalating so rapidly, plus how or why the frequency of the storms have changed from being sporadic, and fairly minor, into these hellishly powerful and tremendously destructive, monstruous hurricanes. We're still waiting for a proper answer to that.

The highly scientific response we *did* get was – 'we just don't know.' Well, jeez that's really informative, not to mention helpful.

One day a small convoy of trucks rolled into Shady Haven ostensibly to give us some assistance, but when the order to *evacuate* came, it wasn't only a shock, it was so unexpected and so pressured. We were ordered, not asked, not invited, but ordered, to get out of our homes. We were given a list of items that each person was to supply, and told to pack only the barest minimum of personal essentials. A few things we might need for the immediate future, and leave everything else, in other words leave our entire lives, behind. So right now, we're like some crazy band of wandering gypsies. Unfortunately for us, we're also missing the fortune teller and her crystal ball…

We were packed up and shoved into the backs of these old trucks, with our bags, boxes, and barrels of water, (as per previously mentioned orders) and shipped out like so much cattle – the only real difference is, cows have a monetary value- and so would be treated with much more consideration – but for us mere humans there was no time to even try to find a way of contacting any family or pass on information.

Oh dear God, *my mother!* If she's been able to get back home only to find me, and just about everyone else in Shady Haven gone – just disappeared … she'll be absolutely out of her mind and totally hysterical by now. I really don't mean to sound quite so selfish or self-centred, and I'm fully aware that I'm not the only person who's been caught up in this damned dreadful situation either. I absolutely do understand that so many other people need to locate their family members, or at the very least to notify them as to their probable whereabouts as well. The way I see it, far too many families have been separated, and unfortunately for many, these marines – while their initial objectives or intentions were probably very honourable, their timing was abysmal, and the initiation of their orders has been nothing less than deplorable. In their haste, they've managed to separate and fragment whole families. Children have been loaded into one truck and sent off in one direction while the truck containing their *parents* has driven off in another direction entirely. We're not total morons, we all know and understand this evacuation was an urgent, spur of the moment change of orders, but the way they just shoved bodies into their trucks, so many and so much in this truck and so many and so much goes in that truck, there was very little, or what's more likely to be the case, absolutely *no* thought or consideration given at all to what might happen to the occupants next. Too much action and zero practical thought. You know what, I bet they keep their guns and bullets together though!

Okay, take that little boy last night, Patrick, Paddy, the cute little kid who came over to hold my hand, well he's a perfect example – I can only presume, and hope, that his parents, his grandparents and his four brothers and sisters are all together, but they're in a different convoy now, and that convoy is headed to goodness only knows where, because they certainly aren't anywhere in this group – I've checked … Bless him, he's just a tiny little kid for heaven sakes. But somehow in all the mad grab, shove and rush, he got mixed up, pushed aside, or else he was going to be the one over the allotted number for that truck, so he's ended up part of this group, except now he's out here on his own. What's supposed to happen to him? I can't begin to imagine how worried sick his family must be. The poor little fellow must feel like an orphan, okay, well that makes two of us, so maybe we can be orphans together. At any rate, he seems to have chosen me to be his stand-in mother for now. Actually, the longer this evacuation and relocation process takes – the more likely our staying together becomes. I just don't know what to think any more, everything's gotten so far out of hand, so mixed and messed up, besides, it sure isn't what anyone expected ...it's borderline madness now; too much of the unexpected has happened, is happening ... and no-one has a clue, let alone knows for sure, what to expect next.

Early on Tuesday morning it was probably nearly a month – maybe five weeks ago now, my mother and grandma hitched the trusty, very old double horse trailer, up to Big Red, that's what my gran calls her equally aged ATV. Mum, gran, and five neighbours all piled into the truck, pretty much the way you'd expect old friends and neighbours to do, and off they went. And you know what, I'll bet that they were all singing *-really badly-* the whole one hundred and thirty-three miles to Solemner Gorge. That's where the biggest market is, ha, what am I saying ... it's where the *only* produce stores and markets are now.

All the other coastal and roadside markets have been washed out! Their plan was to buy enough basic foods to keep themselves, and our other more elderly, neighbours, going for a good while longer. Just in case the main road went underwater too, because even on horseback it'd be impossible to get out again for quite a while. Mum, gran and the others were likely taking the last chance to stock up because there's been so much talk and uncertainty around the ever-increasing storm activity, but whatever the situation – people have *still* got to eat. But they left home twenty whole days *before* our evacuation! Naturally, with the uncertain weather conditions, the timing for their return home was always a bit vague, but they'd expected to be away for only two or three days, four at the most. Although that plan went down the drain pretty much straight away, because anyone who'd gone out to the market that day has been stranded indefinitely, a couple of what they've called 'minor' storms hit very close to Solemner Marketplace meaning the only useful road between Shady Haven and Solemner Gorge was under deep water in low lying areas and the water might have been too deep for my mother to risk driving back home – especially dragging a heavily loaded trailer. After the heart stopping storms yesterday, and the intense lightning storms last night, I've got to admit we've been really fortunate. So far. You might be wondering about the hoary old vehicles my grandma and others are still using and why they haven't changed over to electric vehicles. Well, driving the rough terrain out along the coast, and the long and very rough distances it's necessary to travel, the significantly lighter, far less robust machines that, let's be honest now, are really only suited to smooth roads and short distance city driving, oh and charging the batteries in those vehicles is always a *huge* problem because out here the power supply is pretty 'iffy' most of the time, which is why we still rely on wood burning stoves, oil lamps and candles. This terrain absolutely destroys anything like those flimsy electric cars, so we're still reliant on the very limited supply of fossil fuels for our private 'can go anywhere' vehicles.

We'd covered quite a few miles and had left Shady far behind when we first noticed those fearsome black clouds gathering. We watched them thickening until they blocked out the blazing sun in the distance, we could definitely hear the wind screaming and we most certainly felt the shock waves from the incredible thunder shaking the earth underneath the truck, we could even smell the strong, muddy odour of the rain, but luckily for us the storm turned, it twisted away from where we'd stopped. I don't know how much, or if anything at all will be left standing in Shady Haven for them to go home to. What happens to them if everything's gone? Where else can they go? With no e.web or phones, I can only hope that my beautiful ladies will stay safe and well.

From my earliest childhood memories, storms have always been thrilling for me. I'd ride buttercup, my yellow bicycle, out to the triangle of boulders on the headland. Happily, I was small enough to squeeze in between them. I'd lean my back against the largest stone and with another great big rock on each side - they were like my own personal windbreaks- and watch the storm coming across water. There I'd be, wrapped up warm, and completely dry, inside my grandpas smelly, age blackened oilskin poncho, with my ten-year-old head almost lost inside the huge floppy, man-size hood. I can't tell you how much I delighted in the fat drops of sweet smelling rain falling around me, pinging off the stones and dribbling off the hood, or how, when the thunder crashed so loud my ears popped, or when lightning put on a spectacular show over the ocean, especially for me, but then there were plenty of other times too, when I'd just sit, lost in thought, trying to figure out *how* a breeze, so gentle that it hardly even disturbed the long grass, could suddenly become a violent current of air strong enough to rip leaves and branches right off a tree and whip the little ripples into those enormous, froth capped mountains of water.

But even the biggest, and the baddest of the storms back then, were tame by comparison, and were never, not in the slightest little bit like the savage, unnaturally ferocious storms we've been experiencing lately. I tell you; these really strange weather patterns are so *totally* different from anything, weather related that is, that I've ever seen, felt, or even heard of before. There's no beauty or magnificence in *these* storms that's for sure. The storms coming through now are truly malicious. They drop down out of nowhere, and just smash their way through the land, like colossal waves on the ocean, rolling in one on top of the other and levelling everything in their path. I've heard people saying "it's just pot luck where they come down" but believe me, these storms have purpose, they're hell bent and determined to destroy any, and everything, in whatever path they choose. These storms are just scything their way through everything, and nothing, not a single darned thing, stands a chance against them.

Every time, without exception, and without any kind of normal forewarning, the 'arrival' of a storm isn't a slow build up, it doesn't gradually develop, it's *declared* –like a war. Simultaneously there'll be total and utter blackness, and absolutely outrageous hurricane-force winds. Ahh but then, as if those two together aren't quite ruthless enough on their own, about three heartbeats later, comes a miles wide impenetrable wall of ridiculously heavy, lashing rain which rapidly, and invariably, becomes a floodwater and the incredible power behind that water just rips up and washes away anything and everything in its way. Nothing, no living thing, human or animal, no structure, building, road or rail, regardless of strength, and no vehicle, be it for land, air or sea, can possibly withstand such appalling ferocity.

Ahh yes, and then we have the often-asked question: "What about the impudent, idiotic cretins that triggered this mayhem?" Well, you may as well know the truth - they've disappeared, they've all magically vanished without a trace. To my own mind they're just overconfident, narcissistic, egotistical fools, that turned coward the instant they realised they'd got it wrong. And yet, they'd have the unmitigated gall to call themselves *experts* and *scientists*? – My question to them is *why?* What on *earth*, whatever *possessed* you to even *think* you could get away with such an overconfident, arrogant interference with Nature in the first place? One of the very *first* lessons we are taught in science class is that for every action there's a reaction! Did they happen skip that class altogether, were they all in the bathroom for that part of the lesson or what? Mother Nature's been doing just fine -on her own and without anyone's help- for goodness knows how many eons, so why, for pity's sake, *why* couldn't they just leave things well enough alone instead of subjecting the entire planet to this wholesale slaughter and misery?

The marines tried to lessen my fears a little by telling me that all the townspeople over in Solemner Gorge have been most generous, they told me the locals have arranged good, temporary accommodation, as well as food, clothing and medical assistance, for everyone who's been stranded. Apparently, the ladies have all been settled comfortably into various homes and for any men, the local guild hall has been fitted out with beds and seating areas. However, should evacuation from *there* become necessary, it will most certainly be a 'routine military manoeuvre' and all I can say about that last bit is, if it's anything like our own experience, then heaven help them!

That one, very brief snippet, is the sum total of information any of us have been given, and I'm feeling rather more fortunate than most – at least I've been told *something* even if, as I strongly suspect, it may well be a white lie. Up until now we've heard absolutely zilch from anyone directly. In these strange circumstances, that's understandable, even if it is most unsatisfactory, because with such devastation and seriously rampant carnage causing so much unimaginable damage and outright destruction to infrastructure all over this continent, our nuclear power plants were shut down after the very first round of storms as a precautionary measure. Every area was switched back to the old, very old, standards, but for weeks before the evacuation there'd been no gas or electric power, we didn't even have the old telephone cables to fall back on, and since so many of the communication and signal relay towers have been knocked out or destroyed, the result of that catastrophe is no cell phones. Nothing is working, including Wi-Fi. What that means effectively is that there's no e.web, no news, and therefore no information or communications available to anyone. We've really been thrown backwards in time, and left in the dark – in more ways than one. I don't think any of us actually realised exactly how reliant we are on our devices – we don't know anything else, for us, there *are* no other ways, we rely on our electronics. Without them we're completely cut off from each other and from the rest of the world.

While I myself am quite okay at this point in time, my mother and gran can't know that. They don't know where I am, or what's happening to me, nor where I'll be going (but then of course, neither do I) naturally they're going to be worried sick, and obviously the reverse is also true. I've been *told* they're okay, however I can't help wondering if that's still true. Or even if it *was* true when I was told, perhaps I was being fibbed to in an effort to keep me from worrying or making a fuss. So much can, has, and does, change so quickly now, although it's never a change for the better. In another twenty-four hours who knows where any of us might be, or whether any of us will still be alive, or how much else will have changed? My mother and gran are all I really have in this world. The very last thing gran said to me, with her head stuck out of the truck window was –Now be a good girl and keep a real close watch on the house Sara, if the rains come again, be sure to close and lock up all Grandpas windows won't you now?

That house is a symbol her family, her life, and of her greatest love - my grandpa.

I keep worrying about our perfect old family home, I can't help wondering whether there's even a slim chance that it might be still standing, because it's always been so much more than simply a building, or a roof over our heads. I've got nothing else to do, so I'll tell you why.

When my grandpa was a very handsome twenty-year-old, he began courting my grandma, who was an attractive, but very shy, sixteen-year-old. In preparation for their life together, grandpa purchased forty acres of good farming land, and then he started building what has grown over the years, to be our great big rambling old home. He used beautiful light coloured sandstone blocks that were, each and every one of them, quarried, hand cut and shaped by grandpa himself. Each one of those big stones had to be carried out of the (now long closed) nearby quarry using two mule's and a cart. One single block at a time. Grandma often told us the story of how he built their modest, basic four roomed home, and of how over the years, it just grew and grew, until it ended up with seven bedrooms and four bathrooms; the big wide veranda, the original kitchen, the sitting room and the one bedroom were all opened up into what is now a beautifully proportioned family living room. Each time grandma would say – there's another potato in the pot darling – my grandpa would get a big smile on his face and set off to quarry enough stone to add another large bedroom for each child as it came along. The house was a true labour of love from the very first stone to the last, and each block is infused with grandpa and grandma's deep love for each other love that gave their home a strong heartbeat and a beautiful soul. And that's why on the day I felt the earth moving under my feet, in the safest, most solid place I've ever known, well I don't mind telling you, it absolutely terrified me. I had to leave Grandma's china cabinet lying on its side, knowing that all her precious keepsakes have almost certainly been smashed and broken, and all of those beautiful diamond paned leadlight windows that they painstakingly made by hand, sitting with their heads bent close together working by the light of the old oil lamps, have all been blown in and broken too. Poor gran, she's going to be heartbroken when she sees it - well that's *if* she ever sees it again. Because as she's told us all countless times, every brick, every pane of glass, every floorboard, and every single piece of furniture in this home reminds me of your grandfathers love for me. I'm so glad that at least I have such a beautiful memory to take with me to wherever I might end up.

I tried to save as much as I could by emptying out cupboards and stacking things in the centre of the rooms, I took down the dozens of photographs from the walls, off all the cupboards and knick knack tables, and off the baby grand piano. I wrapped everything and covered as much as possible with heavy blankets, I hope it gave at least a bit of protection, but with the way these storms are, well I just don't know how much difference it might have made. I know in my heart that I tried, and gran will know I did too, she'll know I didn't just walk away. I'm so worried. What's become of them? What's happening with our neighbours and the friends who wouldn't leave the Valley? Will there be somewhere left for my mother and grandma to go back to? Have any of our animals or livestock survived? If they have, are they able to find food to eat? Or will the poor things die from starvation, be crushed and suffering or maybe drown? My mind buzzes with the -if's and when's- If our house and farm are able to be saved will *we* be alive to go back to them? When will we all be able to go home again? Oh, and I don't believe for one little minute it's just me thinking this way either, I believe every person in this convoy, marines included, have their own, where-when-how and what if, lists too. About the only thing we do actually have in common is finding that there are far too many questions in our thoughts and our conversations, but not one single answer to be found anywhere. We're painfully aware that we're helpless to do anything other than what we're doing right now. On one hand we're doing our best to survive, to stay alive, trying to stay positive and hopefully, *hopefully* we'll be able to remain reasonably well.

While on the other hand, our minds scream at us, ahh, but for how long though? How long can any of us survive out in the open and exposed to the elements like this?

On the morning we were evacuated, any stragglers were literally thrown bodily into any available space and even before the last person had found somewhere to sit, the trucks just took off racing along at high speed, and certainly going much too fast to navigate the narrow, debris strewn road that led away from our homes toward the inter-connect, with safety. Why the big rush all of a sudden? I wondered, but then I heard a local man cursing loudly and colourfully, while he was craning his neck to see out the back of the truck, so naturally I had to see what he was looking at too. What we saw happening behind us was heartbreaking, no it was so far beyond heartbreaking it was a tragedy, a disaster. You see there were hundreds of perfectly magnificent, old shade trees growing all the way around the high ridge, trees that have stood tall, wide, and strong, gran called them the Proud Sentinels guarding the Upper Valley Ridge Community, and in hottest part of a summer's day, kindly providing deep cool shade over the houses in the valley below, and those trees had had been doing so for well over two hundred years. It was those trees that gave Shady Haven its name. What we saw happening through the open square of flapping canvas in the back of the truck, clearly explained such an urgent need for speed. And even though it was a truly tragic sight, it appeared to have been choreographed, I could only watch in fascinated horror as one, by one, those magnificent, proud giants, came crashing down the hillside, falling almost gracefully, until their beauty, their strength and their pride were ruined, tumbling, snapping and breaking right behind us as these half dozen old army trucks we'd been crammed into tore off, zigzagging, slithering and sliding through the thick mud smeared over the rock strewn track heading out of Shady Haven and onto the highway, where we joined up with a long column of similarly loaded trucks coming out from the Upper Valley Ridge road, and yet still more trucks joining up on the inter-connect from other, even smaller, more remote hamlets, that are strung out for miles up and down the coast road like pearls on a necklace, and together, all twenty eight trucks were headed toward the safety of a military base one hundred and ninety miles away. The whole convoy crawled to a stop and people were reshuffled around to make more room in some of the dangerously overcrowded trucks, I don't know where, when, or even why, unless they had different orders, the other trucks separated from us, but in doing so, they also separated children and parents. From the five trucks in Shady we grew to a convoy of twenty-eight at the highway, sixteen trucks were supposed to break away, leaving twelve trucks – but somehow, we're thirteen trucks now, so I guess somebody missed a turnoff.

Everything's changing *so* fast, unfortunately it's never a change for the better either. The storms are coming more frequently, and are lasting longer now too.

We've become acutely aware that with each successive storm, the wind velocity increases quite ominously, and is therefore just that bit more destructive than the predecessor.

Over the last, I don't know how many weeks it's been, although when I think back, it's actually been many months since the storm activity transformed from being a pleasure to watch, to truly terrifying. The most frightening aspect of them though, is that they're utterly unpredictable, they just drop out of nowhere.

One minute you'll be looking at clear blue sky, then you blink and the next thing you know it's as black as midnight in a mineshaft. The awful, blood curdling howling winds lead the way every time, then huge, boiling black clouds fill the sky and the incredible heavy rains come hot on their heels.

The terrifying, nerve-wracking winds shrieked around and around the houses and outbuildings worrying away at anything that might be even a little bit loose, well that simply prepared a way for the deluge to find a way in and totally soak contents and further weaken every structure. The whole uncertainty about maybe yes maybe no, storm action, made *any* day to day living extremely hazardous, and impossibly challenging for everyone. But it was particularly hard for the older, less agile people to cope with. So here we are, we have no choice in the matter, were all in it together, and without even being aware of doing it we've been giving and taking strength from each other since the beginning.

The wind and rain are closely followed by incredibly powerful claps of thunder. The kind of thunder that makes the ground beneath your feet buckle and shudder, the thunder that caused all the windows to rattle so hard that they finally shattered. And as if the wind, the rain and the thunder aren't shocking enough on their own, when those thousands upon thousands of lightning bolts are unleashed from the portals of hell, the storms go from being terrifying to absolutely soul destroying. All I wanted to do was run away and hide, because wherever those lightning rods meet earth they just annihilate everything there; there's nothing beautiful, and certainly nothing mysterious or magical about storms for me these days, there's no magic left anywhere, or for anyone, anymore – only blinding fear.

We keep on moving but there's nowhere left to run too, there's not one single place that can be called really safe or truly secure any longer, we've no safe harbours anywhere, not for me, and not for anyone else in this world either. I remember crying tears of blood when I saw the enormous tree that we've always called grandpa's tree, that glorious big old oak tree was actually what had attracted my grandpa to buy that particular acreage all those years ago, the same tree that my aunts and uncles, I myself, my brothers, all our cousins and our friends played in. Years ago, we had our tree house in it too, and the big yellow painted tractor tyre swing- well, the poor tree was sliced completely in two by a bolt of lightning. Split and burned right down through the centre. Countless numbers of mammoth lightning strikes come, they do their butchering and then, just as quickly and as mysteriously as they appeared - they vanish. It's like, there's complete destruction and utter chaos happening all around you one minute, and then 'poof' they're gone, and the sky is clear and blue again, feigning innocence and acting like nothing ever happened. Sometimes, and I know this sounds kinda crazy, but it's as though those lightning bolts would pre-select, or target, the most beautiful things to destroy. And yet, as fearsome as they were, those earliest storms were tame little kittens compared to the wild voracious beasts of prey they've become – and even simply wondering how much more potent they might possibly get– petrifies me.

We've been driving around for what seems to be forever, our only pastime is looking out of the back of the truck, watching what's left, or rather what's *not* left, of our world, falling away behind us. How many times have we come upon a swathe of fresh sticky mud, sometimes miles and miles wide, after a storm has cut through a town, a place where family homes, children's schools, shopping malls, hospitals, playgrounds and all kinds of industrial buildings have been utterly destroyed? A terrifyingly chaotic few minutes and the whole place, including every building, all the people and pets, every living thing who lived, worked and played there, is just wiped off the face of the earth, the whole lot reduced to nothing more than mounds of concrete rubble and matchwood – ahh, but that's only when there's *anything* left behind, well, anything besides the mud that is, and believe me when I say that that foul-smelling sticky stuff is *everywhere*. Although, and we've only actually seen this particular bit of insane improbability twice, on one occasion there were two, and in the second instance there were three houses left standing in a small row, wholly perfect, undamaged and complete, even with most of their gardens intact, but surrounded by a sea of foul-smelling mud instead of other houses! It's all just ten different kinds of crazy...

Oh, I must tell you, there was this one place we drove through, we saw some tangled washing left on a clothesline, there were *no houses* left standing anywhere, they were long gone, it was *only* that *one* clothesline left standing, everything else, every living thing, every building, and every blade of grass around it were all gone. But *how*? I keep asking myself, *how* can such crazy things even be possible?

The storms that affected all of us along with damaging the houses and farm outbuildings in our low-lying valley were, in and of themselves, quite frightening enough, but it was the incredibly huge tidal surges that followed the storms... now *they* became more and more frequent and were really and truly terrifying. When the first big surge occurred, and remember this was really early on, so none of us actually connected it to the storm, most of us were thinking it might have been just a freakishly high –or maybe even a rare, once in a blue moon, *King Tide*, we'd had one or two of those a few years ago, although those tides were stirred up by either an underwater event many miles out to sea or maybe by an earthquake somewhere, everyone had their own pet theory. Anyway, the wall of water I'm talking about was recent, and it behaved in a considerably different way, the wave must have been massive because it actually washed right over the *top* of the little group of shops in the new village centre and the receding waters dragged most of them out to sea. Since that first wave however, so many more of those same wild tides have flooded up from the beach, and travelled at an incredible speed all the way, right into our quiet, sleepy village, and continued on out the other side, miles beyond Shady Haven, and on out into the scrublands, it was only stopped from going any further by the high granite cliffs, let me just tell you that those cliffs are a good eight and a half miles inland from the coast. The way the water forced its way through was frightening enough, but as it receded, it dragged, or sucked away, anything and everything in its path. Most of the lower roads into town have been ripped to shreds and now there's some enormous deep and wide potholes left behind with seriously deep water, meaning anyone with regular electric vehicles are cut off. Unless you have a really high suspension, four-wheel drive vehicle like grans Big Red, or do something like Mr. Waterson, now *he's* one smart man, he used his tractor and just ploughed his way right through all the muck! Some roads were left underwater anywhere from a couple of inches to a few feet deep in places, although the higher roadway, like the one these trucks use, leading out onto the interstate 150-72C is still intact, or at least it *was* when we left.

During the first *really* monstrous storm, the sand right along the full length of the beach was completely washed away, leaving behind nothing but mountains of black, evil smelling seaweed, a muddy, rock-strewn mess, and a long row of huge boulders that had simply appeared out of nowhere, but were sitting half submerged right where the picnic tables and play grounds used to be – and believe me, they sure weren't there before all this craziness started.

The day prior to us leaving Shady Haven, only the very highest point of the headland was still visible, the rest was well and truly under really deep water. In just a few short weeks it went from being an artificially beautified busy tourist destination, to a bare and ugly coastline, to flooded and gone.

Our beach had never been what you'd have ever called a pretty place; I suppose it was quite drab, even ugly really. The water's edge was a good fifty yards from the grassy banks, and tiny sharp black rocks and millions of broken shells instead of sand, but it didn't matter to us because the surf there was always amazing. The Local Government Assembly and the Citizens for Action Groups joined forces around three years ago and had a concentrated 'beach beautifying program' where a long wide strip of tough weedy grass, shells and pebbles was dug out, and then replaced with hundreds of thousands of tonnes of soft, pure white sand that had to be trucked in from goodness only knows where, and dumped along the area they'd cleared to turn it into a beach, one that actually *looked* like a real beach, they'd built nice new toilet and shower facilities, and a terrific children's playground, it was quite unique, colourful, and really eye-catching too, with big salt-water fountains that kids could play in scattered around, and a dozen sculptures of comical marine creatures in various sizes for the little ones to climb on, there were loads of comfortable park benches and plenty of shaded picnic tables that were loosely grouped around token operated gas barbeques.

The main objective was to help our community, by drawing tourists and encouraging visitors to come here, enjoy a day at the beach, and to spend their money in the quirky little kiosk shops, the beauty boutique and the café. It was all done to keep Shady Haven alive. And I must say, it worked *really really* well too. Until….

The new 'One-of-a-Kind Designer Beach Wear', the 'Make-me-Sparkle' handmade jewellery store, Gin-Gin's Espresso Bar, the 'Crooked Spout Teashop' the 'Natures Favourite' for scented oils, candles and bath stuff, the restaurant and little eateries relied heavily on the influx of tourists and visitors to the surf beach. But… they haven't been drawing any busloads of happy day trippers lately, and that's a fact. The flooding meant that those businesses lost everything, overnight. Literally. All they could really do was close up their doors (*if* they still *had* a door to close) and walk away.

All that planning, all the money they'd borrowed to get their businesses up and running, the heavy financial outlay to purchase new equipment and furniture, the expensive machines necessary for coffee, and cooking etc. the fixtures and stock. Months of hard work gone -kaput- all for nothing, well not really nothing I suppose – because they all still had a mountain of debt hanging over their heads. But as it is now, the entire beachfront, and everything that was there, is long gone too.

Amongst the ritzy, seriously uber rich Upper Valley Community – some, actually *most*, of the people who live there may not be very agreeable – but the palatial, grand old sandstone homes on the estates, let me tell you this, those buildings are, or they were, really magnificent and so very stately, quite a few of them would have been comfortable being called Majestic. I'm sad to say that so many of those splendid old homes are probably gone now, lost to the storms. Do you know, that some of those wonderful estates have been passed down through families for four, five, and a few have had *six* generations walk through their corridors? Although many, if not most, of those large estates had already sustained a considerable amount of major structural damage – they'd fared much worse than we had down in the valley – where, mind you, the damage was plenty fierce enough. It's undoubtedly *because* they're positioned so very high on the ridge and are totally exposed, therefore the storm winds were always so much stronger and even more extreme up there. Time after time, with each and every storm brutally assaulting their structures, once even the smallest opening was found, or made, the wind and rain just kept chipping away increasing the damage, leaving them in an ever increasingly deteriorated condition than before, and another step closer to total ruination. And while our farms directly below the ridge community, weren't faring too much better, it's been really distressing for *us* to witness those grand old estates crumbling, so I can't even begin to imagine how terribly distraught their *owners* must feel.

Even though many of the new era, ecological, all organic, all natural, sustainable solar powered farms, with the various associated dwellings and outbuildings spread out along the furthest stretch of the High Ridge road were built in the last ten to fifteen years, from modern, *supposedly* more durable man-made eco building materials, with the strength of modern structural design and construction, as opposed to the three to five hundred year old builds, proves that new and modern, isn't always better, because those ultra-modern high tech buildings were completely demolished really early on, right from the very first of the unnaturally vicious storms actually. The majority of the structures went crashing down in the first wave of storm activity. The enormous crops, and even the large herds and flocks of free-range animals, were all washed, or blown, away and ended up down in the lower valley, along with incalculable tonnes of rich black organic soil, and so much of their costly farming equipment has either been blown away -as if those expensive machines were toys- or else they've gone sliding down the hillside, as have so many goats and other small animals and birds. We saw the back wheels and cabin of a bright yellow tractor standing up nose first, embedded in sludge right up to the windshield, both the big bucket scoop and the big engine were completely buried in muck. That was less than a mile further inland from my home. But even *if* by some whimsical miracle any of those High Ridge Ranches and the owners survive, the breeders will have lost their principal money earners, their prestige breeding stocks, those poor animals have either been drowned, killed by falling debris, like trees and walls, zapped by lightning, while some others have been blown off the cliffs or have simply vanished.

In the weeks prior to losing power, news reports coming from outside our Zone were pretty unnerving, all too often informing the listeners that there'd been further appalling loss of lives and property, listening closely, as we were, we understood that it was due to the exact same weird storm activity we'd begun experiencing right here. All this's so far beyond my range of comprehension. With all the sneaky government watchers, the heavy cyber security and every digitally recorded movement and keystroke imposed on *every* computer, every company large *or* small, all places of education, all businesses and workplaces have government-imposed security up the wazoo, so I purely and simply cannot grasp how *any* of the activity has gone undetected, *or* maybe big money changed hands and it's been *ignored, or* gone *unreported*. Okay yeah, it's only speculation on my part, but what if I'm right… Whatever happened to all the checks and balances the President put in place specifically to *prevent* unscrupulous dealings? This has made her a laughing stock.

Twenty-three marines, working under the officer in charge, arrived in the early morning hours to sandbag Shady. Apparently, it was obvious to the big guy in charge (or so he said) that it was going to be a total waste of their valuable time and the minimal resources available to them. He conveyed the information to his commander, and new actions were sanctioned. Evacuations. The marines were to give us every possible assistance, working alongside us wherever necessary, to get Shady packed up, and be ready to move out at first light the following morning – earlier if possible. Everyone in Shady Haven worked throughout the day and kept going until it was too dark to see what we were doing. Even though the boss marine said we were just wasting time, we wanted get everything possible done by way of securing homes and giving our livestock at least a fighting chance to survive. However, as per the Commanders order we were packed and ready to go by first light. The marines' plan was to meet up with other, similarly loaded trucks that were converging on the highway junction a few miles up the road. Those vehicles were coming from every rural hamlet in the region and together we would travel in convoy. From the meeting point, half the refugees were to be transported to a military base that was safe and secure, a further ninety miles inland, the remainder were headed to outlying military posts in various locations.

The basic plan was: Once we'd all been safely delivered, the marines would return to their own bases and prepare for the next rescue operation. I overheard a conversation between a group of marines who were obviously bored and really impatient to be on the move again, this was their third evacuation detail in a week, and they were tired of chasing after civilians, one even complained that this wasn't the kind of action he'd signed up for!

Well, you know what they always say about the best laid plans don't you?

The troop-carrying area of these darned old army trucks are not in a luxury coach class that's for sure! Jeez, even the ramshackle old orange school bus was more comfortable than these things, and believe me, those school busses were rough! These trucks are so old, (think ancient) and considering just how many vehicles like this one there are, they must have been pulled out from storage facilities across all 42 Militarised Zones! Unpretentious, un-upholstered (splintery) wooden bench seats bolted to the floor and into the sides of the truck body, with 'safety belts' that are, in reality nothing more than cracked and worn loops of fabric for a hand hold, that have been pop riveted into the reinforced steel framework every eighteen inches or so, and then the whole lot is covered with a really thick, suffocatingly heavy camouflage canvas canopies that uniformly stink to high heaven. Like super smelly shoes that have been put away damp.

These military transports are your absolute *basic* everything, they are without any pretence, or promise of *any* form of comfort, however we've been assured that they *are* completely reliable and still highly functional. The passenger, or troop transport area, was built to absolute minimum basic standards and it seems to me that that wouldn't include anything as crude as insulation or cushioning. There's positively *nothing* unnecessary in them, the additional strength was built into the framework and engines of these things. In all likelihood they're left overs, or maybe they're survivors, of The Zone Wars, which means *they're seriously old*. They are, as we've been told repeatedly by the head honcho, extremely tough and safe, but most importantly, they're extremely functional. They have engines powered by bio-diesel and this class of engine just doesn't quit, the bio-diesel engines were designed especially for troop movements, to transfer marines, haul equipment, to get any and all military personnel, ordnance and supplies, into, over, across, around and safely out of, active war zones, whether those zones be located in sandy desserts, rugged mountainous terrain, tropical forests, snow and ice-bound mountains or steaming jungles or swamps. These trucks were also purpose-built to withstand *anything*, harsh terrain, fire and land mines included, it's also why these machines use bio fuel, there were no charging stations in any of those far-flung places back then – there probably still aren't. Imagine being in the midst of a heated battle and the power ran out, you can't simply press pause in combat to pull one of these huge trucks into a charging station halfway up a mountain or in the middle of sand dune or a swamp!

While all that may be true, they were certainly *not* designed, nor were they ever *intended*, to move civilians, certainly not the very young, or elderly townsfolk loaded with their personal belongings, furniture, or the many mixed and weird assortments of caged fowls, or new born lambs and piglets, that *is* for sure. Whose bright idea was it to bring a half the farm nurseries along anyway? Although we're all terribly grateful there are no calves among them.

We're actually sharing this already cramped space with a pair of enormous cages that have tiny baby lambs and squealing piglets, oh and don't those pint-size honeys add their own special little *something* to the general air quality, umm, okay I'll be polite here okay, and call it…their special *aroma*.…

As for where we're headed, well, the fact of the matter is, we have completely no idea anymore. Back in Shady we were told these transports would deliver us to a place called Spring Waters Ridge, however that destination was changed some hours before our arrival when word came through that Spring Waters Ridge had been destroyed, our revised destination was another marine base by the town of Tall Timbers, some one hundred and fifty miles further away. Five minutes ago, one of the marines, Chung, I think he said his name was, came by and said that Tall Timbers has been completely battered. When the convoy stopped for a toilet break a while back, Reba and I climbed out to stretch our backs and legs and there were two soldiers on the other side of the truck talking, I heard one of them say there were no known survivors after that storm either, everyone and everything there, is gone. I'm not a hundred percent positive on this, but I think I heard one of them let out a sob. Well, not surprisingly we were just informed by the sergeant, that there has been no new destination arranged for us - as yet; because the storm activity is tracking in completely unpredictable patterns. 'We however' (he said) 'must keep moving, simply because being stationery is too dangerous.' Please, can somebody explain how constantly moving is somehow safer exactly? He's just *said* the weather patterns are *unpredictable-* so by all means let's all go driving straight into a storm!

Any military site that would have, could have, or should have, been able to provide sufficient accommodation for a large troupe such as ours, is suddenly either preparing for its own hasty evacuation, or has already been destroyed. Look, I know okay, and yes, even to my own ears that sounds *really* cold, callous and uncaring, however, it's just one of the many new, and very uncomfortable facts of our lives right now, there's nothing I can do about it, nor can I change it either way. Believe me, if I *could* change what's been happening, I most certainly would have done so already. We're all feeling a bit 'left out in the cold' so to speak. Actually, I feel like a package that's lost the address label.

Our not-so-fresh-air and the much-reduced view of the outside world comes through a small eighteen by eighteen-inch opening in either a forest green or dirty sand coloured camouflage canvas wall. The sun will be out, shining brightly, and burning fiercely, so much hotter *now* than has ever been recorded - Oh I suppose I ought to inform you that we are in the middle of what *should* be our wintertime, at this time *last year* it was snowing heavily, and children everywhere were skating on frozen ponds and rivers! *This* year however, the daytime temperature is about 130-150 degrees outside, although the temperature *inside* of these canvas boxes is so much hotter. The sun will burn down on us for hours on end, then in the blink of an eye the whole sky for as far as you can see in any direction, will have filled with bloated black churning rain clouds – that's when the wind starts, then comes the thunder and then lightning follows, the next item on the agenda is the impossibly powerful rainfall. This truck convoy (by sheer good fortune) seems to always be a few, miles away from the active storm event. It's just far enough away that we're still kind of safe, but plenty close enough for us to feel many of the effects. There is always a sudden, really dramatic change in the air pressure, it's like the earth has drawn in a deep lungful of air - the canvas covering the trucks sucks right in, and it's difficult for us to get a full breath for a few seconds - and then we feel it - that abrupt, dreadfully dense, concentrated stillness, a real heavy silence, and even the loud engine noises seem to be absorbed and deadened, then within the next few heartbeats all that changes and the only thing we can hear are the hideous, incredibly high pitched whistles and shrieks of immensely powerful winds that have dropped down to ground level out of nowhere – when the horrifying wind starts screaming - the trucks roll to a complete stop. And we wait. We wait for however long it takes, but until the all clear to proceed comes from the scout, nothing, and no-one moves an inch, not one iota. We might be waiting for long, nerve wracking hours, sometimes it's less, but so far, no storm has ever moved on, or ended, in a matter of minutes.

Even at this distance we are able to hear the wind shrieking around, and believe me that sound is clear, petrifyingly clear. Just knowing the wind is tearing trees right out of the earth, and sometimes we can hear the horrible *crump* and *crunching* sounds as buildings are torn apart, demolished, and there's a sickening kind of slurping sucking sound made by roads and highways as they're ripped up, lifted as easily as tape from a table top, the blood chilling screeching of steel and timbers being torn from buildings as they're twisted, snapped and sucked up out of the ground then shredded into a gazillion splinters. We can hear the bestial savagery and the nonstop explosions of heavy toughened glass windows and walls too as they're blown out, then there's the explosions when huge tanks of propane gas erupt in flames and sounding like heavy artillery and mortar fire. Too many times we've *seen* truly massive chunks of concrete, incredibly long sections of heavy steel roofing, and all sorts of building materials being blown around in the sky as if they're nothing more substantial than sheets of paper - until they're mashed together in mid-air, and the whole lot is whipped away by the winds, right along with anything else collected when the storm rampages its way through. These enraged winds are so *unbelievably,* so *incredibly powerful,* strong enough to annihilate all kinds of buildings, no matter how well constructed, how large or how small, with spine-chilling efficiency. From office blocks and houses to giant shopping malls and vehicles, they're all sucked up and sent flying as though they were nothing more than children's toys made from plastic building blocks, obviously size doesn't matter. It doesn't seem to make any difference what's in the storm's path either, be they cars, trucks, busses, cargo ships, planes or trains – they're just picked up effortlessly, and tossed aside, and I know in my heart that hundreds, and in some cases, even many thousands of people, young and old, babies, little children, so many animals and so much precious preserved wildlife just going about their daily business, the howling wind doesn't differentiate - they all suffer the same fate - they just vanish, almost *everything* disappears without a trace, and after the wind has done its share of the damage, along comes the rain to wash away anything the wind might have left behind. Hammering, punishing rain, starts pelting down with such force it actually drills deep craters into the ground. Even before the rain is done, well, then it's the lightning's turn. And oh jeez, what lightning it is too! I have *never*, not in my whole life have I *ever*, not even with all the hundreds of storms I've sat and watched with pleasurable awe, never, ever, ever, have I seen *anything* even in the least bit like these hundreds and hundreds of simultaneous strikes. What's more, I simply could not believe such lethal ferocity as I've witnessed time and time again could even existed in nature. But it does, and then some.

I used to really enjoy watching The Earth Explorers Program, the one where they show the biggest, baddest, and wackiest stuff that nature has to offer, but even that program, which, mind you, has shown some pretty horrific damage, has never filmed *anything* that compares with the pure savagery of these strikes. I'm not talking about just one or two big flashes here and there either; there are, quite literally, thousands and very possibly, hundreds of thousands of colossal, *simultaneous* strikes. The whole earth appears to glow and the air around us crackles. Even from a distance, the static electricity in the air makes our hair stand out like halos around our heads. We've always thrown blankets over the animal cages trying to protect them as much as we can, but it doesn't seem to help the poor little things very much at all. The suddenness and the *sheer strength* of the storms is not only spectacular, even awe-inspiring in a crazy, morbidly fascinating kind of way, it also completely distorts a person's sense of reality and it's truly, truly, terrifying. Within a matter of moments, what was once a nice, quiet, very ordinary community, just going about its regular daily business in this scorching, incredibly hot midwinter sun, with confused bees droning around the flower gardens doing what bees do best, cats and dogs sleeping under trees, on shaded porches and windowsills all over the town, and the odd lawn mower giving off the sweet smell of freshly cut grass, has become what can at best, only be described as a complete disaster area. Other times an entire town has vanished without a trace. All too often the only things that remain, when there *is* anything at all left behind, are a few big piles of smashed up masonry in an immense puddle of yellowish-brown sludge, now and then there might be a few broken pipes sticking up out of the muck in a twisted mess, but there's never much evidence that there were ever dwellings and never any people...

Buildings –oh, and I'm certainly *not* implying that they were old, or flimsy structures either. Many of them, well I suppose that most probably the greater majority of them, would have been relatively new, between seventy and one hundred and twenty storey's each, and like all modern constructions, they'd have had to have been completed to the highest, and most stringent of building codes, every building has to be examined at every stage by inspectors who are really looking for something they can fault. New constructions use high grade steel, steel reinforced concrete blocks, and more often than not, once the basic building has been completed, the outer structure would be wrapped, or finished off, with enormous skins of weatherproof, and fireproof, black, silvery grey, or white manufactured marble or granite, and would have to have had toughened, double or triple glazed windows and doors; all buildings constructed in the last ninety years have been built to withstand earthquakes, floods and hurricanes, but even so, they haven't been able to withstand the immensity or sheer strength of *these* winds. Structures have just been shredded, and either pushed, twisted or ripped, right out of the ground and blown away as though they were made of kiddy building blocks! People, animal's, roadways, rail lines and all manner of transportation vehicles, are suddenly sucked up and become airborne, they're thrown about in the air like soap bubbles, with the exception of only those few, extremely odd and weird incidences I've told you about. Homes along with really large, substantial buildings such as hospitals, schools, shopping malls, prisons, manufacturing plants, and even long stretches of eight and twelve lane highways, InterCity hover lines, bridges, everything goes... nothing is invulnerable. Everything in every zone is recycled so all of the major domestic and commercial centres have gargantuan water recycling plants, metal, plastics, glass and rubbish recycling plants, and they've all been destroyed and blown away, the enormous intercontinental aircraft standing at airports, have all been sucked up and *poof!* They' just *gone*, carried off and disappeared. While *'gone'* they most certainly are, but *where* have they *gone too??* Nothing seems to fall back to earth again – we've always been taught that what goes up must come down eventually – but where is it all?

These new wind patterns aren't typical of tornadoes, *or* cyclones *or* of hurricanes, at least not in a way that we know and recognise – for more than two hundred years Weather Agencies have been able to pretty much accurately predict the strength, the paths and the movements of storm events. However, to try and describe, let alone predict, the new storms; the punishing wind velocity, the utter violence and absolute ferocity are all so far beyond even the *most extreme* conditions of those categories - even if every weather catastrophe in history were all rolled into one big weather event, it couldn't hope to compare to these – because just *one* new storm is so much, so terrifyingly, unbelievably, and so mind bogglingly stronger. No-one has ever seen or even *heard* of storm activity that can, in *any* way, any way at all, be even remotely likened to these. It has been reported that the World Central Bureau of Meteorology has nothing, absolutely nothing in any recent data base nor in any of the innumerable historical records to compare them to, and we're led to believe that they've checked worldwide – in infinite detail- going all the way back to the first recordings ever kept. They've even delved deeply into tribal myths, legends and stories looking for information. I believe that too.

Governments and Scientists are in fact working together on a universal scale now; they're all searching - frantically searching, trying to find *some* solution to these extremely erratic, utterly lethal, weather events.

Oh, and the scientists who set this chaos and pandemonium loose on the world? Well, you've probably already guessed the answer to that, *no one can find them* or *their data!* I dare say that once they realised their horrific mistake, they knew if they hung around there'd be hell to pay, so they removed or destroyed all records and data, and then they just up and vanished without so much as a trace. That means there can *be* no investigation or scrutiny of their data, of any written notes, or settings, or of *anything* even remotely connected with this fiasco, and you *cannot* unbreak an egg, especially not an egg like this one, no matter how clever you think you are. There are hundreds, possibly many thousands, of laboratories world-wide, all trying desperately to unscramble this particular egg. But even with all of best brains and purest intentions in the world, when they've been left with no starting point, no calculations, no records, and no data of any kind – I don't hold out much hope of their success – however, and unfortunately, it's not beyond the realm of possibility, that some scientist, or group, in an effort to undo or rectify the damage, could possibly make things even worse... As for the rogue group responsible – Governments in *every* Zone major *and* minor, worldwide, have contributed sizable amounts to the fund and they've made a united announcement, that there will be an extremely substantial reward for any information leading to the apprehension of any, but preferably all, of those guilty heads.

The international news media have given these storms a bright and shiny new title; they are now titled the 'New World-Wide Weather Phenomenon' or N.3W.P.

They have to be kidding. Really? Just-give-us-a-break-will-you... Do they think that by giving these hideous killer storms a snazzy label, or a catchy title, it's going to make some sort of a magical difference – make them acceptable? Can they *possibly* believe we're all so *stupid?*

The large and tremendously diverse populations of every Zone on this earth have, for the first time in *all* of human history, been united by one single overriding emotion. Stark Terror. Terror, has, miraculously united all mankind.

One of the marines was overheard saying that he'd picked up on the short-wave radio that entire populations in Zones worldwide, were gathering together, they're putting their political, racial, and religious differences aside and joining hands in prayer. Feel free to call me crazy if you want to, but I can't help wondering, how many wars, how much senseless killing, and maiming of innocents, how much futile bloodshed, could have been prevented, and how many valuable lives would have been spared, if this action, this one act of a united humanity, had been taken with an unprejudiced love and respect for each other as fellow human beings, instead of from abject fear, simply looking for a way to save their own terrified hides?

The convoy has made a very much needed rest stop, so that we can all unkink both ends of our spines, unlock our knees, and crawl down from these hopelessly cramped seats and stretch out our leg muscles, (*and* to answer the now, rather urgent, call of nature!)
Hey if we're stopped for long enough, maybe we can get rid of some of the cramps and kinks in our necks and backs, we might even be lucky and get some circulation back in our butts! Understandably, each person here is anxious about what our immediate future holds, but for those in the group who have been separated from their youngsters, partners or parents, that -Need to Know- has become pretty darned desperate now. More than a few of us have lost our families, and even if it is, as the head guy says -only a temporary situation- it's a really awful one for any of us to be in right now. Somehow, I just can't bring myself to believe him though. Don't get me wrong, I'd like to, I really would, but I'm not completely naïve *or* brainless, I can see what's happening to the world all around us too.
The big dark-haired marine (I'm telling you, this guy's built like a mountain) who seems to be in charge, or else he's taken charge, of this whole operation, has just asked us all to meet him under the awning between the lead and second vehicle, it's impossible to gauge anything from that man's expression, I've wondered a few times now if he's a poker player. Because if he *is*, then he's probably a

darn good one, his stony expression certainly gives nothing away that's for sure.

Well, I'm not exactly sure what we're going to do now, the storms seem to have been preceding us and have inflicted some truly horrendous damage. Sargent Tyler (that's the big dark haired marine guy) has just told everyone that we'll have to head even further inland because any town that might have taken us in, within the next *three hundred and ninety-eight miles* in what had been his intended direction, have all been wiped out – *totally* wiped out. He lowered his voice and told us quietly –everything is gone, and there have been no instructions concerning possible survivors. What he *didn't* tell us was he was wished good luck, and told to carry on as best he could by his Commanding Officer.

He revealed to us that at best there is only rubble left above ground, that means no secure shelter, there's no running water and no sanitation; add to that, that there will be no medical assistance available at *any* point, and our future –immediate or otherwise - has obviously just become somewhat even more disturbing. Fortunately, though, no one in our large group is sick, pregnant, extremely elderly, physically incapacitated in any way, or in need of regular medications or medical treatment. There's enough clothing and bedding, we have an excellent supply of dry and preserved food, and who could forget those farm nurseries… actually we have sufficient food supplies to keep us going for quite a few months … double that if we're very careful. No-one dares to ask what becomes of us after that food's gone though.

One of the slightly more modern, and physically much larger supply trucks was supposed to have parted ways with us and continue on as part of another convoy, but perhaps there was a route slipup or mixed messages because one supply truck has remained with us – we've been told that truck is fully loaded with a triple layer of barrels filled with bio fuel, (the boys counted sixty-eight barrels) and there are also twenty-five small pallets filled with a wide variety of boxed dehydrated foodstuffs on board that had been intended for one of the military bases, a base that sadly, no longer exists, but what a great bonus it'll be for us. Add to that, that we were told to bring at least one container of water for each person for bathing and personal use. In regional areas water can be very 'iffy' at times so every household keeps a good supply of fresh water, and it's almost always in two twenty litre stainless steel clip-lock cylinders with folding wheels. Although, in view of this latest information there won't be time for bathing anytime soon, we'll probably be lucky to have what my granny jokingly called ~a lick and a promise~ not that anyone has washed anything besides their face and hands for weeks – and if we aren't able to stop anywhere longer than it takes to eat a sandwich, then these stuffy, unventilated and diabolically hot trucks might just get a shade more uncomfortable for everyone. Although I must say, the young boys seem pretty cheered by the prospect of not being able to bathe for a while longer! Apparently, we have our very own doctor on team refugee too, he even comes with a shiny new diploma (so new it hasn't been unrolled) a complete set of new instruments *and* a full, complete kit of drugs and medical supplies! The poor guy was supposed to be opening a new family health clinic in Landah, that's about fifty miles to the north-west of Shady Haven, but that won't be happening now that's for sure. Once again – it's another huge bonus for us.

Tyler wants to have another talk with us before we re-board the vehicles; he said he's going to head for a small town near a place known as Green Falls Crossing, wherever that is, I can't recall ever having heard of it, and judging by all the curious expressions around the group, nor has anyone else... He's told us to prepare for a very long, and a possibly rough night; (oh joy) each driver will be taking the wheel for two hours on rotation, and they won't be stopping for more than the two minutes it takes to change over for any reason – none at all. (So, I think we had all better go very lightly on the water!)

The grouping in each truck is fixed now, no one changes vehicles anymore, and a captain has been chosen from each group for things like, passing along information, handling, or overseeing the preparation of the food and the distribution of drinking water. We have people dealing with the storage of bedding, and people responsible for a roll call before we disembark or re-board the trucks, just in case someone wanders off and gets lost. It looks like these trucks will continue to be our mobile homes, for the duration. The tenth, eleventh and twelfth trucks have taken on the lion's share of bulky and heavy luggage, like a couple of mysterious huge metal boxes stamped 'air freight' and I saw four quite sizeable packing crates stamped fragile, they're also taking the biggest animal pens for the now not-so-small-animals, and our suitcases, the smaller hand luggage with our extra change of clothing and personal stuff, as well as the extra bulk food supplies. As for the marine's own personal belongings, they're kept behind or under the seats in the truck cabins. The thirteenth, or 'Bonus' truck as I think of it, is filled with, as I said before, the drums of bio fuel and the caterers' crates of dehydrated meats, vegetables and other foods. I would have thought we had everything to do with our traveling arrangements pretty well sorted out, so I can't imagine what he wants to talk to us about this time. Hopefully it won't be any more sad, bad, or worse, news.

Well damn me! Now *that* was just a bit *too* rough! Wow- how about a not so warm *or* hearty welcome to the Marine Corps folks! We have, from the youngest child to the eldest person, without any shadow of a doubt, and in no uncertain terms whatsoever, just been *told!* We are – and I quote: To follow orders, to ask only absolutely necessary… preferably intelligent questions, and oh yeah, basically to follow their instructions, unquestioningly, and To-the-Letter. Aye-aye captain!

When we were little kids, I believe it used to be -sit down, shut up, and do as you are told! I'm really getting a bit sick and tired of all these orders, *and* I'm beginning to get seriously irritated by that Tyler person too, he's just plain *rude*, it's so unfair of him to have that attitude, this disaster is *not* of our making. Oh, but the most annoying thing, is he always looks directly at *me*. Why? What have I done wrong? I'll tell you precisely what I've done wrong –*nothing*, not one single solitary thing, that's what! He is just so, so, uncouth. Yes sir, no sir, and three bags full sir. Oh, now that's just great! He caught me sneering at him and mumbling to myself - Oh bugger blast and damn that man … he's just let me know that he can um, lip read too, woops!

 Night has fallen. But all that really means is that we've managed to survive another exhausting, blistering hot and overcrowded day - and the trucks keep rumbling along.

It's impossible to talk above the noise of the engine, so we are each left with our own thoughts in this bouncing, bone jarring, smelly, stuffy, uncomfortable, blackness of the crowded truck, until we manage to doze off … only to be jerked awake again when the wheels hit yet another deep pothole, and believe you me, there are lots and lots of potholes.

Word has come through that we are about five minutes out from Green Falls Crossing, we can tell by the deeper growling of the engine that the trucks have gone into a low gear and are just rolling along. Thank goodness, now we can bid a fine farewell to Tyler and his crew. With a bit of luck, we might be able to get some information about our families...

Sienna and Katherine are curled up in blankets sleeping like big puppies on the floor, Patrick has his head in my lap and he's fidgeting and twitching in his sleep, but at least he's stopped crying for his mama. For now, anyway. I wish I could sleep too, but my brain refuses to quit, it keeps ticking off all the possible things that could go wrong. I don't want to disturb the little man, but I'll have to poke my head out and get some fresh air soon or I'll be sick… what a way to start the morning, hopefully once we've completed the transfer to Green Falls it will be better. I think keeping this journal is helping me stay sane – well, sort of sane anyway, I'm ready to start the next chapter… Green Falls Crossing here we come!

Oh, my, lord! I just stuck my head for some semi odour free air. Whatever I'd expected to see, it certainly wasn't *that*. Was that really the Green Falls Crossing we we've been looking forward to so much? I sure hope not, because well, because it's been destroyed, it's not there anymore.
The whole scene outside is one that can best be described as one of utter devastation. I saw a few people, well three people anyway, wandering around looking lost and confused, the poor devils are red raw and terribly blistered with sunburn and wading knee deep through a giant stinking mud puddle, a puddle that extends as far as the eye can see in every direction. The trucks have picked up a little more speed now and have kept moving, regardless of those poor wretches out there. What else can they do I suppose? There isn't enough room for extra bodies and we've no way to help them anyway.
Just how much can one person change in a few months? I honestly wonder, because a couple of months ago I *know* I would have jumped down out of this truck, full of vim and vigour, ready and willing, to help in *any* way I possibly could, and be damned to anyone who didn't like it. Yet now, here, today, I can

readily accept that this situation, as awful as it is, is too far beyond my ability to help. I don't think I like this change in me either, not at all.

The rumble and juddering of the trucks is as monotonous as it is continuous, and merciless. I feel sick in the stomach from breathing in the exhaust fumes, every bone in my body is aching, my head is pounding from the incessant deep drone of the huge engine running in a low gear, and from being tossed and batted around like a ping-pong ball with all the mud skids, the potholes, and the sudden sharp turns to avoid piles of mud-covered rocks and junk on the slippery roads... or should I say whatever 'mud-way' that functions as a road now, because there *are* no roads left. I'm not alone, my own physical grumbles would also be applicable to every person in every truck too I'd say!

The time between stops is plain torture, but the stops themselves are in some ways so much worse – because we have to drag ourselves, *and* these poor miserable children, back into the trucks when break-time's over so we can continue on our way. Every time we stop – without fail - the three small ones in our truck ask, 'did my mummy got here yet?' It's awful, and it makes us all feel really horrible, knowing that all this moving around, going from one desperate pile of nothingness to the next, might realistically, all be for nothing in the long run. The little ones look at us with sad puppy eyes that don't understand why they're being punished, or why we've taken them away from their families, or why we won't let them out to play. The worst part is it's not like we can give them any decent answers when they ask where mummy or daddy is, *or* even where we're going either, and you can only say –I don't really know sweetie – so often.

But I swear, I really do, I may well jump down and lay myself under the trucks wheels if I hear – Where are we going? Or, will we be there soon? Or the worst one, where's my mummy. One-More-Time.

We haven't seen anywhere, or any*thing*, in hundreds of hours of non-stop driving that hasn't been totally obliterated by a storm and turned into a sludge pit. At our last stop Tyler informed us that his last radio contact with his superior officer was 37 hours ago; there has been nothing since that communication; not even static. Whenever I see him, I watch his stiff poker face, because he's starting to show some small signs of concern, or, dare I even say it? Fear. Even *thinking* that he's afraid, or that anxiety is even a possibility for him, is far scarier to me than the storms are.

Whenever we have even a brief rest stop, all the marines get together, mind you, they keep a good distance from us, and talk among themselves in low voices. They'll have a quick look in our direction every now and then, and, well I mean, we're not complete morons, we *know* they're talking about us, but then if we *do*, by some mischance, make eye contact, their immediate reaction is to switch their gazes to the sky or to the ground or else just pretend to be looking past us. You know, I think their reactions are far more disturbing to us - to me anyway, than all the miles and miles of the flattened muddy landscape we're constantly surrounded by.

It's kind of like they *know* something, yet for some reason they're either not willing, or maybe not *allowed*, to share that information with us. As for that darned Tyler, he just keeps pushing us on – I honestly believe that he's totally oblivious to our grumbles and squawks of discomfort, it's alright for him, *he* has a proper cushioned seat to bounce around on – let him trade places for a whole day and night jammed in the back here, sliding and bouncing around like a tethered ping pong ball, and we'll see how fast he changes his attitude! He could have stopped in any one of twenty-six dozen places so that we could have a decent break, heck, he could stop right here – after all, it's all the same darned mud, but oh no, no, no, he just has to stay on the move. *He* has to be sure. *He* wants to find a place that *he* considers both a perfect enough, *and* a safe enough area to stop so everyone – marines and refugees alike- can take a decent break; hopefully he'll find that magical place *before* our collective bladders rupture! Yes I know, I know, I'm being bitchy now, and yes, I also know he's probably right -*again*.

There's such a nice older lady in this truck, her name's Mrs Beatty. She'd call us to come over to her side to have a look-see at anything she saw that was a bit different or a bit more interesting than the usual M.U.D. Her husband though, has very much the exact opposite temperament, he's *not* a nice person at all, in actual fact he's a really nasty, mean mouthed, mean minded, mean spirited and cantankerous old bugger.

 Oh wow, *finally*, we're stopping for a *real* break. (My butt truly gives thanks)

He wins again. This's easily the best, and the only *intact place* we've seen for many (far too many) days. He's stumbled across a lovely, well-appointed, clean and *green*, picnic ground. Tyler's directed the drivers to take the trucks down into what looks like either a deep gully, or else a dried up river bed. It's most likely a river bed because I saw a little bridge over on the side and another one a bit further along. Ah, yeah, and those rusty ladders along the sides sort of give it away too. How weird is it that - with all the water and mud we've been driving through for - well, I don't really know how long anymore- that we've managed to find some shelter in a riverbed that is well and truly dried up! Anyway, it was around ten feet deep where I was looking out at first – almost level with the top of my head, then a little way ahead the side walls rose up steeply from about twelve to possibly twenty feet deep/high and then rose to over well over thirty feet high with fairly straight, very rough rock walls or I suppose they were actually, once-upon-a-time, river banks. Except where we've stopped it's a kind of big square cut out, maybe it was for mooring boats or something. I briefly glimpsed lots of pretty, colourful, flower gardens scattered all around the park too, oh grandma would have really enjoyed walking around this park so much.

Once we'd stopped, Tyler started shouting out his never-ending lists of 'do this and don't' do that, giving instructions left right and centre. Our truck stopped right alongside a ladder, the trucks were all parked in a pretty higgledy-piggledy way, and I think the drivers were as anxious as us to stretch their bones. The girls and I thought we were going to be the lucky ones to be given the go ahead to have a quick run up to the bathrooms. Hooray *real* toilets!

Not a chance…Tyler said "there's too much stuff to be done right here first"…but the crestfallen looks made him give in and he told us to go "*Go* get going then *run!* But make sure you hurry straight back again, and *no* dawdling." Tyler, Liam, Sanchez, Zahan and half a dozen more of the men had their heads stuck in truck engines checking –I suppose whatever it is that men check in truck engines.

Tyler had to give us a boost up to the bottom rung of the ladder then the girls and I bolted upwards and ran to the toilets, we did what we had to do, and ran straight back to help Tyler again. I have never appreciated the simple act of using a real toilet and being able to wash my hands under cool running water so much! That wild girl staring back at me from the mirror was a bit scary looking though! Once we'd arrived back -and received 'the nod of approval' from Tyler (hey, that's really high praise from him!) we started by helping to unpack the food boxes and set one of the folding tables up with plates for the evening meal. Sienna called out to me – "eh Sara, just take a look at that lot will you, oh for gosh sakes! She snapped angrily- I don't *believe* those people! What's the bet that they'll all be starving and want something to eat in a few minutes, but will they stay and help out? *Nooo!* Not them, not a chance!" She was on a rant… Against all of Tyler's multitudinous instructions, like – 'this is neither the time, nor is it the *place*, to go walking off' and – 'we're all very aware of how suddenly things can, and *do*, change now, and -

'don't anyone even *think* of leaving the immediate area' - and all the dozens of other dire warnings to 'stay close by so you can get back in a hurry'… but in spite of all his instructions - a whole truck load of people- I haven't a clue who most of them are, but I *do* know that at least a couple of them are from the Upper Valley Eco Farmers group, but it's just so typical of that lot to totally ignore every single word the man said. He might just as well have saved his breath. They've all sauntered off, taking themselves out for a nice revitalising walk along the lovely pathways winding through a pretty wooded area. I intend to go up there with Paddy after we've eaten. Okay yeah, I *do* understand that they're probably walking off some travel sickness or the stiffness from just sitting down for too long, *of course* I understand that, but hey… we're *all* just as *travel sick* and just as *stiff* and our butts are just as bruised *and as sore* as each other's now!

The youngsters were getting in some much-needed exercise, playing chasings, running around and around the trucks like crazy clowns burning off a bit of extra energy. I called out to Patrick, asking him if he wanted to eat with us, or with the men this time, and he opted to eat with the men. Naturally. Everyone, marines and evacuees alike were happy to have their feet on dry, solid ground for the first time in ages. So relaxed were we that when Sanchez pulled out his guitar and started singing a song that was really popular on a teen music program - KrayZeez Sounz - a few of us joined in, Carol and Deidre even started dancing! It was such a great feeling to laugh and be silly again, it's been ages since anyone sang a song *or* laughed. Tyler started walking toward us, he'd just called out my name when suddenly… without any warning at all, the sky overhead turned from soft friendly blue to pitch-black. It was as though a giant light switch had been turned off so dark did it become.

Tyler shouted for his men to -drop everything and close-rank these trucks together get those noses hard up against the wall. Liam! Get 'em in man, tight as you can, and I don't give a shit about the damned paintwork! DO IT! … *RIGHT NOW! Chung-* stow those tools. *MOVE IT! Rawlins* round the kids up and get 'em inside the trucks, just grab and chuck 'em in don't wait.

Engine hoods slammed shut, motors kicked over and gears crunched as powerful engines roared back to life, the drivers spun the trucks noses to the wall and side by side until they were crammed tightly against each other and the bars protecting the engine covers were scraping the stone wall; they were parked so close and so tight that the drivers had to climb out of their window and into cab of the next truck and the next- all the way down the line. Tyler was bug eyed and practically foaming at the mouth once he realised just how far some people had strayed from our base. He had to shout at full volume to be heard above the roar of the engines and the howl of the strengthening wind.

'Call out to them, oh for shits sake, try to get those freakin idiots back down here before all hell breaks loose. *BUT YOU DO NOT LEAVE!*" He snapped out furiously.

Rawlins had almost thrown the older women and every kid he found, into trucks to get them out of the fast-rising wind, Mark jumped in behind them and managed to get half a dozen or so terrified kids down and as safe as he could make them, then he vaulted back over the tailgate to help Tyler. Any marine who wasn't assigned a task joined in our efforts to call back the wanderers. Well, we shouted, we yelled, we whistled, and we screamed out to the walkers to come back, but any sounds we made - and it didn't make any difference, or matter, how loudly we screamed, our voices were simply snatched away by the rising wind. In a fit of urgency some of the soldiers started sounding the truck horns in urgent bursts of loud noise, but again, the wind carried even those clamorous sounds away. Everything was lashed down as quickly as was humanly possible, anything that had been removed from the trucks like food, jugs of water etc in preparation for our meal- too bad there was no time - it was just left wherever it was; we couldn't take the time to be packing anything up, and there was certainly nothing out there worth dying for. Tyler was shouting at the top of his lungs – "Leave the end trucks empty - hopefully those fools will make it back and manage to get into one!" The winds were really picking up and were much stronger than gale force already, bits and pieces of our food and meal making equipment were whipping past us, the bamboo dinner plates seemed to fly up and then begin to blow around in slow, even lazy spirals and circle over our heads before suddenly zipping off like flying saucers. By this time anyone still outside really had to hang on for dear life as they worked their way along the length of the convoy, grabbing hold of the rails tightly, we were definitely careful not to let go of one hand before we had a really strong grip further along the next rail, (the thick metal rails used for roping down the heavy canvas) in case the wind snatched us away. I'm so grateful that all the kids were moved inside when they were, because my own feet were lifted right off the ground quite a few times – I've *never* been so scared in my entire life. Each person moved as fast as they dared, nevertheless if you wanted to live, extra caution was essential inching along, hand over hand along the row. There was barely even enough time for people to climb in or to be pushed or shoved into which ever truck they were closest to. My heart almost stopped when I felt myself being snatched high off the ground! Tyler came running from behind and grabbed both my arms at the elbows, lifted me clean off the ground and ran me past the press of people cramming themselves into the next truck, he stopped behind a truck, picked me up bodily and practically threw me into the third truck along the row shouting above the wind for me to "damn well get in there with Paddy and for god sakes Sara stay the hell down." He yelled out to me, "Paddy's in there, you know what to do" and he was gone again. We were told very early on to lay down flat and 'hunker down into the floorboards' as a safety precaution, however, bodies squashed up together like thirty sardines in tin that was only meant to hold ten, would be a more accurate description of us right now. Somehow, in all the crazy, chaotic confusion, a couple of the animal pens had either fallen open, burst open, or else they had been *helped* open by one or more of the children. So now we were sharing this impossibly overcrowded space with maybe a dozen of the now not so tiny and cute two-month-old lambs, and all of the goodness only knows how many escapee chickens have taken refuge in any small space they can find, and I don't know how many, maybe it was only five or six of the three dozen of the, once again, not so tiny and definitely not cute anymore, squealing piglets got out somehow and were squirming around our bodies. Boy oh boy did I ever get shoved into the wrong truck! I feel like I've been tumbled in with Old MacDonald! I grabbed a l blanket that had fallen off the seat and rolled Paddy and myself into it and I shunted myself backwards, snuggling Paddy to me and wedged both of us as tightly as I could underneath a bench seat. I remember humming into the back of his head.

Please tell me if you can, how do you comfort a very young, utterly terrified child, when you're scared clean out of your wits yourself? When things are really bad, like trying not to die, we just have to make do with whatever we have.
 The wind howling around us was like a living thing writhing in torment. It shrieked and clawed at everything above ground level. Suddenly all the air was being sucked right out of our lungs while a crushing weight from the inky black sky pressed down on us. My ears started ringing, then I felt queasy and dreadfully light-headed, but for the life of me, no matter *how hard I tried*, I *couldn't* drag in a full breath.   Everyone, adult and child alike were

absolutely petrified that the truck would be sucked right out of that river bed, all I could think of was -if buildings are sucked up so easily – then this one measly truck is no obstacle at all, we could easily be very, very dead, in the next few minutes. Feeling the heaving vibrations as our truck was lifted up off the ground by the wind then dropped back down, hearing and feeling the scraping of metal against metal, the harsh grinding of metal against the rock through the floorboards as the trucks pitched and rocked getting wedged even tighter against the trucks on either side made my teeth ache. The violent shaking and bucking had the top layer of people inside the truck rolling across each other. Now I understood the urgency behind Tyler's barked commands to park them (the trucks) broadside and - so damned close they lose paint... or words to that effect. His quick thinking –that, and being inside the squared off dock area which seemed to be the deepest part of the riverbed- is, I am positive, the *only* thing that saved any of us from learning how to fly. From the sky above, lightening scythed through the darkness, it was razor sharp, and so dazzlingly bright that grotesque shadows were thrown across the multi layered human carpet spread across the floor of the truck. Thousands of simultaneous flashes of wild electricity illuminated the gloomy interiors making the murky dimness brighter than midday despite the thickness of the canvas canopy. In all honesty I couldn't tell you how many of us were squeezed together inside that truck, but there were lots of us, and we were being shaken around like an old slipper in some gigantic dog's mouth. I heard a voice calling on God to 'help me, save me, stop this storm and I promise to be a better person' and there was more, lots more, the constant wail of fear, terrified screaming, not only from the children, but from grown men and women alike. Hey, we were all petrified okay. No, to be honest, by that time we were all *way* past being merely petrified. In fact, most of us (myself included) honestly thought this was it, we were going to die. Right there. Right then. Game over. Goodbye.

The wind screamed and howled, raging around the trucks while pulling and straining everything to almost breaking point, scratching frenziedly at the ropes. We can only thank our combined good fortune, the ropes that had taken the combined strength of two very strong marines to tie and tighten as securely as they could had held, because they knew that when those ropes were saturated, they'd hold strong against all the torment. But for those inside, it was knowing that the comparatively flimsy canvas was the *only* thing between us, and the insane wind trying to suck us out, that turned our bones to jello. Even though the canvas was stiff and thick, and it had been pulled drum tight, it still flapped and snapped like a thousand bull whips around our heads. Our ears pulsed and ached from the deafening clamour, our lungs craved, and struggled to drag in sufficient air, while our eyes and ears throbbed from the impossible air pressure. Loud bangs and thumps sounded all around us as the trucks were struck repeatedly by large, or at least by heavy *sounding* objects, and torrential rain sliced down into the earth like knives, gouging deep furrows beneath the tyres, and causing the trucks to tip and tilt, forcing them to lean further against each other at some weird and crazy angles, as a result we, the human sardines inside the tins called trucks, were forced by gravity, to roll, ensuring we were squished up together even harder. The terrible squeals of fear, the frantic pleadings, the bargaining, and all the deals and promises to God became almost a mantra. Blend into that cacophony, the frightened squawking of birds, the piercing squeals of the piglets and pitiful bleating of lambs and, well, you might get some small idea of what it was like. Uninterrupted blasts of rolling thunder roared overhead and caused the earth below us to shudder, to roll and tremble. Phenomenal amounts of sheet lightning flashed incessantly, and the wind – oh my god, *that wind!* All I can say with absolute certainty, is that that wind tried really hard to suck us up and out of our hiding place like spaghetti from a bowl, and in a few truly horrifying instances – it very nearly succeeded. The wind strained and stressed the canvas canopy to the point of shredding. And the more ferocious the storm became, the louder –and creepier– were the pleadings and false promises being sent heavenwards. The demonstration of raw power and savagery was brutal, and seemed to go on, and on for hours. Time, as we know it, had ceased to exist, and our entire universe had shrunk to be wholly contained within the interior of that truck, our sense of reality, *if* it still even existed at that point, was doubtful at best.

After what seemed an eternity of being emotionally overwhelmed, rigid with fear and anxiety, not to mention being absolutely terrified out of our collective minds, *everything-just-stopped....* The world outside went deadly silent. I can still remember trying to pop my ears, thinking I'd gone deaf, because there was not one single solitary sound to be heard from outside at all. Even though inside the truck, the whimpering, the pleadings, prayers and promises continued unabated -until realisation that the horrific maelstrom had finally passed- dawned on them and they too slowly fell silent again. Bit by bit my hearing returned to normal, however apart from someone's mutterings, the occasional groan, or a cough, the silence inside was profound – the only thing we heard was a constant dribble of water as it ran off the saturated canopies in a long continuous drizzle. Even though the terror had passed, my fingers still had a death grip on the bench seat above me. I was still holding on for dear life. The next sound I recognised was a tad muffled, but it was definitely heartbroken sobbing. My sense of direction was still way out of kilter, it took a few moments until I realised the sobbing sounded pretty close by me, I lifted my head up and twisted my head around as far as possible, listening but still unable to locate the source of the crying, until I grasped that it was coming from *underneath* me. Poor little Patrick, he was curled up in a tight little ball under the bench seat we were laying under –somehow, undoubtedly from all the rolling around, I'd somehow gone from being on my side with Patrick cuddled into me, to laying on my back, but with him stuck behind me so I was almost on top of him. The poor little darling, his wrenching sobs were enough to break your heart. I knew talking – even if I *had* been capable of speech at that moment - which I quite sincerely doubt - wasn't going to do any good this time because we were all still scared stiff; there's no point denying it, not even to, well *especially* not to the children. Because children are, by nature, all knowing, all seeing, all hearing, living breathing lie detectors.

It wasn't what you'd call an easy exercise, but by wriggling around I finally managed to turn slightly, just enough to unlock one very stiff, very sore arm, from around the seat my nose was squashed against, I squirmed until I was back laying on my side again, there was just enough space for my hand to rub softly back and forth across his little shoulder and arm, hoping the contact might give him at least some small measure of comfort and reassurance, or maybe so he simply wouldn't feel so completely abandoned. The poor frightened little man twisted himself around and grabbed my hand in both of his and hugged it to him like it was a life preserver out on the ocean. I could feel his hot tears sliding across my knuckles. It took a while but once he'd realised the truck wasn't moving anymore, he began to calm down. Then he started giving me soft little hiccupping rabbit kisses on the back of my hand. We stayed like that – unmoving- for maybe fifteen or twenty minutes, until we got the all clear from Salvatore came and had to shout through the canvas wall to be heard above the noises of some still howling occupants. He was checking to make sure we were all okay, but he asked us to stay where we were just for -un pocotino momento por favor- a little bit longer please. Patrick refused to let go of my hand, which was perfectly fine with me, I needed some reassuring human contact myself – however one of the little brown chickens had perched itself on my hip, and was busily pecking at the accumulated crud, dirt, and heaven only knows *what else* was stuck on my jeans, it wasn't really helping the situation at all, although when Paddy saw it pecking away at me, he thought it was the most hilarious thing he'd ever seen! Sanity... saved by a hungry chicken... Who would've guessed?!

A couple of marines had made several failed attempts to undo the ropes that kept the canvas closed, eventually it was Tyler who managed to get the waterlogged, stressed and swollen knots released by using the biggest darned screwdriver I've ever seen in my life, to pry and wiggle in between the turns in order to release the soaking knots and pull back the saturated canvas flap that had, thankfully, remained intact and very firmly secured at the rear of the truck. The positive outcome was basically due to the excellent design and first-rate workmanship in the manufacture of the truck bodies and these canopies, and when you consider that they've been left sitting in storage untouched, and not maintained for more than forty years, it's totally amazing. He stuck his big, sopping wet head through the gap he'd made, to see for himself that we were all okay, and enquired whether anyone had been hurt. While his query was certainly very brief, only a few words really, I did notice that his normally strong, commanding voice, was unusually flat and quite husky with concern. His relief was also very real.

To the best of my knowledge, it was the first time the man had shown anything akin to a genuine human emotion, pleasure or unease. I remember thinking to myself that if *he* was looking quite so thoroughly shaken up, then you can believe me; that in itself was enough to scare me senseless all over again. When Paddy saw the pain and fear in his hero's eyes, it scared him so much that he squeezed impossibly closer to me until we were virtually glued together; and just for good measure, he held onto my hand even tighter.

Slowly and stiffly, we started making the uncomfortable, and in some cases very embarrassing attempts, to firstly locate, then untangle or separate cramped arms and legs from under, on top of, or around each other, and make an attempt to stand upright, oh well, semi-upright anyway, and start shuffling toward the exit without stamping on – tripping on, or falling over, any stray limbs, bodies, or animals, still down on the floor. While it wasn't as easy as it sounds by any means, and we probably looked more like the cast of The Drunken Sailors in a stage drama, than anything else. Tyler offered each person a strong arm and a firm steadying hand to assist us to climb down, and he was really good too, because he made sure each one of us could stand unaided before letting go. Patrick and I were the last ones to get out. And, oh I don't know, maybe it was only my still very active, well overactive, imagination – but I swear, he stared right into my eyes, and held me a bit tighter, a bit closer and for a little longer than was strictly necessary. Nevertheless, I suppose I can admit it really *was* a nice feeling though. He stood Patrick up on the tailgate, shook his hand then he gave him a real snappy parade ground salute, and thanked him for keeping everyone on his watch safe in the face of such grave danger. Patrick, bless his big heart, stood tall, had a big wet sniff, wiped his nose on his grotty sleeve then wiped it along the leg of his even grottier jeans before returning the salute -with the wrong hand- and told Tyler he was welcome! However, once my big brave little protector was back down on the ground again, he grabbed hold of my hand, and we trotted off together, slipping and sliding through ankle deep mud until we caught up with the rest of the group.

As each person in their turn had approached the tailgate to get a helping hand to climb down, we'd all looked past Tyler's broad, khaki clad shoulders, and no-one could help but stare in morbid fascination at the horrific transformation in what had, only a relatively short time ago, been a truly beautiful place. When we'd stopped initially, Tyler's sole intention had been to have an unhurried lunch break and give the children a safe space to run around in, while the rest of us would be able to have some much-needed respite from this gruelling journey to – well to wherever we eventually end up I suppose.... A while ago the area right where we're standing, had been dry to the point of being dusty – and now we're ankle deep in stinking brown sludge.

One after the other we'd followed Tyler and his men, climbing up that long, rusted ladder all the way to the top where one by one we stopped dead in our tracks until the ones coming behind shoved their way through the human blockage. From the first person to the last, we were struck dumb. No-one could do anything except stand in complete silence, and stare out across what had been the park, no words were spoken, no-one there seemed capable of speech, we just stood and stared, most of us with our mouths hanging open in true and total disbelief. The entire area and for as far as the eye could see, the land was empty and bare. The perfect place we'd found to get out and relax for a little while had vanished. That lovely park and everything there was gone, completely and utterly destroyed, reduced to nothing more than an absolutely depressing splodge of ugly gooey nothingness.

"Oh-my-lord, where did it all go, where *is* everything?" I heard someone in front say – I certainly had no answer for them, my brain seemed to be having a complete shutdown, because, for perhaps the first time in my life I was incapable of coherent *thought*, let alone understanding what it was my eyes were seeing – or more accurately – what they were *not* seeing.

We stopped here, it would have been how long ago - maybe a smidgen over two hours or an absolute *maximum* of three? When we first arrived, there had been well maintained lawns and lush, green grassy slopes, there were colourful flower gardens, and more than a dozen of those split log style, all-in-one four-sided covered picnic tables with plenty of barbeques and open picnic settings scattered around. In fact, we'd counted on using one or two of those barbeques to toast some of the stale flat bread and maybe buy some sausages and meat patties so we could enjoy having something hot to eat for a change. Those picnic area barbeques were built to last for many, many years. They were, at least they *had been*, very well-constructed. The equipment appeared to be very similar to what had been used in the beach beautifying project back in Shady Haven, only on a much grander scale here. Solid, good-looking gas cookers constructed using very durable sandstone and cement, with heavy-duty, stainless-steel hotplates. They'd been positioned at regular intervals in a circle all the way around the really large picnic area. I kept trying to bring back a clear picture in my mind of the park as it was a little while ago. The big 'His n Hers' log cabin style amenities, the sparkling clean bathrooms and showers that I heard so many of the group had been anxious to put to good use after we'd eaten. I don't think I've ever felt more excited by the prospect of a shower and shampoo in my life! I also remember reading a neat little signboard that said all sorts of wonderful things like soap, shampoo, fresh fruits, salads and vegetables, hot dogs, fries, fresh burgers, patties, fresh meats and sausages for the barbeques. Another sign told us the store kept fresh bread, rolls, butter, ketchup, hot coffee, cold drinks and that first aid items were available at the Log Cabin convenience store, and I could have rented a nice clean towel, for a few cents. I remember Lara laughed when she saw the sign as we'd hurried past it on our way to the toilets, she said "that's something we'll need for our shower's girls, who's got some coin?" If you'd taken a little walk along the winding path past the shop there had been such a pretty wooded area with tall, wonderfully fragrant pine trees, and we'd seen a small herd of tame deer. Patrick had wanted to feed those cute little deer so badly too.

As if we were one body, the entire group, marines and evacuees alike, simply stood there, and stared in silence. It was as though we'd been pinned to the spot, we hadn't of course, but we were still human beings, and being confronted by this overwhelming, this heartbreaking up close and personal loss and devastation, we were being forced yet again to acknowledge our own fragility, to remember and to appreciate the very tenuous hold we have on this life, and as such we were equally awestruck by the brutality, the strength and the savagery. We were left speechless because by divine intervention (as one lady put it) we'd lived through that horror to bear witness this dreadful aftermath.

I got a whiff of something, it was something quite familiar too, unpleasant but less pungent than the stink of the mud, but then, in the foggy confusion of the moment I couldn't properly identify the odour.
Looking over what had been -until a few heartbeats ago- an ideal, perfectly groomed park, only to see another lake of muddy brown goop, miles and miles wide, in its place. The amenities block, the shop, barbeques, the gardens and the picnic tables were gone; the only evidence left to indicate that they had ever existed, and weren't simply a figment of our collective imaginations, were a few small blobs of smashed up concrete, and twisted pipes that were sticking up through the mud like so many skeletal fingers.
Oh! Sweet mother of mercy, my brain clicked and I recognised the smell -it was gas! – it made no difference that the barbeques were gone, there were

still mangled bits of pipe poking up out of the mud like bony fingers pointing skyward, and those pipes were still connected to the gas mains, and right now they were releasing very volatile gas!

I had, and even now, so many days later, as I write, I am still having great difficulty equating what should have been right there in front of me.... with the wretched muddy nothingness that was actually there. I remember I turned around –very, very slowly– my bare feet sinking deeper into the gluey mud, taking in more and more of my surroundings. Oh, good grief! My whole body began to shiver and shake, I thought I was going to be sick. My first impulse was to run away, I just wanted to run, to find a place to hide, I wanted to *be* somewhere else, *anywhere* else... as long as it wasn't *here*. I wanted to go home, but then I had to question myself on that too. Go home? Okay, that's all well and good- but go home to what!? Would there even *be* anything left of it now? Anything? Anything at all, or has Shady Haven been left looking exactly the same as this place, exactly the same as far too many other places? I fully understand, and I really do appreciate that Tyler wants to find *something good, somewhere safe* for us but *is* there anything left out there or even a place that's more than this filthy mud and slop?

That's when it hit me, in that very distinct, very precise instant, I finally admitted the truth to myself, it took only that one very fleeting, but very illuminating flash, and I understood that my whole world, my every hope, and every dream I've ever dreamed for my future, the future I'd studied and worked so hard for had been taken, stolen from me, replaced by this, this cataclysmic disaster, this most pathetic of poor excuses for a once beautiful world. Somewhere behind me someone let out a piercing, terrified shriek, sharp enough that it brought my mind crashing back to this barren pig puddle again. *'Where are all the trees? Why aren't there any trees here?'* Her screams dragged not only *my* mind back to all the ugliness of our surroundings, but seeing the utter naked misery evident on so many other faces around me, and I knew then that all our thoughts had been drifting along those same lines. All I could do now was resume my examination of the area. I looked across to where the lovely little forest had been, and wondered...Where *have* those magnificent, tall, dignified, and wonderfully fragrant pine trees gone? Every branch, every sweet-smelling sprig had disappeared, not one single stick, no branch or blade of grass had survived for as far as anyone could see in any direction. What happens, what really *does* become of all the birds, all the deer and the other helpless little creatures and insects that had made their homes in there?

I was overcome by a sudden weakness. I could barely stand, my throat was hot, dry, and terribly sour, it was suddenly so tight I felt as though I was choking, and my mouth filled with nauseating, bitter saliva, but I couldn't swallow. I wanted to vomit, but couldn't even do that either. And it was impossible to speak. I just stood there with my mouth opening and closing like a stranded fish, it took every scrap of energy I possessed just to wipe away the big fat salty tears that were sliding down my dirty cheeks in slow rivers. I felt crushed, defeated, miserable, and extremely insignificant in the midst of all this chaos. This couldn't have happened surely? It's just not possible. But it has, it did, and obviously, it is. I thought about it for a while, and then got to wondering if we *were really alive* or, maybe we *really are dead this time*. I wasn't sure, and to be perfectly honest, the truth is, at that point I don't think I actually cared one way or the other. Until I looked down on the upturned, sweet but frightened face of the little boy holding my hand.

The tomblike stillness and the deathly silence were broken once more, by the same woman, she'd started to sing in a soft, trembling off key tear-filled voice, she was singing just the one line from a really old-time folk song that I vaguely remembered my great-grandmama used to sing sometimes, usually when mother drove us up to the city.

'Where have all the flowers gone, long time – something- something-something' I can't recall anymore words. Mr. Ruiz shouted at her "eh ya stupida crazy, why you don't justa shut the hell up?" But she was deaf to the world outside her own head, she simply kept on singing in her achingly sweet, off-key voice, sitting in the mud and swaying slowly from side to side, with her arms wrapped tightly around herself, crying and singing that one lonely line of a long-forgotten song, completely oblivious to his harsh disapproval.

There we were; standing in the midst of yet another ocean of that evil smelling sticky brown goop and the reeking odour of gas. Mr. Ruiz said –rather too loudly- "we're alla so damma lucky to be haliva still!"

Although, at that moment, I couldn't stop myself wondering… Really? *Is that really true? Are we? Are we lucky to be alive?*

I don't know how to answer that question objectively, but when I looked around me, for the umpteenth time, knowing that all there was to see, no matter which way I looked, there would always be more and more devastation, more fearful faces, more death, and more of the mud covered, desperately broken world surrounding me – I suspect the real answer to that question is, in all likelihood *no, we're not lucky at all….*

 For mercy's sake, how many places have we seen, have driven right on through, that were left looking *exactly* like this? I looked down onto the now crooked line of trucks, but something snagged my attention. Something seemed to be a bit off, no, something most definitely *wasn't right* down there. Truly, I don't want to remember what happened next, because it still troubles me deeply, but I have made a promise to keep this journal as a true, and as accurate an account for whoever might find it and read it after we're all dead and gone. I'm pretty sure that that time can't be very far off now.

Anyway, I refocused and checked along the row once again, this time counting out loud, and ticking the numbers off on my fingers as I went…one, two, three, four, five, six, seven, eight, nine ten. Ten trucks, ten. Ah hell's bell's…where were eleven, twelve and thirteen? There should have been *thirteen*. I counted again to be sure. There were still ten. Ten and only ten trucks, I couldn't make it any more than that. *Where were* the other trucks? *Holy cheese n biscuits!* Where *were* those trucks? And the people? Holy Moley!

Those poor people! What about the people who were inside them? What, *where are they?* Then I remembered the wanderers and wondered did they even make it back to those waiting trucks in time - just to be blown away anyhow? A picture flashed through my mind – a big group of people rambling off...I spun around searching the landscape once again, but nothing out there had changed, it was still the same emptiness and sludge. I could hear Tyler calmly calling us all together, now that's something very much out of character for him, *plus,* he even stood and *waited patiently* until everyone had stopped talking! Well, this must be serious indeed. Once he had silence, he started speaking, but for the first time ever his voice was so quiet that we could barely hear him. Something wasn't right with him, I mean there was something seriously not right – this was so unlike him that, well I didn't know what the heck to think, so I paid very close attention to his mannerisms and his words. He was telling us -in such a soft voice he had everyone either stepping in closer or leaning in closer to hear- that his men had each done a head count and they'd all come up with the same numbers, but those numbers didn't match up with the amount of people who'd arrived a few hours ago. Not everyone had made it back into the trucks. Even though I was still shaking like a leaf myself, I observed him closely, his weary bloodshot eyes were telling me their own story, a tale of profound sadness, of deep, genuine grief and true, heartfelt sorrow. But then in the blink of an eye, his face, and his whole demeanour changed, his expression went kind of blank, his mouth hung a little slack and his gaze was far away, like his spirit had suddenly stepped out for a while, and had left his body unoccupied. That condition lasted maybe twenty seconds and he was back again. The full fleshed lips of moments ago were now pressed together into a wide, hard, bloodless slash, I watched his strong jaw clenching fiercely, I watched the muscles bunching repeatedly along his jaw and somewhere along the line he'd developed a twitchy nervous tick in his right eyelid too, the rapid changes were all pretty unsettling but then I looked down at his hands and saw those big, capable hands were shaking violently. That was all bad enough, but unfortunately there was worse to come. When he spoke, there was an almost frightening change in the quality of his voice that really disturbed me, yes, it was deeper and a great deal huskier than usual, I'd anticipated as much, but when he started speaking to us in that awful, ghastly flat monotone, my blood ran cold. His words were totally lacking any kind of expression or emotion, and I knew he was keeping himself tightly controlled. His bearing was extremely rigid and forcefully controlled. He was wound up tighter than a spring and ready to pop.

However, once he started talking he started repeating himself again, and again, over and over, each word becoming increasingly terse, harsh, ragged, angry, pained and so very dreadful to hear. His eyes weren't looking *at* us anymore, now they'd become flat, dull and unfocused. I believe the shock of today's losses, coming on top of weeks and months of unrelenting strain had caused his mind go off somewhere else, but wherever that place was, it was an awfully troubling and very painful place for him to be.

He started to mumble something, although at that point his words were indistinct and impossible to understand - at first. Oh, but then he started repeating himself same as before, over, and over, and over again; and this time his voice was getting louder, and more aggressive, more emotionally charged and *angrier* with each repetition, until he was almost screaming like a wildman. "*I told them,* didn't I? I *did* tell them, *I know* I told them, I told *all of you,* time and *time again* I told them. *Not* to wander off, to *stay close* by the trucks; *why didn't they listen to me!?*" He was really bellowing now. Patrick was upset, anxious and really scared, seeing his hero breaking down right there in front of him, but being only three years old, he couldn't understand why. In his own confusion and fear he grabbed hold of my hand and burst into tears. I picked him up and held onto him tightly, probably a bit too tightly if I'm to tell the truth, because I wanted to get him away from there but because everyone was standing so close together, I couldn't move an inch in any direction, or take my eyes off the man standing only one small step in front of me. Tyler was in dreadful torment, he was suffering *so* cruelly, and I was powerless to help, or to even *do* anything for him.

Tyler was yelling out, really screaming now, but in all honesty, I sincerely doubt whether he was even *aware* of anyone else at all. Being close enough, but not game enough, to reach out and touch him, I could see tears' glistening in his eyes, however, if there's one thing I'm absolutely, one hundred and ten percent sure of, it's that it was the final scrap of the tattered remnants of his inflexible, absolutely single-minded, pig-headed self-discipline, that prevented those tears from falling. We turned towards the sound of boots splashing and squelching through the thick gooey mud and a voice calling out – "Gunny! Sergeant! Hey Tyler! Sergeant Tyler *Sir*! *Master Gunnery Sergeant Tyler, SIR*! Requesting permission to speak *Sir*." Two of the marines, Chung and Rivers had broken ranks and came over to stand close to him, very, very, close, taking a position one on each side of him. Rivers spoke quietly and calmly, directly into Tyler's ear before they turned him around and had to practically drag him away from the flabbergasted assembly.

A few minutes later we heard Tyler's loud, wounded, terribly outraged *roar*, yelling angrily. "*Hells freaking bells man; just exactly what the hell do you expect of me? We have lost over a dozen civilian lives here today. Lives that we are – NO, not we- lives that I am- responsible for! Lives we promised to protect. No! No! Sorry, wrong again - Lives I promised to protect!*"

Each word was like a gun shot, and after a while there were just indistinct rumbling mumbles.

I can't say for sure who it was that made the suggestion, but I'm thinking now that it was more than likely Mr. Costa, he asked for everyone to go and stand alongside the same person they sat next to on the way here, if that person wasn't present, then we were to leave a space. Thank goodness all the kids were accounted for, but there are still an awful lot of empty spaces indicating how many people were missing, none of them were from our area or from the ridge area either, not that that makes any difference whatsoever really, they were all just as much a part of this convoy, as me, or anyone else here.

I could hear Grace crying (poor thing, she was in shock too) she kept repeating over and over. "But *where's* Jeremy? He's going to miss out on the opening night if he doesn't come back soon. Come *on* Jeremy hurry *up* will you? Where are all the others? I'm hungry. Does anyone know where the toilets are? I can't find Jeremy's staff now either. They can't have just disappeared, not completely, Jeremy. Where's Jeremy? I need to go to the toilet now, but where is everyone why aren't they getting ready?" Over, and over, and over again, she just kept reciting those same mixed up unanswerable questions… and rocking…rocking back and forth, back and forth. I snapped back to reality and sent Patrick off to Mrs Beatty, she was keeping an eye on the children while there was no-one else looking after them.

Meanwhile I managed to get some of the shady girls to help me to get Grace cleaned up (poor lady, she didn't need the toilets anymore) I think I must have something like a built-in autopilot, because I seemed to be able to do the necessary things without even thinking about it.

Lunch had been completely forgotten, although now a few of the boys were complaining of stomach ache, while the men just sat around in the back of the trucks without talking or making a sound just waiting for the next instructions– I must admit that it was a welcome change too - Mrs. Beatty and Mrs. Armstrong had scraped together a meal of sorts, and asked everyone to eat at least something. Reba helped me find fresh clothing so we could get Grace cleaned up, after we'd sorted her out, we hand fed her a sandwich and even got her to drink a few sips of lukewarm tea, but by that time her eyes were starting to droop, so we tucked her up in the back of a truck using someone's blankets and pillows, I neither knew nor cared whether or not the owner would object to her using them. In fact, by that stage, if someone *had* complained - I would have enjoyed a good old-fashioned 'donnybrook', as my gran called an argument- something to relieve a bit of the tension knotting up my back and shoulders.

Any conversations were carried out quietly, not that there was anything much left to say, and admittedly, the subject on everyone's mind, was also the one no-one was ready to talk about yet, so mostly we just sat, tried to sleep, or read a book but by then the daylight was fading. After about probably two hours or so, Tyler surprised everyone when he called out for us to come down out of the vehicles and gather around. Incredible but true, he seemed to be rock steady and completely in control of himself once again.

He started by saying "Today everyone here has suffered two very traumatic experiences, and even though we'd survived that shocking storm, it was only to find out that we'd also lost a good many of our travelling companions, so it's quite understandable that we might feel the need to have an experienced councillor to talk to. Corporal Rivers has been trained extensively in this area, so if anyone does feel the need to have a talk with him, I will make sure he's available. Today, we have lost nineteen of our companions, and that is just so very tragic for every person in this group. My men have undertaken a localized search for our missing members, although to be perfectly open and honest with you, outside of a miracle, there is no hope of us finding any of them alive. We have seen all too often the damage left behind – but today is the first time we've experienced, and been affected by a storm, fortunately it wasn't as strong as it could have been. Now we've experienced, and seen with our own eyes, the level of violence and damage done by that storm. I cannot imagine any man, or any woman, surviving a storm of that measure, and certainly not out in the open. I am still amazed that *any of us* have survived. When you do start to think about what happened today, and about those we've lost -and you will- maybe not today or tomorrow, but those thoughts will come, there are certain things that must be considered and understood, okay? If those solid brick and concrete buildings, the gas cooking appliances and that grove of trees could be torn up out of the ground so easily and have vanished, ask yourself this question, how much more fragile is a human body? It's imperative that we get on with our operation now, now more so than ever; in so far as getting you all to a place of safety, and returning to our base, nothing has changed." I think I detected a slight hitch in his voice as he spoke. He continued on with an disturbingly long list of damages and loss. "That storm also took out three trucks completely, well five really, when you count the two with severe damages. If you will all recall, the first truck parked at each end was left empty for the walkers to climb into, well those trucks are gone now" (there were murmurs of absurd things like – it was divine intervention, or, it was their time, and one... Oh - my god, it was their destiny, it was their fate, or another, it was providence. Josh Woods slowly turned his face away and said solemnly, "God's will hath been done", and Mr. Ruiz, being as sensitive and sentimental as always, pointed to Tyler and commented "da stupid idiots shoulda listen at him n dey wouldn't a got dead." Tyler continued speaking. "The other truck was carrying an assortment of your personal wares... Mrs. Beatty cried out "no oh no, oh *please*! Not my sewing things? Please tell me the big kit's not gone, is it?" without answering her Tyler continued "and both of the remaining outer vehicles on each end, the one containing heavier belongings such as furniture and crates of some sort – have been severely damaged, the other truck, the one that had been transporting the marines, some boxes of dried food, and some of our gear – well the truth is, both of those trucks are badly damaged, and far beyond our ability to repair or make operative. In our present location we simply don't have the tools or equipment necessary. We have to abandon those vehicles. Therefore, it will be necessary to load the extra fuel, food supplies, the animals, and only carry enough water necessary for our survival, as best we can, into the eight remaining trucks."

That was when he dropped his bombshell...he told us that in view of this unfortunate situation, certain *individual sacrifices* would have to be made, we would –he said– have to dispose of some, certainly not all, but some, of our unnecessary personal possessions. The goods would be locked inside the abandoned vehicles as securely as possible, but we simply *cannot take* any of the larger things with us right now, or *anything* that is not essential to our immediate survival. Anita suggested the girls should get rid of a lot of useless clothing and she'd be more than willing to share her clothes with anyone who didn't pack enough practical clothing. Sienna got a fit of the giggles and admitted she'd packed mostly her formal or best going out clothes, oh and that cute red dress she wore at her sister's wedding as well. Quite a surprising number of the other women and girls had done exactly the same thing; they had packed their best, most expensive clothes and shoes, and left their comfy everyday wear behind. I wondered to myself, why would you only pack evening and formal wear? Who the heck wears a ball gown as their everyday clothes? Myself, I had packed plenty of underwear, a few pairs of jeans, shorts, a stack of tee shirts, pyjamas, a few warm jumpers, a coat, socks and extra runners, toiletries, a couple of towels, a thick blanket and my big feather down quilt which were rolled up tightly and squeezed into grandad's old waterproof duffel bag, a double sleeping bag, two bed sheets and my pillow with six pillow cases on it – just in case... but not a fancy dress or a pair of snazzy shoes anywhere! Even though I was supposed to be packing only my personal items to evacuate, I had the thought that where there were children, there should be education available, so I grabbed as many books and necessary school equipment as I had strong enough boxes to pack them into.

"No!! No more I tell you! I will *no* part with my precious antique armoires! Leave behind all zi zuitcases, zose nonsenses in boxes, my beautiful armoires, zey *are* comink viz me!" Mr. Diaz started to call something out but his wife's high pitched, and extremely annoying nasal voice cut across him – *"My* zuitcases and *all* off my baggages I vill most *certainly* be taking viz me, and *you*, as a man of zi vorld sergeant" she said trying to look sexily at Tyler- "I know you unnerstand it no, I vill need to be keep my computers *and* my cam-era e-quipments *and* my music collections vis me, *in* zeir *completeness also, yes!* Zi moo-zic is so relaxating for everyone no!? I am zi *artiste* so I must remain allvays relax-ed for my vork. So *no*, Senor Ty-ler, zese sings I *cannot* be expec-ted to liff vizout, if zere is not zi space for everysing, zi choice is, ah it is so, so zimple- just leave all off zose dirty and smelling animals behind!"

Tyler closed his eyes for a second (I think it *really was* a count to ten moment) then he took a good deep breath and said to everyone. "It's pretty straightforward folks, we will carry as much as possible, but there simply *will not* be *sufficient* space for everything that we have packed into those vehicles. Not unless *you*" (he pointed around the group) "are prepared to take your chances, you can get out and walk, and sleep, alongside the trucks." Mr and Mrs Ruiz were shouting at Tyler, at us, at the marines and at each other- in rapid, completely incomprehensible Pandushi, red faced and waving their arms around, pointing at their possessions that were now sitting in the mud outside the truck alongside a huge assortment of offloaded boxes and baggage. One of the marines strode over to them and snapped off a mouthful of something in Pandu-Shi, very loud, and I must say, very *effective* Pandu-Shi! I have no idea what he said, but whatever it was, it worked a treat! Because both Mr *and* Mrs Ruiz's mouths snapped shut and they turned away even redder faced and more infuriated -if that's even possible, than before! Mr Ruiz stalked off - oh, well yeah, if a man who is barely five feet tall, wearing a cheap, filthy dirty, creased and badly stained suit, with mud encrusted high heeled western boots and wearing an ill-fitting, crooked, and badly discoloured synthetic toupee, and a scruffy overgrown moustache, *can stalk off* -well, I think he might have managed it!

There were plenty of stifled giggles coming from those watching him. However, before we commenced the difficult business of sorting through our most personal, and in fact our *only* belongings, a short prayer was said for our missing companions, eight youngish couples, 2 young single men, and one elderly gentleman. Nineteen people who'd shared breakfast with us this morning had vanished from the face of the earth in a matter of seconds. We have all learned a very hard, but also a very important and valuable lesson first hand today, concerning the indiscriminate cruelty the sheer *unpredictability*, and the heart stopping savagery of this weather. Many of the complaining nay sayers had learned quite an essential lesson from this awful tragedy too - Listen to Tyler, and heed his advice, the man *knows* what he's talking about.

The marines had turned the trucks around and the headlights gave us enough light to work by.

The sorting out wasn't at all the big deal I thought it would be, mainly because the marines guided us on what each of us should, or probably should not, keep. For instance, things we would need wherever we ended up, as opposed to things that would not only take up valuable space and weigh us down (and thereby use up more of the precious fuel) but would, in the long run be worthless to us, like antique furniture or thirty pairs of shoes, or two thousand music discs, oh and not to mention all those large heavy air cargo boxes filled with weighty audio-visual, lighting and camera equipment *and* their corresponding computers! Because without electrical power they're all totally useless anyway. (That they were ever loaded at all has Tyler turning purple!) However, things that would soon be priceless to us, like personal toiletries, soap, a toothbrush and toothpaste, shampoo, a few spare changes of underwear and clothing each, extra runners and socks, and if we had them, a hat, scarf, jumper and a coat would be sensible too, as would our personal sleeping pillow, two or three towels and a couple of blankets each, bed sheets also have many uses, and these were the things may well prove to be invaluable to us. I was among the fortunate few who didn't have to discard any of my things, whereas a number of women and girls were left with very little to wear.

One of the marines helping us, suggested we could lay all the blankets and towels along the seats and use our pillows as back rests, by doing it that way –he said- they weren't actually taking up any *extra* space, and we would be able to stow more things in our luggage – and if there was anything extra that we thought we might need, well we might have to keep it on our laps for the duration of the journey.

Oh dear, oh *wow!* Now didn't that kind and very thoughtful suggestion earn him a scathing look from his boss! There simply wasn't going to be enough space available. The remaining water and provisions, the cases and boxes of medicines and medical instruments, First Med Assistance, Green X and Blue Support boxes together with all practical and utilitarian goods, were pooled and packed tightly, *really* tightly, into each and every possible nook and cranny of the three remaining trucks. The marines were being really considerate to us this time, and whatever space, no matter how small it was, we could add our precious and other non-essential belongings. The Boss man came to me and asked me what I was studying, I told him I am, well, I *had* been - a senior teaching assistant for Special Needs and Physically Challenged Children, I'd also hoped to work in Zone forty-one, with Indigenous children someday. I asked him why he was so interested. He replied that he'd noticed I'd put out some boxes of what looked to him to be various levels of educational text books and a large crate of writing books, writing equipment and pencils. The next words out of his mouth completely stunned me, he told me he'd salvaged them, along with all the school books and writing implements from the other students we had on board. He said he'd been able to fit everything in by separating them into smaller bundles and tucking them, under seats, on top of, in-between, and behind other things.

"Educational equipment, and teaching resources are far too valuable to lose; those things must *never* be disrespected *or* thrown away" he said. That man is just such a walking contradiction! Strangely enough though, neither of the antique armoires, the computers, camera equipment, the cases of music discs, or the trunks and chests filled with designer gowns, shoes and suits made it onto the truck. Those things, along with the rest of the unusable luggage and a few unnecessary things belonging to the missing folks, along with all the rest of the groups discarded possessions, have been sealed up and left inside the abandoned trucks.

 Although, and at Tyler's direction, Williams and Fitzgerald sorted through all the luggage and the boxes belonging to the missing people, they selected and repacked every scrap of suitable clothing, toiletries, bedding and blankets that we were now really short of. (Remember we have a lot of lost children and their luggage didn't come with them) They were stunned to find two big crates containing beautiful sets of restaurant quality cooking pots and pans in super large sizes, and in another crate they discovered a complete set of professional chef's knives, ranging from a small paring knife right up through the range to massive bone cleavers, there were boxes of cutlery and all the utensils any chef or cook could wish for packed in with two dozen each of crisp white, dark blue, red, black and yellow linen tablecloths! I wondered who they'd belonged to, because whoever it was, when they'd decided to take what was supposed to be a relaxing walk, not only they themselves, but all their plans, their hopes, and their dreams for the future were lost too. Fitzgerald had the bright idea that instead of discarding the dozen or more big stainless steel clip top locking water drums, to empty them instead and fill them with awkward things that had to be packed anyway, since many of the flimsy containers we'd used were falling, or had already fallen apart. The drums would roll easily whenever they had to be moved and could be reused for years to come. Not only did Tyler actually *approve* of the idea, he even commended him on the suggestion.

 Fortunately for us all, if we were careful, there would now be enough of everything that we'd need for our survival, at least in the short term.

Tyler was - to all outward appearances completely calm and absolutely unconcerned. But it was all one big act he was putting on for our benefit. *I* could tell by the way he was walking, by the high set of his shoulders, and by the way he was constantly looking all around searching and scanning the immediate area and beyond, that he was feeling really uneasy about something, and I proved to be right, because as it turned out, he was one very anxious man indeed. When our journey eventually resumed, the marines were all heavily armed and marines were assigned to guard the safety and security, of not only the passengers and drivers, but also the trucks packed with the animals, the foodstuffs, and our remaining goods and belongings. Even the scout has been issued with a high-powered machine rifle that he wore slung across his shoulders. One of the older boys started teasing the scout about having a rifle hanging down his back saying it would be less than useless in an attack – but before the last three words were out of his mouth the kid was looking down the barrel of that not so 'useless' rifle! They were guarding us yes, but against who, or what? Was he edgy about the possibility of an attack and if so, where did he expect it to come from? Or perhaps he was worried about thieves? Although, the only other human being we'd seen was the old woman in the little store – and she'd met the same fate as our walkers, and we hadn't seen another living soul for weeks. We had been told that Rivers, Martinez and Chung (Michael, Josh and Chris) would be riding shotgun at the back of our truck once we got moving again, and judging by their weapons, they seriously meant business too. Patrick, well not only Patrick really, it was *all* of the boys in our truck, they were awestruck and goggle eyed by those big ugly weapons and impressed by the many long belts of wicked looking bullets they had draped across their shoulders and pooling like long coiled snakes on the floor behind them. Right from the very beginning when we left Shady, I've had the feeling that they found this assignment really frustrating. If you recall, their initial assignment, had been one that had started out being so straightforward, so well-ordered, clear-cut and uncomplicated, exactly the same as their previous relocation assignments. But *this* assignment has, right from that very first day, well, it has just refused to go according to their plans. It felt to me as though, he (Tyler) was now on high alert, and expecting some major trouble to be coming our way. And even though I wracked my brains and scoured my memory I even went back through the pages of this journal for clues, I couldn't find so much as a single hint of what it could possibly be, *unless* the terrible loss of life and equipment or perhaps the shock of the storm has special significance for him.

There was an uncomfortable air of expectancy surrounding him that had the flow-on effect of making everyone else jittery, and constantly looking over their shoulders. We all shared the one thought - wondering who, or *what* it could be that he was suddenly, and so obviously concerned about.

The job of disentangling the damaged vehicles without having the benefit of heavy machinery was a major feat in itself, and it certainly showcased the physical strength, and sheer *ingenuity* of these men, who worked tirelessly all throughout the night even after such a long and emotionally tough day. The separation was successful but they weren't finished yet, not by a long way, they then had to go about stripping the trucks that were to be abandoned bare of any and everything that might be useful. They completely filled one truck and almost half filled a second truck with all of the salvaged parts, tools, any undamaged canvas was swapped over (but not discarded) for any canopies that had been ripped or damaged by the storm, the bucket seats were removed (I asked Tyler if he would allow the two older ladies to have a seat each, and to my surprise he not only gave them the seats, but he managed to anchor them securely as well) a couple of spare truck wheels were taken on board and every last drop of the fuel was siphoned from the fuel tanks and most of it was transferred to the active vehicles while the remainder was 'canned' (as Chung called it) into the drums already on board, the batteries, auxiliary spot lights, welding equipment, some really unusual looking tools and even stranger tool kits, engine covers, wooden bench seats ropes and anything else we might possibly be able to make use of, and although it was an extraordinary process, it was also quite a disturbing thing to witness. Looking at that stockpile of spare parts has, in some peculiar way, really opened our eyes, and brought home to some -as nothing else had so far – that we actually *were* in fact, in some really serious trouble now. The realisation had finally dawned, that of every awful thing that had happened and *was happening* all around us, one fact was irrefutable now; we were, each and every single one of us, in genuine physical danger of both serious injuries, of dying – or of being killed. Whether we met our demise via a storm or some other as yet unknown threat, time alone would tell. Until that moment, for some of the evacuees/refugees none of it had been quite real. I noticed a man standing by himself behind one of the stripped-down trucks who seemed a bit preoccupied, but not in a good way. I asked him if he was feeling okay, because he didn't look well. I was really surprised when he came right out and admitted that "so far, it's been sort of like we were watching all the storm drama unfold on a television program. Because it *couldn't* be real. But now" he said "I get it, I finally *get it.*" He added "the fact that there had been so many millions of people out there, who weren't there anymore, and every one of them had been a real person just like, well like me, with real families, real jobs, real hobbies and real lives who'd lived in all of those wrecked and battered places that we've passed through, but the truth that they, along with people we've actually known and shared a table with, are disappearing, and dying, and they're dying in the most hideous ways imaginable out there – I just didn't *want* it to be real... and it is, it *is* real, too damned real and today I realised you, me, any, or *all* of us, could so very easily be next and, and...I know now that I'll never see my wife and kids again. They were put into another truck before the last Pick-up (Shady Haven) and I think they're all dead now." He covered his face with his hands and walked away, bent almost double and sobbing hard.

I've also been having serious doubts as to whether my mother my gran, or my brothers either for that matter, could possibly still be alive. My heart's crumbling, feeling so broken and so heavy inside my chest, because I can't honestly believe that they *are* still alive. Now, more than ever, I wish I'd stayed at home, but did they make it home at all? I don't want to be left in the world all alone; I'd be much better if we'd all gone together.

Somehow, over the course of the last few days this horror has all become real, much, much *too* real ... and this overwhelming feeling of imminent danger and disaster is beyond hideous. I know this will sound a bit trivial, but, well this whole evacuation thing started out being a bit frightening, what with all the storm damage to our farms and our homes, the rising waters and everything, and everyone being pushed to pack up and get out - but in another way, it was really sort of exciting for us too; you know, it was all a bit of a hoot, and practically all the younger ones like me, just saw it as excitement, a great big adventure, we were breaking out, running away from the small town boredom, and escaping the small minded community attitude, getting a chance to live a bit for once. We just didn't understand or *appreciate* all the wonderful, worthwhile things we had. Our families and friends, our busy farms, our animals, our work or schooling – and now? Well right now, we have *nothing*, absolutely *nothing* at all.

The recent events have demonstrated the grim reality of our situation, of what our lives are now. Reality has raised its ugly head, and it's turning out to be a complete nightmare for *everyone* on this journey.

Oh, for goodness' sake, not those two *again*! What, are they still twelve years old? Reba's just told me that Angie and Janice are having a cat fight. I wouldn't mind betting it's over one of the marines too. The funny thing is, neither of those two airheads would even *consider* it for two seconds; but the men/man they're fighting over, probably doesn't even know those two girls are *alive*. To them we are, *if* we're anything at all, we're simply part of another job to them, although those two nutcases are too brainless to recognise that simple truth. Oh well, I suppose it gives them something else to do and think about. Hopefully there won't be blood spilled.

The marines have to keep their strength and fitness levels up, and seeing as they can't spare the time required to stop and do their normal daily exercise routines, Tyler's come up with a solution –of sorts. Instead of sitting idle in a truck getting doughy bums, (like us) the men who aren't driving or on guard duty…well folks, they run. They run with a 'lightweight' sixty-pound pack and a heavy weapon, *plus* a full belt of ammunition too, and that ammo *isn't* lightweight, not in any man's language. They run either alongside or in front of the moving vehicles (but never behind the truck). The runners and our guards changed over every ten miles. I'm exhausted from just watching them!

And so, we drive on… for mile, after bone jarring, emotion pounding, spirit destroying, overloaded mile. The number of people that were in four packed trucks before – are now squeezed up into two, now no-one can even scratch themselves without scratching their neighbour as well, but I suppose I shouldn't be complaining because a least we aren't sharing the limited space with lambs, pigs or birds anymore, and riding still beats walking any day of the week. One look at the runners confirms that thought. No matter where we look, no matter which direction we drive, there's never been anything that even faintly resembled a roadway, or human habitation, it's always the same stark, tragic scene.

The only thing to see anywhere was mud, sludge, muck, slush, mire, ooze, quagmire, goop, bog, call it whatever you like, we were surrounded by a loathsome, foul-smelling ocean of it. The trucks drove over it, and the marines ran through it, all day -and often the greater part of the long nights too. The storms have (fortunately??) either preceded us, or else followed some ways behind us, but always seemingly keeping a safe enough distance from our convoy all the way.

Occasionally we'd see a small cluster of houses that had suffered only slight damage –maybe they had only been caught by the weakened tail end or else been side swiped by a lesser storm, and there'd be a few blistered and burned people outside trying to carry out hasty repairs. But most times we would see what must have been extensive municipalities, once busy places called home by a million people or more that had been ripped up, torn down and blown away, leaving behind no hint of life whatsoever.

Some of the places we drove through, the only things that hadn't been wiped out would be the odd broken chimney, or sometimes we saw a washed-out swimming pool that had filled up with, and was surrounded by, tiny scraps little bits and pieces of brick, concrete and splinters of wood that would scarcely be good enough for kindling. Although when you think about it, all of those things, in all of those places had probably once been symbols of pride, of success, maybe a secure, safe home and financial security to some nice, every day average family, a family that judging by the evidence all around us, no longer existed. Where were they now?

Yes, that's a very good question, where *have* all those people, all the animals, the houses, the buildings, all the manufacturing plants, the transportation vehicles…. where has everything gone *too*? I mean it must all still be out there somewhere, logic, science, the law of physics and good old common sense tells us that it all had to fall back down to earth *somewhere*, but where?

I really should steer my brain away from these kinds of questions, because any answers I might come up with, paint a picture too horrific to think about. The trucks have slowed down to a crawl, crunching over the few wretched remains of what had once probably been a medium sized township, every scrap and fragment was completely coated with a thick layer of sludge. If you had a mind to gather up every stick and nail that was left behind after one of the storms had raged through, there wouldn't even be enough to build a toy doghouse. Michael pounded twice on the side of the truck as he jogged alongside, something, about ten yards off to the left, had caught his eye, Tyler must have told him to go and take a look, and report what he found- it was so depressing and grim to be confronted by such complete and fearsome destruction, time, after time, after time. Michael's heart was racing as he approached the object he'd seen laying in the mud. As he bent to pick it up his heart sank and rose again within a single beat. He'd found a life size baby doll, wearing a very muddied hand knitted baby dress, the dress somehow still showed small patches of light pink, a knitted bonnet covered the dirty hair, and one knitted bootee sock covered the dolls foot, the relief on his face, that it *was* actually a toy, was unmistakable. He held it up for Tyler to see then dropped it back onto the ground and jogged back into position. Although, the fleeting expressions of dread and relief on his face for those few seconds absolutely did reflect the thoughts and feelings of just about every other person who'd seen him with the muddied toy in his hand... what about the little girl who'd played with it? Where is she now? The dolls clothing had probably been lovingly hand made by a doting mother or grandmother for a very special little girl. Chris, another marine, jogged over to the truck to show us something that he'd found while Michael was checking out the doll. What he held in his hand was really and truly awe inspiring, amazing actually, and quite truthfully, it was a mystery way above and beyond simple amazement; a long thin sliver of wood about half the thickness of a toothpick *had pierced* a *house brick* clean through! Good heavens! *What kind* of force is even *capable* of doing that? Well, we've known for months that the winds are tremendously powerful, but honestly, just how strong *are* those winds? Where will they be coming from next time... and the time after that? Will we, the people in this group, will we eventually fall victim to them as well?

What have those idiotic whiz kid scientists done to us? What have they done to our planet? How could they *possibly* have gotten it *so wrong?* What mistake, what miscalculation did they make that has brought so much hideous death and destruction raining down on our heads? What error or inaccuracy did they make in their calculations that it triggered such catastrophic warlike devastation, bringing about the total and widespread annihilation of so many and so much? The inestimable number of horrific human deaths, and who knows how many of earths other unique life forms have vanished and are most probably gone forever? The only thing left behind after these storms is this absolutely sickening nothingness, the thousands upon thousands of miles of once fertile land bursting with life and potential, has been laid waste, fouled for hundreds, maybe even thousands of years to come. What will be the ultimate outcome be for our once rich, incredibly diverse and beautiful world?

The muddy 'highway' kept churning beneath our wheels. Occasionally, far off in the distance we'd see other vehicles, although we couldn't tell whether they were abandoned, broken down, or, if like so many other things, they'd been blown away and fell to earth in that place, it was incredibly rare to see any people, and whenever we did, those who were still capable of movement were walking around, their skin blistered and burned beyond belief, their manner dazed and confused.

Oh, there is just so much I don't want to think about, much less remember, and writing it all down is, well sometimes it's not only difficult, it's really and truly stomach-turning for me. But I have to keep reminding myself that within these pages, this horror story needs to be told and it *must* be told exactly the way it's happening, in spite of my own feelings, because with this journal – it really is everything or nothing, and hopefully one day someone will read these pages and know the truth, maybe they won't understand it all any more than we do, but they'll know what *really* happened to all the people, to the world. Because unless things like news reports, and the governments insane insistence on secrecy, and their habit of covering up, or sugar coating the truth, unless it changes a great deal after this, any future generations will *never* know the realities, or the truth, they'll only know, or be taught, what the Administration of the day *wants* them to know and to *believe*. But *we, the people*, have learned only too well that all Governments and Rulers lie, they cheat, they also steal and become tremendously wealthy by employing downright dishonesty, and they will most certainly gloss over, cover up, deny or what's most likely, they'll bury the real truth, and bury it so deep they'll think no-one will ever find it. But the truth *will* be found.

There was this one place we drove through that was, oh my god, it just stank so bad, so *incredibly* bad, but there was nothing outside, or nothing we could see that might cause such an unspeakable stench either, there was really nothing around outside at all - except for the omnipresent sea of mud … Until we crested a hill - and there it was…

Never, not in all the years spent living on a farm have I smelled anything so, so, well, so foully rotten. Fetid or putrid are about the only words I can think of, but even *they* can't even *begin* to touch, let alone to *describe* that horrendous stink, it was such a stomach-churning rancid stench. The air was thick with the vomitus smell of putrid, rotting, decomposing meat, it made everyone gag. Rivers stood up – he'd tied a wet handkerchief around his face- to look around outside- and yelled at Chung, hey quick man, secure that canvas! But he was too late, we'd already seen them. At first my brain couldn't quite grasp *what* I was actually seeing, and then in a split second my eyes and brain focused and I'd recognised them for what they were. They were bodies, dead bodies, mountains and mountains of them, *so impossibly many* yards, probably even *miles* deep, and those poor, poor dead people were strewn about, thrown all over the ground like some giant, evil tempered child, had thrown all her boxes of toy soldiers and dolls away, there were possibly, god only knows how many millions of dead bodies out there, humans, and animals too, all mixed up together with tonnes of smashed up vehicles, machinery of every conceivable type, and mixed in there were mountains of twisted metal and building debris mashed together with dead bodies. It went on like that for a good two miles, goodness only knows how deep or how wide those mountains of misery were. It looked for all the world like one gargantuan dumping ground.

Although, and as ugly, and as horrible and as cruel as it sounds, I suppose it *has* answered the question of where did they all go, but it's just, oh god, it's just so appalling, so, overwhelming, so incredibly heartbreaking, horrifying and wicked. Worse, it's such a tragic senseless waste of humanity.

All these hours and hours later, and all the miles we've covered since, I can still see it, and I can still smell it. I think I'll carry the smell and the memory of that frightful place in my head forever.

There was one poor man, such an unfortunate soul, he was really and truly wretched. This lone man, burned so badly the blisters were hanging off his face and body like brown water filled balloons and he was horribly injured, the poor soul had clearly lost his mind, but he still hobbled after us, one terribly damaged arm hanging by his side, the other arm waving a machete around, and as he tried to run, the poor man was tripping over blackened and bloated corpses and the various body parts of humans and animals alike, he just kept chasing us screaming and shouting out hysterically that we've already been judged by God and this is how we're paying for our sins! *"YOU AREN'T DEAD YET BUT YOU'RE ALREADY IN HELLLL!"* This outburst was followed by a long string of the filthiest obscenities I have ever heard... Thankfully the trucks gathered speed and swerved away from the nauseating, and absolutely the most emotionally and mentally disturbing scene any human being could witness in ten lifetimes.

It was started by the Upper Valley people, mainly that one nasty old man, but the other older men, took up the fight and started yelling some really horrible, shocking and truly revolting abuse at Tyler, thumping on the closed connecting window between the passenger area and the cab of the truck, bellowing and him – yelling out that it was *his duty* to stop and give assistance to those poor wretches wandering around out there, or to at least have the decency to go over and bury the dead. Someone else shrieked at him to remember that he'd taken an oath to serve and protect the public. Tyler crashed the window back and responded savagely by saying – "It would not only be dangerous; it would be suicidal for the men and also hazardous for every passenger. Besides anything else it'd be completely pointless for us to stop, because we have nothing to spare for them, and like 'machete man' over there, each and every one of those people out there needed hospitalisation and some serious professional help" but there was no way known to man, that he was going to subject *his* men to *those* conditions! "Just how long do you think it would take us to do a mass burial on such a vast scale? And I'm telling *you, you morons, it's not our* duty, who knows what kind, or how many deadly diseases have developed and festered out there? Get your forces right before you open your useless big mouth too, you damned brainless fool, it's the motto of the *Police Force, they* promise to -Serve and Protect- I'm a *Marine* and *I* follow my *orders*, so putting it bluntly *sir* - I can't offer any help."

No one could possibly know when we would run into trouble, or another storm, and as Tyler was forced to explain yet again, "We have precious little left for our own needs now, so how many do suggest we assist eh? 1? 25? 100? Do I feed them the last crumbs of *your* food today? Just how many of those poor miserable souls do you think we could actually help eh? And that's providing of course that we aren't all murdered before we could even *start* to do anything for them. Oh, and when the little food we *do* have left runs out, then what?" Tyler's voice was getting louder and harder. "What?" He said pointing to Patrick and Shannon. "Losing their parents isn't enough hardship, or enough punishment for these kids, is that what you think? Is that it? *You'd* allow these *little children* to go *hungry* as well as being heartbroken and terrified every minute of the day and night? Is that *really* what you want!? Well okay then, so what happens after tomorrow night eh? *Tell me!* C'mon then, *you're* making yourself out to be the big man, you're the one with the big mouth giving *me* orders! Or are you too gutless, too spineless… that's really it isn't it? You're just straight out-and-out blow-hards, *cowards*! All mouth and no substance- well mister tell me – come on now, it's time to prove what you are *really* made of, *you've* started this, now *you* have to finish it. So, tell me what-are-you-going-to-do? I'm listening – but I can't hear you, speak up man. Oh, so now all of a sudden, you've gone really quiet, all out of suggestions eh, nothing more to say now, is that right? Well, now *everyone* in this whole group knows *exactly* what-you-are-*really*-made-of mister." Mr Beatty just sat there red, almost purple faced, and fuming to the point of physically shaking, while his poor wife was pale faced and trembling, looking thoroughly mortified by his reprehensible behaviour.

"Please, now I'm asking you to all to listen to me, everybody, it's by far the best, *and* the safest option for everyone, if we to keep to ourselves, to remain together, as we are - a whole group. That is unless *you'd* like to volunteer *your* services sir? You can get down out of this truck, I can stop *right now*, this very minute, *you* can leave this group; you sir, and any likeminded people or person who wishes to join you, are perfectly at liberty to go over there and you can do whatever you think you can do. I'll even give you a few shovels to dig that grave with! But rest assured that *we*, the rest of this company, will keep right on moving, and we will keep on moving until I can find somewhere that's safe enough to make camp." Tyler took a deep breath, but he couldn't stop until he'd had his say.

"But *you* –it's Mr Beatty, right? You, well *you* can leave right now sir; and no-one will even try and stop you, nor will we wait for you. I'm damned sorry for their plight, but I cannot offer anyone else, anything at all as things stand today. If, or should I say *when*, we find a place that is undamaged and functioning properly, *then* I'll *immediately* report to the relative authorities exactly what we've seen here today, and I'll see to it that the necessary arrangements to get the proper medical assistance sent out here. I can, and I will, do no more than that. It's all very well for you to throw your very considerable weight around and to give me and my men orders to do what you yourself are *too cowardly to do.* You sir, you and your ilk disgust me." Tyler wiped his mouth with the back of his hand and seemed surprised at the amount of spittle he'd raised. I could well understand and empathise, as to why he was so very angry, and so totally frustrated by, not only his inability to change our present situation, or that he had to turn away from fellow human beings in such blatant distress and obvious need, but that he even found it *necessary* to have to explain himself so repetitively, to these supposedly intelligent people, when the most obvious, the most practical necessity of keeping us all as safe as possible, and the need to find a safe place to stay, was one that even the youngest of these children seemed to be able to grasp. For goodness sakes *Patrick* understands and he's only three years old! However, Tyler's statement had made its point. Although none of the men who were, only a few minutes ago, mouthing off and disparaging him, volunteered to leave the convoy either. Tyler glared at men with undisguised loathing and disgust before snapping closed the window in the cab.

The next hours were dreadfully uncomfortable and spent in absolute rigid silence. No-one wanted to talk about the experience, although as soon as we had safely passed out of the area all the canvas backs and side curtains were rolled up to allow the flow of clean air, even though it was as hot as the fire pits of hell, to wash over us for a few minutes in an effort to get rid of that putrid, sickening odour. Shortly after the convoy had safely cleared the area, and we could breathe properly again, Tyler brought the convoy to a stop and had everyone outside while he addressed the latest situation – and thereby short circuiting the rumour mill. He detailed the complaint, *and* the complainant, fully explaining all the reasons for our negative action, hopefully, for the last time. Once that issue had been discussed and finalised he gave us some pretty grave news "I am unable to communicate with my base Commander, so my original orders must stand unchanged – and they are - to take you all to safety.

I will carry out those orders to the very best of my ability. Anyone who objects to that is welcome to have their belongings unpacked and remain here. We will all wait until you have had time to think over the situation." A voice from the back shouted "Just leave him *and* his trouble making buddies right here, we don't need to feed the likes of them." Not surprisingly the speaker had quite a surprising number of supporters for his suggestion too, but Tyler told them to be quiet. A few minutes later, and having had no further responses from the group, he asked us to resume our seats, where we again sat in deep, uncomfortable silence, I was trying not to look at Mr Beatty, or his poor, thoroughly mortified, and very, very angry wife. But no-one was amused by Beatty's big mouth and he was smart enough to sit there and mind his business.

The much-abbreviated convoy got underway again and we kept moving - on and on and on, day in and day out, for ages, time had lost any semblance of meaning. Generally uneventful days and nights rolled into each other so I've lost all track of the days, weeks, it could be months or maybe even years, I just didn't know or even care anymore. We'd lost any hint of time completely, besides, it had no real meaning.

Storms came at fairly frequent intervals and with varying degrees of ferocity. Fortunately for us, we've incurred no really serious injuries other than a few bruises, some cuts and a few scratches, but luckily, even though one truck did sustain some minor damage, there has been no further major loss to the convoy – I only wish the same could be said about the human element. What's happened to our morale, well now *that*'s a very different story; the group spirits are seriously fractured; tempers are unravelling so there are far more nit-picking arguments, and snide remarks than there are conversations. A lot of the Upper Valley people, Mr Beatty, his friends and neighbours in particular, would argue that day was night at the best of times but even more so since Tyler had called them all out, and from the day when it was proposed they be left behind, they've spat poison and contempt at any opportunity. While they've never been entertaining or companionable, they've become increasingly nasty and more spiteful to travel with – if that's possible.

Their main topic of conversation has essentially been a litany of what *they* perceived as major flaws in Tyler's character and behaviour, his actions and his attitude, I.E., how *dare* the likes of him take *that* tone with such a highly respected man, from such a highly respected community and so on and so on, blah, blah, yadda, yadda, yadda. But never *once* admitting that the old man is, was, and has been, behaving like a complete idiot since day one. They carried on with their senseless whining until I wished I had a bat, or a lump of wood to whop them all around the ears with. Anything, just to shut them up, even if it was only for a little while, an hour or forty-eight would do nicely. I'd ask to change places with someone, but there was no-one else I disliked enough to inflict Mr Beatty and Co on.

The trucks continued to rumble on, squishing, squelching, and sliding their way across the never-ending sea of thick brown goop, narrowly avoiding large chunks of debris concealed by thick layers of mud that rendered them invisible until the last possible moment. Nor did we find anywhere worthwhile to stop for more than the few minutes it took for a very short nature break. The stops where the marines would climb up on top of the trucks and check to see that all the salvaged engine covers and tyres and whatever else they had tied up there was still secured seemed to give Beatty and his cohorts a reason to grumble and curse again. If there was anything that you could call a positive thing, about the storms, well they *were* giving us plenty of fresh water, although we'd reached the point about, oh I don't know maybe two, three or four months ago, when no one felt the slightest inclination to stop and bathe. We were mostly all still wearing the same stinking, filthy dirty, mud and crud encrusted clothes we'd put on the morning we were evacuated. So right now, we all looked, felt, and smelled, equally bad, but honestly, who even noticed or even *cared* anymore? We were was just too tired and too dispirited to give a damn about anything as pretentious as basic hygiene or appearance. Everyone that is, except for the marines. Even though they were all just as smelly, as unwashed, and for the most part even muckier than the rest of us, somehow those marines still managed to have an almost parade ground bearing about them. Their shirts, and they really *are* seriously filthy, are always tucked in neatly, they personally, always appear to be washed, even if they weren't clean shaven any more, far from it, actually most of them had heavy beards now, and yes, they were all very much in need of a barber, but their hair is kept under their caps so it still *looks* reasonably tidy. I'm seriously considering a buzz cut myself! Nevertheless, I *have* managed keep my long hair tightly plaited, I re-do it every morning, so it's not getting *too* awfully tatty, just desperately in need of a thorough shampooing and a good brushing. I can't imagine what it must look like now because my head has even stopped itching! When I think, that I'd washed my hair every Sunday morning and always showered morning and night…

We'd been traveling for somewhere between one and a thousand days - no-one, not even Tyler himself, really has any idea at all now. We had not a single clue among us, nary a one, not even a sideways glimmer of an idea as to how long we've been travelling. Nor do we know where we are, could be, or even *might* be either, for all we know we've been going around in giant circles. Oh, for sure, the marines have all the maps of course; in fact, they had multiple maps covering every inch of the fourteen zones, eighteen if you count the zones that divided a while back. But those maps are less than useless now, simply because any of the practical map references, like highways, military bases, cities, towns, schools, hospitals, train lines or airfields, have been totally obliterated by the storms. We haven't even seen a sign that says 'Welcome to' somewhere/anywhere, the one and only thing we *do* know for an absolute certainty, is that we haven't actually left the planet – yet. Our fuel supply is perilously low too, all the drums of fuel are empty, and there's talk amongst the marines of 'milking' all the fuel tanks into two trucks, then we'd move only at night due to the sweltering heat, because we'd all have to take turns in walking and riding, and while it wasn't an ideal strategy, at least it was a plan.

It was probably around five o'clock in the morning, the trucks were barely crawling along in low gear as a last-ditch effort to conserve fuel, when we had a surprise encounter with an incredibly large (totally unknown, and un-named) rock formation that spread out for long miles in both directions, just before first light. Our drivers agreed that in the murky pre dawn light it had appeared to be a long fog bank. So, in hindsight, it was just as well they *had* slowed down to crawl along, because they actually drove into the 'fog' which was, in reality, a solid stone wall. The sudden unexpected stop sent most of the drowsy passengers on the bench seats sprawling on top of the people on the floor… Curious to see why we'd stopped, a crowd jumped down to have a look around at this big rock wall we could hear the marines talking about. They were right, the thing was enormous, incredibly high and long. So long I couldn't see how far along it went before it disappeared into the distance.

It wasn't my eyes playing up, everyone else was looking too, and no-one had better luck. Although someone had pulled out a pair of binoculars, but even with those they still couldn't see where the wall ended either. It was certainly very, very high, and even though we looked left and right along its length, we could see no end to it, so maybe it curved away. Tyler and a few of the drivers had their large laminated maps spread out across the truck bonnet, and with the aid of two huge torches, they were trying to find something, a name, a record, a reference, *anything*, at this stage even a fleeting *mention* of this incredible, massive landmark would do – because surely, something the size of this thing, well it *had* to be marked or at the *very least* - noted somewhere – except that it wasn't. Certainly not on any of the two dozen interconnecting maps they had covering every microscopic inch -in minute detail- every part of every zone on the continent anyway, so we were left no wiser than before. To say it plainly - we didn't have an inkling, as to *where* we could possibly be, and as our zone system is separated from the others by an ocean on two sides, and bridges over two extremely wide, deep rivers, one bridge is six and the other is eleven miles across, on the other two sides. That being the case, common logic tells us that we still have to be *somewhere within* the eighteen zones! But, as one of the marines commented "since we haven't crossed a river or an ocean" (the muddy ones don't count) "we still *had* to be on our continent." Now since *that* has to be true, and seeing as this rock formation is so vast, it *must* have a name or an identifying reference number, then it *must* appear on, or at the very least be mentioned, on at least *one* of the military maps. And it would be absolutely great if it did - except that it doesn't. And when you consider the sheer immensity of this lump of rock, or is it a mountain, a range or a barrier, oh I'll just call it The Big Rock Thingy, (I think that's scientific enough for now don't you agree?) anyway from where we've stopped, it's like at least twenty big city blocks in length in *both* directions! So, for it *not* to show up *anywhere* on *any* of the maps at all? – Well, that's extraordinarily weird to say the least. Those maps are taken from satellites circling above the earth – all I can say about that is that the vital military satellite must have one huge blind spot!

The men had been out, walking and searching along the length of the wall for ages, trying to find a way into, or a passageway through, the formation, they've been carefully examining it, practically finger-combing the walls in both directions. In the end it was the first group of marines who discovered an opening. It was so easily overlooked too; there was a relatively low but deep archway, and it'd been choked up by thick dried mud and dead bushes that'd obviously blown in when there were still trees and vegetation growing in the surrounding area, however they'd concealed the entry so well that it'd been overlooked, not once, not twice, but three times! The entry was roughly about a quarter of a mile to the left of where the trucks had stopped. Tyler and the marines spent a few sweltering hours clearing the passageway but unfortunately, the vehicles were much too wide to fit through the narrow opening.

From where he was standing at the entrance Tyler was saying he guessed that at the widest part it would only be about seven feet from the uneven ground to the top of the stone arch and five, maybe six feet across, give or take a bump or two in the contours, although it looked as though it narrowed quite significantly further along, where the passageway turned a corner, around there it looked to be only about three to five feet maximum. If he's right about that, it might be a bit of a tight squeeze to get some of our luggage and other stuff through, especially if it gets any narrower further in.

Tyler sent three men in to see where the passageway led and they were to report back as quickly as possible with their findings. He came to stand beside me and half speaking half mumbling said "*if* it leads anywhere at, all maybe it stops at the bend. It could very well be a dead end after all." We all sat together on a conveniently low rock ledge enjoying a tiny, but very welcome, cup of coffee the lovely Mrs Beatty had offered -much to her appalling husband's very obvious disapproval- while we kept nervous eyes on the sky and waited rather impatiently in the rising heat for their return.

While the three men were gone, we tried to encourage the poor worn out, bored and incredibly travel weary children to cheer up a bit, we exaggerated wildly and attempted to out do each other with our tall stories and by guessing what might be waiting for us around that mysterious corner! Would there be dinosaurs? Or maybe - maybe there's an inland sea with dolphins and mermaids! Privately though, most of us just hoped there wouldn't be another all-encompassing sea of sloppy mud waiting for us.

I couldn't help myself; I kept wishing they'd get a move on, hurry themselves up a bit more and get back to us. It's an awful feeling, and I do hate to admit it, but I was every bit as nervy and jittery, as everyone else was, but then again, after all the gruesome and frightening things we've seen and lived through, we were all, and I believe quite justifiably so, really, really nervous. I know that I shouldn't harp on it, but when you've had nineteen people, all with whom you've shared meals, who have sat next to you, and have at some point, more than likely slept next to you, and you realise that they just went out for a short, simple walk, and vanished off the face of the earth, or when you've driven so many wretched miles through what was essentially an open grave. Well to tell you the absolute, the basic, but most honest truth, not one of us relished being out in the open, we all felt far too exposed, and far too vulnerable. It was infinitely more preferable being squished up like sardines inside the trucks than being out in the open like this, feeling terribly unprotected... Not that a sheet of canvas would offer any protection whatsoever against a storm of the magnitude it takes to demolish a city, but it *was,* as illogical as that might sound, it *was* a comfort to hide away inside those dark trucks. Maybe it goes back to the time when I was only a very small girl, and my grandpa would play hide n seek with me, I'd squeeze my eyes closed – and if I couldn't see…. then I thought I couldn't be seen either – well that's what I assumed back then! Bottom line is, we all knew how unpredictable the weather is and we were all scared.

I suppose in reality, the marines hadn't been gone for very long at all really; because we'd just finished our coffees when they all came running out to their sergeant, who was waiting just outside the entryway watching for them to come back like an anxious mother hen waiting to count her missing chicks. They came through that wall with shining eyes and *huge* ear to ear grins plastered across their faces. Tyler pulled them aside and they talked – with the marines first, naturally, and then he called over the team leaders. While he was conferring with them there were lots of excited hand gestures, much laughter and nodding of heads and fingers pointing back toward whatever lay beyond the rock passage, then we knew *we* were being spoken about, more pointing, firstly at us this time then at the rock passage, and then Tyler was looking back over his shoulder at us again …after a longish wait (it felt like for-ev-er) he called the rest of us over and told us that the recon party had found a large area of undisturbed land covered in green grass, it was clean, it was dry, and it was very habitable. "There's no mud Sara!" There, he's done it again…*me again*, why me, why does he *do* that, why is it when there's dozens of other people standing around waiting expectantly - he singles me out?

We would have had to have been completely out of our tiny minds to pass up such a god given opportunity, to even *try* to continue on. Actually, our two options came down to these (a) stay here where it appears to be safe and dry, or (b) to turn our backs on this place, to keep on going, and be stranded out in the open with no fuel…and certainly die horribly, and to die sooner, rather than later. To me it was a no brainer, stay where we were. But how typical of the few morons we were unfortunately stuck with that Tyler had to treat them with silk gloves instead of a solid club around the ears… and explain what they already knew was happening.

"Our fuel supplies are all but gone, and in all likelihood, we won't *get* another opportunity like this." As usual Beatty contradicted him at every turn – but surprise, surprise, Tyler had finally had a gutful of Beatty and his band of argumentative idiots. Tyler had made his decision, and this time it was absolutely final, and most definitely non- negotiable. His next step was to order his men to reverse each of the trucks in turn, right up to the entrance, unload them and carry everything, our possessions, the dwindling supplies of provisions, and the now undeniably not-small-at-all animals through the passageway and into the new area. After they'd been unloaded, the trucks were then driven away from the entrance a few hundred yards - purely as a precautionary measure. Tyler said although he didn't know exactly what we'd find inside – but it had to be infinitely better than what we were leaving here outside. Looking around at the totally barren, smelly, mud-covered landscape (mudscape?) we could only agree. Besides, we had to agree with Tyler especially when his next statement was "without the fuel to go any further, I'd be negligent in my duty toward you, if I was to turn away from this outwardly safe refuge, and continue on, to take you all back out into acute and definite danger, and certainly to our deaths. We've all been more than fortunate thus far – it's better not to push that good fortune any further…"

Part Two. Safe.

He called the marines over to join in and he spoke to us as a complete group.
"Well, this is it people, we're going to be staying right here for as long as these storms last, we have no more fuel, therefore we have no transportation. It's been quite a number of months since I've been able to make radio contact with my commanding officer, *or* anyone else, and that being the case, there can *be* no rescue team alerted to our plight, even if we knew where we are, which we *don't*. Therefore, ladies and *gentlemen* (he directed this at Mr Beatty) I suggest we adopt an optimistic mind set and make the very best of whatever we have here, and hope that we are somehow able to sustain ourselves until some form of help arrives. Whatever lies at the end of this passage is what we have, we've no actual choice in the matter, we can either all try to get along or you can decide to be miserable, that's entirely your choice it's up to the individual, or of course you can choose to leave, but the majority will show good sense and stay. Sooner or later, we will be missed and a search will be mounted for our return."

While he was talking, I was recalling the hundreds upon hundreds of thousands possibly *millions* of dead bodies of unknown, unidentifiable people, in *one*, of goodness only knows how many other locations, who are perhaps all presumed to be missing, or displaced as well, and it made me wonder just where, and how far down, would *our names be* on anyone's missing list? Who would even *know* if we were alive-or dead? And who would even be bothered looking for *us* specifically, when so very many millions have disappeared and died?

The men from Upper Valley sat together in a group and started cat calling him again, so he simply jingled the ignition keys and offered them the trucks – which they rudely and very crudely declined.

The entranceway was narrow enough to begin with, and in some places, it narrowed quite suddenly *and* significantly; so much so, that bags or boxes that required two people to carry, now had to be pushed and shoved in front, or else dragged along behind, still others, which unfortunately, proved to be either too large or too awkward to manhandle, needed to be emptied out and carried in by the armful. I felt really sorry for our sweet, always agreeable always good-natured, never offensive or offended, Mr. Callaghan - he's a very tall very 'well-built' man (more like a human two in one) well, the poor man managed to scrape himself quite painfully on some sharp protrusions jutting from the rough stone walls, however it only served to make him more determined than ever not to be left behind, *or* to shirk doing his share of the heavy lifting, so he forced himself to squeeze through and even joked about feeling lucky that we had a doctor handy! The children were all wide eyed and *so* excited (ah, but they were all just a little bit jumpy too) Perhaps by the possibility of dinosaurs, alligators or a giant octopus?! Maybe so, but they were still every bit as enthusiastic and as eager to see what lay at the end of the passageway as the rest of us were. I didn't know that such childlike enthusiasm was so contagious! It was so unbelievably terrific to actually *feel* excited about something again.

Tyler called the captains together and we did a head count, we totalled ninety-two people including Tyler and his marines. Once everyone was accounted for, we were broken up into groups, each group taking some of the children, and some of the animals. The passageway was long, about sixty or more yards long and full of twists and turns, oh and it also had loads of sneaky razor-sharp pointy bits sticking out to catch the unwary arm or hip... Our sliced and torn flesh was a really well bloodied demonstration of that. Mr. Callaghan found it easier, safer, and *considerably* less painful, to crawl on his hands and knees through the narrower sections, as most of the protrusions which were shoulder and head height on me were around waist and shoulder height for him, but unlike the rest of us, because of his great height he had to watch out for the top of his head too. He had loads strapped to his back and also gave the little ones 'pony rides' to add a few laughs and happy giggles into the exercise! Like I said before – he's a really lovely man.

By the time I'd managed to reach the end I was half dropping, and half dragging my bundle and the canvas bag I was carrying was not only cumbersome it was darned heavy as well – but when I reached the end of the winding passageway I did exactly what everyone before me had done. I dropped everything and just stood there with my eyes wide and my mouth hanging open saying...oh w-o-w!

This place was so totally, so unbelievably, *beautiful!* The whole gorgeous place is truly a living paradise. A sweet smelling, *dry,* spectacularly *perfect* paradise! We stood at the entrance to an unbelievably gigantic, a vast, immense area of luxurious thick green grass; away in the distance there were tall trees dotted about creating small shady spots, and a carpet of very pretty, but really extraordinary coloured wild flowers, all set in an absolutely gargantuan oval rock bowl. I suppose the best way to describe it is –it's sort of like a really big volcano with a large section of the top removed, or a sports stadium, one that's really, really wide and round at the base but narrows ever so gradually towards the top, which was about as high as a thirty (or more) level building – well anyway, it's really high. Tyler voiced my own thoughts when he commented that somehow, this place seems to have been left untouched and unaffected by the weather outside. He was so excited! He called out to me; will you look at the crazy colours of those flowers Sara, and they're all alive and in full bloom! Me – *again!* It's so darned embarrassing because heads swivel and people stare at me. Why does he do it? I don't know, but I really wish he wouldn't. It took us quite a few hours of hard schlepping back and forth, with almost everyone being loaded down with stuff like donkeys in the olden-day. Not before asking Mr Beatty and his unsavoury comrades one last time if they were absolutely sure they didn't want a truck, were the remaining, unwanted, trucks not only emptied, but gutted and stripped bare of any and everything that might one day be useable.

Once everyone was safely inside, and all the luggage, the baggage, all the bits and pieces off the trucks, lots of heavy, unusual-looking equipment and loads of even stranger looking tools had been hauled in, Tyler once again took charge and set about getting some night-time shelters organised. He started by utilising the canvas from the trucks, and using bench seats from the back of each truck which had mostly been dismantled for easier portability. There were six long bench seats in each truck, and these were turned on their ends, tied together and two sets of them used as 'A' frames with some canvas dropped over the top. "Just something quick and easy for the first night, he said. Two marines were assigned the task of setting up a bush kitchen well away from the sleeping areas; I was recruited to be David's assistant, and Mark took Kristy as his assistant. Apparently, we had to find out as much as we could about our new living space. "In military speak" Mark said, "we had to carry out reconnaissance." For once it was an order I was happy to follow through with, it certainly beat unpacking!

I remember commenting to Reba at the time, that the grass was simply gorgeous, such a rich luxurious green. Although at that point, I'd only run my hands over it but hadn't actually felt it under my bare feet. Something that was quickly remedied in the short half minute it took to unclip and kick off my mud encrusted runners and socks! My whole life I've run around with bare feet, at any and every opportunity, although, with all the many surfaces my feet have known, I have never felt such thick, bouncy, velvet soft grass before. It's a dream to walk on it barefoot, but naturally, David insisted I put my shoes back on because- In his words (and sounding exactly like my mother when she cautioned me) "you have *no* idea what might be hiding in this grass Miss Sara, there could be broken glass or bits of metal, snakes, all sorts of biting things, creepy crawlies, there may well be anything at all here Miss Sara, so it's either shoes on, or stay behind" he made me feel like a naughty little girl... but I put my stiff smelly socks and filthy runners back on.

The four of us set off heading in the direction of the far wall. Mark spotted some rabbits hopping around but when we approached, they stopped and sat very still, just looking up at us... a distracting flash of brilliant colour zipped by and eight eyes followed where it went, it flew into a pretty little grove of trees where there were dozens and dozens of tree branches all bursting with beautiful, brightly coloured birds, and for some strange reason it gave me a bit of an unsettling feeling to know our every move was being scrutinized by probably thousands of curious eyes.

We'd covered about half the distance to the far wall, and were on the other side of the grove of trees and their unusual brightly plumaged occupants, when we discovered a natural rockpool, it was huge too, I mean it looks to be about double the size of an Olympic swimming pool, and it was brim full of fresh, crystal-clear water that was teeming with different kinds of fish, to me they looked really big, and really colourful rather exotic looking fish, and we could hear, but not see, heaps of frogs croaking away happily in the thick undergrowth. Mark was enthusiastically pulling small glass, rubber stoppered bottles and a roll of white sticky labels from his pockets, then taking samples of everything he saw, the water, grass, soil, a plant here and a flower over there, clicking away with great enthusiasm making a photographic record of these most unusual looking birds and fish. He carried on clicking until he realised his camera wasn't, and hadn't been working, since he started taking his happy snaps. We were about to turn and head back, when David suggested that instead of retracing our steps, we could walk the long way back following the wall around to the camp area again. After being jammed into the back of a moving truck for so many months it was pure joy to be able to stretch our legs and enjoy a guilt free, fear free walk. But by jeez, my unused leg muscles were beginning to feel a bit wobbly now.

It was Kristy who spotted the water spout; it was only about two feet off the ground and ran into a gravel trough (sorry, but I can't think of a better description) before it disappeared through the wall again, we decided that it probably fed the pool with a constant supply of fresh water. While I was busily looking at everything at once, I spied a largish hole in the wall so I called over and pointed it out to David, it was about seven feet off the ground, or two feet above my head where I was standing. The next thing I knew he was crouched over with his hands on his knees and Mark was climbing up onto his shoulders to inspect this big hole I'd found! A minute later Mark's arm reached down and grabbed hold of David and hauled him up the wall too – then they both disappeared into the hole! It turned out to be much more than merely a big hole though, much, much more. The *hole* was actually a bit more than that as it opened into a large cavern, although Mark said it was real dark further in so he couldn't see very much, David said that from walking around in there, and judging by the echoes, the area was *big*, it could be as much as thirty by thirty-five feet across, possibly even larger. He had seen a very faint light, more of a lighter shade of darkness –if that makes sense- and he thinks if it's not one big area, then it could, quite possibly have some more caves running off from it, but they'd really need proper lights and ropes to explore it thoroughly, although -he said- if it's as big as it feels and sounds, it might just make an ideal night-time and bad weather shelter for everyone.

Feeling pleased and excited that at least we had some good news to take back, we opted to take the most direct route across the grass to meet up with the main group again instead of continuing to follow the wall. Mark and David informed Sergeant Tyler of our findings. No sooner had he been given a brief description of what we'd found, than he started barking orders to his men, Hank and Davy volunteered to go too, but they were told it would be best if the experienced marines did the initial investigating, however they could help the women set up the camp while they were gone. Ouch! What a letdown for the poor guys, not to mention some seriously injured masculine pride there. I felt really sorry for them too.

Tyler issued five of his marines with canteens of water, pack rations, chemical glow-light torches, ropes, heavy duty leather gloves, and big white marker chalks he'd taped onto long pieces of wood to be dragged along behind to mark the way back and solar powered walkie talkies so they could report any discoveries back to him immediately if they found anything worthwhile. Kristy and I weren't allowed to go with them either. My protest that they wouldn't have anything *to* explore if I hadn't found the entrance in the first place, made not one scrap of difference to Tyler, we were told it was marine's work, and we were to stay put in the camp area and make ourselves useful.

His next instructions to us made our position perfectly clear. We were to help unpack and to prepare a meal, once that was done, we should set up our sleeping areas with warm blankets for the night ahead. Honestly, it really bugs me the way Tyler is always giving *me* orders too; I'm *not* one of his darned soldiers and I'm certainly *not* in the habit of taking orders from just anyone - my mother and gran are different!

Right then there was a downright unnerving growl, the familiar deep, truly menacing rumble of thunder began bouncing around the walls, and spurring us all into action. The sky above turned from the stunning clear blue of the early morning sky, to inky midnight black in a heartbeat, the almost impossibly huge quantities of bright blue and white bolts and sheets of lightning, followed by sounds of crashing thunder combined with the blast of solid, pelting rain had all of us cowering together under the big canvas sheets. But-nothing-happened. There was no wind blowing a gale and tearing the place apart, nor was there any rain falling around us this time, only plenty of fireworks and the deafening peals of thunder. After about forty-five minutes the storm had passed and the sky was back to being a perfectly innocent blue again. We all agreed that that was *the* most terrifying and bizarre storm we'd ever encountered – or not encountered.

The marines didn't arrive back for the late midday meal, they were still out at nightfall, and they weren't back by the time we had our late supper either. They *still* hadn't returned by the time we were advised to go to our tents and get some sleep. Sleep! Who could sleep? I sure as heck couldn't, my ever-so-slightly overactive imagination was busily churning out all the possible – right along with all of those really *impossible*- reasons for their delayed return.

Even though, young Patrick seems to be quite relaxed and comfortable; he's wrapped up in my big feather down quilt on the floor of the tent. I swear, that child can sleep anywhere, and under any conditions. I'm so jealous! Sienna's in here with us too, she's another lucky one, she must have fallen asleep before her head even hit the pillow, but oh jeez… ahh, well now, wouldn't you know it, she darn well snores, she's loud too. I couldn't hear her snoring in the truck…. because of the roar or growl of the engine, but boy oh boy, I can sure hear her now! There is *no way* I can get to sleep with that buzz saw going full tilt either! Ahh, it's no good and I can't help it, my mind just refuses to switch off; (Sienna's dreamers giggles, snorts, grunts and mumbles aren't greatly helpful in the sleeping department either) My brain keeps searching for answers among the millions of stars I can see in the big triangle of night sky that's showing through the opening in our canvas shelter.

Writing in this big journal helps me focus my thoughts, this one is the first book in a set of three, and they were (a very strange gift for a nine-year-old) from my grandma years ago and I really didn't think I'd ever use them because I've always used my computer for everything. To be perfectly honest, I don't even know *why* I packed them, but now, well I'm kinda really glad that I did, because in some ways keeping this journal is helping me a lot. I feel closer to gran when I write in it, *plus,* I really want people to *know* what has happened to us, in case we *don't* make it back again, even though now that we've stopped moving, and dare I hope, are a lot safer. I'm more confident now, about eventually getting home, than I was yesterday.

Gee-wiz, I'm jumping at every noise tonight, probably because I'm a teensy bit anxious about our intrepid explorers. I've been having this crazy-weird two-way conversation in my head for hours now, and I think I'm losing, or possibly have already lost, my mind. Finally.

Could they be lost?

No, you idiot – remember the chalk, they've marked their route.

Well, maybe one of them is injured so badly that they can't leave him.

Nope, that's no good either; two could still stay while two came back for help.

Maybe there's been a cave in?

Not a chance, we would have heard that much noise for sure.

Well, what if they've been overcome by some kind of ancient poisonous gas? Maybe they've been bitten by swarms of strange insects, or snakes? Oh, good life! What if there really *are* things like pre historic creatures in there?

Okay Sara, you're getting beyond ridiculous now and you know it, *and* you've seen way too many sci-fi movies.

Sienna stirred and mumbled groggily "ehwhaaatjasay?"

Oh great, now I'm talking out loud to myself! Even so, there's got to be *some* reason for them to be taking so long. Oh jeez, now I've started answering myself as well…

Sleep-I *really* do need to get some sleep.

 My thoughts spun around continuously, chasing one another around and around, and around, until my head was in danger of imploding. I tried everything, but the thoughts *would not* be stopped. Finally, at around four in the morning, I heard the men quietly returning to our new camp. If I really strained, I could distinguish Tyler's deep voice amongst all the other deep voices, but the actual content of their conversation was unintelligible to me. I would just have to wait until Tyler was good and ready to talk to us. That man is just *so* annoying, in *so* many ways, but thank goodness he's safe, and the rest of the men too of course.

I must have dropped off to sleep then, because we were woken at sunrise by the sound of Tyler calling everyone out for breakfast. Honestly, I'm beginning to wonder if that man really *is* an *actual* human being or if he's a robot prototype. He must have only had about an hour of sleep - at the very most – but just have a look at him will you! He's standing there, tall, and strong, and as bright and shiny as a new penny. Never mind that he's also looking like he's shared a full eight hours with his favourite pillow in a nice comfy bed. He looks freshly bathed, his dark hair is really long now and starting to curl up below his collar, but it's neatly combed, and his uniform, although granted it's still absolutely filthy, it's as brushed and as neat as always. The whole refugee group, along with the soldier boys, gathered around the makeshift kitchen and shared a simple breakfast of delicious oatcakes and a small cup of unsweetened black coffee, or fresh water. We were each issued a short list of instructions for the day and broken up into task groups. The only exceptions were the older women, or those with really young children …oh, and apparently the *genteel* men from Upper Valley, they will, as they informed Tyler, be quite content to sit around and play cards today.

Tyler called back the ones who were already starting off. "Before any of you leave, I would like to give you some good news for a change. And I do mean some really good news." He waited until he had everyone's attention before speaking again.

"As you are all aware, last night, myself and Sergeant Rawlins along with Corporals James, McIntosh, Rivers and Private Bush, entered a cavern that was discovered by your neighbour, Sara" he dipped his head toward me and *almost* half smiled an acknowledgement "it has turned out that that particular cavern is just one part of a *very extensive* system of interconnected, habitable caves, and it appears that each cave is large enough to be occupied quite comfortably. As well as being large, they are clean, dry, vermin and insect free, so we can easily make them to be as comfortable as possible in these most unusual circumstances that we have found ourselves in. Although, and equally important for us, these caves will protect us from any bad weather, extreme cold or strong heat." A rumble of comments started, but before anyone could start asking questions Tyler interrupted again "However, before we make the move over there, my men will further investigate the extent of the cave system in daylight. Therefore, none of my men will be available for duty today and very possibly tomorrow as well, so I suggest you all stay close to camp in case there is a storm. I would strongly suggest also, that once your small lists of tasks have been completed, you all take this opportunity to have a good rest. Because once these caves have been properly examined, and *if* they are as suitable in daylight as we *think* they are, we will all be busy clearing this area and moving everything across. Without means of transportation, we will remain living within these caves until such time as the storms have run their course and we can contact the outside world again. Okay, so once it's safe to leave here, we will find a way to return you all to your homes, or if that isn't possible for any one of a hundred reasons, you will be moved to a suitable alternative location." I had a sneaky suspicion that he was about to say 'dismissed or stand down' but he caught himself just in time and simply said, "Have a nice day everyone." Kristy and I were joined by six of the other girls who lived on neighbouring farms; we've known each other forever and have been friends, or at least friendly, all our lives. Suzy and Amelia are cousins and we're all in our early to middle 20's, single and wondering what the near future will bring our way. We're all pretty sure that it won't be very much. And while there wasn't much male company on offer for any of the young girls back home – there's significantly less available here. Ha, oh my goodness, just have a look at those two will you! I might have known Janice and Angie would be getting up close and cosy with the men. Those poor guys, they probably don't have any idea, but if those two have their way, they can probably count their 'single' days on one hand now.

We all wandered across the grassy expanse heading to the pool, on the way we stopped to watch a little group of bunnies playing on a grassy mound, but the thing we found so strange about them was that they were totally unafraid of us, which, when you think about it, really is pretty odd, the rabbits around home would run for their lives the minute anyone came into view, even if they were still a hundred yards away. Oh wowza! The rock pool is so totally *amazing* and it looks to be even bigger than I first thought it was, a whole lot bigger really. The water is sparkling and crystal clear and, oh jeez, it's really quite chilly too!

We found, much to our surprise, that it's also incredibly deep.

We've all been surprised by the so called 'wildlife' here, because they're actually quite tame and inquisitive, a little bit shy, but super friendly too. First it was the rabbits, now it's the fishes, those little guys are so curious that they swam right up to us; we can actually *touch* them without them swimming frantically away from us, which you must admit, *is* a bit unusual.

After a while we'd all tired of swimming, so we stripped off down to our underwear and spread our (now very clean) clothes out to dry and lay down in the longish soft grass and chatted together. It was Amelia who noticed the birds first; dozens and dozens and lots more dozens of them, had lined up along the branches filling up all the space in the trees. They were just perched in complete silence watching us, their little heads turning this way and that, they looked for all the world like they were trying to figure out what we were! We had to admit that all the wildlife we'd seen in this place so far, was extraordinarily un-wild; it's almost like they've never seen a human before.

Having dried our clothing off and dressed again, Suzy suggested we should get back and start helping with the chores, or we might not be too welcome at dinner tonight.

The walk back to camp was like being in a dream. After so many months of being filthy dirty, scared half to death, dealing with the endless meanness and spite of certain people, the being shaken and the bounced around, the seemingly endless loud noises and the smell of fuel exhaust. This place is quiet, it's peaceful, the air is wonderfully fragrant and soothing, not to mention that now for the first time in goodness knows how many months we were clean! In fact, we all felt *so* good we practically danced the whole way back, with the soft grass springing gently under our feet it was like walking on a carpet of soft foam. The air is so fresh, so clean and so clear here as well, it's almost as though this whole place, even though it's obviously very ancient, was really only born when we arrived yesterday. It's really interesting, because everything here is *so* interested in *us* and so friendly.

"Hey…has anyone seen any roaches or spiders or a web anywhere, or any other insect? What about moths? No? I didn't think so. Well then how about a fly or a mosquito?" Asked Amelia. Suzy replied that she'd seen a big swarm of bees around the flowers, but nothing else.

I looked around at the others to see their response, and we all shook our heads and said "Nope, nothing like that." She continued. "*And* another thing, how come it's so clean? I haven't seen a scrap of rubbish or litter of any kind anywhere on the ground either, not even an old gum wrapper or a bottle cap! Hey, and what about all these fantastic big walls without a single bit of graffiti in sight, and I didn't see any outside either, did anyone else see any? Well, I for one have never seen *anywhere* so immaculately clean, c'mon now be honest, have you, have any of you?" We all shook our heads in agreement once again; all waiting for her to come to the point…. but apparently there wasn't one, she just sighed and said "Oh well, we'd better try and make ourselves useful – there's nothing else to do around here that's for sure."

As they wandered closer to the rest of the group, they saw the young boys running around with their arms loaded with dry sticks. Back in the camp area, the older ladies had been busily turning total chaos into as near perfect order as possible. When I asked Mrs Beatty why they'd gone to so much trouble if we're just going to have to move anyway?

"Oh Sara" –she said, looking at her close friend and helper Mrs Armstrong, as they both turned their heads to glare at a pair of lazy husbands busy playing cards "if we don't keep ourselves busy, we might give in to temptation and do murder!"

As soon as we'd arrived here, Tyler made sure that all the food stores had been sorted and stacked together for easy accessibility. Mrs Beatty and her small team of Kitchen Wonders had done the hard work of organising it all. Dry foods and canned food had been sorted into vegetables, fruits, fish, meat, beans and they'd been pleasantly surprised to find there were still quite a lot of caterer size cans of powdered milk. The fresh produce – of which a surprisingly large amount still remained, although they were mostly pumpkins, potatoes and other root vegetables, had been carefully stored away from the sun and kept up off the ground, although just about every single vegetable had started sprouting, a lot of them looked as though they were crying out for some dirt to grow in! All the water barrels were arranged neatly in rows, and the huge, still vacuum sealed stainless-steel drums of flour, oats, dried corn cobs and corn meal that had been marked with an X of tape, so that the vacuum seal wouldn't be broken until another container was empty, were elevated and well ventilated to prevent damp and spoiling. There were still several enormous sacks of rice too, they'd been put on top of the sealed containers to prevent damp. Reba walked over and asked me what was going on with all the food shuffling, I had a bit of a chuckle and told her why they're going to so much trouble, she laughed out loud and told Mrs B if she'd like to have some rest, she'd be glad to offer her assistance with 'the other thing!', "I'd be more than happy to help with that too!" Several voices said at once. "Oh, me too girls, and I've got my own candidate for the chopper-stopper too if you know what I mean!" Said Mrs Armstrong. At least the ladies were able to have a bit of a giggle … even if it was at their husband's expense. Those two ladies are incredibly good sports, and I think they'll be a lot of fun to have around, unlike *some* of the others.

They gave a big thanks to all the younger boys, they'd wanted something to do so they've been scouring the grounds for sticks and fallen branches, and now there's a big pile of neatly stacked firewood, with a big steel bucket of rich black soil standing nearby in case the fire had to be doused in a hurry. Large stones had been carried over from somewhere and the younger men/older boys, take your pick… were making a primitive, but effective fireplace for Mrs B and Mrs Armstrong to prepare the large quantities of food they'd be cooking to feed us all, and a low fire would be kept burning at night for comfort and light, mainly light. I had to laugh at the antics of our cooks, they'd broken open those big crates of pots, pans, and utensils which had more than likely been destined for a large restaurant kitchen, and it was so entertaining watching their antics, because they were almost swooning over the quality and the terrific range of super-sized pots! Well, that's a first for me! I have *never* seen anyone cuddle a great big soup pot before, dance with a monstrous skillet *or* kiss a huge ladle! Apparently, there *is* a first time for everything!

Nevertheless, in spite of the obvious effort they'd put into making it nice and 'homey' it still resembled a gypsy camp. Except for the omnipresent coffee pot. Mr Beatty claims he would *never survive* without his fresh coffee. I overheard Suzy's comment to Jessica that she hoped he's bought a really good supply with him, because it looks like he'll be here for *quite a while*…but on the other hand… drink it all up Beatty boy because the alternative is perfectly okay with us too. Naughty girl!

We worked together all day, doing odd jobs here and there for Mrs Beatty, we sang pop songs, we talked about movie stars, our plans for the future, who we liked in the group- and more interestingly- those we didn't, and some rather surprising names popped up in that particular selection. Oh meow! Were we being catty…much?

Before we knew it the lunch bell (the long stainless-steel ladle vigorously applied to the bottom of a big stainless steel and copper pot) was being sounded, so we all headed over towards the fire where a delicious smell started sending our salivary glands into overdrive. Mrs Beatty had, once again, made the most delicious meal out of practically nothing. We feasted on hot corn cakes, pan fried (reconstituted) ham steaks with some tender fresh field mushrooms that she'd found growing in an over-abundance right next to her kitchen, as well as fried wild onions, with some unusual but quite pleasant tasting fresh salad greens on the side, they were also found growing in great abundance nearby. Mrs. Costa had made a really refreshing cold tea with some of Mrs Beatty's own honey (apparently, she'd kept bees too) and some absolutely delicious preserved lemons. The children ate like they'd never seen food before. There's no need to worry about any of these kids having fussy appetites that's for sure. Pretty soon they're all going to be as bad as Max and Luke – meaning there simply isn't enough food in the entire world to fill those two up! After we'd eaten, my friends and I got together and took care of the cleaning up.

Later on, when the tidying up was finished, most of the group sat down on the grass together like we were at a big family picnic, and talked. We told jokes and found out a little bit more about each other. Even though we'd been traveling together for months, and in spite of Tyler's best intentions, the whole noisy truck situation just made things impossible as far as having conversations or getting to know one another is concerned, but now we shared our hopes and dreams, and our now heavily revised expectations for the future, and of someday, hopefully, finding our missing families and loved ones again, along with the occasional funny story. It was so nice, just to be able to stay still, to sit or lay down and really relax, to have *time* to have a good talk and to enjoy having a laugh together. Instead of always being squished up together and uncomfortable sharing the very confined space with far too many people, (something that was made even more difficult and stressful when we lost the other trucks) constantly being on the move, unable to relax, being forever anxious, and months of only being able to sleep in tiny snatches. Although, or I suppose *because* we had all been thrown together somewhat haphazardly, we're actually a very interesting cross section of our very multicultural society, looking around at all these faces, I'm almost certain that we have at least one person from every Nation-State and Zone on our planet! Unfortunately, however, not everyone could be bothered joining with us, nor were they willing to be friendly enough, to be a part of it. It isn't surprising although it really is a shame that not one single member of the older Upper Valley people (except for the two lovely cooking ladies) joined in, we'd all have liked to have their stories, their opinions, their views, suggestions, and their comments, every bit as much as getting to know them and about them.

After all we *are* all caught up in the same predicament, and for good or ill, we're all in here together. I can't help wondering *why* they insist on keeping themselves apart from us, the Lower Valley farmers, because it would be so much more entertaining, not to mention more comfortable, if we could all mix in together.

The afternoon passed quickly, Mr Armstrong (no relation to our lovely Mrs Armstrong though) had pulled out a ball from somewhere and the young kids have made up a game of their own, with rules (?!) that I'm pretty sure, have been taken from just about every ballgame imaginable; from ping pong and golf, right through to tennis, baseball and soccer! But they had so much fun, they laughed a lot, and joked round and used up loads of their accumulated energy, a huge improvement on our recent nomadic meanderings.

 Mr. Costa had some packs of playing cards, so that took care of the greater majority of the other men. Those who weren't playing, were advising those who were. Mind you, most of them were cheating like crazy too!

Mrs Beatty hadn't seemed to be her normal cheerful self all morning, and grumbled quietly to herself as she grabbed up a big heap of dirty clothing and a monstrous bar of washing soap and pushed the lot into two great big buckets, the girls and I took turns sharing the load and we chatted to her as we walked. Katherine asked her if she was alright, because she seemed to be very sad or upset about something, I don't think any of us were at all surprised by her answer either; she told us that she was "so heartily sick and tired of her husband, all he ever does is bemoan his fate and complain, him and his self-opinionated cronies –oh, I'm quite sure you know they're all from the Upper Valley *Gentleman's* Club, but honestly, with their attitudes, and the way they egg each other on to be so hateful to everyone else, they definitely *aren't* gentlemanly and they *really don't* deserve to be here at all, and certainly not to be a part of this otherwise very happy group." She told us that "she wishes she'd locked him in with his precious bulls and have done with the whole wretched 45 years of being stuck in a miserable marriage. There are a couple of really nice young girls and some young mothers from our area too, but unfortunately they all have husbands who're exactly like Fred; they're all, every darned one of them, more of the same mean-spirited bullies. It's really sad for everyone else but there isn't *one* that you could call a nice or a decent man among them at all. Their poor wives and children are actively discouraged from mixing with anyone who's different from them, honestly, the way those men talk, you'd swear we've all come from different planets." Mrs Beatty seemed to study the grass for a few minutes, and when she lifted her head again, she was quite angry. "Such a wretched miserable lot they are girls, so please don't be too disappointed when the ladies and girls won't join in, they really can't, not without creating a whole lot more painful trouble for themselves, but will you please at least *try* to get friendly with the young ones - if you can? Or at least let them know you're open to friendships? They really do need to have some friends now. In that fancy nancey Upper Valley Society, parents don't even mix with their own children. Goodness gracious me, mix? They don't even *speak* to each other! It's awful, just awful for any woman married to one of those – excuse me for saying this girls, but those men are just jerks!" her unnecessary apology made us laugh and that seemed to give her spirits a healthy lift.

A few moments later, Mrs Beatty's dispirited blue eyes positively sparkled when we showed her the pond and her eyes grew big and wide, she surprised us when she just plopped down onto her knees to have a closer look at the pretty strange looking fishes swimming up to the surface to look right back at her, the sweet lady was utterly mesmerised and remained in that kneeling position without moving a muscle, until we called out for her to look over the other side of the pool at the trees, which had once again silently filled with hundreds of stunning, brightly coloured birds that, at a distance, seemed more like big flowers growing on the branches than anything birdlike. "Oooh, oh my word aren't they simply magnificent! Do any of you know what kind of birds they are? I've never seen anything like them before, oh my goodness aren't they simply gorgeous! Just look at all those outlandish colours will you!" Reba described the unusual curiosity, and tameness, of all the animals and wondered out loud -once again- as to the reason for it, however Mrs B could provide no answers either, she could only offer more questions, same as the rest of us.

We filled her buckets with water for washing and then again for fresh water rinse the clothes - because we didn't want to pollute the freshness of the water for the animals who probably go there to drink- or the washing soap might even kill the curious fish. After everything in the pile was clean, we took turns to carry the now wet, and therefore much heavier load back to camp where we spread everything out to dry on the grass. There's no stopping Mrs B once she gets going, she'd asked everyone to bring her anything that needed mending, she hunted around gathering up any clothing, blankets, sheets etc. that had been torn or damaged and was in need of repair, because as she reminded everyone "what we have with us is *all* we have... there will be no calls made to our favourite shops, or any online purchases that will be delivered, that's for sure!" She lamented the loss of her great grandmothers ancient relic of a sewing machine, because it was able to use a treadle – she had to explain what that was to us as we'd never even heard of such a thing until now –"Movement on the treadle, that's the plate that controls the machine, by pushing back and forth on the plate with your feet which in turn engages the gears and produces the mechanical movement without requiring mains power," but she said, "I still have my two hands and my trusty sewing kit" everyone had been so surprised when Sargent Tyler had allowed himself to be persuaded into allowing her to bring it along because honestly, her sewing kit is almost the size of a small vehicle - *and* it took up a fair bit of the floor space of a truck all on its own! But I suppose even Tyler could see the value in having it along, simply because it *was* a very useful, even necessary thing to have; and as she said when she was bargaining with him; she could make, or repair, anything that made from any kind of woven cloth or leather. Mrs B told us that a great many of the contents had actually belonged to *her* grandmother, and some had even belonged to her *great grandmother* before her, meaning that many of the contents had quite a significant age to them, and much of it was no longer available to anyone, anywhere in the world, and after looking into her sewing hamper I think we were all inclined to agree with her! There were dozens and dozens of neatly folded lengths of different fabrics, in such a wide variety of colours; she also had a large industrial size spool of almost indestructible thread in every colour, and shade variety imaginable, not to mention the many different strengths of thread, from the finest silk right through to some that are about as thick as twine. Oh, and she had so many bundles of packets of every size of needle to sew with, to knit with or to crochet with. There was also quite an impressive array of scissors in there as well. From teeny tiny nail scissors to heavy monstrous industrial sized shears, and there was another kind with serrated teeth, also in a few different sizes - and goodness gracious me, the assortment of buttons in that box was incredible… imagine a colour and it was there, all the different sizes too, and then there were her pins, well, some of those were so strange looking to us, and until she'd explained what each shape was used for, we could never have imagined or even dreamed they'd ever existed, let alone what they might be used for! There were short straight pins for holding the edges of fabric together, longer much finer lace pins -for lace – naturally enough! She had extra-long quilting pins, a cushion filled with real long, deadly looking beaded hat pins, apparently a great many years ago, they were pushed through the hat, through the hair and back through the hat again, to hold a soft or a straw hat on your head… oh and she had what she called - safety pins- now those pins are really weird looking things, and she had them in every size from tiny delicate gold coloured pins to long stitch minders and kilt pins, Mrs B explained that many years ago in some cultures men used to wear a sort of wrap around skirt called a kilt, and according to history, no undergarments were ever worn, and they used those pins to stop them from blowing open at the wrong time! She showed us long thin 'stitch' minding pins apparently used for knitting, she even showed us two dozen of what she called her most precious, most secret treasures – they were (a bit weird looking too) safety locking pins, from a time long, long, forgotten when she said all babies wore napkins made from a reusable absorbent cotton fabric, they had belonged to her great grandmother as well. Mrs B said she always kept a few of them handy, in what she called her small *quick fix bag*. "My dears" she said laughing; "these old locking pins will hold almost anything together! Many's the time they've had to hold up the hem of a lady's dress, and Mr Beatty's often used them to secure his ugly old bull's parade number onto the harness, wonderful old inventions that are just beyond impossible to find nowadays, such a shame too really." She turned around and smiled at Hank and Max, and laughingly said "we should all thank them, because they were the ones who'd really had such a tough struggle with the jolly old thing to get it in here, but truly, I couldn't part with this box, I'd rather lose a limb – my great, great, great grandpapa made it himself, if ever it's empty you will see 'To Rosamunde with my deepest love forever, Ibrahim'. They passed within twenty-four hours of each other, Gran was ninety-four and grandad was ninety-eight, theirs was a true love story."

Once she'd settled herself, quite contentedly, into one of the bucket seats that had been salvaged from a truck, she was in her element and started humming to herself cheerfully, as she sorted through her afternoons work.

That left us Shady girls to our own devices.

I think perhaps it's time I introduced everyone in our rather mixed lot, Katherine has just turned 25, Suzy, Janice, Alicia, Jessica and Nikki are all 21, Amelia, Emma, Rachel, Loakai and myself are all turning 23, then there's, Colleen and Carol, Angie, Reba, Magdalena (Maggi) and Sienna are 24 and Kristy and Zoë along with Laksha, Collette and Mardi, are 22, Nina, Conchita (Connie) and Xiao-Linh (Lin) who are the 'babies' at 17 and 18. Somehow two very definite groups have emerged, the 'over 23's and the under 23's! We're borderline but we chose the 'unders' on account of they're more fun to be with – not so *grown-up*, or serious! So, we all sat around on the grass sunning our legs and doing each others hair, wishing one of us had thought to bring a manicure set and some tweezers, because after months of neglect, we'd all become hairy scary mono-brows. Right then Reba had a brilliant idea, her step sister Katherine was *the* most organised person she knew, and maybe, well hopefully, she'd thought to pack some of those female- grooming necessaries in with her personal toiletries.

We all sat back and watched Reba run over to Katherine, oh gosh, we had to laugh at her antics, we could tell from watching her that she was trying to sound as though she didn't really care whether she got the goodies or not, but Katherine (bless her catalogued heart) went straight into her tent and handed over two little purple bundles to her sister, who promptly dropped a kiss on her cheek and ran giggling back over to us, waving the bundles over her head like a trophy. I've never noticed it before, but that girl has *the* oddest running style...

Oh! Oh my! Oh, good lor…ouch! Pain! More pain! Ouch! *Too much pain now*! I swear, I will never, ever, *ever,* let Kristy pluck my eyebrows *never-ever-ever* again! Not unless, or until, I lose all my limbs and senses. My poor eyelids have never been so pinched and pulled at in all my life!! I really don't know who felt worse, Kristy, or me, (although, yeah, coming to think of it, I think it's probably me!) however it certainly *was* an experience – and one *never* to be repeated. *Ever.* On the other hand (no pun intended) she *does* do a beautiful manicure, and her pedicures are to die for. She manicured each of us in turn, filing down all the chips and cracks in our fingernails, trimming off all the torn cuticles and making each of us feel really good, and I have to admit, that we certainly felt a lot more feminine again. Kristy's really smart too, she used the white, almost powder fine sand we found around the edges of the pond to buff away the rough skin on our hands, and our feet too. Never in a million years would I have thought to use it, especially in that way. She massaged our tootsies and repeated her handiwork with the cuticles on our toenails and then trimmed, shaped and buffed our toenails until they were shining and pink. After another swim we were all very delighted at how silky and soft our hair felt, since we'd used no shampoo or hair products of any kind, our hair was simply washed clean in the pure fresh water as we swam. Poor Reba, she has possibly *the* curliest hair in the world! And without her straightening serum or hair straightening tools, it's an extravaganza of wild wild weed indeed!

While I waited for my hair to be braided, I was

watching Katherine and her two closest friends, Angie and Sienna, even though they aren't very much older than us - they really are - if you know what I mean? They seem to project a certain poise and sophistication that we simply do not, and probably never will, possess. (Actually, they make us feel as though we should still be walking around pushing our baby dolls in toy push chairs) I watched them, watching the guys playing touch football - not that they aren't well worth watching mind you!! Max is 28 although he's much too timid and quiet for either of them, Luke's all right, he's about 26, I think, and Hank is a real hunk, but at 24, he's all good looks and big muscles, but unfortunately, well, let me just say he's not too busy in the brains department, Brodie is about the same age as Hank (I think) and he's sort of more normal, but seriously business minded -which for most of us, equals - pretty boring. That leaves Davy, poor Davy, he really is probably *the sweetest* guy on earth, but he's just so lost. He's *such* a cutie and at 21 he's muscular, and built like a weightlifter, he's seriously good looking too, in a curly blonde haired, baby blue eyed sort of way, but poor thing is terribly, painfully shy, and he's out on his own. By that I mean he's too old for the kids, and too young for the men in the group. He'd be welcome to come over and sit with us, but we know he won't – not only because he's so awfully shy, but he's fully aware that Connie has had her eye on him ever since she was about twelve years old! And he'd probably be the first guy in history to actually die from embarrassment!

There are 10 young ones (there are more with the Upper Valley group too) and they're all good kids, except for five-year-old Loretta, who is so-so-so spoiled and can be *quite* badly behaved at times. For one so young, she has *the* most *awful* temper, and she's certainly not afraid to use it to get her own way, as often as she thinks is necessary, which seems to be pretty much most of the time, unfortunately. The children's ages range from the baby, who must be about eight, maybe nine months old now, a one-year-old, and then there's Patrick, who is, I'm guessing, probably around three, the others are ranging through to thirteen years. I'm afraid I can't offer any information about the marines because we still don't even know all their names yet.

Well, I think I've introduced everyone that I can now. I don't know the story behind the children's' missing parents and families, or what really happened to some of these kids; all I *do* know is that they came into the convoy on the second day when all the trucks joined up, and in Tyler's never-ending shuffling us around, he managed to get everyone thoroughly mixed up. Although, I have heard since then that some of the kids had been separated from their parents even *before* they joined us, or else didn't want to go for a walk when we stopped at the picnic ground and the storm hit taking some of our people. So, I'm really not sure what, or in what order, things happened, and I'm not certainly not game enough to ask. We have absolutely no way of tracing any family that might still be living, or letting them know that even though the children's parents have disappeared, the kids themselves are all okay and are being well cared for. Anyway, that's a problem for Tyler and the

Marine Brass to work out at a later date, it's not up to me.

Yippee, now it's my turn to have my hair braided!

I just love having my hair played with, my grandma used to do all sorts of fun things to my hair when I was little, but it got too long and too thick and heavy for her arthritic fingers to handle, until eventually when her hands got too bad, all she could do was brush it for me every morning before I went to work. So, this is an extra special treat for me. I feel so relaxed and so happy right now, I was just at the point of dropping off to sleep when we heard the marines coming back across the field singing some sort of macho, males only marching chant. They certainly looked dog tired and they're all covered in dirt and a fine, powdery white dust, they're even dirtier *now* – than they were before, but they look happy and really excited too. Reba said "There's something about a man in uniform that's just *so* attractive" and from behind me I heard a chorus of "ooh yeah!" From the other girls. "Big broad shoulders, flat stomachs, tight tushes', muscly arms and long strong thighs, will get my full attention every time." I'm not positive, because it was more of a whisper, but I'm pretty sure it was Angie! Although it's a well-known fact that Angie adores *anything* in long pants!

Tyler shouted across the short distance for me to get everyone to gather around in the dining area (I swear he treats us, well *me* mostly, as though we're his new recruits) but one thing's for sure, when he shouts at me – I move. Besides, he said he had some good news for us, and I for one want to hear it.

Once we were all in the dining area and he'd finally managed to get the children calmed down and fairly quiet again, he began by telling us that "his men had found a new, safe and secure valley. One that's easily twice, maybe three times -possibly even more- the size of this place, beyond those caves." Someone said, "*Oh come on fella* make-up yer mind how big it is will ya?" "Okay, okay" shouted Tyler, "I haven't measured *either* space alright… anyway, it's *really big*, is *that* better? There's plenty of good clean shelter within the caves, also the new valley should provide us all with much more than this area does." Everything got a bit confusing after that because everyone started shouting out questions at the same time, so Tyler simply held up his hands and said we were all to start packing up our gear and make ready to move out immediately. Luckily for Tyler he was looking the other way and didn't see the look on the faces of the two older ladies – because they were half way through preparing a meal, and man-oh-man when they turned those twin laser beam stares at him, the term that came to my mind screamed …you're a dead-man!... Actually, with all the dirty looks he got, he's quite lucky not to have been turned to ashes on the spot! The older women were so totally unimpressed by his bit of news; that for a minute there I thought they might either mutiny, or physically assault him right there where he stood. The Upper Valley men started grumbling and kicking up a big fuss too, simply because they quite enjoyed sitting in the sun playing cards, drinking tea and doing nothing useful…and besides, they didn't want that to change. Although I had to have a little giggle at the way they suddenly backed down when Tyler told them he wasn't forcing anyone to move, so they were more than welcome to stay right where they were with their card game if that's what they wanted to do!

I swear I don't know what sort of energy reserves those soldiers were running on, because they must be absolutely so far beyond exhausted by now. Not one of those men have had a proper, restful, or even a chance to have a deep refreshing sleep, for at least a few months, and now, so late in the day after they've been exploring, caving, and climbing around since the very early morning hours, now he's got them organising us into groups, and issuing each of the different groups with very precise instructions, so that there will be very little, or if at all possible, *no* double handling of belongings, or misunderstandings as to what each person; right down to the very youngest -capable- child had to do.
Watching the boys trying to catch and cage up the chickens was simply hilarious! But when Tyler and two of his men told the boys to stand aside and attempted to show them *how it should be done,* we were literally rolling around on the ground and howling with laughter! Those cheeky birds outwitted the marines with every cluck and flap of their wings. Mrs B stood by with her hands firmly planted on her hips (probably to stop herself from knocking down a few marines with her bare hands) watching three grown men making absolute fools of themselves, but about five minutes later, when she'd had enough of their

shenanigans, she stepped in and shoved them aside, she then proceeded to show them the *right* way to do the job. "For pity's sake you're all useless, just go, get away and leave the poor little things alone. All of you –go on now, get away, right away. Shoo. Go! *You too, get*" she pointed at the offenders "get on about your business, and let me deal with these poor creatures, I'll let them calm down again." All she had to do was give them a few seconds to walk around before spreading some feed grain in a short thin line leading up to the opening, then after sprinkling a little dried bread inside the cages the birds found their own way in. That left the marines looking a little embarrassed and feeling stupid, as for Mrs B she simply walked off to finish off her own packing, although I did hear her mumbling away to herself- "Men! They think they know everything, when they don't know the first thing about anything that doesn't have horns, bullets or wheels, honestly!" Tyler turned his somewhat self-conscious face to one of the older boys and asked him to get something from Mrs Beatty to scrape up all the animal poop and drop it all into the fire ring, once he'd done that, he could empty the bucket of soil over the whole lot and stamp it down...

Everyone had finished their packing up well inside the two-hour time limit we'd been given. Every single item we'd carried in with us had been disassembled, repacked, and the engine covers that had done duty as walls for some of the tents last night had today been reborn as sleds. They'd been loaded up and tied down securely, before having a drag handle attached, simply by using a length of rope, and that made it a lot easier for the soldiers or the young men to drag them along behind. The women and children carried the smaller, less bulky items and less weighty supplies.

By sundown no-one would ever have known that anyone had even been there, except for the fire ring, which had been disassembled the rocks removed and the ashes concealed, along with the animal droppings, with the dirt from the bucket, there was some crushed grass in the sitting area and the cropped patch where the lambs and piglets had been penned up, they'd all been nibbling away so very happily on the sweet grass. But even so, come the morning, any crushed grass would have sprung back up again anyway.

Well, here we go again, following Tyler and his Men blindly into…what? Where? None of us had any real idea of what we might find on the other side of this cave, we only had Tyler's word that it was something special. But his word was good enough for almost everyone, he'd earned our trust. To tell the truth though, I was a bit sad to leave this little bit of paradise, but in the course of the past months we've all come to rely on, to put our lives, and our trust in their decisions entirely, so if the marines think it's good, and if, as they say, it's really a much better, more suitable place for everyone, then it must be okay. And in any case the soldiers really do seem happy to be going back over there.

We were just past the half way point, in our crossing toward the caves when all of a sudden, we were standing in total darkness. Deafening thunder rolled and cracked in the distance, terrifying levels of ferocious lightning slashed through the blackness, and we used those momentary bursts of brilliance to light our way across the grassy field, I thought we were lucky this time, because it didn't start to rain.

Oh! Wow, hey look up there c'mon, can you, cn you see it, shouted one of the boys. Like we were automatons we stopped and looked up to watch the almost painfully brilliant, purest white clouds being chased across the sky by heaving black storm clouds, both were moving at an incredible speed, racing wildly and recklessly across the sky. One second it was dazzling sunshine, and the next second it was dark again, and within seconds the sky had filled with big fluffy clouds, but in the blink of an eye those same fluffy clouds were pushed aside by menacing clouds, clouds that were thick black and boiling, but before our brains could properly process these rapid changes, the sky would be beautifully clear and innocently blue once again! Down here at ground level, surrounded by the high walls in this very strange, magically sheltered world, the sweetly perfumed air remained completely calm, there wasn't even a breath of wind.

"Come *on* people *move it along will you!* Tyler growled. I want everyone in and everything to be set up well before nightfall, now stop gawking at the sky and *keep moving.*"

The marines had, quite by chance, found another entry point, fortunately it was one that gave us a much easier access to the big cave. After having dropped his torch down what he thought was a hole, Mark had found a much wider and much easier entrance that curved and sloped gently upwards like a natural ramp. This second entrance had been well concealed by an enormous cluster of exquisitely coloured flowering bushes which had grown all the way across the rock wall and concealed the second entrance.

Tyler had instructed the Men to very, very carefully, tie the bushes back and away from the opening, however, under *no* circumstances were those bushes to be visibly damaged and if any stems, flowers or branches *did* happen to break off they were to be collected and taken inside out of sight. The entrance was to remain obscured in case there were unwanted intruders. As Tyler spoke, one of the Upper Valley men started jeering and making a joke of all Tyler's instructions and his attention to detail "well, see the thing is Mr. Morgan, *we* found it didn't we? Well then, it only stands to reason that someone else could too. At any point in time, another person or maybe even another group of people, could stumble across the way in, in exactly the same way we've done, and as you are all aware, there's absolutely no guarantee that they'll be friendly folk either, now is there? And I for one Mr. Morgan, have no desire to have to fight for the right to stay here. Do you?" His point was clear, valid and well made, so we all did whatever he told us to do. Which was, quite coincidently, just the way he liked it. The discovery of the alternative entrance meant that there was no need to climb up and squeeze everything through the first and much more awkward opening, therefore each individual person's share of the provisions, and personal belongings, could be managed with relative ease. Although mind you, there was still plenty of grumbling, and non-stop whining, with a large side dish of cranky. There were complaints about everything, from a couple of the refugees and *far too many* really loud, downright offensive remarks, totally uncalled for filthy obscenities and criticisms, coming from the *supposedly* morally superior and oh-so-very-refined Upper Valley people, or UVs, as they were being referred to by the marines now. The term 'UV' was practically being used as a swear word! Admittedly the trouble had been brewing for months, but at some stage in the twenty-four hours since our arrival it had reached flashpoint. I can't honestly say exactly *when* it started, but a very unpleasant, very clear, and very definite division, has been established between the two groups, fortunately for us, the marines have placed themselves firmly on the side of the Shadey's and all who are with us. I did notice it before, but only slightly though, because the times we stopped to eat or stretch cramped limbs were always short, but now that the travelling is over, well *now* it's blatantly obvious - to the point where the UVs have become downright aggressive. Strangely enough, or no, perhaps it's not so strange at all, but it's only the people from the Upper Valley who are being *relentless* when it comes to finding fault with absolutely *everything* Tyler is doing, or is *trying* to do, for all of us. We all know fully well, and so do they, that he's doing the very best he can, and heaven only knows, the man has few enough resources to call on, however there's just no pleasing some people is there?

Even I have to admit that after a while, moving and manoeuvring our way through these caves while being loaded to the gunnels, wasn't such easy going.

Patrick had spent most of the day running and playing, and now he was too tired to walk any further, so I snuggled him in amongst the huge load of bedding on my sled and let him rest.

We're country stock, all of us working-farm raised, so we're well and truly accustomed to hard and heavy work, but what we're *not* used to doing is clambering around on uneven stone floors when we're weighed down by heavy loads that seem to be getting heavier, and more difficult to manage, with every step in semi-darkness! Especially since we've all lost a fair amount of muscle tone over the last few months while we've been carted around the countryside like so much cattle. We've all developed what I affectionately call 'truckers butt' brought on by sitting and bouncing around on our behinds in the back of the truck's day in and day out, with no opportunity for anything like real exercise at all, certainly nothing to keep our muscles in their tip top pre-evacuation condition. So, feeling fatigued due to this unaccustomed form of exertion brought out a completely unnecessary, and an all too often, much nastier side of quite a few people. The transfer seemed to be taking for-ever and was a considerably longer distance than Tyler had suggested it would be. If you combine that, with the UVs constant criticisms aimed directly at him, it's no surprise that he was in a pretty touchy mood as well. He practically exploded with fury when the strap gave way and a large cooking pot slipped off from where it had been tied onto poor Mrs. B's back pack; he really roared and, well he basically flew right off the handle and straight into a full-blown rage at her! The racket made by the pot crashing onto stone was one thing, but couple that with Tyler's outraged shouts echoing and reverberating endlessly inside the rocky cavern, it was like being trapped inside a gigantic Chinese gong that was being beaten on by a madman wielding a hammer. It was so loud, and echoed so much, that my poor eardrums ducked for cover and my eyeballs wobbled! You have to give her full credits though, Mrs B gave him back every bit as much as she got! We saw a side of Mrs B that day that we'd never have thought possible, she stood there with her hands firmly planted on her hips, and drew herself up to her full height -five feet one inch- (*with* her trainers on) and faced up to his strapping, solid-muscle six-foot something frame, and she actually spoke *down* to him. Her tone was very stern, more like he was a recalcitrant child. She stood her ground and told him "I've had *quite enough,* I am *not* one of your marines sir, and what's more I *will not* stand by quietly and allow you to *treat* me like one! *What I am,* Mr Tyler" (she said) "is a woman who is quite old enough to be your *mother,* and in the future young man, *you* will afford *me, exactly* the same level of courtesy *and* the *respect* that you would give to her. *if she were here instead of me...* I will also make one single, and most definitely *non-negotiable* demand of you Mr Tyler, and please *do not* misunderstand, *or* misinterpret what I'm about to say. It's *not* a request- it's a *demand* regarding yourself, *and* your men. I *insist* on also receiving the same degree of courtesy and respect from each and every one of your marines, *if any one of you*" (she turned to face the marines grouped behind Tyler) "*ever* disrespect me again, you will *all* find out first hand, *exactly* what it's like to be fending for yourselves. You would all be well advised to remember that, *if* you want to eat a decent meal ever again, so just keep that thought in the forefront of you minds gentlemen. This has been your one and your *only* warning, the alternative is to cook, and care, for yourselves as best you can. Because if you *ever* show anything less than full respect, I will cut you off completely. The choice is entirely up to you gents." Then without a backward glance she readjusted her pack, gathered up her dignity, retied her big pot, and continued walking. Oh-my-goodness-golly-gosh! That was just so great to see!

Big Bully Boy Tyler, being brought to heel, by an itty-bitty little woman, it was all we refugees could do not to clap and laugh out loud. As for his men, well, they just stood around stony faced and stiff with indignation. I don't suppose these soldier boys are accustomed to being given a direct order by a civilian, and by a civilian *woman* no less! She hadn't left them with a great deal of choice, and not so much as an inch of wriggle room in the matter either. She's one very shrewd lady! I'd been watching Tyler closely, and was taken aback by his rather extraordinary reaction to her severe reprimand. I noticed that his customary unsmiling mouth had compressed down even further into a hard thin slash, his nostrils flared angrily and although his ears and his thick neck had both turned bright red, his face had gone as white as a sheet under his tan. Nevertheless, Mrs B had made her point and she'd made it crystal clear. Tyler called out for her to wait a minute. "Please Mrs Beatty wait a moment."

WOW! I can't believe it; he actually knows how to say the word *please!* He then gave her a rather stiff apology and begged her pardon, saying he had meant her no disrespect, then he negated every word by adding, "Okay people, we've wasted enough time, we really need to get a move on if we're to finish the crossing before sundown."
Corporal Zahan called on everyone to "FALL IN" his words echoed and bounced around the ancient chambers while each person collected and resettled their packs once more and continued playing follow the leader.

This cave system was absolutely huge, gigantic even! And the metal sleds that were loaded with the bulk of the larger and heavier goods, food supplies, mechanical stuff and various bits out of the trucks, bedding, and one very small boy… were acting like giant cheese graters on our central nervous systems. The ghastly noise made by metal being dragged across uneven contours of the rock floor and echoing loudly, had us all gritting our teeth so hard our jaws ached… add to that, that each of the marine's hobnail booted footfalls vibrated all around us, making each step sound very similar to the sharp report of a gunshot, all those sounds combined, rebounded, and echoed for ages. Our ears were ringing, our heads were throbbing to the beat of our stumbling march forward, and too many muscles burned and ached in protest. To top it off, tempers on both sides were becoming even further unravelled. Oh, but when Jeremiah, one of the youngest of the boys called out "Hey, mithta Tyler! I fink we've been going around in a thircle thir!" He knew beyond any shadow of a doubt that he'd been in this exact same spot at least once already.

Well... didn't Tyler round on him! He accusing him of being nothing but a lazy little trouble making brat who would never make a half decent marine because he couldn't take the pace. The youngster didn't need to make a reply, he simply pointed to a place by the wall and said "Look... juth over there thir, a few minuths ago, when you wath having your um, talk, wif Mithuth Beatty, I had a pee over there, if you don't believe me, take a look for yourthelf a'cause ith's thtill wet thir!"

Mr. Uppity (as I'd nicknamed Mr Beatty) yelled out "So how come we're goin' aroun' an aroun' in circles eh Tyler? Couldn't be that you marine boys are *lost* or somethin could it, eh?" At first Tyler looked quite taken aback, then shocked, and then actually embarrassed, but then he just got really, *really,* mad. He shouted back at Mr Beatty that he was only trying to protect us, he only wanted for us to be safe, and be secure over in the new area; he didn't want anyone trying to find the way out alone, with so many twists and turns, a person might take a wrong turn and become lost, it could be dangerous too. So, he'd done the only thing he could, he tried to discourage us, he said, by making the way back out seem longer and more challenging in an effort to protect us.

This newest revelation caused a really uncomfortable ripple to run through both sides of the tired and worn-out groups. So exactly what, or who, did he suspect that he was protecting us from? Was there something these marines knew, but weren't passing on to us? I started thinking about the heavily armed guards in the trucks. What had had him so worried, even back then? And what, or who, would we need protecting from? And why would we even *want* to leave the security being part of the group gave us? Does he honestly think any of us is that crazy? But even if someone *was* stupid enough, and really wanted to leave, wasn't it after all, their *own* personal choice to make? Or is he perhaps, concerned about any future reprisals against him personally, more than an individual person making a choice?

But at the moment, and even though we were all thinking along the same lines, no-one was game enough, or should I say *stupid enough*, to speak their thoughts out loud. Then again, as for asking him for some clarification about his fears, the pain it would undoubtedly cause in our heads and ears, simply wasn't worth the question, the answer, *or* the risk! All jokes aside, everyone's ears were still ringing from the loud echoes instigated by the heated exchanges rebounding back at us from every direction. Oh well, at least that explained why I thought the caves all looked so much alike... Tyler looked over at me with something that appeared to be pleading in his eyes... and I pulled a cross-eyed face and poked my tongue out at him! By way of saying- ha, so there *Mr Smarty pants* – Oh yes, I know, beyond any shadow of a doubt- sometimes I can be *extremely* mature...just not today!

Within minutes following that last, very intense verbal exchange, we rounded a corner and came out into dazzling sunlight. The next thing to be heard was everyone groaning in unison! Ahh, the simple pleasure of being able to put our loads down again, even if it would only be for a little while. Sienna dropped her small bundle of blankets, shook her hair out from under her cap and asked if anyone had a cigarette and a wine, she was rather less than underwhelmed by the one hundred percent negative response she received. Max and Brodie were getting really impatient, they wanted to be rid of the heavy sacks they were carrying strapped to their backs, and were trying to wangle their way past Katherine and Angie as they shuffled along, walking sideways like two crabs with their shared, but very awkward, and lopsided load, looking all around to see where there was enough space to put it down.

Once they'd cleared themselves a pathway through the tangle of people and saw where we had come out, Brodie and Max, holding true to their bloodlines and indigenous ancestors, let out a truly ear-splitting traditional Indian war whoop, and then called back to Luke, Davy and Hank. "Wow come over here you guys quick! Come on, you've just *gotta* see this, it's so, just oh it's wow, oh man this is, it's, wow, this's *so* fantastic!"

Standing crowded up together on the high and wide stage-like ledge that overlooked the valley floor that was much, so much more, than merely fantastic, the view from the high stage, allowed us to see right across the valley floor, and it was purely breathtaking. What we were seeing down below us, was nothing short of absolutely spectacular, although that word really isn't big enough, or dramatic enough, to do justice to such a magnificent vision. I was spellbound, and totally awestruck. To think that every morning I would be waking up to such incredible beauty gave me a rush of the happiness tingles.

This new area was vast, beyond huge, in reality, it was absolutely, incredibly immense. More like six or seven maybe ten times larger than the area we'd left behind, not the three times bigger that Tyler had given it, and it is formed in *exactly* the same way as the previous canyon, in that this canyon too, and although it is a natural formation, it looks like an enormous stone walled fortress, it's a massive oval, an immense light blue/grey granite bowl. The surrounding walls must be at *least* seventy to ninety feet high, and were even higher in some places. And here too, the walls have that same strange characteristic of sloping ever so slightly inward like the other area, it almost looks like the opening of a volcano. The walls here however, appeared to be much lighter, a softer shade of the same soft blue/grey granite and the strong afternoon sunlight picked out something like crystal that makes them gleam and glint with sparkling pin points, like diamonds and silver, as though they want to make you aware of their immense strength, and that they're strong enough to keep you safe, and sheltered from the storms. Tyler walked up to me and handed me his binoculars, he said – "here, have a good look." The main difference between the two canyons though is in the overall space, over on the other side, in the first canyon, which by the way, we all thought was huge enough, is by comparison, in fact a great deal smaller and the ground over there is fairly flat like a sporting field, whereas over here, there are some gentle grassy slopes and an immense, and absolutely stunning waterfall way over in the distance.

"Wait 'til you see it up close Sara, it really is the most beautiful thing, you can't see it from this angle, but the water pours in through a huge horizontal slot really high up in the wall, and falls into a gigantic smooth stone basin, that's easily three times the size of your 'pond' over the other side, which in turn, flows into that little river over there, can you see it? And that river winds its way across the canyon and disappears again under the wall on the far side" he explained. I moved around to the very end of the stage, and there it was, the waterfall, and I felt so privileged to see it in all its glorious magnificence… Right now, the waterfall was giving off a delicate, fine, water spray, or maybe it could be described as a heavy mist, but whatever you might want to call it, it's positively alive with pretty, delicate colourful rainbows, I've never seen *anything* as stunning, or as beautiful, as this in my whole life.

Exactly as there had been in the other area, there's a multitude of spectacularly colourful birds that have gathered to sit quietly, without moving a single feather, all jam packed together along the fragrant branches in another forest of tall trees. All those eyes, observing our every movement from their hiding places amid the thick foliage of the trees growing along the opposite bank of the stream, I wondered if they were the same birds, or if these ones lived here.

Through the binoculars I could see another grove of much smaller trees, situated further along the stream, although each of individual trees had thick, really dense foliage, and a large number of those extraordinary looking, and impossibly coloured trees appeared to be growing fruits of some kind. Through Tyler's binoculars I could see some animals grazing in the distance, and here too, there were rabbit-like animals galore, I laughed when one of the boys called out that he could see a horse... and could he have it please?

Once again, we kicked off our shoes and walked on grass that's so velvet soft, and so cool under our hot, tired aching feet. Pure bliss.

I started comparing the physical appearances, and the actual similarities, as opposed to the contrasts between the two areas. Obviously, the main difference here, besides the sheer immensity of the area, and the breathtaking natural beauty, is the myriad variety and the fascinating, if somewhat peculiarly coloured flowers. My mother and grandparents have always been devoted and enthusiastic, more like fanatical, gardeners. From the time I was just a babe in arms, right the way through to my late teens, but more so when I was a little girl, we'd spent many days and weekends in gardens of one kind or another, be they various magnificent Botanical gardens, admiring beautiful flower gardens around grand houses, or in the public parks, or sometimes wandering around the gardens of stately old institutions on visitors' days, or the vegetable gardens and orchards belonging to, or around the various farms in and for miles around, Shady Haven. However, in all of the gardens, and the many hundreds of flower-shows I was taken to, and all the many plant varieties my grandfather grew, or pictured in the dozens of big gardening and flower arranging books my grandma collected, I have never, in all my life, seen flowers that bear so much as a slight resemblance to anything like these, not to mention the sheer variety *and* the exquisite brilliance of them. There are certainly lots and lots of unexpected, even confusing colours among them too. Totally new, never before seen, nameless colours and shades. There are colours here, that neither I, nor anyone else, has ever seen anywhere else before. These truly strange and mysterious colours were enough to make even Tyler stand in silent awe of Mother Nature's more pleasurable handiwork. We have come to a veritable paradise; maybe, oh hey, what if we have accidently stumbled into a cousin of those fabled Gardens of Eden!?

 Privately though, I'm feeling just a little uneasy about these canyons, these very *secretive* canyons. I can't help but wonder about the undeniable fact that according to the marines' many and very precise and accurately detailed maps, they don't exist, but at the same time I'm marvelling at them, I'm also seriously questioning just *how* all of this magnificence has not only survived, but *how* has it's remained undiscovered and untouched? And how is it that *this* place has survived probably many thousands of those violent, completely wild storms, when so many other places have been destroyed, wiped from the face of the earth so completely? Storms that are so severe, and so unrelenting, yet seem to be growing increasingly stronger and more violent, are only a few feet away on the other side of these high walls. Storm furies that by some strange, and inexplicable quirk of nature, have left these gardens completely intact and unscathed… but when you think about it, they're only a relatively short distance away from the outside world.

Another thing that is really unsettling for me, is how come it doesn't rain *in* here? We can stand, or sit and *watch* the clouds changing from an innocent fluffy white to boiling, heavy black storm clouds. We can *see* the lightening flashing and hear it crackling, it even sends up showers of sparks when an occasional strike touches the top of the walls; we can *hear* the savage, blood curdling ferocity of the wind as it rages and shrieks in a mad frenzy of destruction all around the outside walls, we can *see and hear* the pulverizing rain falling, although what's even more incredible, to me at least, is while there's the unbelievable blast furnace like temperatures outside, here inside, the temperature's so mild, it's really just comfortably warm. Yes, we can see, and we can hear, *everything*, but we *feel nothing*. Every living thing within these walls remains completely dry, undisturbed, and totally untouched; this whole place is a garden of complete, and gentle calm, a peaceful oasis in the midst of outrageous carnage.

"Stand To" came the order from Hans, the burly Corporal, snapping us all back into the moment at hand. I looked up at Tyler and as I returned his binoculars, I couldn't help but notice that he was finally starting to show how excruciatingly exhausted he must be. Deep dark circles had been etched under his thoughtful, terribly bloodshot blue eyes, those nasty scrapes on his hands had opened up and were bleeding freely again too, he desperately needed to bathe and sleep. For his own wellbeing, he had to allow himself to wind down, at the very least until his body has recovered from the incredible stress it has been absorbing for months. His big broad shoulders and strong wide back weren't anywhere near as parade ground perfect as they usually are. It comes as no great surprise either, considering that, and even putting aside the punishing pace he's set himself, and everything else he's been doing for months, the load he carried over here by himself today, well that alone was more than heavy enough for three normal men! He just doesn't seem to know how to be an average, or even a just above, average human – he has to prove he's the superior alpha male. But even alpha's need to sleep occasionally.

Without his cap on, his previously buzz cut hair has grown quite long and is starting to curl around his head and neck. Maybe he *is* part human after all.
"Come on folks, there's still a great deal of work to be done before it gets dark" barked Tyler, "and if you want to have any sort of comfort and shelter tonight then I strongly recommend you all attend to your prescribed duties" (oh jeez, there he goes, he's doing it *again*, why? for goodness' sake, *why* does he *always* look straight at *me* when he's dishing out his orders?) "Starting *right now people.*" And with that little spell breaker, we all started to shuffle around, locate and reorganise our various loads, we had to get all the belongings and stores sorted into at least *some* semblance of order, all over again. Anything used in

the kitchen; cooking hardware, crockery etcetera, was stacked up in one place ready for Mrs B and her team to sort out again, all foodstuffs were allotted a place and the ~~soldiers~~ (darn it, why do I keep calling them that?) the *marines* began erecting a temporary storage shelter for them.

Following *that* exhausting bit of exercise, we were given instructions regarding the sleeping quarters. Yesterday, when they came here to investigate, Tyler's men had found a multitude of much smaller caves, and overall, these caves are like one enormous honeycomb, only in rock; they have each been inspected thoroughly for wildlife or vermin (none found) and were therefore pronounced ready to be occupied. The caves chosen as being the most suitable for sleeping quarters, once they had been declared large enough, and safe to use, were easily identified by a number neatly written using a waterproof wax marker on the wall (this time they used bright yellow) The numbers served a dual purpose, the first was identifying the safe sites, and the second was so that each person would know which *room* to go back to until we got our bearings, or I should say, until the area becomes familiar.

These caves were also convenient insofar as many of them were interconnected and they all branched off from a very large, very bright, sun drenched and stunningly beautiful, central cave. The central cave in turn is situated high above the ground and dominated the spectacularly exquisite view across the entire valley floor below. Tyler suggested that we all take a good look around and decide whether or not we were all in agreeance, because he thought it could make an ideal living centre for all of us to use in case of inclement weather, if we ever have any! The central, or main cave is, as I have said, simply stunning and a truly beautiful piece of natures' amazing architecture. The high walls are pale golden honey-coloured stone. I was running my fingers across some of the irregularities and was surprised to find the stone's really quite smooth. The extraordinary cathedral-like ceiling is an almost perfect oval, the wall rises up from about fifteen or so feet on the outer edges, gently increasing to about twenty-five feet, then the wall rises sharply to I guess around fifty-plus feet in the centre, more than anything else, it reminded me of the stage in the Grand Opera House my grandpa took me to once, and I could imagine an enormous crystal chandelier hanging down with thousands of twinkling lights. The stone floor is almost level, oh naturally, it has a few slight dips and bumps of course, but there's nothing dangerous like an open channel or a deep hole, and with a good clean out it will make a terrific general living area, or a big family room overlooking, as it does, the valley floor about fifteen feet below. The smaller caves, of which there seemed to be dozens upon dozens, will be perfect as sleeping areas, or a quiet place we can go if we need some peace and privacy, or as grandma always called it –a bit of *me* time. There's also another very large, open fronted cave just around the corner and to the immediate left of the last bedroom. Unfortunately, that particular cave has a largish opening about a foot and a half wide, right in the centre of the high, dome-like roof, there is a really wide but narrow open area behind, with lots and lots of small irregular ledges. Mrs B, who had been inspecting the whole area, because she was on the look-out for a place with some specific qualities, and when she found this one she asked if they could use this space in particular, for their kitchen. Because as she explained to Tyler, it has ample spaces that would be too small for regular storage but would be perfect for storing the food supplies, it also afforded good protection for the cooks, and with that hole above, it would permit the smoke from the cooking fires to escape, and *if* the marines were able, and *if* they could erect some sort of manoeuvrable canopy over that hole - one that would be able to withstand the onslaught of the wind and rain preferably... an adaptable cover over the top would make it a perfect companion to the rest of the living area. Tyler thought about it, and commented, somewhat grudgingly, to his most senior engineer, that her idea actually made really good, and very practical sense.

The location of the newly designated kitchen would avoid altogether any need to create a canvas cook house that could actually be a serious fire hazard, it also avoided the necessity of carrying foodstuffs back and forth in bad weather as well. So, it was decided that Mrs B's suggestion would be taken up, and that the next morning, weather permitting, a work party (who were all now very eager to stay in Mrs B's good book) would climb up to see exactly what they would be dealing with, thus allowing them to go ahead and work out a practical design for a strong, but still easily manoeuvred canopy over the hole. Well, it looks like those truck engine covers will be reborn anew, said Sanchez with a big grin. I looked over at the ladies and giggled to myself because more than anything else, Mrs B's expression was a lot like that of a cat who'd found a whole bowl of fresh cream! She has established herself as the undisputed queen of her new domain, and right at this moment, she was one very satisfied queen indeed. Her personal celebration was simple, singing and humming happily while she did some serious sorting out and prepared to cook up another delicious meal. Which would be devoured in no time by this ravenously hungry hoard!

Here, in these canyons, we've become aware that in the evening, sundown is more of an extended twilight rather than nightfall proper. Even though I am surrounded by so much incredible beauty, I really do miss not having a horizon to look at. These high, strong walls are really beautiful, but they mean there's no way I can enjoy the spectacular sunsets these storms have given us, maybe they're supposed to be some sort of compensation because the fantastic sunsets are most definitely the *only* good thing to come out of this misery. But I suppose if our safety and security does come at a price, then my personal payment is living without spectacular sunsets.

Tall shadows indicating the onset of evening, have lengthened and deepened into a deep purply-black the whole way around the towering rock perimeter, and while the sunlight has faded away, we haven't been left in complete darkness since the daylight has been replaced by the delicate rays of cool silvery moonlight streaming down, bathing the centre of the valley in a soothing pale light that delays the onset of complete night-time darkness for a while longer.

In the first area, if we sat quietly for long enough, we would sometimes hear small scurrying animal noises from time to time, but that won't be happening tonight, sitting down for *any* length of time is positively not an option. With so much work still waiting to be done - and with Tyler frequently calling out directions, it was all hands-on-deck, and shoulders to the wheel, so to speak. Aye, aye captain! Oh no *not again!* I swear, if that man keeps looking at me while he's yelling out his orders, I'll start screaming out a few of my own!

Those two older ladies must work really well together, because in no time at all, they've settled into an easy and relaxed rhythm, getting on with the huge task of setting their kitchen and storage up, getting all the provisions unpacked and organised, emptying those huge boxes of crockery and linens, finding places for them, then there's all those oversize cooking pots and utensils – quite a big task for two, not-so-young, ladies. While the rest of us were busy searching through all these mixed-up loads to find, and sort out, our own few belongings in the central chamber, by some mystical sleight of hand, those ladies have accomplished the impossible – they've prepared a meal for everyone in the midst of what can, at best, only be described as total chaos! We were all invited to choose the room we wanted for our own use. As one would expect, this room selection, was something that *should* have been a pretty much straightforward and easy thing to do right? But with the UV's around, *nothing* has a chance of going smoothly. It would seem there was an incident, or a clash, and it comes as no surprise at all that it's caused a wee bit of dissent within *certain parties* in the group. It happened when a couple of people *both* wanted the same room, and for some reason –and one known only to themselves- the UV group member believed that they were *entitled* to have the first choice! Although I cannot, for one second imagine why! Therefore, Tyler decided that the only fair and reasonable thing to do was to conduct a lottery.

 One of the marines wrote the name of each person onto small slips of paper, folded, and placed them into another marine's cap, he then wrote the allotted number of each cave-room on another slip, which was also folded and placed into a second cap. Patrick was called upon to take one slip of paper from each cap and pass them first to the eldest group member, Mr. Costa, to read; the slips were then passed over to Tyler and he read them out loud. There was no room for argument, although, and only if both parties agreed were we permitted to swap rooms. Married couples were given two rooms, connecting wherever possible, although some of the married people elected to have their own very separate space, which simply meant a cave-room each. At least Tyler tried to allow them sleeping quarters as well as some personal space for privacy. I do have to admit, he *does try* to be very fair to everyone, and so often he has to ignore just how out-and-out *rude* some people are to him. That enormous, battle scarred 'Kit' Mrs B's big old sewing chest, the one that has been responsible for so many aching backs, bashed up knees, banged up ankles, and countless bruises, sore muscles, trapped fingers and squashed toes (I suppose I'll be diplomatic and *not* mention the couple of rather blazing arguments it caused along the way) the monstrosity that has been carted all over the countryside for months, is probably going to prove to be invaluable to us, and I'm quite certain it will be doing a great deal of extra duty, and really justifying its place in the community very soon, that's for sure. Mainly because we'll all want to find a way to secure a privacy screen, or some kind of closure across the cave-room openings, that are currently affording no privacy at all to anyone, however, until the engineers, or some other clever person, can come up with an idea for some sort of door or curtain arrangement, we'll have to warn each other of our approach or close our eyes! As Mrs B suggested, I think we might end up using willow fronds from the abundant collection of weeping willow trees growing along the river bank, once woven and fixed to a frame they might make reasonable screens. The room Patrick and I will share is at the very end of the honeycombed curve, which means its sort of facing away from the other rooms and is closer to the main chamber, so at least we'll have a little extra privacy when compared to a lot of the others, and the view, (even though it's a little bit cut off) is still wonderful. Fortunately, our room is quite spacious, although I've only just now realised how uneven and bumpy the floor is, so it looks like I'll need to learn how to sleep in a hammock for a while after all! I plan to ask Tyler in a few days (when he's not so busy) if he knows of an easy way to smooth it down or maybe fill in the bumps and holes with soil or sand to level it out a bit more, and be safer, to walk on. I'd hate for one of us to be tripping or falling over in the pitch dark all the time, I need a twisted ankle like I need a hole in the head.

Oh no! No, oh jeez, now that's just *so not fair,* as if I haven't had enough bad luck already. No, *really?* You've got to be kidding me! *Tyler* has taken the empty room right next door to mine. Oh well that's just great. *I don't think.* I've been hoping for a girly neighbour, well so much for *that* wish. Tyler's about as girly as a grizzly bear with a thorn in its foot.

 The twin problems of latrines and showers have also been handed to the engineers. We've been told that this sort of thing is actually their forte, and it's part of their typical work routine. As the man said "it's what we do best." Apparently, they go into regions and zones that have been badly damaged, if not totally destroyed, by earthquakes, tidal waves, fires, floods, conflict etc. and their job is to take control of restoring water supply, and essential, even if a somewhat rudimentary sanitation system, that's necessary for basic day to day health and survival for the people, while all the rest of the digging, demolishing and repairs or rebuilding of their homes etc. takes place. I think this job should be a piece of cake by comparison, seeing as there's no damage, no danger of buildings collapsing under, on top of, or around them, no dead bodies, nor is there the threat of disease or a war for them to work around.

As everyone got on with the business of settling in, I began hearing snippets of various conversations, mostly wondering how they were going to get used to this cave living, and while I'm not sure who was talking, it was coming from one of the UV rooms and unfortunately, there were some really ugly words being passed back and forth. Young Davy is talking to the Boss because he's worried about how long the food will last, and Tyler's told him to hold onto that thought until after our meal tonight and he will add his concerns to the list of topics up for discussion. Max, Brodie and Luke wanted to survey the whole area as soon as possible, they were told to go ahead, and knock themselves out! Amelia, who suffers from arachnophobia, was terrified that she'd have some creepy crawlies either in her room or worse - in her bedding. Fabs, one of the marines, gave a wicked chuckle and suggested that he would be only too happy take care of her, *personally*. Much to her blushing delight! Then Mr. Armstrong demanded that Tyler stop what he was doing and supply him with immediate answers to all sorts of impossible, and totally ridiculous questions. Tyler's reply was simple, if I can, I'll answer your questions, but it won't be 'til later on, because right now I'm just too busy. Apparently, the Upper Valley people have elected Kevin Blanchard to be their (very unlikely) spokesperson. Mr Blanchard is a man who is extremely short in stature, with a slender (scrawny) build, he has receding fine grey hair, an unfortunate nervous stutter, and he wears thick, heavy brown framed spectacles, that are far too big for his thin face and make him look like an owl, oh, and he's extremely timid. The poor unsuspecting fellow was shoved forward and told to ask the engineers how soon the *electricity* would be connected for their lights! The group of engineers didn't utter a single word, they just stared him down, well the poor man blushed furiously, mumbled a 'thanks for your time' and scuttled away with his head tucked below his shoulders to deliver the unwelcome answer, while the rest of us, had to stifle our giggles and pretend we hadn't seen or heard anything, and hurried to get our own jobs completed.

After the tense, very physically, and emotionally exhausting day we've had, we wanted to get back into Tyler's good books. We're all *so* absolutely sick and tired of his never ending complaints, saying we're too slow, or we're dawdling, and a little while ago he even asked us if we were enjoying our Sunday stroll. *Why* for goodness' sake I mean, it's not like we'll be *going* anywhere anytime soon, so what's his big hurry?

Suddenly, as if we were one single body, we stopped whatever we were doing and froze, the whole place had been plunged into sudden, impenetrable darkness, a darkness that was broken only momentarily by irregular bursts of dazzling lightening, and the bellowing roar of crashing thunder. We'd thought the noise was loud outside but when you're *inside* the caves, the thunder is loud enough to send a body deaf! One really smart marine had had the foresight to make up about a dozen fire torches and he'd dug them deep into the ground at intervals, so that we weren't all left wandering around as blind as bats. The dinner gong sounded and a few moments later we all filed out, gingerly shuffling along the unfamiliar, slightly uneven floor in semi darkness until we'd made it into the 'downstairs' dining area, where those flaming torches had been evenly spaced behind the long tables. The marines had made tables by using the wide wooden siding salvaged from the trucks, and thanks to the quick thinking (and downright sneakiness) of one marine, each of the four massive table legs had been cut into four pieces lengthways giving us sixteen strong table legs, unknowingly supplied courtesy of Mr. Ruiz's precious antique furniture!

The improvised tables had been set up with an odd assortment of crockery and flatware for us to eat from, and the splintery wooden bench seats from the trucks had been covered with strips of torn canvas, to serve as our seating. I wasn't the only one who was suitably impressed by just how quickly these marines were able to, not only secure a site, but make it – if not exactly cozy, then at least liveable, and even if it's not all that comfortable, pretty, or fancy right now, if today's efforts are anything to go by, it jolly well soon will be!

Even though tonight's meal, had been prepared in a rush, you'd never know it because once again everything was just delicious, our miracle workers Mrs B, Mrs Armstrong and a few other ladies who offered to step in to give the cooks a helping hand, are all well pleased with the new kitchen, and they're particularly happy with the vastly improved cooking appointments, no more crouching, bending or squatting on their haunches over hot pots and pans that were balanced, rather precariously, over a somewhat wobbly rock fireplace, for which their poor (and no longer young) backs and thighs are extremely grateful. In the new kitchen area, there's a very long and deep, natural rock ledge that sits just below their hip height, it has been utilized for the cooking fires, and believe me, Mrs B already has big plans for quite a few additional improvements as well. I overheard something about grinding out a long basin like section in the shelf for the cooking fires and a steel plate and a grate over the top. Interesting times are ahead for her domain…

Oh my, lord save me! I apparently made the unforgivable blunder of calling one of the 'All Powerful and Mighty Marines' a *Soldier* in Tyler's hearing yesterday! So, he's just spent the last half hour *enlightening* me as to the many and varied differences between (the *vastly superior*) marines, and what he rather disparagingly calls common foot soldiers. Wow, I can't believe the unbelievable *conceit* of these men! What's *really* funny though, is that Tyler, for some crazy reason, and one known only to himself, thought that I actually *cared*! When really, I couldn't give a raspberry flavoured hoot about the differences! Nevertheless, I *will* watch what I say from now on, but *only* because I know that the man will have another huge ego trip while he's giving me another seriously boring ear bashing!

We had just started making our way outside into the fresh air, in fact I'd only taken a couple of tentative steps, when dozens upon dozens of massive forks of lightning carved through the otherwise pitch-black night sky, and as before, each of the strikes were very closely, in fact almost instantly, followed by a deafening peal of ground shuddering thunder and hundreds of smaller, but definitely *not* insignificant, flashes of electrical energy. The beautiful diamond encrusted veil of stars above us had been wiped out in the blink of an eye, only to be replaced by an inky expanse of blackness so deep, you couldn't even see your own hand right in front of your face, and every time the thunder clapped and roared above, for those still inside the main cave, it was like being stuck inside a huge kettle drum being beaten with a steel pipe wielded by the same madman who'd attacked the Chinese gong on the way over! Once we were outside again, we could hear the deadly rip-roaring winds shrieking like an out-of-control freight train directly above us and screaming around and around the outer walls like wild banshee's; most of us have had to agree that some of the strangest phenomenon any of us have ever encountered, seem to take place right here in these mysterious canyons. How *can* it be possible that while directly over our heads, a storm of incredible, absolutely lethal proportions is raging, yet down here on the ground, there isn't even the slightest whisper of a breeze to tickle the grass, and not one single drop of rain ever falls? When according to science, these almost circular canyons *should* act like a vortex, sucking the storm activity down, where it would naturally obliterate everything? Something completely unnatural is happening here. In my mind I keep going back to the maps, to the undeniable fact that this seemingly ancient stone monster doesn't have a place marked or is named anywhere. The comment someone made that it seemed to be born especially for us creeps me right out – but what if that's true?

Someone just stumbled into me, apologised and shuffled off into the darkness, I can hear the sound made by, what I know only too well must be torrential, flooding rain, and the intensified roar as probably thousands of gallons of water pour over the waterfall. It's all really mysterious though. This storm, like so many others in the thirty or so hours since our arrival, while sounding ever so much more ruthless than the one we experienced first hand on the outside, it has caused us no harm what-so-ever, and yet, this storm, like others very recently, was unquestionably right over the top of us. The deadly wind, the teeming rain, the resounding claps of thunder and the incalculable brilliant, blinding blazes of lightening, continued on for hours – while leaving every one of us, down in these canyons not all that far below, safe, dry and completely untouched. While the phenomenon is positively beyond our understanding, well to be perfectly honest I'm not alone, it's got everyone else totally baffled too, but you won't hear anyone around here complaining about it, that's for sure.

After I'd made my journal entry last night, and while Patrick slept soundly in his cocoon of soft blankets, I tried to master the hammock: *tried*, being the operative word here. After more than a dozen attempts, and just as many lumps and bruises, I knew that unless I was ready to sleep on the hard rock floor (which I wasn't) I had no choice but to call on my very amused neighbour Sergeant Tyler, and ask him to hold the darned thing steady so that I could at least get into it and centre myself well enough so as not to finish up looking at his big bare feet - again. It took me another full fifteen minutes, *and* a few more bruises to add to the ever-growing collection of purple dots covering my body, before I managed to, not so much get *comfortable,* as to not to fall out. To be honest, I don't think I dared to move all night either – just in case. Unfortunately for my poor behind, knees, shoulders and elbows, I found out the hard way this morning that getting back *out* of a hammock unscathed, is every bit as tricky as getting *into* one… for me anyway, the only benefit of getting out - is you only have to fall once!

After the incredible storms of last night, this morning broke bright and warm, the beautiful clear blue sky looked washed and fresh once more. The waterfall sparkled and gave me some spectacular rainbows to enjoy, and the grass seemed even springier and softer underfoot than ever. I've gladly put my shoes away, because really, what's the point of wearing them out when I prefer to walk around bare foot anyway?

I could hear the ~~soldier's~~ *marines* executing their gruelling daily callisthenics, working their way through the mandatory exercise program, the same as they'd probably done every morning on their base without fail … Noisily. Very noisily in fact, especially with Tyler's bull roar voice shouting orders and insults that they've gotten lazy and soft riding around like girls. Apparently, the months they spent running and carrying a full field pack on their backs, beside the trucks for mile after muddy mile don't count. I've heard some excited whispers that we're *all* going to have to start doing those same exercise routines soon. I can only hope and pray they have defective hearing. Now… let me put this in writing, *for the record;* I *do not* find the prospect of all that sweating, *or* panting *or* grunting, while someone yells at me to jump higher, or drop and give them ten more push-ups (I *might,* at a pinch, be able to manage to do *one) or* to go and climb up that rope, but not *both,* let alone be able to accomplish whatever other forms of torture, or physical torment, they may have in mind to prescribe - all that terribly appealing. In fact, unless it's farm work or surfing, physical exertion and I, have *never* been on particularly sociable terms, and most definitely *never* on a first name basis, so *no,* the proposed exercise program does *not* please, or appeal to me, at all, not-one-little-bit.

As Tyler walked toward us, I thought, he'd been for a swim. If you had eyes in your head, you couldn't help but notice just how *good* the man was looking, freshly bathed and his damp hair – now well and truly in need of a good cut- was combed straight back off his strong tanned face. I can see by the looser fit of his pants and shirts that he's lost a little weight, although his already muscular physique, has become rock-hard and much more defined, most likely due to all the heavy work and walking/running he's been doing. I saw him a few days ago without his shirt on and he's looking, very ah, *solid*. He stopped right in front of me and just stood there staring down at me without saying a single word. He stood there, towering over me, looking completely refreshed and ready for anything, while I was fidgeting from foot to foot and trying to straighten up my clothes and messy hair. I've been doing some serious sweeping this morning, so I must be looking, and probably smelling, pretty grotesque by now. Surprisingly he sidestepped around me and told us all to take the rest of the morning off. What a strange, strange man he is! He said to go out in small groups to just relax and explore our new home and see what we could find, we *were,* he added, due for a well-earned rest. He also told us to be on the lookout for anything that looked like edible plants, or animals that we could use for food - and if it was possible, to see if there were any fish big enough for eating. He grinned and looked directly at me *again,* before adding that he and his men would finish off making up as many beds as they had supplies for and once that task had been completed, they'd begin to work on some of our other basic furniture requirements. I understood his cheeky reference to beds, *and* the reason for his silly grin only too well. Meanwhile another part of his team would be working with the engineers, they would get the showers planned out and make a start on the temporary latrines while we were all away. Mrs B gave her husband explicit instructions as to what she wanted him to look for, and he retorted that he had no intention of moving from his seat in the sun... Mrs B stood her ground with him for once, she said straight out that in that case, he could stay sitting all day if he wanted to "as long as you don't expect anything to eat today Fred, because you'll get *nothing* anymore, not unless you work for it, the same as everyone else does! In fact, that goes for everyone who wants to be waited on – no work, no food!" If looks could kill... she'd have dropped dead on the spot. She also asked each group to bring a small selection of flowers back, because she was hoping that at least some of them might be edible. Her only request was -please make a mental note as to where they could be found again. Some of the young men rigged up fishing lines and took an empty tin can to hold any worms they were able to dig up.

I suppose, when I think about it, it's really fortunate that practically all of us have come from a farming background, basically because we all know how to utilize animals, plants and even most of the common vegetation, for food. We can live and eat quite well here, whereas a town or a city raised person might – only through inexperience- die from starvation, even while they were standing in the midst of plenty.

Kristy, Reba and I headed off chattering away as usual, then we started singing some of our favorite songs - until we ran out of the ones, we knew the words to, after that we just dawdled along with our arms linked together in comfy silence, each lost in her own thoughts.

Reba spotted the strange little creature first, now it was either one really *big* rabbit, or else really small goat-like creature, its fur was a light golden-brown colour, and it was sunning itself on a rock ledge about twelve feet above the ground, and goodness only knows how it got up there because from where we were standing it seemed to be a sheer surface. Kristy took her ever present drawing pad out of her back pocket and quickly sketched what she saw; it had a hairy coat like a long-haired goat, but it was a great deal smaller than any goat we'd ever seen, except for kids (babies) it also had really super-long floppy ears - exactly like a rabbit, and a kind of rabbity face! But from down below, we couldn't tell if it had hooves or soft padded feet because it was lying down with its feet tucked under it, like a cat, although I couldn't be certain because it was so high up, but when it looked down at us, and while it didn't have a typical goats face, I thought it might have had those crazy goat eyes. We debated a little as to whether mamma was a rabbit, and papa was a goat, so maybe the poor little go-bit (as we called it) was simply a poor confused baby. I couldn't wait to tell Tyler about it when we got back. We continued on as before, giggling and joking about Tyler and a couple of the nicer ~~soldier's~~ *marines* when it hit me like a bolt out of the blue.

What was *wrong* with me? – Am I losing my ever lovin mind now? I actually *wanted* to see Tyler! Not just to tell him about the go-bit either, I think, oh god I think I just want to see *him*, to be near *him*, and talk with *him*. This, cannot be good, Oh-My-Goodness… *noooo,* don't tell me…it can't be… I can't… he, I think, no, no, no, I couldn't possibly *fancy Tyler!* Could I, can I? Oh, lordy lord this is, it's just, no, can't be, oh it's awful. *He's* awful, he's rude and he's always, *always* angry about something, he's loud, obnoxious and so, so bossy, he's insensitive, moody, not to mention that he's a brute *and* a bully…. but he does have the body of a god … and the nicest blue eyes. Oh, jumpin jiminy and hallelujah, *that's all I need*, to fall for an amazonian brute who thinks he's all that *and* quite a bit more. But he really *has* got such nice blue eyes and his facial features aren't too bad either, actually they're really nice… well, they are when he's not scowling at me, and those arms… oh jeez for pities sake Sara stop it! Think girl *think*, when did it happen? Damn the when, *how* on *earth* did it happen! I wasn't aware of their scrutiny, but the girls had been watching me closely. Kristy asked me if I was feeling alright; she said I looked as though I was going to throw up. Well, she wasn't too far off either! Reba agreed and asked if I'd eaten anything other than food from the breakfast table? I waved away their questions, I felt sick suddenly, I wanted to cry, my hands were shaking and they'd gone all clammy and sweaty. I felt my knees start to wobble and said – I we, I, please, I have to sit down for a while because I need to talk some um, girly, besty friend, girl type stuff with you. I could hear myself babbling a lot of nonsense and the girls were looking at me really queerly. After a bit more babbling, we sat down and I confessed about my newly discovered feelings for Tyler. They just sat there, totally silent - like a pair of rocks... and I hadn't expected a non-response like that. Honestly? I thought they'd laugh until their sides split, but they didn't. They just looked at each other then grinned at me wickedly; Reba smirked and held her hand out to Kristy and said "Ha! You my friend, owe me five." To say I was shocked by their reaction, or rather, by their *lack of reaction*, was like saying that water's wet. I didn't know what to say. I blurted out; you *knew*? *Both of you?* You *both* knew? You guys *knew* but you didn't bother to tell *me, why*? What kind of friends are you anyway? I felt like crying, but we all started laughing instead. Reba told me she'd guessed which way the wind was blowing a few months ago. When Tyler was always watching where I was, making sure I was safe, or else finding any and every excuse to come and talk to me, and I was doing the same thing with him. Okay, alright, so how come *I* don't remember it like that? Seemingly, I was the only person in the whole camp – with the possible exception of Tyler- who *didn't* know we really fancied each other. I felt so stupid. And then I rolled around on the grass laughing - until I realised just what the implications of a possible relationship between us would mean. It was hopeless, impossible, totally. Nope, no; not happening, it's completely, it's *absolutely* out of the question. I couldn't possibly have *any* kind of a serious relationship with him. He must be at least ten years older than me, and what if it didn't work out and we were still stuck in this place? We'd have to see each other *all* the time and *that* would be disastrous. Even worse, what if it *did* work out? There can't be any kind of future for us here. Oh-my-God, can you even *imagine* what my mother's reaction to a man like Tyler would be? Hell's bells and halleluiah, my ever-so-correct-and-strictly-by-the-rules grandma would *flip,* man-oh-man, she'd really pop her corset if I got myself into a relationship here, where no-one could marry us. Oh please, and what happens if, or when, we eventually leave? He's a career Marine *and* an Officer. With him it's all heads up, eyes front, back straight, bum tight and shoulders squared, oooh, and don't forget the biggest biggy of all, the *discipline* either, orders are orders and always followed with unquestioning obedience, starched uniforms, mirror finished boots and parade ground drills! These things are not only *important* to him, they're, well, they're as much a part of him as breathing, they're his *whole life,* and I'm, well I'm just not any of those things at all. And anyway, oh let's just forget about it eh? And besides all of that – he's such a big bully. I expected my first crush to be on someone like the boy next door! I certainly never thought it'd be anyone like Tyler!

"Well, you're not alone in that canoe my friend, if we're being all honest and opening up a nice new can of worms now Sara, you're not the only one of us Shady Ladies who's taken a fancy to a man in uniform. Don't let on that I've told you, will you? But Angie's told me she likes Mike –a lot, the really big, the, well you know, the *huge* kind of *a lot*, and Janice has been making eyes at Josh too, *and* he's batting his baby blue's right back at her!" Reba chimed in with "Hey has anyone noticed how Amelia's eyes shine like search beams whenever that Fabs guy is around? You mark my words; things are going to be getting very interesting around here in the not-too-distant future my friends." We all started laughing, then "Oh hell, no! Here they come again!" We all shouted in unison grabbing hold of each other's hands. The sky which had been so incredibly blue, and so clear, suddenly turned black, the three of us sat huddled up together and watched the thick, lumbering, treacherous looking black-grey clouds that heaved and rolled about overhead weighted down with water; goodness only knows how much lightening flashed and zapped across the sky, a couple of lightning bolts struck the top of the walls sending massive showers of sparks flying and the static raised all the hair on our bodies and heads, the deafening peals of thunder hurt our ears as the noise bounced and echoed back and forth on these stone walls. From inside the walls the sound of the wind was like some prehistoric wild beast snarling in a fury, howling and shrieking threateningly directly overhead and all around us; yet we seemed to be perfectly safe down here, protected from the nightmarish horrors that raged continued to devastate the already tortured world outside the walls. Although the oval walls in this place amplified any sounds, and the booming thunder made the ground vibrate, we were still warm, dry and untouched by them, time and time again. But how? How is that logical, or even possible? It goes against every law of physics. After all it's not as though these valleys are so minuscule that the rain can't get in – because they're not, these valleys are so darned gigantic you could lose a dozen or more whole sports stadiums *and* arenas in them!? I seem to have developed a habit of probing that same question with nearly every storm, and I would dearly love to find an answer. Oh jeez, will you listen to me trying to make it sound like I have a real brain!! Even though I teach, I know enough to know I don't know enough. Seriously though, I do want to try and work it out. These storms don't build up slowly, as has always been our earthly standard, because now, since the failed *experiments*, storms just arrive -suddenly and fully developed, but there's no hint, or warning, of their impending arrival whatsoever, we don't get the gradual cooling down or heavy clouds moving in. There's nothing gradual about the weather changes now -they just happen. A storm can last anywhere from a few brief moments, to many long hours, but then every bit as suddenly as they start, they stop, like someone's flipped a switch, or closed a door. This whole place seems to be, well I can only think of it as being enchanted, or charmed somehow. I suppose that's going to have to be my quick fix answer. Never, not even once down here, have we been caught up in any of the furies, all we ever have are the effects – the noises of wind and rain, the blinding sheets of lightning and the darkness, the waterfall is definitely being fed by some unseen channels high up on top of the walls that must carry the overflow from the rain into, well I suppose it has to be some sort of underground reservoir, so the grass is always green, the plants thrive, and there is always an abundance of fresh water. It can still be very frightening though, especially if you're near an edge or halfway up a to the next level, being suddenly blinded by utter blackness, and the rapid changes between light and dark of the racing clouds, the lightning strikes, the showers of sparks and crazy loud crackling, it makes me, and practically everyone else just a little nervous.

This place is so secretive - in so many, many ways. At night when I'm trying to settle down to sleep, I can admit I'm kind of frightened by it, even though we are all somehow shielded and protected here, from all the dangers outside, and I know I can't even really justify my fears, but I suppose that's just the way I'm made. Okay it's as if all the horrible things that scare most people, have been taken away, spiders, bugs, snakes and animals, and because there's no vermin, there aren't any cats etc. every living thing inside is friendly – apart from some horrible humans that is… I heard someone comment to one of the children yesterday, that not even the birds or smallest animals have any reaction to the sounds coming from the world outside; whereas normally they would run or fly to safety. Even our lambs and piglets seem to know they're safe within these walls as well, the chickens do too, they couldn't care less one way or the other, and the animals just love it here.

So, does that mean a pig or a chicken really *is* smarter than me?

The weather we've had, or I should say heard, today, is following the same erratic pattern that it has day after day, night after night, and week after week for however long it's been going on. Time has kind of become irrelevant, it doesn't really matter anymore.

Kristy had a really odd, very unkristy-like look on her face, when she glanced over in my direction and I asked her what she was thinking about. She stayed quiet for a good five minutes but when she did finally speak, her voice was so choked and husky, I could tell she was on the verge of something a lot bigger than tears.

"So-So what! What's the big deal if we don't ever leave here? Honestly Sara, would it *really be so bad?* Well, would it? D'you want to know something? I've been thinking a whole lot about what we've really and truly left behind, well c'mon tell me, what *did* I leave huh? My dad took off with that woman two years ago, and good damned riddance to the pair of them. I couldn't find a job anywhere, my family has gone all to hell with one brother on drugs, because he couldn't handle what his goddam useless father did to mum, and another in prison for peddling drugs, because he saw what his idiot brother was willing to do for a hit and how much money was in it, now he has ten more years to think about it. The wonderful, amazingly gentle and loving mother I've always *known,* is gone, she's been replaced by a cold-hearted look-alike, who's an emotional wreck and always looking for her next drink. I've hated being anywhere near them Sara, I absolutely *hated* it, it's been like living with strangers. I've been so afraid of *becoming like them* – and, and besides, haven't we really all been wondering if *anything* could even be left standing, or if *anyone* is still *alive* out there anymore? You saw it, heck we *all* saw it. We've been seeing it with our very own eyes, in how many places, how many countless small villages, towns, whole big cities even, they'd been picked up and blown away, trucks, cars, buses, trains and even the inter-zone connector freeways and air-rail lines, they're all gone now too, – wiped out. We all *know* we've all *seen* what's happened, and in all probability is *still* happening, and will *continue* happening to the world outside until there's nothing and no-one left. Everything's been turned into one enormous puddle of pig slop. Now, I'm no hypocrite, and I know full well that we didn't have a chance to get to know those people in the other trucks, okay, not very well anyhow, but we're all very aware that if that wind had been a bit more serious, if it'd dropped down a little bit more, it could so easily have been *us* that got blown to hell and gone that day too, *but it wasn't us, was it? Why? Why* were *we* saved? Can you tell me? Does anyone know? There *has* to be a reason, and a very *good reason* why we've been allowed to live! I want to know what I'm supposed to be doing" Kristy was on her knees now sobbing hard and painfully. Somehow, she still managed to keep talking, even though it was between the sobs and sniffles, and with all her snorts and dribbles; I only understood about half of what she was trying so hard to say... But now she'd got me thinking too, going back over all of the television news stories we'd watched every evening for years, and every night those news stories were full of nothing but bad news, continually reporting on the wicked, the horrible, and the ugly, telling us all the truly evil things people would be doing to each other, then there were all the magazines and newspapers that were packed with more of the same kind of stories, about wanted murderers, crime waves, brutal kidnappings, and bashings, the all too common drive by killings, the senseless bombings, break-ins, the cruel rapes and murders, and different brutal teen gangs, men, women, kids and grandparents dying in ridiculous turf wars that seemed to be over nothing more than 'owning' a corner were happening everywhere, more and more frequently. It had gotten so bad that we were even afraid to walk alone in our own quiet little town - in case we were grabbed, or beaten up, murdered or raped! None of us wanted to live with that fear, who would? And what about those awful pictures of little children and tiny babies dying in their mothers' arms from starvation or disease? All that misery Sara, maybe it's all still out there somewhere, and if by some miracle it is, what if it's waiting for *us*? Would staying right here, would it *truly* be so awful? Look around you, open up your scared small-town eyes, and take a good, a really *good long hard look around you*. Here, it's so peaceful, and it's clean, and for the most part, quiet. We all know, deep down we know it, there wasn't much of anything or anywhere, or even any*one*, left out there, our families and everyone we ever knew was certainly long dead by the time we found this place. And that must have been at least, um I don't know, how long ago now? Okay, oh and that's another thing; does anyone remember what day of the week it is? Or the date? No, well how about the month? Can you tell me for *sure* what month it is? And does *any* of it really and truly count, *or even matter* anymore?" I thought about this journal, but even here, I'd left it for days and days, even weeks at a time without writing anything, because in the trucks every day was mostly just a repeat of the day before, so no, I had absolutely no idea of the date, time *or* month, any more, and she was right about it not mattering anymore too.

The next thing we knew she was wiping the tears from her face - and then she started laughing! She said, oh look, it's just me having a dose of the crazies okay, forget I even spoke. Just forget I said anything okay? She stood up and started walking really slowly, looking down to the ground at the flowers and every now and then bending down to pick something for Mrs B.

Reba turned around and looked at me with a huge grin on her face and said – "okay, that's made it official, she's gone nuts, yep, the poor kid's gone completely loony, stark raving bonkers, loopy, she's cracked! Totally lost the plot! But ya know something else Sara? She's *so* right about everything she said too, and we *both* know it… I don't think I want to leave here either, what about you? What have I, what have you, or *any one* of us here, in actual, honest fact, *what have we got to go back too*, or even to look forward to finding, out there anymore? Honestly? An' Kristy's dead right about another thing too – there wasn't much of anything left, except lots n lotsa mud outside. I wonder, hey Sara, d'you remember that crazy clothes line we saw? I wonder if it's still standing."

And that, my friend, is how the whole honest-to-goodness acknowledgment of our current situation came about. I'm pretty sure that were amongst the first people out of the entire group to openly, and honestly, question the reality of our collective future…out loud, to another person.
I suppose every one of us – the marines included-have thought about it all privately, probably at night laying in the deep stillness, while they're trying to get to sleep, but as far as I know, no-one has really expressed themselves, their thoughts and fears, as openly, *or* as honestly, to another person. Until now.
We sat and talked, oh we talked for hours, we were *still* talking when Michael (one of the nicest marines) came looking for us. Ah here you are. We've been searching the caves for you girls, it's pretty late and y'all should be getting back for the evening meal, the Boss is pretty concerned. Both Reba and Kristy looked at me and smiled. Reba nudged Kristy and winked in rather an over exaggerated fashion. Michael saw it and just grinned as well…I felt myself blushing to the soles of my feet! Then Michael fell into step alongside Reba and they chatted away quite happily all the way back.
Somewhere in the course of our conversation, my go-bit news for Tyler had been completely forgotten.
Anyhow, with all of my newfound self-awareness, I was a really unwilling to see, much less speak to him

now in any case. It would, in all likelihood, be for the best if I just ignored my feelings, maybe, hopefully, they'd die away naturally and leave me alone, or he'd find someone else. Now why on earth did the thought of that happening upset me so much?

After the evening meal, it was good for everyone to sit around and all join in for a noisy sing along, we sang all sorts of songs, from stage musicals to jazz and popular songs, to ballads, and even some gospel songs. After we'd exhausted our musical repertoire, then came the really special treats. Stories! The stories our older group members told the younger ones were such a delight to hear. The selection of tales varied widely, some of the older ladies would tell *really old-time* morality stories, they called them fairy tales, *really* old ones, like Sleeping Beauty, Red Riding Hood, Robin Hood, The Three Bears, and there were others who told us their own life stories, and then there were others who just invented terrific stories as they went along, and I think those were my real favourites! The marines seemed to specialise in scary stories about ghosts and monsters, terrifying sea creatures, and (Patricks favourites) creatures from outer space and renegade robots... thanks guys really, because then it was *our* job to try and settle over-excited or terrified little children down to sleep!

When the new daily routine and work rosters were worked out, the group's time management wasn't quite so measured, that meant more free time was enjoyed by everyone, and for the most part we made an effort to live together more or less comfortably; although we did try to keep to fairly regular hours for sleeping, waking, and those dreaded, now compulsory, morning exercises, yoga and meditation (my salvation) Meal times were, by order of the cooks, kept fairly static. But having said that, our daily lives were more in line with a holiday camp where everyone helped out with the chores, and we had a lot of fun as well, with the glaring exception being the Upper Valley people. Oh well, you can't *force* someone to be happy if they *choose* not to be. Many of those people still refused to mix with us, and they try very hard to keep their young men and women and even their *children*, separated from us, they've actually *forbidden* anyone to become friendly with the marines *or* the Shady Ladies as we jokingly called ourselves, though the children *are* permitted to attend my classes. The children's school lessons take up, on average, three hours every second morning, alternating with life lessons on the other day. I had recruited Laksha as another teacher for our younger children, she had the skills, and most importantly, she had the patience they required, while I took on teaching the older kids as many subjects as I had text books for, after that, their life lessons rounded out their education nicely. Gardening and crop work were commenced in the very early mornings by the men folk, although once their school lessons had been completed, the children quite happily joined the men in the gardens. There they learn the value and the rewards of real, physical work, and they've helped to create the various gardens needed to grow the food that they and their families would be eating, or to tend and care for the animals that each and every one of our lives depended on. Everyone had tasks designed to keep our little community fed, and humming along contentedly.

Time as we have known it, and have lived by all our lives, had ceased to matter, and anyway, even if it *had* mattered, none of our wristwatches, clocks, portable radios tablets or cell phones worked anymore anyway.

Tyler and his Men had laid out four -Time Stones- in a line, they'd used fire and heavy rocks on four of the heavy gauge aluminium chequer plates that made up the tyre shields. Somehow, they'd been able to curve each shield enough to cover a stone, using only the heat of the fire, rocks and their brute strength. Just when the men thought they'd finished the job, they got to the second stage! Tyler had the men rubbing at them for days with stones and the coarse sand they made by pulverising small rocks to grind off the baked-on cream and grey camouflage paint, so that when the sun shone directly down onto a stone, it lighted up like a burnished mirror and that gave us our approximate times for Breakfast, mid-morning, midday, mid-afternoon, and by the time the shadows reached the first line of torches it was about time for the evening meal, nothing further or more exact than that was necessary.

Time has just slipped by, comfortably for the most part I suppose, and if I can judge by how much taller Patrick has grown, and by how long everyone's hair is, or how baby Anna is growing, and how many sharp little teeth she has now, or how hard she's trying to talk, that we have been here for close on a year. There are always going to be some difficulties and snags, but we've tried to deal with each problem or incident as they've come along. I am almost completely happy now. Oh yes, we all have our own memories and our personal ghosts that disturb our composure from time to time, people from our past that we've loved, and miss, and sometimes still wondered about, but we can't *do* anything about them, or for them, so we try to let their memory sleep. I was wandering around the pool in the early morning as is my regular habit now, I enjoy watching the mist rising up from the water, and listening to the soft morning sounds all around me, when I finally had to admit to myself that Tyler has grown to be a really important, and most probably, even a necessary part of my life. I'm still not too sure *how* that happened either, because he really has been a really huge pain in the butt from day one, he really has, and sometimes still is. I realised ages ago that I had some strong feelings for him, but because of our ages and the unique situation we're living in, I've also tried to ignore them. The ignoring thing, yeah, well it's all well and good, in theory, *but* it's just not working for me anymore, and that *really* bothers me. I waste so much time and emotion on that man, and you know what? I don't know if he's even remotely interested in me now, *if* he ever was, and besides, he most likely lost any interest he *may* have had, long ago. So, all this worry, all the over-thinking is, almost certainly, just a big fat waste of time. Ahh well, at least time is something I have plenty of.

The whole time that we were traipsing all over the countryside like a lost band of gypsies, looking for a safe place to stay, I was so thoroughly self-absorbed, and *because* I was being a selfish brat, I resented his constant commands and demands, and even though I knew all along that it was for my own good, it was still irksome, much like taking nasty medicine. Patrick quickly became my lifeline, and he still is my main man, we need each other and we've grown to love, and to trust each other totally and without question as well. Paddy's such an absolute joy to have around, and he's smart and devoted too, he's taught me so much about who I really am. But Tyler and I, well, we really are so different, in far too many ways; I take things as they come, I'm a bit laid back, kinda cruisy and easy going. Whereas he could best be described as being pedantic, not to mention nit-picking, finicky, pernickety and he can often be a complete pain in the neck. He's still as bossy as anything, oh, well yes, I suppose it *is* his job to be, but I swear, sometimes I think he gets paid an extra special bonus for being downright mean and insensitive! Oh yeah, and that's another thing, he's got absolutely *no* sense of humour, whereas I love to laugh and joke around. Ahh jeez, let's face it he's like a cactus in a broken glass pot.... just plain prickly all over, with lots of sharp edges. I talk *all* the time about anything and everything or nothing at all - While the sum total of his spoken words amounts to ordering everyone around or telling them what to do, when, and how, to do it. In all the time this group has been together, I have never, not even once, seen or heard him have a genuine pleasant conversation, with anyone. Yes, he gives orders, yes, he gives instructions, and yes, he gives criticisms, *all-day-long*, but as for any sort of pleasant or even mundane dialog – well, he doesn't seem to have it in him. For a grown man that's just not normal. *He's* not normal! What the heck's he so afraid of? Of being seen as an actual, genuine, flesh and blood human being, who may have real feelings, and have normal human wants and needs? I wonder if he ever gets lonely on his private emotional island? Since settling down here in New Eden, as we've decided to call it, he *has* been marginally (*very marginally*) more relaxed and on the rare occasion he's actually allowed himself to become a tad more human, or should I call his behaviour humane?

Lately I've been wondering how it's humanly possible for one person to be so rigid, so switched on, and so inflexible, so consistently. Not only to the marines under his command either, he acts the same way to every member of this large group *all the time*. Except when it comes to the children, with the children he laughs and sometimes he even allows himself time to play with them but even then, it's only for a moment or two. I don't, and I cannot, understand his behaviour at all, it's just so contradictory to the way I am. To the way *most* human beings are. Although, when I started to seriously question his motives and what it could be that drives him so hard, a strange thing happened. I also started to realise just what a colossal undertaking has been forced upon him; he certainly hadn't bargained on this. A lesser man might well have just dropped us off out there and left us to take our chances. He most definitely wasn't supposed to be in *this* situation at all, and it's for damned sure he didn't volunteer for it. His revised orders had been simple and straightforward; to evacuate as many people and their belongings as the trucks would hold. Leaving from the last pick-up point, which was Shady Haven, he and his men were supposed to transport us all to a nominated place where we would be safe, and they were to leave us there. Following our safe transfer, he was to return with his men, and re-join the other marines at their base camp. End of story. But Nature took the reins.

How many times have I noted the marines looked frustrated or irritated? Or that they couldn't win a trick with this weather? The expected time required for the entire operation was – one week, possibly up to, but not exceeding the two-week maximum. Well, it's been well over a whole *year* at least, quite possibly closer to two now. I spent an hour or so, reading back over the pages in my journal, reliving and remembering some of those horrific days and nights. It's been a pretty upsetting activity for the most part, but I made quite an astounding discovery in those meticulously written pages today. I'll give you the thoughts that went through my head while I was revising…

-Oh, hells tinny bells! How could I possibly have been *so dumb!* It's been staring me in the face this whole time… scratching away at my sub-conscious for goodness knows how many months, and I've been just too plain stupid to see it- The realisation startled, and I don't mind admitting, annoyed me so much. I had started regarding him differently, from that first day when our original destination was destroyed. I must have subconsciously acknowledged his really tough predicament, and starting from that point in time, my *subconscious* attitude changed, while my conscious opinion continued to fight him. Now that my eyes have been opened, I'm finally able to understand what's been happening, the respect I had been giving to him unconsciously all along, had been quietly growing into something a whole lot different, and morphing into a much stronger emotion, without me understanding, or even being aware that it was happening. I'm not sure what, if there's anything, I can do about it either. Unfortunately, we can't stay here indefinitely, except maybe in our dreams, no matter how badly Kristy and Reba want to. I'm willing to admit that it would be perfectly wonderful to just forget that the rest of the world exists, but the trouble with that is - that it does – well at least I truly hope it still does- we need to remember that when these storms finally blow themselves out; and while their frequency and severity haven't changed, *yet*, we all know that they *can't* possibly last forever, Tyler says there will be people out searching for us. So pretty soon we'll have to leave this heaven on earth and find our way back to the ugly, but true reality, the one that our lives, our families and our jobs represent. Or, if the damage done to our homes and towns is even greater than we think, then we'll have to rebuild and start over again. All too soon our time here will become a treasured memory, an incredible interlude, but it will always only ever be a well-loved dream that was born from a nightmare.

Hopefully, for many of us there *will* be something to go back to. That's such a big part of our fear too, the not knowing what, or if anything, or even if *anyone* is still out there. I really worry about these children too; they're missing out on all sides. No parents, no extended family or familiar friends, no appropriate schooling, in here they're learning none of the things, or any of the actual skills they'll be needing once they're back in the outside world. There are no real celebrations, and they have no toys, they don't have, and therefore they aren't learning to use, the various pieces of electronic equipment necessary, and required, to continue in the different areas of their education, so what will happen when it's time for them to join the workforce? I hope Patrick is going to be okay, he's grown to be like my own son now, he spends most of the time, when he's not playing, when he's not in class or learning in the gardens, apart from those times he is with me, we also share my sleeping cave at night. Although when he's *not* with me or having lessons, he has what he calls special *boy's only* time with Tyler and the marines doing *real man* stuff, as he's so fond of telling me.

We –Tyler and I- often discuss what we should be doing for the kids, because we feel that they're missing out on so much of a normal life by being here, yet having just said that, it's the *children* who have adjusted to this way of living so much better, faster, and easier, than anyone else has. That's especially true when I watch the Upper Valley people, they are always so darn restless, always resentful and intolerant, and *so angry,* at, and about, any and every thing. They will argue and bicker about anything, *any little thing at all, all* the time. If one of them is asked to lend a hand, or to help with a few simple tasks, or even to do a small job, all hell breaks loose! If Tyler says yellow, they say red, they are, each and every single one of them, hell bent and determined to make every moment of the time they spend here just as awkward, unpleasant, and as difficult as is humanly possible for everyone else. But why? What can they *possibly* hope to gain? They have utterly unreasonable and unrealistic expectations when it comes to Tyler's abilities. I often hear Mr Beatty arguing with his wife when he thinks no-one can hear him, (with the way this place echoes, you must be joking – there's no such thing as privacy- that's just a fond memory!) He's a bit of dictator is our Mr Beatty, and yes, he does physically abuse poor Mrs B, he often slaps her and I actually saw him punch her once. I told her she *had* to speak up about his abuse, but she says –it's the price I pay for peace and quiet- she never wants to complain. But he rants and rages at her because the house that's been in his family for five generations has been left abandoned, all because *she* got scared, and *why* you might ask, did she get scared? Just because her arms and back were cut up, and her legs badly hurt, covered in cuts and bruises when the back wall and roof blew out and flying chunks of masonry and broken roof tiles rained down on her! I think I'd have been damned scared too! He *never* stops to acknowledge the fact that *he* has walked away from the house too! Now he just wants to get *out*! To be out and to be far away from Eden, in the worst possible way, and he's not going to stop stirring up trouble until we leave here, of *that* I am quite certain.

But it's a catch twenty-two situation, we *can't* leave until we are sure it's safe, and that will not happen while ever the storms continue. And judging by the sounds and the frequency of them, the end of the storm activity is nowhere in sight for a good long while yet. Unfortunately for Mr Beatty and his friends, they're going to have to accept at some point, that controlling the weather is something completely beyond Tyler's ability. Mr Beatty also seems to conveniently overlook the fact that it was that very act of attempting to control the weather that has landed us here in the first place! Seriously though, they need to relax (or as grandma would say 'chill out') and at least make *some* effort to make the best of whatever length of time we're able to stay here. But we know all too well, they've been tying themselves, and each other, up in emotional knots from the day we left Shady Haven in the transports, so relaxing and getting comfortable in Eden, may not be the easiest notion for the majority of our UV members to take on board.

I for one know I could live here, and very contentedly too – for as long as is necessary – or longer. Kristy and ninety nine percent, if not all, of the other Shady Haveners, along with our group of children, would jump at the chance to make Eden our permanent home as well. Although I often wonder, if they were given the choice, what would the marines choose? I have a sneaking suspicion they'd choose Eden as well.

But right now the sun is coming up, and the misty light is creeping across the grass to the morning marker, that means my pre-dawn walk is over and I'd better get back to lend a hand preparing the breakfasts, and then get myself organised for the dreaded exercise program, after that little torture session I'll call the class together for this morning's maths and writing lessons.

In the shadowy morning light, I could see Tyler heading straight toward me across the grass; his ramrod straight back, plus the fixed set of his shoulders, and his determined stride weren't lost on me. I could see that whatever was on his mind, he seriously meant business. My mind raced, trying to think what I'd done wrong this time. Ah jeez! This was definitely *not* a good start for my day. Damn the man! Oh, cheese n bikkies, that'd be right, now my belly's gone all giddy and my stupid knees are shaking.

Sunrise, my favorite time of the day, is about to be ruined by this lumbering great ox and his bad temper. As he got closer, I was able to see his face a little bit more clearly. I tried reading his features; I was looking for the familiar warning sign. Yep, and there it was. When someone was due for a right royal telling off, there were twin frown lines at the bridge of his nose that almost joined his thick black eyebrows together in a straight line -and there they were – but hang on, no wait a minute, there's something else there too, what is it? The early morning light is making shadows on his face. I can't tell, there are too many differing and shifting expressions in play. Dammit... now I don't know what to expect. Ha! What am I saying, with him I'm *never* sure! He was satisfied he'd found me, (*glad* he'd found me is maybe a bit too strong) I could see that he was worried about something too, now *that, really* concerned me - a lot; him being 'worried' did not bode well for me at all, because his 'worried' voice could cause deafness. By the time the last thought had flicked through my

mind we were almost face to face. Or should I say my face was almost meeting his chest. I'm telling you this (whoever you may be) so that you can get a mental picture. I'm five foot two and weigh about ninety pounds, fully clothed and dripping wet, whereas Tyler, he's at least six foot six, and weighs somewhere around two hundred and twenty pounds naked and bone dry! So yes, I'm *always* polite! -Yes sir! No sir! Whatever you say sir!
Then the strangest thing happened.

His mouth broke into the most beautiful wide smile, and, oh, those eyes… his blue eyes crinkled up at the corners. I have never, not once, in *all* the time that we've spent together, seen him actually smile. Oh of course, I've seen him angry, infuriated, embarrassed, frustrated, and enraged; I've seen him concerned, anxious, worried and downright irate! But I've *never* seen his genuine smile before. It has transformed him so completely. "Good morning Pretty Lady, have you enjoyed your walk this morning?" I could only nod my head like a brainless twit because I was totally speechless! I (carefully) fell into step with him and we chatted cautiously as we made our way back toward the dining area. About twenty yards from home, he pointed to a ledge on a rocky outcrop, and we sat down. Then he dropped a bombshell on me. "I'm going outside the valley with half a dozen of my men later today" (I felt my stomach drop to my feet) "We need to find out what's been happening out there, I've tried making radio contact with my commander again, well with *anyone* to be honest, but as you know there's no reception anywhere within these canyons.

For some peculiar reason the storms don't affect us in here, not that I'm complaining mind, but there is definitely something in here that blocks all reception and kills batteries or anything powered and we have *got* to try and find some radio reception, and to do that we need to go out into the open air. You've got to be aware how rapidly things are escalating with Mr Beatty and his cronies? I need to make some kind of contact and arrange a military extraction team *if* it's humanly possible. Although the storms still sound like they're doing major damage outside, and I need to find out where we stand – safety wise. The attitudes of the whole Upper Valley Group – with the only exception being a few of the older ladies, the little children, a couple of the younger women, oh, and two of the young mothers – has become intolerable, they're ridiculously agitated and restless, they just want to leave here and get back to their lives. Although personally Sara, I don't believe there's much, if anything at all, left out there to go back too, but from inside this valley it's impossible for me to know that for certain. We'll probably be gone for about a week;" (my heart dropped down to join my stomach) "and I won't be able to see you in that time. You must know that I've wanted to talk to you for months and, well I can't go out, I can't just leave things as they are between us. I don't know what we'll find out there, but I do need to know where we –you and I- stand, before I leave Sara. There's no way I can say this except straight out. I've fallen in love with you, I hope you have some feelings for mm" the rest was cut off by my mouth covering his. My arms slipped around his neck and I felt myself lifted up from the ledge as he stood up and held me in his strong but surprisingly gentle arms. Time, simply stopped. My heart was pounding in my ears and there were sky rockets going off behind my closed eyelids, the long hair on his face was soft and smooth and his lips were unimaginably soft, and tasted of honey and lemon tea. I could feel his heart thumping against my belly and chest. Slowly, ever so slowly, we separated and I felt my feet touch the ground again, albeit a bit wobbly kneed at first. I don't know who got the biggest shock; him or me!

All I heard was his deep, husky voice saying "So, okay yes, well um, that's, okay, yes, right, well that's all settled then. I'm glad you agree with me," was all he could manage to say. At least he (unlike myself) was capable of semi-coherent speech. We finished the walk back hand in hand, both of us grinning from ear to ear like idiots! There were quite a few more surprises in store for us when we arrived back though. It seemed that Tyler wasn't the only marine to declare himself to his chosen lady before breakfast! Michael and Reba were as close as two peas in a pod, no great surprise there, they'd been making goo-goo eyes at each other since the early days. Nicholas and Suzy were wearing huge silly grins as well, and Fabs- I really should find out why they call him that- was all cozied up with Amelia, Sienna and David were making happy eyes at each other as well, and Angie and Mike, Janice and Josh along with Kristy and Mark had all gone missing...

Yesterday we had nearly all single people; this morning we had almost a dozen new couples! And while none of us were exactly thrilled about the necessity of the men having to go outside on recon for nearly a week, we understood the reason that made it so necessary. Besides, Tyler had made a plan, and that was that. This pairing up situation was all brand new to us and we really wanted to explore our new feelings -and we would – we'd just have to wait a while that's all. The outside world had been worse than any war zone; actually, it resembled more what I imagine an Alien Landscape might look like -when we left it; how much worse would it be now? It really is much too dangerous for them to go out into that, and really terrifying for us. I truly don't believe any of us even want to think about the enormous risk they are prepared to take, especially because the reason for having to take such a terrible risk in the first place, is due to a group of completely self-obsessed, ungrateful, lazy, and useless, and mostly worthless, troublemaking bigots.

For now, all these new feelings and budding emotions, on both sides, will just have to wait. At least I wasn't going to be all alone in the waiting. Although that isn't really much of a consolation.

After breakfast we all gathered around in a circle, we joined hands and said a short prayer together, asking that these men be returned to us safely and speedily. We all stood quietly, still holding hands for a minute before they shouldered their ropes, settled their minimal equipment and survival packs more comfortably and securely on their backs, and kissed us goodbye, before disappearing into the colonnade of caves.

I could see in his eyes that he'd told the truth when he said he loved me, and I know he didn't want to have to leave like this. I also know, only *too* well, that whatever he considers to be his responsibility, or his duty, will be a firm commitment and always his primary course of action.

Better get used to it Sara, and make good and sure that you *can* honestly live with that, because you know he will never change, was all I could think…The remainder of the group was very reluctant to move, so we all sat around and talked – and talked - to each other about the way we'd lived our lives before the onset of the storms, and the way we've lived for the past, I don't know, could it be a full two years, when we actually did some sums, it worked out that baby anna was only less than a week old when the trucks came, now she was walking and starting to say words, so it's been quite a while.

Ever since the day when Kristy, Reba and I had had our talk by the pool, we'd consciously avoided having exactly this kind of conversation –but now the time had come again for complete openness, and total honesty. How we each felt about living here together, the many things we'd left behind, and all kinds of things we really missed about living in modern civilization. We spoke openly and truthfully, Colleen had sneaked away from the UV group to be with us, and she told us that so many of the UV members are totally fed up with being *forced* to stay in New Eden, because it is, in their eyes, far too primitive and prison-like, they were constantly complaining that food was hard come by (not that many of them actually *worked* to produce any of it) the common conveniences they'd always taken so much for granted just don't exist here, there are no cars, radio, or television, there are no computers or games of chance machines, no theatres or cinemas, they have no newspapers, magazines or stock reports, and there are no fashion or lingerie boutiques, no jewellery stores, shoe stores, or hairdressers, restaurants, café's, bars, and the men hate not having their cigars *or* alcohol and the women miss the wine that helps them cope with their menfolk!

Strangely` enough, all the things that *they* hated most about Eden -were the very things that myself and so many of the others found to be an easy and very welcome change. Aren't we humans a queer lot? The things the rest of us missed most, ranged from our close family members to television programs, mooching around the shopping malls and grocery stores, and pets, to a beautician, although Sienna said she'd be almost willing to die for a hamburger and a double choc-malt shake! The next most popular things were a hair straightener (poor Reba!) hairspray and of all things -lipstick! (That was Janice) On the other hand the greater majority of the Upper Valley residents wanted, and needed, their status symbols like money, expensive perfumes and cosmetics, jewels, rare silks and even rarer furs, classy restaurants, their chauffer driven transports, and their stock brokers. Mrs. Diaz wanted to go back home to get the jewellery she'd forgotten to pack, and her husband was sure their estate had been robbed, completely cleaned out, right down to the wine cellar by now, therefore he was anxious to return and get the insurances sorted out!? He's crazy…his *estate* was sitting halfway down a cliff before we'd even cleared Shady Haven! There *was* nothing left *to* rob, much less for them to go back to! Mr and Mrs Maloney just wanted to get themselves back to civilisation again. To 'attend the opera my dear' in *our* social circle, one simply cannot *exist* without being seen at the opera! Although their neighbours, Hugo and Lizabetta Katzaina wanted to get to a bar –any bar would do- and crawl inside a very large bottle of something (anything) and stay in there for at *least* a week! I don't think anyone was surprised by the fact that just about every single (older) Upper Valley person, not only *wanted* to get out, they were *desperate* to do so, and they wanted to do it *right now*!

None, not a single solitary one of those people placed *any* value on the fact that they were *still alive* and healthy at all, in fact they're all probably the healthiest they've been for decades! Their only interest lay in a bunch of stupid superficial or financial matters. A great number of them are being so nasty, and so horribly insulting towards us….and Mr Ramirez has, only this morning, referred to us as nothing but a pack of filthy peasants! That was when we 'peasants' decided that a confrontation wasn't worth it, besides there was still work to be done. We're well aware that Tyler would certainly be annoyed if we slackened off just because he wasn't here to tell us exactly what to do, and I dread to think what his reaction to open hostilities on our part would be. Katherine was only half joking when she said "we don't want to have any lovers' tiffs over that bunch of blithering UV idiots and poor work ethics, now do we?" But she's absolutely right. Carol and Colleen came over and quietly apologised for their parent's terribly insensitive and rude behaviour. "You know that we don't think the same way they do, we both love it here and wish we could stay too, however we know they're all planning on making everything really, really unbearable, the minute Mr Tyler and the other men come back. They've already started, as you all know, we think they're using this time without Tyler around as a solid test run, so please be smarter than them and don't buy into anything they try to start. Mr Beatty's over there right now talking them all into a frenzy, they're getting organised and they've started making plans to leave already. I'm so, so, sorry it's turning out this way, but what can we do?" Said Carol, the poor girl had tears in her eyes. They didn't wait for a reply, they just turned away and walked slowly back toward their appalling group with their heads hanging down like two condemned prisoners walking to the gallows.

Just as Mrs B had asked, in her good-natured way, for one of us 'love struck ladies' to give her a helping hand to prepare the lunch vegetables; the sky turned pitch-black and another storm raged wildly over our heads. Even though the children have experienced these storms hundreds and hundreds of times, two of the younger boys are still a bit scared by the loud noises and always look to us to give them comfort and some security, usually by cuddling up on a lap and being told a story until it had passed. The feeling of strength, and the innate sense of security that Tyler and his intrepid band of men have long represented, and the steadying influence they project, has, unfortunately, gone with them, and both were being sorely missed already. I was praying quietly that our men had been able to find some form of shelter as well. Although I'm thinking that they might not have actually cleared the first area yet, because they'd said they wanted to climb out over the walls, instead of taking down the concealed doorway. Big Murphy came over and patted my arm gently saying "they'll be alright Miss Sara, they're all well trained and we're all stronger and even fitter now than any of us have ever been in our lives before, so they'll be okay, don't you be worrying too much now."

 I crossed my fingers stamped my foot and blinked twice for luck. Well heck, I've already told you how mature I can be sometimes, haven't I? Murphy watched me and laughed, "That's right Miss Sara, now I'm purely positive that they'll be alright for sure!"

Our valley remained as rain free as always, although the waterfall could be heard fairly blasting fresh rainwater into the giant water basin, it really is a wonder that the fish don't get dumped out onto the grass when the water hits so hard. A little while later the storm ended every bit as suddenly as it had started, although the waterfall continued to buzz for another hour or more. The bright, cloudless blue sky had returned, so we carried on with our normal working day (outwardly at least) as if nothing had changed. But I knew we were all wondering how *our men* were faring on the outside with no protection whatsoever available to them, and having only each other to rely on...

Today the lunch break was a very subdued affair, the remaining marines all seemed to be disappointed at being left behind to watch over us (I overheard the term *babysitters* being used) and the other girls were, like me, just wishing we'd all had more time with our new beau's. I spoke to Zahan and gently reminded him that he and the others weren't babysitters, they're his trusted deputies, and they'll be acting in Tyler's place. They've being entrusted with trying to keep the peace, I said we'd all be doing our part by not responding to taunts, by keeping busy and staying out of the way. The next week is going to struggle by so excruciatingly slowly, and *all* the men folk, every single one of them, from the youngest marine to the oldest civilian man, felt they'd been treated unfairly this time, being left behind with the women and children. But at least the marines and the engineers continued to put in a good day's work. They were getting on with whatever tasks, or modifications, they were currently working on (they were always coming up with brilliant new ideas) instead of sitting around grumbling, and without lifting a finger to do anything constructive – like *some* other people. The bathroom facilities were very nearly completed, they're actually reaching the end of the final stage now, all these many months of physically exhausting, and mentally challenging work they've put into this project, and goodness only knows how many countless hours of brainstorming and trying to remember all the small, but vital details, of the ancient Roman and Greek architecture they'd studied all those years ago - I just hoped they'd receive some richly deserved acclaim for their amazing accomplishments.

The people from the Upper Valley just sit around complaining loudly, whining about anything and everything, and most of the farmers who usually work a few hours in the gardens, have joined the free loaders as well. What an incredible difference Tyler's absence has made already!

After the necessary tidying up and cleaning had been done, as well as our afternoon chores having been attended to; the majority of us *peasants* sat quietly, or lazed around the waterfall with our thoughts and conversations, while keeping ourselves well away from the UV's. This sort of lacklustre behaviour is just so uncharacteristic of our group; normally we'd joke around, or amuse ourselves in a dozen different ways. But in our present mood, it isn't going to happen, not today anyway.

 Night time came and settled quietly around us, although without Tyler's busy routine of noisily issuing a series of directions, our meal was taken in almost complete silence. The whole family atmosphere we've all enjoyed so much has shifted, it almost feels as though someone has died. No one was in the mood for a sing-along, and the children didn't want to hear any stories tonight either, so that being the case, most of us sought out our beds much earlier than we usually do. I think most of us wanted really to be alone with our thoughts, and to remember the extraordinary and wonderful way this day had started for us. For a while the deep grumbling voice of a man could be heard, until Mrs B had had quite enough, and told her husband - in *no* uncertain terms - "Oh for goodness' sake Fred just *stop* your small minded, stupid, ignorant, and ungrateful damned complaining will you, and let us all get some sleep. Fredrick Beatty, if you were thirty years younger and seventy pounds lighter, I'd have pushed you out through that colonnade with those brave boys myself! Now for pity's sake, *will you be quiet."* I heard someone say – "that's right, you give it to him good Mrs B!"

It still took a while, and there were a few more angry outbursts from the UV ranks, but in due course, silence took over the valley. Although it was such a thick, heavy, and very depressing silence, one that had me feeling so much more alone than I've ever felt before. Not even a long walk in the moonlight could lift my mood tonight, and for the first time ever, it actually made me feel considerably worse. After a while I gave up and wandered back to my bed where I'd left little Patrick curled up and sleeping like a puppy, but knowing full well I myself wouldn't be able to sleep a wink.

Oh lordy, the long days, and even longer nights are just dragging by so sluggishly. There are so many questions that need asking, and so many of us needing to hear the answers. One way or another we've managed to keep our fears to ourselves – because speaking them aloud would only serve to make them even more real – but still, our eyes spoke volumes that even a blind man could read. The children picked up on our unusually quiet moods, and as a result they're really subdued, their anxiety has made them irritable as well. Paddy stuck to me like glue, never leaving my side for a moment, the little sweetheart kept finding ways to keep me busy, and continually reminding me of how big and how strong Tyler is, and frequently repeating that they're all *real marines*, so they'll be okay, and they'll be back with us really, really soon Sara. I don't think I would have managed quite so well without my great little supporter beside me. I know for sure that Tyler will be super proud of him too.

The men have been gone for six days so far, but for us girls, and for our group as a whole actually, it feels more like they've been gone for six months. I'm trying to stay optimistic, and I keep promising myself that they'll come back to Eden in a day or two.

Those dreadful men from the Upper Valley – *and* a lot of the brainless UV women have taken up honorary membership with the men's Grumble-Guts Club now – oh good lord, those people really need some serious sorting out - once and for all. For people who categorize themselves as being the 'elite' class, their behaviour is just deplorable, they're so vulgar, and the obscene language they're using, even in front of their children, is absolutely inexcusable, they've taken their all too evident disapproval of Eden ten steps too far, and way beyond any form of excusable behaviour now. They openly belittle and insult anyone who doesn't come from the *Their Upper Valley Ridge Community*, they've even gone so far as to extend their shameful attitudes toward the *children* now too, and they vilify these poor marines, who are, after all, simply trying to keep the whole operation here progressing smoothly, but they're being abused, cussed out and sworn at in the rudest and crudest ways, one UV woman went too far when she spat on poor Bush! She actually spat in his face! Insulting an inoffensive gentle giant like Bush, Bush of all people! He's always the first one to offer a helping hand, he deserves her gratitude not her insane ferocity! And when those men *aren't* being abused, they're being completely ignored! If they dared to ask for some assistance, if they needed an extra pair of hands for five minutes, to help with something, or if they have *no* other option *but* to ask if some of the Upper Valley men would give a bit of a helping hand with the work in and around the gardens, all they get, instead of the help they've asked for, is a mouthful of obscene gutter-trash language instead, and the women are disgusting, they're just as rude, every bit as crude, horribly offensive, vulgar and totally uncooperative as well. They won't even allow their children to attend lessons now. It's like some evil disease that's spreading through almost one half of our community. They've come to be really hostile; they're revolting and just downright spiteful to everyone else, and for what? The rest of us are having to work double time in the gardens now, because without Tyler's presence and authority, the UV men have just downed tools and walked away from their assigned areas completely. But you can bet your boots that they all present themselves at the dining tables at mealtimes!

We've decided the only way to avoid what would, without doubt, be an ugly, open confrontation, is to stay completely separated. The marines applauded our decision to remove the children and ourselves from the common areas, even at mealtimes, it's the only possible way we can maintain any semblance of peace. Mrs B said she wouldn't feed them if they won't help, but I had to calm her down and warn her that if she did that, they'd probably go on an all-out rampage and start destroying things in her kitchen. To which she reluctantly agreed. It's not an easy, nor is it in any way a satisfying solution to the problem, especially not when we all live so closely together.

I'd been keeping to my regular routine, and was always the first person awake, it was still pitch dark, with only soft moonbeams lighting my way through the centre of the valley, exactly the way I liked it for my morning walk, no-one else stirred from their sleep until the sky lightened a little more, and even then, it was only ever the ladies on breakfast roster.

So, you can imagine my surprise when I found Tyler and the marines sitting around a small makeshift campfire about thirty yards away. They'd kept a good distance and blocked the firelight specifically to avoid disturbing anyone too early.

Tyler knew I'd be the first one up, so he was patiently waiting for me with a crooked smile that didn't quite manage to reach his eyes. Somewhere, right down deep inside me something did a long, slow, nauseating roll. Every instinct told me there was something very wrong here. All the hair on my body stood up on end and I had almost painful goose bumps over my scalp, arms and legs. Something's not feeling right, but what is it?

I wanted to know everything, and I wanted to know it all at once. How come they were back so soon? What had taken so long? I quickly counted heads (twice to be sure) and breathed a sigh of relief when all the men were accounted for. So *why* did I have that horrible, sickly, sinking feeling, that *something* was dreadfully wrong? And *why* did they all have such awful blank expressions? Yes, something was going on and whatever it was, it wasn't good. The alarm on my 'need to know meter' was howling.

"I'm not up to saying it all twice Sara." His voice sounded so drained, so flat and lifeless. In fact, he sounded almost defeated, and that wasn't like the Tyler I knew, but no-one else was talking, at all. They were back, and the whole team had made it home, so they should have been in high spirits, or at least in a far better mood than they were, but not so much as one single word came from any of them, and I think their unified silence was actually more frightening to me than anything. Tyler said "we either wake everyone up, or else we'll wait until breakfast to break the news." "Break *what* news Tyler? Oh God! What happened out there? For goodness sakes, tell me, *please*, don't you dare keep me in the dark, *what's happened*? Tell me dammit!" I stamped my foot down, but a tired smile and "you're so darned cute when you're mad Sara" was all I got for my effort. I looked around, from one face to another, searching each one, desperate for a clue, any clue, but they were all wearing their very best, military issue, poker faces, this morning.

I said simply, "alright then GO... go and wake them all up then, go on, anyway you know full well that they'll want to know you're all back home safely, and *we* all need to know how things are out there, because believe you me, it's been pretty unbearable living here with the way those horrid people are behaving now." Tyler must have thought I was going to cry because he put his arm around my shoulders and steered me toward the fire. We sat down close together facing the other men. The slow flickering of the flames made crazy wobbly shadows across their faces, and when they finally did speak, even though it was only a few short words, their mouths didn't seem to be moving in time with the words, it was like watching a badly dubbed foreign movie. Tyler and Michael went to wake up all the adults; I'd asked that the children be allowed to sleep on, because whatever had to be said might only serve to frighten them needlessly right now, and they've been walking on eggshells because of the terrible behaviour of the UV's this week as it is. The next ten or fifteen minutes were spent in very uncomfortable silences, or else in sporadic, short, stiff, overly-polite exchanges, that quickly dried up. It was as though we'd become total strangers again in the days since they left.

It wasn't long before the sounds of slow shuffling movements over at the cave entrance could be heard; I looked across the gardens and saw small groups, and people walking in pairs, were starting to straggle over. I sat up straighter and tried to prepare myself for, for...I didn't know what. As relieved as I was to have these men back safely, I was every bit as uncertain as to what our collective future might have in store for us. Frankly, I had no idea what was going to happen; I suppose I was just fiddling about to cover my fears. Judging by their behaviour, and by the miserly few hints I'd been given, there isn't going to be any good news being celebrated this morning. But was the bad news that it was okay to leave? Or was the bad news even worse than that? I moved over a bit so Sienna, Kristy and Mrs B could sit down with me. Kristy slid her hand into mine on one side and Sienna did the same on the other side, and Mrs B was holding onto Sienna's hand for dear life... she seemed deathly afraid of what we were about to be told as well.

Tyler stood beside his men, and calmly, without any dramatics or embellishments, relayed the information they'd gathered over the last six days, and offered the conclusions they'd been presented with.

" I'm going to be honest, completely honest with you, there's no alternative, and I can't, I won't, pretty it up to make it more palatable, nor will I tell you a lie, there's no point. Okay the outlook, as far as anyone leaving here and heading back to wherever, or whatever you believe might, or might not, be left of civilisation – is, in a word, grim. Putting it in plain, simple terms, there is *nothing left* out there, and when I say *nothing* - I mean there is *absolutely nothing left*. I have no way of knowing what was here, or in this area, before the storms started. When we initially found the passageway in, it was blocked by large tree branches, different fruit trees, a whole lot of dried vegetation of some sort, and broken building materials, so there was definitely life, and people living around here, but whatever *was* here before is long gone, right now it's totally empty. Exactly the same as when we first arrived, there are no roads; no buildings, no towns, and no farms, there are no trees, plants, animals or birds out there anywhere, we didn't even see one single insect, and there are certainly no *people* left alive. *Everything is gone.* We saw nothing that was even remotely connected to human, or even animal habitation for that matter, in all the time we were out. Even in places where we're fairly certain there *must* have been farms and fields, well it's exactly the same as we've seen so many times over, this whole area, and for a great many miles around, the land has just been scoured, laid waste of any, and every, form of life. There is not a tree, not even a single blade of grass left anywhere that we could find. And not long after day break the temperature reaches inferno level and stays there until dark and then the temperature suddenly drops to around freezing. In the days we were outside, we walked the entire perimeter of this quadruple canyon system, and we climbed right up to the very top of the outer walls to get a better view with the binoculars, and I'm telling you right here and now, that there is nothing, literally *nothing* out there at all, with the sole exception of that brown mud that is thick and sticky in the daytime and almost freezes just after sundown - in every direction. The entire place is dead. There's nothing out there except for boiling heat and the mud and let me tell you, there are hundreds and hundreds probably even many thousands of miles of that sticky brown stuff, and any hills or variations in ground levels have been levelled out flat. These binoculars (he held up a large set of day/night vision military binoculars) allow me to see for between zero and two hundred miles over the flat terrain, and the terrain outside is as flat as a pancake in all directions so you can believe me when I tell you that that's all there is out there. Mud, incredible cold, and deadly heat. And sudden, very deadly storms.

Remember the trucks we stripped and left behind? Well, they're all gone... and before anyone says otherwise - it's impossible to even *think* they were stolen – because, even if there *was* anyone to steal them, there's no way they could have been driven, not if you remember how well we'd stripped them down, but even stripped they were still, heavy armour-plated vehicles. No, the only answer is that just like everything else, they've been blown away. You all know that they were big old vehicles, super heavy-duty trucks that were designed to transport military personnel in wartime; those machines were purpose built with armour plated cabins and toughened steel chassis, able to withstand machine-gunfire, IED's, landmines, bombs, mortar attacks and fire. The trucks that we parked up against the outer walls have, like so many other things, the buildings, trains, the highways, and we've *all been eye witnesses* to them being smashed down before being picked up and blown away. *Exactly* as *you yourselves* saw happening in so many different places before we stumbled upon this place, the same as we witnessed the buildings right next to us in the park, and how could anyone forget that our own people were picked up and blown away like so many dry leaves that day?" Everyone, sitting or standing, could hear the pain and distress in his voice at the merest mention of our lost companions. The marines that had had to stay behind were paying close attention to the body language, and to the words spoken by their commanding officer and their comrades. I could see that they too had been strongly affected by Tyler's report, because that report forced them to accept that they did, after all, have *some* human limitations, and the very confronting awareness, that this time, in spite of their having excelled in a great many categories of unarmed, physical and combat training, or the numerous, and incredibly diverse courses they'd studied, and despite their being as prepared for anything, or as well-resourced as they are by having all of the combined, multifaceted knowledge, right at their fingertips, after putting in so much time and effort, doing the hard yards, in achieving their expertise, often painfully, and sharing the incredible can-do, and know-how attitude, they also had the solid comradery that's part of being a marine. Yet even with all those things at their disposal, they had to admit, that in these, terribly unpleasant circumstances, when it came to such belligerent people, people who were quite literally, people ready to do anything, anything at all, people who were ready to die, just to get away from here. The marines had to accept that they were helpless, all their achievements, all their qualifications amounted to nothing now, because they're of absolutely no use to them, and they were unable to change the situation. And that didn't sit too well on them *at all*. It was alien to the very nature of being a marine. Tyler finished his report by saying "It's all over to you now, each person here is going to have to make their own individual choice. But, and mark my words, no-one can make a decision, or speak on behalf of, or *for, any* other person this time. Either we stay together, and continue growing this safe and secure place into a sustainable village, for however long it takes until we're found, *if ever* that time comes, and *if there is anyone left* out there to find us, or to even look specifically for *us,* among the millions of missing persons. However, you are equally free to choose to take your chances and leave." He paused to give anyone who wanted to speak a chance to do so…

"I'm not about to go telling you anything you don't already know. On one hand we have a place that *you all know* is safe and secure, or, on the other hand you are free to choose the absolute, guaranteed deadly peril, on the outside.

I cannot, and I *will not* try to stop you, if you are so determined and you choose to leave. No-one here is going to force you to stay.

I *cannot* change anything; I *cannot do anything* about the situation we're in.

But understand this, I *cannot,* and *will not,* provide *any* military assistance, *or* support, for anyone who chooses to leave. You will be relying *entirely* on your own resources.

My men and I have discussed each, and every possible alternative, at great length, but the simple, straightforward and undeniable facts of the matter are, that they come down to only the two possible choices that I have already put to you. In case you weren't paying attention, I'll give those choices again. They are -1. *Leave*, and take your chances with the weather. Temperatures reach about 140 degrees *plus*, and drop to around 2 degrees after dark, and the storm activity, well you already know all about that. So, the chances for your survival, which can only be rated as exceedingly poor at the very best, to zero, which realistically equates to nothing short of *suicidal*. Or -2. *Stay*. We can all stay here together, and we *can* begin again, re-adjust our way of thinking, to accept everything that we have, and building a new life here for as long as it is necessary.

There *IS a third choice* for those who want to leave *this* group, but not risk the outside world. There are four of these canyons, you could make your home in the first area which is the smallest and most accessible of the four, or you could move to one of the other two. But leaving the security of these walls or the safety of another canyon, is probably not only the most unwise, but very likely the last decision you'll make in this lifetime." He stopped just long enough to catch his breath before continuing. "*BUT*, I feel I must warn you, again and again, for *anyone* who is considering leaving this security we were so darned fortunate to find, it is highly doubtful that anyone will survive even twenty-four hours out in the open, in all probability it will be much, much less than that, because as you are already aware, the storms seem to come about every one hour forty-seven minutes, and have been lasting anywhere from twenty-eight minutes to twenty hours. Once you are *outside* beyond the safety of these walls, and away from the shelter, *even if you change your mind*, it may well already be too late to save yourself. You'd all do well to think about what I've just told you, think long and hard *-when*, not *if-* but *when* that first storm comes through *you will die, as will your wives, your husbands and your children, they will also die...* Do you remember the massive grave site we drove through? Do *not* dismiss it! Because *you* will all most assuredly become a part of it, or else another one just like it. You *all know* the power of these storms; you've *all seen* first-hand, the devastation they are capable of, and don't forget the countless towns and cities that have *ceased to exist.* This is *not* some movie, and it certainly isn't a game. This is as *real as it gets,* and we're talking about your own life, and the lives of *your own* children. No-one *has* to go, no-one is being forced to leave this place, quite the contrary, I'm sure that any differences *can* be sorted out *if* you are *willing* to do so. But to do that we must sit down together and talk things through, you need to discuss your feelings with us, and I'm positive we'll be able to work out *something* that will be suitable and agreeable, to everyone."

There were loud, strong, very negative sounding mumbles, and grunts of derision coming from the Upper Valley group, so Tyler said, "I really am sorry you feel that way, but I will once again state clearly here and now, in case you didn't hear me, *or didn't believe me,* the first time; I will not, I *repeat, I will not* jeopardise the life of a single one of my men, *I* will *not* go, nor will I send even one of my men out to help you. If you do make the ill-advised decision to leave, then you will be out there completely and utterly on your own, with no vehicles, no phones, no communicators or lifesaving equipment of *any* kind, you will be, as I've just stated, completely and utterly on your own, and you will be relying solely on whatever survival skills you may, or may not possess to walk probably a thousand miles through mud, and take the risk of not finding any kind of life or assistance anywhere." Tyler paused briefly and looked around before continuing. "These storms are the real deal, and you all know only too well that they are. They are extremely, and unnaturally powerful, *and* they are one hundred percent lethal. You all *know* this is true. I cannot stress strongly enough just how barren, how totally devoid of anything even resembling shelter or protection, there's absolutely *nothing* out there at all. If anyone ventures beyond these walls that action can be summed up in a single word – fatal. It was bad when we arrived – it still is. We will hold a whole community discussion tomorrow afternoon after lunch duties have been cleared. I suggest anyone who *is* dissatisfied with the life here, and we all know who you are, that you think long and hard, and discuss your decision *plus* the real life versus death ramifications of that decision. Look into the eyes of your children and tell yourself they are going to die if you leave here – it might change your mind. If so, we can work with that. We are more than willing to facilitate any changes that are humanly possible – but we can't do it without your co-operation and your whole group's effort."

As he spoke, the morning sun poked the first long fingers of golden light down and bathed us in its gentle warming glow.

"But right now, my men and I need to bathe, eat and sleep, in that order. The sun is coming in now so let's all be getting on with the day."

I had been sitting with my head bent, intent on listening, and focusing on everything that was being said, but now that the sky was brightening, I looked over at the marines. And I don't mind telling you, that I was thoroughly shocked and horrified by what I saw, and I wasn't the only one who'd been knocked for six by their pathetic condition, or by the numerous and extreme physical changes that one week outside had made to each one of them. They were all suffering from acute sunburn, there were big yellow blisters covering every part of their body that'd been exposed, which was almost their entire body, they all had horribly blistered faces, backs, legs, hands, necks and shoulders, they'd all lost a great deal of weight, and their supposedly protective, *virtually indestructible* camouflage uniforms, were nothing but rags now, and essentially left them almost indecent! The super tough fabric of their shirts hung down in long strips around their shoulders and their heavy-duty cargo pants, or rather, what little there was left of them, had been ripped to shreds too, even their military-grade Kevlar ranger boots had been worn all the way through from climbing around the rough stone walls. Their poor faces, necks, shoulders, arms, hands and legs were all just a huge mass of big yellow blisters, crisscrossed cuts, long and awfully deep grazes, and heavily blood and mud caked gashes. Each man had some dreadful, absolutely appalling, injuries. Michael told me very briefly how they came by some of them. Those really nauseating deep rope burns across their stomachs, shoulders, backs, thighs and wrists happened when they'd had to rope themselves together around a stumpy stone column because they couldn't find anything more secure quickly enough. Tyler would no doubt tell me all about it later; actually, I'd darned well *make* him talk about it if he wouldn't do it freely. I could see a very large patch of dried blood in the back of Michaels's terribly matted and muddy normally blonde hair, in reality, every single one of our marine adventurers had numerous, wounds and seriously bloodied body parts. Oh Yuk... I've just noticed that none of them have *any* skin left on their knees, knuckles or elbows either... they're all just raw flesh crusted over with blood and dirt! Taken individually, each man looked as though he must be experiencing some serious, really god-awful pain, and collectively - well taken collectively, they were a real mess, and under any normal circumstances they would have been taken by ambulance to a hospital emergency room for assessment and treatment, and more than likely kept there in Critical Care until they healed ... although nothing about us has been what anyone could call *normal* for quite some time now.

Each man looked out through a pair of the weariest, most horribly bloodshot eyes I think I've ever seen. Brown dirt was deeply etched into the lines around and underneath their ears, eyes, noses, mouths, and necks, and well, their hair and beards were just stiff with dried mud and blood, giving their faces a strange mask like appearance.

Tyler, was always the leader, always in control, but this morning, trying hard though he might be, he just couldn't hold himself up straight, he simply couldn't do it, he looked exactly what he was - totally shattered, and he was, like all of them, so far beyond exhausted it's a wonder he could even stand up at all. I'd never seen him like this before, and I pray that I never see him like this again – ever. His back, his neck and shoulders were drooping, past the point of being slouched over, his head was hanging so low that his chin was almost resting on his chest. Seeing him like this, with his clothes hanging off him in rags, his long hair and beard solidly matted and caked with blood and mud, his body was almost completely covered in splatters of dried grey-brown mud, he bore a striking resemblance to a picture I'd seen as a child of a wild man from the mountains. But story books aside - he looked, and without a doubt felt, completely and utterly exhausted; exactly the same as every other incredible member of his amazing team. I could well appreciate their wanting nothing more than to eat, bathe and sleep.

While this small team of ~~soldier's~~ *marines* had been reconnoitring outside, the larger group that stayed behind had continued to very enthusiastically, and ever so creatively, adapt our meagre supplies of hardware to make up useful apparatus like plumbing the water for the showers, and a couple of *real* flushing toilets. The engineers had risen to the task, and had finally completed the unbelievably difficult challenge of converting every single one of the large portable stainless steel water containers that we'd taken from our farms. The first two into solar heated water storage for the kitchens, and then converting the larger water tanks that had been removed from the trucks, into additional, much larger, water storage for the solar heated showers. While they were investigating the various possible water sources, the engineers had come across a very deep and wide rain water collection channel running right the way around and just below the upper rim of the canyon. The biggest challenge they'd faced way up there, had been how to divert *some* of the water away from its natural course and into their tanks, so that they were kept filled with clean fresh rainwater for bathing, without depriving the waterfall of an adequate supply. Their next experiment came in the form of adapting the (thoroughly scrubbed clean) disused fuel tanks; they had, by sheer creativity and hard work, managed to modify and turn them into cisterns that were kept filled with excess rain water and would be used for flushing the toilets that had, over the past months, been painstakingly cut, pounded, broken and then cleaned up and smoothed, Greco-Roman Style, from the solid stone with partitions between the carved wooden bench style seats. We are all so very grateful to the engineers, because those men have done an unbelievably amazing job in a relatively short time. Plumbing genius's they are! And right now, it was time for Tyler and his men to be the very first to enjoy the results of the brilliant engineer's long and extremely difficult, but totally ingenious labours. Once that was done, only then could Tyler and his extraordinary team begin the job of recovering from their own hard work. The large, gleaming stainless steel water tanks, were situated in the deep natural stone gully high above the new bathing rooms where the sun reaches first, and long before it comes in to brighten up the canyon floor and gardens, so the water should be quite pleasantly warm now, allowing the men to have a relaxing warm shower, instead of an icy cold swim. However, with all the plumbing and the incredibly extensive pipe work they have done, there isn't a single piece of tubing left – they even adapted and used the exhaust pipes from the trucks, and now, every last oxy-acetylene tank is completely empty. It's to be hoped that Tyler had no special plans that involved welding, especially ones that his engineers weren't aware of, because from this point on, we'll have to rely solely on sheer inventiveness!! Although it seems to me that a special brand of resourcefulness is something we have a plentiful supply of.

Fortunately for the marines, they had, as was military practice, carried spare fatigues, uniforms, underwear, boots and gear, along with a full-dress uniform in their kits, in case their assignments took them away from their home base for more than a few days, so clothing wasn't an immediate problem - for them. However, the clothing shortage was going to be a really significant issue for some of us here, in the not-too-distant future.

After they'd bathed and eaten, they went to their sleeping quarters and slept like dead men until nearly sunset. While they were sleeping, two longish (a little more than an hour and a half each) and three short - but very sharp- storms, swept through the heavens overhead. We'd realised early on why the canyons were so pristine, and so lovely, it was because while the storms never-ever touched the ground *inside* the canyons, the rainwater kept everything fresh and growing beautifully. Although under normal circumstances the children rarely, if ever, reacted to them in the daytime anymore, at night time though, the storms were still disturbing for some of them, I think it's mostly because at night-time they're so much more visual, the lightning is terrifically dazzling and the thunder seems to roll more deafeningly around the walls after dark when everything else is so quiet.

Once breakfast was over, we sat together in our usual

little groups and there were some serious conversations about the topic on everyone's mind. Go or stay? Stay or go? I myself had already given this a great deal of thought in the weeks and months leading up to today, and I wanted to stay. Especially now if, as Tyler has said, there was more than likely nothing, and no-one, left alive in the outside world to go back to. We could just stay and carry on with our new start right here; we have almost everything we'll ever need to live quite well. Okay, so we don't have the regular and previously, taken-for-granted-things, like gas or electricity, and there are none of the modern conveniences we'd been accustomed to (but have learned to do without surprisingly easily) oh yes, and one *teensy weensy trifling detail* … in a year or less we'd have no clothing either!! Fortunately, we were mostly young, and with a lot of help from the marines we've found we're surprisingly adaptable *and* really resourceful. I firmly believe we are able to live quite well and healthily, as long as we're all prepared to roll up our sleeves (*if we still have any!*) and work together as a real team or family. Listening to myself I've just had a sudden funny thought - Oh Yeah that's it, I've finally gone crazy. Even to myself I sound like I'm recruiting for a hippy commune...

On the *downside*, we don't have very much in the way of long-term medical provisions. But we've agreed that there is almost nothing we can't do, or make, between us. While we were sitting around talking, we realised that some parts of our old lives may well prove to be very useful here, although other parts of our learning would be a whole lot less than useless…

While I sat soaking up the warm morning sun, I let the conversations flow around me. I was mulling over everything in my mind, I am certain that by staying I'm doing what is right for me *and* for Paddy- before all this happened I had been preparing to sit my final exams and graduate from teachers college, I'd already secured a position as a junior teacher in an excellent private boys school, and I've been tutoring in Math's, History and English for school students after school and in vacation time, for a few years, so a good basic education for the children here won't be a problem, *however*, any teaching resources, will naturally be rudimentary at best, because my limited supplies can't last forever. Overall, there are lots of things we will need, things that we simply do not have. But then the other side of my brain said that what we don't have we can either, improvise, make things ourselves as best we can, or else we'll simply do without. We will manage to live with, and use, whatever we do have. If all those hundreds of thousands of early pioneers could do it, well then, so could we.

When I was just a little girl, my Granddad would say -Sara my little darling -its sink or swim time now- although, being so young, it made no sense to me at all, but now I think I understand what he was trying to tell me way back then. Making a serious decision, like this one was, I think, exactly what he meant. I need to stand up and make a judgment *by* myself *for* myself, one way or the other, and if I *do* make *the wrong* choice, I can't blame anyone else, or complain about it, afterwards.

The girls and I spent the early part of the day gathering up enough vegetables and plants for the next meal, and delivered them to the kitchen where the ladies were preparing some rabbits for the spit. Once that job was completed, we went across to the pond to catch something to go together with the rest of the evening meal, although the whole time we were out, one of us kept looking back over to the caves to see if any of the men had woken up or had made an appearance outside yet.

Ultimately it was the delicious aroma of rabbits being slowly roasted on the spit wafting through the air that enticed them from their slumbers…

The atmosphere around the dinner table was so on edge and so tense tonight, making conversations difficult to start, although once started, they quickly faltered and died, so our meals were either eaten in record time, or else food was pushed around the plates and left uneaten, something completely unheard of before today. The only ones happy about the uneaten meals were the pigs and the chickens, and I must say, they were *most* appreciative!

Unfortunately –even though the men's safe return *was* cause for celebration- in view of the seriousness of the situation, any form of happy atmosphere or celebration, was completely lost to us. There was none of the light hearted joking or the easy teasing banter that we generally enjoyed so much, and for the first time since we arrived here, I was afraid of what the immediate future might hold for so many. As soon as the children had finished eating Kristy and I took them up to the inside play area where we set them up with games and some story books. We asked them to stay in there together for a while, they knew that we'd be close by, over in the dining area with the other adults, unless they really needed our help with something, we said they were to try and ignore us, and not to be worried or frightened, if we got a bit too noisy.

While we were settling the children, Mrs B and the other ladies cleared all the dishes from the tables and returned with a tray of cups and a big jug of hot fresh lemon and wild mint tea. As she put the jug down Tyler stood up and made his way over to the children, he thanked them for being so brave, and for helping his marines to take such good care of the ladies while the team had been away. He smiled to himself as he watched each one of them proudly sit up a bit taller and straighter -then he read one chapter of a favourite story to the youngest ones before handing the book over to Lawrence, one of the older boys, to finish reading. As he walked away, he heard a little voice saying "ah not like that Lawrence, Tyra says it better'n that…"

Tyler felt a burning need deep in his gut, to make each one of us fully understand just how very high the stakes were. He was genuinely concerned that while he knew that some people were intolerant of the very basic standard of living, which is what we have here, they refused to accept that we're ten times blessed to have anything at all, they didn't seem to want, or were willing to acknowledge either the danger, or the downright brutality of the conditions they knew first hand, still existed outside our sheltered valley. However, I'm quite sure his impassioned explanations and protestations weren't even being listened to as they should have been, by *any* of the Upper Valley people. Someone had worked really hard to make sure that their collective closed minds had been made up *for* them. Primarily by Mr Beatty's irresponsible and ignorant blathering's, although a couple of his 'converts' had invested a lot of their time, and their acquired hatred, in persuading the remaining few uncertain members of their group. What astounded me, and many others too, was that the UV community was a highly intelligent group of business owners, clever, very sharp minded people – but now it seemed that between them they couldn't summon an original, or a logical thought or idea between them. Mr Beatty was contradicting, ridiculing, and even laughing loudly at everything Tyler said, he was literally hyping all of the others up to follow his own narrow-minded point of view – and they took the bait, hook line and sinker... The discussion as to whether to leave or stay, was supposed to take place tomorrow afternoon, after due considerations had been given to the seriousness of their *individual* decisions, but it simply wasn't going to happen that way, not with Mr Beatty pushing his own egotistic, and perilous, agenda so hard.

What followed that evening, in spite of all of Tyler's best efforts at getting them to at least acknowledge even *one* of the many perils they would most certainly be facing, and wanting desperately to get the information through their thick sculls, was singularly *the* most *unpleasant* and *uncomfortable* hour I have ever had to endure in my entire life.

Tyler spoke clearly and fervently; he described the endless expanses of tortured barren landscape they would be faced with once they stepped outside of these protecting valleys. "It was bad enough before, you know it, and I know it, so just *what exactly* do you think you're going to find? We passed no cities, no towns or even small villages that were still standing, and as the storms haven't abated any, there's *still* going to be nothing for you to find or go to. Even *if* you make it through the first storm, that in itself will be a miracle, but you could be walking for *months* without seeing another soul, and between the fierce heat and near freezing cold, how will you fare? What will you eat? Where will you be able to rest? There's *nothing left out there - anywhere!*"

It certainly wasn't a pleasant picture that he painted for us. Nor was it meant to be. He spoke softly, but earnestly, about his fears for the life of anyone who ventured outside, whether it was on their own or with a whole platoon. In fact, he said he honestly felt that anyone, even *with* thorough, suitable survival training, would be committing certain suicide by venturing too far outside. Another one of his team members spoke up lending his support, saying that even though Tyler's team were all young, and in absolute peak physical condition, and were trained to be aware of the fluctuations in air temperature and air pressure, of both the subtle, and the very sudden variations in weather conditions, as well as the constant necessity to locate and secure any available shelter sufficient for their *small* group, he also told them that even being as aware *and* as prepared as they could be, they almost *didn't* make it through a couple of the storms - and they were all extremely well trained in survival techniques. Then Rivers stood up and said "You intrigue me Mr. Beatty, I seriously have to question just *how, you,* a man of more than seventy years of age, who is grossly overweight, in woeful physical health and seriously unfit, who has *no* leadership training, and a man who doesn't possess even the most *basic* forward planning skills, can survive. Do you think you'll be taking these people and their children for a short walk in a park? Do you even comprehend *anything* you've been told today? Do your followers understand that you really don't have even the *first clue* about surviving? So I have to ask, just how *do* you plan to lead such a large disorganised group of untrained, unfit, and utterly unprepared civilians? Quite a large number of those people are themselves no longer young, nor are they physically capable of walking *one single mile*, let alone *hundreds* of miles, and that's *why* I'm asking you, *how* do you plan to move them, *and* those tiny little children, when they are too tired, too sick, too exhausted, or too weak, too thirsty and too hungry to go on? Those people, both adults and children, can't walk very far sir, so who's going to carry them? That means *you* sir, will be faced with *the triple burden* of trying to lead a group of physically and mentally unprepared older people, *with* a number of very young very dependent children, *plus* carry the food supplies manage their luggage, *and* to somehow make a trek of *around one thousand miles* at the very *least* across an extremely hostile landscape, with *no* shelter *or* protection, and no way to get additional food supplies or fresh water, for your large group, or assistance of any kind whatsoever? You, a sick, old and infirm man are going up against the most extreme daytime heat this planet has experienced since the dinosaur age, then there's the storms and you all know what they can do, how will *anyone* survive the freezing night time temperatures? You must have a plan and provisions we know nothing about, otherwise you wouldn't be leading these people, these babies and children to their deaths... or would you? *How* you plan to do it is beyond our collective comprehension. Mr Beatty, do you actually *have* a plan? Or are you just going to take these utterly unprepared, totally clueless people outside, and walk away from the *guaranteed and proven safety* of this place, and you'll what... just keep your fingers crossed and hope for the best? That's it isn't it Mr Beatty – you're just going to hope for the best in an impossible situation."

Burns stood up and voiced his opinion by saying; "I want to address the followers now, what Mr Beatty here, is planning to do is logistically impossible, if this was a military operation, or even a children's school outing, it would be planned right down to the last can of beans and bottle of water. What will you have to eat and how much water will you be able to carry? The already very fit, very *experienced* personnel would have been in a training program specifically modelled on such a trek, they'd be being geared up and working in heating and chilling units to build up tolerances twenty-four hours a day, *for at least six months*. May I be bold and ask what *your* team preparations have been so far? We know none of you have ever joined us for the exercise routines which, given time, would have been of at least some assistance in building basic stamina, so I ask again, *how* are you going to do it?"

Once the marines began talking from their own, very considerable store of experiences, and putting forth their own reservations. Tyler sat back and listened with an increasingly heavy heart to the sarcasm, the belligerence and downright arrogance, and the pure *ignorance* that responses to the marine's words received from the Upper Valley people, and while he studied the differing facial expressions around the table, he was silently sipping his tea through painfully swollen, cracked and blistered lips. The expressions on the women's faces varied widely, from sneering, to total disbelief, to uncertainty, to abject fear, while the men's expressions alternated between overconfidence, fear, doubt and total arrogance.

It soon became obvious that the Upper Valley men had been talking and discussing the pros and cons of staying here with us, or leaving to make their way back to their respective homes again. It was also clearly evident they weren't willing to believe the marines' story of the total desolation outside caused by the storms, even though they *knew* it to be the truth, they'd *seen* it all with their own eyes, they'd *witnessed* the ever-increasing nothingness spreading far and wide all around them for months and months before we stumbled upon Eden. Tyler told the rest of his team to stand up and take off their shirts, then he asked them to turn around slowly so everyone could see the damage for themselves. "Now I want you all to take a real good look at my men, the burned and blistered skin will be the least of your problems – unless they become infected, in which case you will be very sick indeed, you won't be able to walk, you will need medical attention probably for at least a few days. Now Mr Beatty, how in the name of sanity do you think they're going to survive sir? Tyler looked from one to another before asking them all, what he could possibly hope to gain by lying, or by reminding them what it was like outside when they first found this place. Mr Beatty must have felt the commitment of many of his followers' wavering, so heaved himself up out of his seat and stabbed a crooked arthritic finger savagely towards Tyler, saying he suspected him (Tyler) and his cowardly good-for-nothing playtime marines, of being tired of military life and so they thought this was a real good way of deserting, without ever being found out! "I betcha you had this place all planned out an' ready to come right on in and *find it* eh, yeah, I reckon I've hit that smack bang on the target ain't that right? I reckon *that's* a whole lot more likely than what y'all asayin here! Rivers of mud!? Whole towns and even them big military ve-hickles been blowed away? Well now, I ain't seed no trucks a'flyin through the air lately, have you Morris? How about you Jeremiah? Flyin trucks eh? Mighty interestin! Just ezacly what kind of B.S. are you tryin' to feed us here son? *I* think you're all just tryin' to scare us, to keep us locked up an' all trapped in here like we're your own personal slaves! It's a whole lot more likely that there's nothin more'n a noisy old rainstorm or two left out there nowadays nohow. Well now jes take a good look around you – there ain't no harm bin done around here is there? He turned and scanned the faces looking up at him expectantly. (They reminded me for a moment of baby chicks waiting to be fed by their mother) Have *any* of you folks seen any rivers of mud, or mayhap some flyin ve-hickles lately? Granted, and mebbe we *did* see some mighty gosh-awful things a-happenin before, but them storms have blowed theyselves all to hell n gone by now I'd reckon. Don't go being shy now – If'n ya think different, then speak right up."

Mark stood up and shouted at them "You're all behaving like a bunch of dim-witted lunatics! *Why?* Tell me *why* will you? *Can* you? You've all seen it -*first hand*- what's happened out there, well goddammit old man, it's *still* happening! Listen…" Mr Beatty started to interrupt "Sit down and shut the hell up Beatty - now *you* hear *me* out, and you hear me good. *I heard you* with my own two ears, I heard you all *screaming, crying* and *praying* in sheer *terror*, I *heard* you making bargains with Almighty God Himself to save your sorry hides promising to change your ways to be better people! Remember that huh? *Because I certainly do*. We drove through those same muddy wastelands for weeks, *months*. Dear Lord above! Tell me, *please* tell me *how* can any of you *possibly* have *forgotten* that? It hasn't gone away, if anything it's a thousand times *worse now*! "

But he might just as well have saved his breath, because Mr Beatty continued on loudly, and rudely, talking over him as though no-one else had spoken a single word, as if there had been no interruption at all.

The Upper Valley people were all shaking their heads – "No, I didn't think so – What about rain? Have you seed any drowning rain Claymore? Have we had *any* rain at all? I sure as hell haven't felt any! Anybody even been wet from a little rain shower? NO! NO! NO! And NO again!" His vicious snarling face had transformed into an evil mask of pure hatred as he whipped his huge, flabby body, around to face Tyler. Once his jowls eventually stopped swaying, they started jiggling in time with his jaw movements instead. "Just stands to reason that you're nothing but a snivelling low life, and a *filthy-dirty-liar, Mista Tyla.*" He heaved his bulk around again, this time to face those of us who were sitting on the opposite side of the table. "You're all gonna die *real slow n painful* y'all know that doncha? If y'all stay here with this lying no account cowboy! Hell, you ain't got no *proper* food, *no real meat,* where you gonna get clothes from huh, you tell me that? What'll happen if someone breaks a leg or worse? YOU..." he said pointing his bent and twisted finger at Tyler again..." mister-think-yerself-better'n-the-rest-of-us-big time-bullshit-talkin-marine-boy-Tyler, are nuthin more than a lowly, yeller belly coward, an' the worst kind of a lying fool! We'd all rather take our chances with a little water n mud than be slowly starving to death and watching our precious wives n babies die too, by staying here heedin' the likes of you!"

Tyler rose, ever so slowly from his seat, pushing himself up and resting his damaged knuckles on the table as he lowered his huge frame toward Mr Beatty (who backed away real fast, so fast that he almost fell backwards over the seat) and spoke in a low, very clear, but fiercely controlled voice; "You are entitled to your own opinion Mr Beatty, but I am not now, nor have I ever been, a coward, nor am I a liar. Everything

I've told you here is the complete, honest, and unadulterated truth. There is absolutely *no* reason on earth for *me*, or for anyone else, to be telling anyone lies here. Why would we? Tell me sirs, and ladies," he said looking around at all the Upper Valley men and women, *"what possible reason* could I have for wanting to keep a pack of entirely useless, bone idle and lazy, unproductive, trouble making, *greedy mean-spirited* people such as yourselves, here? Unlike Mr Beatty, I am concerned *only* for your safety, and for the wellbeing of your families." Tyler turned back to face Mr Beatty. "I have told you truthfully all I can, to save your miserable, mean, lazy and totally worthless hide. As you, and anyone who's foolish enough to follow you will find out for themselves if you leave. It will be on *your* head Beatty, between you and The Almighty, but it will *not* be on *my* conscience."

The discussion –if you could call it that- ended right then and there.

Their attitudes confused me, it seemingly made no difference that they had all *seen* Tyler and the team when they had returned. They *saw* the marines come back with their own eyes, they *saw*, oh hells bells, they could *still* see that all of their many wounds were very real indeed; every one of the men had suffered acute sunburn, they'd been battered, badly injured and bruised, with their clothing all but ripped off their bloodied and torn bodies. The men belonging to that side of the group simply didn't *want* to hear the truth, or what would be the safest choice for them to make, and the heated arguments between husbands, who wanted to risk everything and follow Beatty, and their wives, who wanted to stay and settle down, raged on long into the night. Poor Mrs B had been white faced, tight lipped, and very obviously shaking with rage when she left the table. Her head was bent low in shame and loathing after her husbands' disgusting and cruel outbursts. For the first time since I'd met her, I knew that her fabulous sense of humour wasn't going to win the day for her, not this time, and not this day either. They were some really vicious and spiteful lies her husband had told, and she was mortified, deeply, deeply embarrassed, completely humiliated and totally ashamed *of* him, and *for* him. Her thunderous expression spoke volumes for her state of mind and emotions. I was so glad my name wasn't Mr Beatty, because my guess was that their next conversation wasn't going to be easy *or* pleasant, in any way, shape, or form.

The meeting that Tyler had held such high hopes for, had ended appallingly. There was nothing more that could possibly be said. I could do nothing to improve the outcome, or his current mood, so I went to the children and stayed with them reading story books until it was their bedtime.

It took a long, long time, but eventually an uneasy silence descended over the caves, there was the odd irritated hiss, a cough or grunt, but nothing more. The deepening silence was shattered by a vicious storm ripping through the night. This time I stopped what I was doing, and for the first time in a very long time, I really paid attention to the terrifying savagery being unleashed just on the other side of the walls, mere yards from where I was standing. I gave this one my undivided attention. I listened to the booming thunder rolls that bounced and echoed around the valley – I watched as the lightening streaked, and forked brilliantly and repeatedly, every so often sending a great shower of sparks flying skyward as it struck the rocky ridge and showed up the gardens as brightly as noonday. I smelled the ozone that came with the lightning, I watched the clouds drop their load and I heard the heavy, hammering rain, and the powering up of the waterfall, and wondered miserably if anyone else was paying closer attention tonight too.

How - I asked myself - *how,* how could *anyone* in their supposed right mind, dismiss these terrible killer storms as just *a little rain n mud* but nothing to be overly concerned about!? Tyler came over to me and we started to walk out into the cool, refreshing night air, he said he wanted to talk over some of the things that had happened while he was outside. We headed for the new stairway leading down to the ground below, we were walking very quietly, our bare feet making no sound on the stone floor, and out into the deepening night shadows, holding hands and talking quietly. Tyler turned me around to face him and began to lower his battered blistered and bruised face to kiss me, when there was a soft but clear, "uh hum, please excuse us for interrupting Mr Tyler, Sara, but if you don't mind, could we talk to you, just for a moment please?" Instead of kissing our eyes met and we smiled at each other, then turned to see both Mrs Armstrong and Mrs Beatty standing anxiously by the bench seats. Mrs Beatty had the beginning of a brand-new bruise starting to colour up her right cheek, that matched the swollen lid of her right eye and a fresh, still bleeding cut on her bottom lip, and Mrs Armstrong had similar fresh marks on her face, her neck, and on her wrists. "Good evening, ladies, how can I help you tonight?" Mrs Armstrong looked at Mrs B and nudged her with her elbow, "you talk to him Bea, I'm afraid I'll commence to danged-well cussing if *I* do." "Okay then, well, the thing is you see, well the thing is this Mr Tyler, we don't *want* to leave here, our husbands can go wherever, and do whatever they please, and with whomever they choose to do it with, but we don't want to go with them, and they're saying we don't *have any choice* about whether we go or not, because we're married and that's the end of it. What *we*, both of us that is, need to know, is, is, well can they *force* us to go out there with them? Our marriages haven't been going too well for a long, a very long time, Fred has become a real tyrant these past too many years, and now I have an excellent chance to start fresh and make a good life for myself, with good, decent and kindly people, but I don't want him to go and spoil things for me, not again, not anymore, Millie here feels the same way about her life with Monty. Do you mind us asking what our chances are of staying on here as cooks, or we'll be *whatever* you might want us to be?" "Ladies, today I asked all of our people here to choose, and it would appear that you two lovely ladies have done *exactly* that, so all that's really left to say to you both now is, welcome aboard! Oh, and don't worry about a thing, if there's any trouble, my men and I will sort it out; *no-one* will be forcing *anyone*

to leave here tomorrow, whether someone has chosen leave or chosen to stay, then that's what they'll do. You ladies have done only what I've asked each and every person here to do, you've both made your feelings clear, and we really welcome your decision. So go back to bed and try to get some sleep, or if that's going to be a problem, you're both welcome to use my room instead of your own - if you'd prefer - because tomorrow is going to be very hard for everyone."
We said goodnight to two very happy and very relieved women, before we continued on with our um, moonlight walk and talk.

By first light most of the older men, along with a few of their wives, some of the older boys and girls and unfortunately some really young children too, and a dear sweet little girl who'd been a newborn, only two or three days old when this journey began, Annie was barely even a toddler, but her parents were packed up and ready to go. We weren't surprised to see that they were, each and every one of them, from the Upper Valley community either. The men stubbornly refused to listen to anything that might change their minds, and their wives took their lead from them – the poor children, well they were given absolutely no choice. Tyler noticed two of the older girls were looking very nervous, and staying close together instead of being with their family group. A little while ago I'd heard Carol tell her mother that she and Colleen would be up front with the men, and that they wanted to walk out with the only other teenagers –the gentlest, most sweet natured twins Randy and

Cliff- but Colleen had told her father not to worry about them because they'd wait and walk at the back with the other women and children. It occurred to me that they were a bit confused, although I thought no more about them because I heard Mrs Cullum shouting in stage whispers to her husband that she didn't give a damn *what* he did with himself anymore, but she was leaving this hell-hole with him, or without him! After a meal, the eighteen adults, four teenagers and six small children, that had decided to leave, were led back through the caves, they were carrying their own possessions and enough food and water rations to last them at least a week. Most of their belongings had been packed onto makeshift sleds –long poles with blankets tied at the corners and the bundles tied on- to make things a bit easier for them. They all walked in complete silence through the beautifully lush First Area, following the twin furrows made by the poles. The huge piles of dead branches and wood that had been stacked up behind the concealed gateway months and months ago were pushed and pulled aside and the *Homeward Bound* group went out through the passageway and then out into the totally barren, bleak, muddy and super-heated landscape. Tyler asked them all once again that even if *they* were still determined to leave, would they at least spare their children and allow them to live, he even told them they could come back and get them once they were back home.

Mr Beatty's response to the offer was very negative, very abusive and very, very final. (It was also a physical impossibility)

Every single member of Mr Beatty's group, and even

Beatty himself, visibly recoiled, and some folk even took a few involuntary steps backwards, the children and some of their mothers started to cry when they saw that it really was *exactly* as Tyler had described it to be yesterday. We could almost hear their thoughts; Tyler and the other marines *weren't* lying, they *did* describe it as it really is, what if everything else they said is true too? Tyler asked them all one last time, if *anyone* had had a change of heart or, now that they could see the ruin for themselves, if *any* parent would now be willing to allow their children to stay, or now wanted stay themselves. Randy spoke to his twin, laughing loudly and saying "Ha-ha-ha Cliffy, it all muddy here n we gonna be gettin' real dirty now, we got good fun now Cliffy!" With a silent, but deeply intense anger, I looked at the faces of those men, and understood only one thing - Pride is a dreadful obsession, even at this late stage their foolish pride wouldn't allow them back down, or even permit their precious little children to be spared the horrors waiting out there. And so it was that Beatty, bent over, shuffling and leaning heavily on a thick walking staff, led his ragtag band of people away from the safety and security of the cave areas, and out into a very bleak, already blistering hot, extremely uncertain, definitely dangerous, and doubtlessly, a very fleeting future.

As we turned away from the entrance to go back inside, I heard a woman calling out to me as she came running toward us. Before we knew what was happening, she pushed little Anna into the small gap between Tyler and me, she was almost hysterical, crying "please, oh please keep her here, oh for God sakes I love her so, please, please, will you take her back inside?" Then without another word she turned and ran back to her husband who was waiting for her with his arms outstretched to her and tears streaming down his cheeks. Tyler said quietly that he'd leave the gate open for a day or two – just in case…

As I settled the confused, almost hysterical child into a comfortable position on my hip, I wondered *why* she and her husband didn't just turn around and stay here as well. What could they *possibly* be thinking? Save their child, but go out to die anyway? They'd obviously realised they weren't going to make it back home. Pride, once again, stupid suicidal brain numbing damned pride, oh Mr Beatty, what *have* you done to these people?

When I spoke my thoughts to Tyler, he put his arm around me and little Anna then said quietly and simply that there *couldn't possibly* be any rational thought processes working in *any* of their heads. What was so much worse, and what was so impossible for me to understand was *how*, even after *seeing* what was outside, *why* did they all still follow him? Each person now *knowing full well* that there's *no possible future* for any of them, it simply beggars' comprehension. Anna, as small children tend to do, quickly became completely at ease and comfortable with me, we'd spent a lot of time playing games and we'd started pre-learning things like colours, shapes, and different plant names together, so she'd calmed down in no time at all. By the time we'd all walked across the big grassy park to the entrance of the caves, she wanted to get down, so holding onto my finger she toddled along by herself for a while. When we were almost to the entrance, she turned to face the direction we'd just come from and waved her little hand then said in her piping little girl voice, mum-mum gonned way. Then, just as we were about to step up into the first of the cave colonnades, the skies above turned inky black, the wind screamed like a pack of wild banshees around the outside walls and fierce bolts of lightening streaked brilliantly across the sky while the deafening roar of thunder began crashing and banging above us. Tyler turned his face away from me but not before I saw the tears glistening in his eyes, and I knew then, just as he did, that they were all more than likely gone, and already dead, or broken and dying somewhere. I picked up the toddler and made a silent promise to her parents that their child would be safe, and she would be loved. We made our way back through the caves again in silence. No one had any inclination to speak. Right down to the last person, we were emotionally very fragile, our nerves were raw, and our tears were too close to falling. So just paying attention to putting one foot in front of the other was the best thing to do right now.

However, there was quite a surprise waiting for us just around the corner. Crouched down and out of sight in a dark recess, sat Carol and Colleen. They'd both slipped away unnoticed from the main group and had just sat on their bundles in an emotional turmoil of uncertainty, and waited until we came back through again. My heart broke for them, this would have been such a difficult thing to do, but at least now I understood the conflicting messages they'd given to their parents. All of a sudden, I felt as though I was a hundred years old, old and bone weary, completely emotionally drained, and tired, oh, so very, very, tired. Tyler gently called out and asked them to step over and talk to him. Colleen and Carol both looked up at him through red puffy eyes. Those poor girls, their noses were red and running, their cheeks were blotchy and they had dirty wet dust stains smeared all over their faces. "Mr T-Tyler c-can we p-please st-tay here w-with you? We don't ever want to g-go we l-love it here." Tyler smiled sadly down at them and said ever so softly and gently, "come on, come, let's all go home together now." The girls had been hiding away inside the caves, they probably hadn't realised the significance of the storm that was still passing over…they, oh gosh, they didn't realise that they were already orphans. Well, that awful pain can be delayed for a while longer, but come, it most certainly would.

Necessity required that our days became a little bit more structured now, since a few of the professional farmers had chosen to leave, even though not many of them actually *worked* in the gardens, or with the livestock, for quite a while, it was their knowledge that had been so valuable. We would all need to hunker down together and pick up any shortfall in the gardens now. These gardens are –after all- the real lifeblood of Eden, they feed us. The flip side of that coin is that there weren't as many unproductive mouths to feed now either.

Tyler and his men called the remaining members of the group together and everyone sat in a loose circle around the main chamber for a family meeting.

He started out by saying – "Since we had all, in one way or another, been thrown together a year or so ago, we have survived some of the worst things any individual can expect to live through. I have no way of knowing if anyone from the military is still alive out there, or if there are, whether they will ever look for us, simply because of the millions of people who have died, we will probably be assumed to be another number added to the overall losses, so I seriously doubt whether we will ever be found here. You might have noticed I didn't say 'rescued' because I believe we were all brought together for some reason, maybe it *was* purely by chance, but then again maybe it's fate, or maybe I've been out in the sun too long, or banged my head once too often, but to my mind this valley is a gift, it's given a second chance to all of us to begin over again, to undo some of the countless wrongs, give us the chance to reverse actions that have, over the years, done real damage to society, and treated innocent people so badly, the dreadful ongoing conflicts between religions since those in power attempted to roll all beliefs into one, the so called *Newly Combined World Order* that has enforced so many outrageous, unreasonable, and ridiculous, compulsory standards. We need to scrap them, every single one, every irrational, and every impractical one of them, they don't belong, nor will they *ever* have any place here. We can start over, we can, and we will make it work this time. However, the biggest difference *now* is that we'll be doing it *by* ourselves – *for* ourselves. Now, we all know that today has not been a good day, far from it. I confess that the one thing I have been fearful about for so long *has* come to pass. I have been anxious for many months that due to the combined, unreasonable expectations, of my inability to provide amenities like electricity, and the deep resentment at having lost all their worldly possessions, that we'd experience a severe split in the group, and regrettably, that happened. Though I must confess that I never imagined for one minute they'd actually pack up and *leave* Eden." There was a groundswell of murmurings. "But please, please, hear me out for a moment, as saddened as we are all feeling about our many losses today, we have no choice but to move forward, together. *Together. That* is the secret. Together - is the key to our successes in the future. What will benefit you, will *also* benefit your neighbour and your friends. You all heard the things that were said last night about the condition of the world outside, and we all heard Mr Beatty, along with some of the others saying some pretty appalling, and some extremely negative, and cruel things about our future here. There's no doubt in my mind that at least some of those things will have made you feel uneasy, and sadly that was the intention. However, I want you all to pay close attention to me now, and truly *hear* what I'm going to say to you, because what we, that means everyone here, myself included, what *we* do from this moment on, will determine whether those grim predictions are proven to be right, *or* whether by working *together* we will prove them to not only be *wrong*, but show them –and ourselves– how we'll find different ways to overcome any obstacles. And we will grow, and we will be a strong community." There was a small chorus of "hear, hear, yes!"

"For the past months we've been skimming by, all the aggression and negativity had a definite impact, it was inevitable, and we were doing little by way of really getting ahead, *I* think, and I'm truly hoping that you will all agree, that what transpired today has brought us to a turning point, right now, right here, today. From this moment forward we need to come together and strive to not merely survive. We *can* thrive, *we can do it* – no one person can do it alone – our community *will flourish* if we work at things *together*."

Tyler was on a roll now, and he knew he had everyone excited for the future, so while he had their full attention – he kept it...

"Throughout our lives we, each and every person here tonight, have accumulated various talents, now it might be something we've been taught, or studied, perhaps it's a profession, or a craft, perhaps it's a hobby, maybe you have a trade, or perhaps you were born with a natural gift, or maybe a special skill, or, I don't know, maybe an interest that has been developed, or maybe just things we've picked up along the way. As a community, we need to know what each person can do, or, what each person is good at. I'm talking about everything from planting seeds, nurturing the growing plants, right through to harvesting crops, from animal breeding to skinning rabbits, shearing the sheep and go-bits for wool, to butchering the animals for meat, some may have a talent for drawing pictures, telling stories, keeping records of events, stitching up wounds, building furniture, sewing, knitting, or know the correct way to go about chopping down a tree – and well, everything in between. If we are to survive, and really grow, we all - each and every one of us- will firstly need to realise, and to acknowledge what *our own* individual gifts or talents are, in order to be able to teach them to others wherever it's possible. *We all have something special, to offer each other.* Mrs Beatty and Mrs Armstrong will be able to teach the younger women and girls sewing, knitting, and cooking. Mr Costa will continue on as our chief gardener, and I'm sure he will, in time, instruct all of us as to how, and when, we should plant and harvest, we will need to find ways to safely and securely, store our harvests, fortunately for us, we aren't cramped for dry storage space. Many new ways, different ways or methods of doing things will need to be found or worked out..." Mr Costa spoke up and said he'd already worked out the where and the how for the storage. He was having a chuckle as he said – "I'm a street ahead of you on that one Mr Tyler Sir." In reply Tyler gave an exaggerated sweeping bow and raised an imaginary hat to Mr Costa while he continued speaking. "His skill with all sorts of gardening and growing things is quite legendary -or so I've been told. Mrs Armstrong called it his 'green thumb' I imagine he also has a veritable wealth of life stories to tell as well." He stopped for a moment to look around the upturned faces, many of them were looking thoughtful.

"Hank, I'll say this for any amongst us who might have been hiding ever since we arrived, and mightn't know about you. When we picked you up, you had recently completed six years of medical studies, and are a fully qualified general practitioner, you were, in fact, about to open your own clinic isn't that right?"

Hank nodded his head and smiled and looked around at all the now familiar faces. "In that case, would you have any objection to teaching some of the many things you have learned to the younger ones, that way we can have good Primary Aid and help available should we need it? Later on, we will discuss training another young person to be your assistant or support person, as well. As you're aware we don't have an inexhaustible quantity of medical supplies, but this New Eden we've found, I honestly believe it will provide us with almost everything we will ever need.

This evening I propose that we will have a special 'exchange of gifts' celebration. Each person will be given time to tell us what form their own special gift to the family might take. We aren't expecting everyone to be able to do great big things, or important sounding things either. Remember our trucks? Do you remember how big and tough they were? Well, if you took out one single fuse about half the size of a thumbnail, those trucks wouldn't have gone anywhere. So please, keep in mind that it takes lots and lots of small things, to make really big things happen. Everyone here has a special something to offer. It might be as simple as being able to play a game, climb a tree or as complex as removing an appendix. But just let me remind you all, every gift, every ability we have, is equally important, and going forward into the future your gift may well prove invaluable to the wellbeing of this community.

But I know for certain that at one time or another, our community, our new extended family, will call on *your* particular talents.

Now I suggest we all take an hour or so of time out, anyone who wants to talk about what has happened today, or if there is perhaps something else concerning or upsetting you, we're here... We've lost a great deal today, but we must always keep in our minds that it was *their* wish, *their* choice and *their own desire*, to leave us. I tried, believe me I tried, your marine brothers tried too, in every way we knew how, to convince them to stay, but getting away from here was, for some reason that I don't think any of us here will ever truly understand, so tremendously important to them. Some of you I know, had recently formed friendships, for others, well you may have been a longtime friend or neighbour of someone who left us today.

I sincerely hope you will talk about your feelings and emotions, if you aren't quite ready to talk things through yet, well that's okay too, but please remember that we are all here together, we are here to lean on, and to be supportive of each other. You can talk whenever, and wherever, you are feeling the need. My recommendation to every one of you, is *never* keep anything locked up inside, it's not healthy. So, take a walk, have some rest, or get together and have a talk before our celebration tonight. I will be available to anyone who wants to chat, or who may have some questions they want to ask." He started walking over towards me and he had such a tender smile on his poor, sore, battered face, looking down at us he said – "this is possibly the most beautiful thing I've ever seen Sara" I had Anna curled up on my lap and she'd fallen asleep with the chubby little thumb of one hand plugged firmly in her mouth, and with the little fingers of the other hand twisted through my long hair, where she'd been 'twizzling' it between her fingers while she dropped off to sleep. "Well dear sir, it may present a pretty picture to you, but my back is about to break, and I'm afraid to move, in case I disturb her, and I know she's going to want her mother when she wakes up." Tyler disappeared for a few minutes, and when he came back again, he was carrying a wooden crate that he'd packed with some soft woollen blankets. He lifted her ever so gently out of my arms and tucked her up into the little nest he'd made for her. This new Tyler really had become a surprise a minute, and I was feeling quite humbled by him. Honestly though, who knew that *this* side of him could possibly exist? Who would have thought *this* was the same man who only a few months ago, told us quite tactlessly to dump some of our precious possessions - or walk? Obviously, I liked *this* Tyler so much more; he is proving that he will make a good, solid, caring, and an honest leader for our future. We all know he has the strength, the courage, and the intelligence, to get the job done, but what's more important right now; is that he's demonstrating that he also has the instincts, a good understanding, and the *compassion*, necessary to be a strong and respected leader.

With the last of the daylight came a colossal storm, as it passed overhead, the lightening and thunder caused all of our conversations to stall. I'm sure everyone here was thinking about the ones who'd left. Carol and Colleen both burst into tears and ran from the table with Katherine and Reba running close behind them. Chung excused himself from us and made sure the tall torch fires were lighted before we sat down around the tables for our evening meal.

The change within the group was palpable, while there was no overly loud cheery banter tonight, neither was there the increasingly open hostility, and seething anger we'd had to deal with over so many months. A sense of easy harmony flowed around dinner table, quiet conversations flowed freely without interruption of sarcastic or contemptuous comments, and best of all there was the wonderful tinkle of childish laughter. Everything about tonight was comfortable and for the first time ever, there was a feeling of everything being so *right* for a change. Manuel surprised us by standing up and asking everyone to join hands. "I appeal to The Heavenly One to watch over the souls of the people who have left our company, and to please watch over and guide the hearts of all who share this table, to lead us with gentle hands, convey Your wisdom to us, and teach us Your patience and compassion." Then we all started chattering and passing the dishes around. Peace to all.

A few moments later, the four girls returned to the table, Colleen stood for a moment to address the diners.

"Most of you know that my father married Carol's mother a few years ago, we have been best friends since we were little and our bad times were bearable only because we always had each other, so Carol and I want to thank you all, from the bottom of our hearts, for giving us another chance. We both promise to give back double, all the love, the encouragement and friendship. We are so appreciative of all the amazing support you have given so freely, we want to thank each and every one of you too, because it was knowing we had so much generous love and support that gave us the courage to step away from my father's brutality and violence, our only regret is that our mother, Lydia, wouldn't stay here with us. In one way or another we've all lost someone close or someone special this year. And today when our world –Carols and mine, fell apart, well, at one time or another today each person at this table came to talk to us, to encourage us, and to lift our spirits, and do you know what we felt? We felt like we were talking to another sister or brother, an aunt or an uncle, or at least a very dear and caring family member who not only understood, but who really *cared* about how deeply we were hurting. You're all such wonderful friends and we want you all to know how very thankful we are for having such a wonderful new family and such a beautiful home."

As with so many historical events; no-one recognised the moment for what it was at the time, but looking back on that night later, we all realised that Colleen and Carol's acknowledgement, was our defining moment. It was the moment our New Eden Family was born.

At the end of the meal Mrs B carried out jugs of honey and lemon tea, Tyler pointed to Rivers and asked him to start the night off by telling us all something about himself, and what gifts he was able to offer to the family… By the time everyone had taken their turn to talk, we had made some truly significant, and remarkable discoveries about each other – even about those we thought we already knew really well. In our midst we were most fortunate to have two wonderful cooks and seamstresses, one of whom is also a Bee Keeper, she also knew how to spin a raw fleece into thread, how to turn the thread into knitting yarn, or to complete the process by weaving it into cloth; we had an extremely talented artist and gifted singer, an ordained pastor of the church who was by trade a carpenter and builder; we had a florist, and a newly graduated doctor of medicine –complete with medical instruments and supplies, he had also practiced yoga since he was four years old, and he had qualified as a yoga instructor at the age of fifteen. He firmly believes many of society's ills can be relieved by attending to our physical and subconscious needs, and he may well be right. We had a marine who was born and raised on a large cattle ranch, he is an accomplished animal breeder and is registered under strict Zone Law Animal Control, he has also earned many blue ribbons competing in the area of producing 'all natural' garments made from leather, this means he's successfully competed in an area where the competitor is required to complete the entire five step process. It involves the method of slaughter, the clean removal of the hide with minimum waste, butchering the beast. To complete the hide tanning process, right through to the finished product, using *only* natural products – no chemicals or machinery. There is a weaver of baskets, hats and floor mats, we have a hairdresser (well almost) she was evacuated two weeks prior to graduation. Then we have our horticulturalist, herbalist and arborist...there are three fully qualified mechanics, and a tool maker, we have a champion potter, who also happens to be a qualified plumber (a very odd combination!) We also have a good skipper and jumper (Shannon is aged 6) he also likes to ice skate. Not to mention we have a really good reader and tree climber (Rosie is nine years old). We have a keen gymnast and fisherman in Lawrence (he's thirteen) and Rosie piped up again and said she can do just 'everything' and I bet I could feed a cat too - if I had one! There is also a musician who is also a wood artist, he carves all manner of instruments along with ornamental and household goods. Then Colleen stood up and told us all that last year she and Carol had completed a three-year course in naturopathy, Colleen's hobby was developing and distilling her own essential oils and blending them into new fragrances, while Carol's interest lay in developing natural cosmetics and skincare in her spare time. They'd opened their own shop called Natures Place, eight months before they were evacuated. I remembered their shop; I'd brought my grandmother some really nice, classic English Rose oil for her birthday in March. That remembrance suddenly made me feel so very sad, because now it feels as though the memory belongs to someone else, from another lifetime. I think that in times to come, these journals will be so important; they will help me to remember who I am, and where I came from. Sara Anastacia Johnson. Home; No. 11 via Ebor, Shady Haven. New Brunstelle. Zone twelve. Daughter of Hilton and Evangeline Johnson – Granddaughter of Isabelle and Jude MacTavish.

By the end of the evening everyone was surprised by the range of practical skills present in this small group of people. Without question we had the essential requirements –and more- to establish a community. The question remains will we have enough to hold our own without outside help? Even though we've come to understand only too well that getting outside help simply isn't an option. We'll have to be very creative and resourceful!

Just before we said our goodnights and went off to our own quarters for the night, young Marcus piped up and reminded everyone that we had a lot more space in the complex now, so if no-one minded, he would be changing his room for a larger one. That raised yet another suggestion from within the group. Reba asked "would it be at all possible to group some of the rooms and create some little family units, not only to maintain privacy, but so we don't feel as though we're all rattling around in that great big place!" Well...*that* started the engineers off! They were really excited, saying "We've already had some really good and very achievable ideas about making what Reba had called family units, by closing off some of the cave entrances, and opening doorways in the rock walls to join up others. I'm not certain whether you've realised this or not" said Arron "but there are, quite apart from all the ones we already have in use, more than one hundred and forty really good-sized caves right here?" He said pointing to the floor. "Not only those, but directly above this level, we found eighty-eight really large areas, actually they border on being enormous rooms, when we were up top, installing Mrs B's kitchen cover, we discovered there's a large pipeline or passageway, it might not be high enough for Tyler or some of the other marines to walk through, but certainly fine for just about anyone else. It leads to another level, that's directly below where we're standing right now! We're pretty sure there's still a whole lot more of them waiting for us to find too. It will be so easy to convert some of the units into twin levels later on, we have all the necessary tools, we've got all the knowhow, and best of all, we have all the time in the world." Tyler stood up, he was laughing and holding his hands up in surrender. "Tomorrow, you guys, okay? Tomorrow we'll start listing all the new projects and identifying the most necessary ones first okay? It's been a long, very emotional day today, so I think it'd be a good idea if we all got some rest now. Oh, I nearly forgot, I have a suggestion, how would you all feel about calling tomorrow Eden-Day One?" And with those words a tremendous clap of thunder sent a vibration shuddering around the walls, and had most of us scampering off into our rooms.

I was joined on my pre-dawn walk this morning by my rather delightful beau, who has informed me that his given name, in case I wanted to use it, is Wade, (I can only think of him as Tyler) as we walked over to the waterfall, I told him how he's become a constant source of amazement to me lately. Just the way he's been changing, so fast, and *so* completely. Who could possibly have guessed that his true personality is that of a really gentle, and very caring man, or perhaps living in this beautiful place, his truest self, was able to claim him back, from the tough, hard hearted, very cynical "Gunnery Sergeant Tyler that we were all so accustomed to? I hardly recognise the old Tyler anymore. I laughed and said – "If you'd been like *this* the whole time, I would have fallen head over heels in love with you on the very first day!" His voice softened when he said, luckily for him something in me had sensed his true nature had been buried under years of training, because I'd fallen for him anyway. Tyler slowed his walk almost to a stop, he gently put his hands on my shoulders and he asked me -if I would honour him by becoming his wife- then he went and spoiled that special, wonderfully magical moment … he panicked! He kept asking if he was moving too fast, saying too much? Oh goodness, he rambled on and on about nothing at all – the poor man was scared half to death. I put him out of his misery and said of course, I'd love to be his wife, but how can that happen, here? "How *can* we be married Tyler? We have no marriage license, no church, we don't even a *vicar* to give us a blessing or a marriage certificate or anything..."

"C'mon Sara, don't think like that honey, Eden is our chance to start over, to make a brand new beginning, and this place is an opportunity for a whole new start for all of us. Naturally, we'll have to have some suitable guidelines and rules to live by, only *this* time Sara, this time we'll really try to get it right, we've learned so much from the old mistakes, and we need to bear in mind that a whole lot of things from *before*, will *never* apply to any of us living here - ever. Although, okay yes, I do agree that you have raised a *very* valid point here, when you mentioned the marriage license and certificate," I could almost hear his mind ticking off the points. "We're going to need some sort of council, and it's going to be essential to have a reliable system of record keeping in place, we'll also need to have some basic laws that are suited to life in Eden and appropriate penalties if we're going to remain a civilised community. Sara, this is fantastic! Well, this is going to open the first exciting chapter in New Eden's Book!" Tyler looked down at me and gave a low, wicked, naughty boy laugh. "Ooh, but you are *so mistaken* about one thing my love, although I totally agree with you, we *don't* have a *vicar* or a *church*... We *do* however - if you'd care to recall last night's exchange of gifts - just happen to have an ordained *pastor* my prissy little miss, so we *can* be married whenever we want to! Just look around us Sara, look at these blue stone walls, the pool and the waterfall, look at these beautiful gardens and the magnificent flowers and trees, feel the softness of this green grass beneath our feet, and ask yourself, what *church* could *possibly* compare with all this?" As he spoke his arms drew a wide arc while he slowly turned around and around to embrace the whole of our spectacular surroundings. Above us billions of tiny stars were brilliant pinpoints of silver in the blackness. Thunder rattled and banged around somewhere further out, but we were so totally focused on each other we were almost oblivious to the sounds.

We strolled arm in arm and talked, we'd walked the entire perimeter of Eden, and we were *still* talking! We discovered things about each other that almost no other living soul had ever known, we laughed a lot, and yes, we also had a little cry each, but then we laughed again afterwards. There's a lot more, a *whole lot more* to this man Tyler, than he would *ever* let anyone know. He is emotionally very complex, however I'm very thankful that he's nowhere near as cynical, *or* as severe as he has had to be, nor is his nature as harsh or as inflexible as he's been trained to be. The true man is gentle, loving, caring and, well yes, this new Tyler, he cries too.

He'd been raised by an aunt from the age of about two and a half, when his parents were both killed in a collision after a drug and alcohol fuelled night out with friends. He spoke so lovingly of his aunt, his voice warmed and softened, it was almost a caress to her memory, he told me "She'd scrubbed floors, she'd waited tables and then she had tutored older kids in Ancient History, Math's and English after their school hours, and at times, she even cleaned filthy dirty public bathrooms, and Sara, I never heard her complain, not once, about having to do it for me." She'd told him many times that she would do almost anything to earn enough money to educate him properly, because she said he was an exceptionally bright child" she'd soon realised that he had inherited the best genes from his multi-talented mother and academically gifted father, and she believed that he deserved a decent education, even if it had to be in a government run school. But there was no way that she was going to let him waste himself, or throw his life away, not the way his foolish parents had done. He told me, speaking so softly that I had to lean in closer to hear his words, that "he would have gladly died by fire for that woman; she was just turned twenty-four when she took him in and saved him from living his life locked into the overburdened welfare system, where he would have been moved constantly from one foster family to another, or else placed into an institution. She'd heard so many stories of child molestation, and the severe mistreatment, and of the many serious mental health issues, that went untreated for lack of funding, and of young people becoming completely emotionally crippled and unable to function normally so they turned to drugs and crime in order to cope in the outside world, all due to a lack of care and appropriate treatment; she felt, that as her sisters' only child, I deserved so much more than a life like that. She was, at the time of her sisters' death, engaged to be married to a man she loved very much, he was all that she'd dreamed of; a good man, with solid family values -or so she'd believed- he was well connected, and steadily working his way up the highly competitive corporate ladder in a prestigious Zone AAA law firm, with his eye set firmly on one day running for the senate. But her fiancé simply wasn't prepared to take on an instant family, especially when he took into consideration the manner in which I'd been orphaned." He'd asked her bluntly "Have you completely lost your mind? Have you given any thought, *any thought at all* about what having that brat tied to us would do to my career, to *my entire future?*" Tyler stopped and seemed lost in thought for a few moments before continuing "She was completely and utterly devastated by his disapproval, and astounded by his readiness to carelessly abandon an innocent two-year-old child, because he *might* prove to be an *inconvenience* to his carefully laid plans, and was fully prepared to willingly *and* knowingly, condemn him to a shocking and indescribably miserable life locked into the cripplingly overworked system. She made no fuss, gave him no argument, she simply handed him back the emerald and diamond engagement ring he'd given her, before she turned around and walked away without ever looking back. Strangely enough, I never knew anything about that, she'd never ever mentioned it to me, none of it. Her best friend, Eleanor, told me on the day I had to bury her. Aunt Liz, her name was Elizabeth-Maree, she died after a long, and hard-fought battle with lung cancer. I really think God just wanted her all for Himself, she had never smoked *any* kind of cigarette in her life, she never drank more than one small glass of wine; but oh Sara, how she laughed! And she sang all the time, and she always told me she was the luckiest woman in the whole wide world to love, and to be loved by, such a handsome little man. D'you want to know something funny Sara?" He gave a soft chuckle at the memory and said, "she always called me -her little man- even when I was six 'n a half feet tall and needed to duck down under the doorways. She was so special, so *very* special, much more special than any other mother in the whole world, because she really did give up *everything* for me, when she could just as easily have said I wasn't her problem. She could have been a social butterfly, she could have lived in a magnificent grand house with cooks and maids, worn beautiful clothes and jewellery, and never have to worry about money, instead of that cold, roach infested public housing building, wearing clothes she bought super cheap from the local goodwill store. When she died, she was worn out, worn down, and bone weary, and she was only thirty-nine years old. I held her thin, cold little hand and she made me *promise* her that I'd make something of myself, and I vowed to become someone she'd be really proud of. I held her close and tried so hard to keep her here with me, but she needed to go, she had to spend some time with the other angels." (In a flash I understood *why* he'd gone so deathly pale when Mrs B had told him to give her the same respect he'd give to his own mother!) "Soon after she passed away, I packed up her few belongings and put them into storage.

I was barely seventeen years old, I was too tall for regular jobs, and just too plain angry with the whole world for taking her away from me to care much about anything at all. I didn't have any other family I could turn to, and I had absolutely no idea what I was, or might even *be* capable of doing, and I sure as hell had no money to go anywhere. But I'd made her a promise, so I had to find some way to keep it. I was walking down Central Street and saw a recruitment poster for the Air Force, they said I was much too tall for a flier, and far too big for a mechanic or a cook, I looked at the Army too, but it really looked too boring for me, so, in the end I joined the Marines. She must have been guiding me you know, because it turned out to be the best thing I've ever done, the hardest, but still the best. I started out with *the* absolute meanest, most cold-blooded, toughest, and most unyielding drill sergeant in the entire Marine Corps. His attitude was to keep 'em going 'til they get it right then beat 'em to death if they don't keep it tight. He damn near killed all of us, he made life *really tough* for us, and he worked us so hard, and for so long that even our butts screamed out for mercy. I've got to tell you, we all ached in places we didn't even know a body had. In addition to all that, he was just so damned merciless that some of the new recruits who had Daddy's that *knew people in high places,* got themselves transferred out of his squad, while the rest of us busted our guts and our butts to try and earn his approval. Oh, but Sara, there was one kid who just didn't have it in him to be a Marine pure and simple, he wasn't cut out for anything physical at all. He should have joined the local library instead of the marines, nonetheless I have to admit, the Sarge tried really hard with him. Our Sarge said he honestly believed he could make a marine out of *any* man who wanted it badly enough. So, he pushed, and he pushed, and he pushed at him some more. Well, this kid, Ramsey was his name, he didn't have no Daddy, and he didn't have any family he could go to for help, and he just knew he was gonna keep falling way short of the Sergeants standard, so he hanged himself in the shower block. There was an inquiry and accusations, and finger pointing from all directions, and there were reports flying all over the place, some of the high Brass called for his resignation, but they didn't get it. They told him he had to reign in his methods, he carried on just the same way as always, and he was constantly reminding us, and drumming it into our heads, that it'd be no good if he started going all soft on us and treating us like little girls, 'cause the *enemy* sure as hell wouldn't. But one thing's for sure Sara, one way or another, he certainly made men out of the rest of us. On the day I graduated he took me out to a bar and got me blind roaring drunk… While we were drinking, he told me that he'd known my story from my first day, he looked me over and decided. He'd made up his mind *exactly* what track my future would take, right then and there. Well, I got all maudlin' and told him about my aunt, and he got drunk enough to tell me how he still had nightmares about finding Ramsey hanging in the shower block. He really wasn't the cruel bad ass bastard that everyone thought he was. But he *was* a fine, honourable man, and a *great marine*. He had only one fear, and that was sending his men out unprepared for the enemy. Somehow don't ask me how – but he got me from the bar, back to the base and rolled me onto a bunk. Since graduation day he's become a close personal friend. I'll never forget him, or his decency, or his many kindnesses to me over the years, every Easter, Thanksgiving and Christmas when we could both get leave, he'd take me to his family home for the holidays, instead of leaving me in the barracks alone. What about you? What was growing up like for you? Got any deep dark secrets?"

"Do you *really* want to know? Well, and no, I wasn't as roughly done by as you were, you poor thing. My father left us; he ran off with my mother's best friend when I was a just little girl. I'd always been his special princess, so I couldn't understand *why* he'd gone and left me behind, but I honestly believed he'd be coming back for me. I waited, and I waited for him, I was so sure he'd come walking back up the garden pathway to get me, he'd come and take me away with him, but after he left, he never did look back, not even once. I sat on those front steps of our house every day and every night for a whole month, with my bag of clothes and stuff, just waiting for him to walk up that path and say c'mon princess lets go! He's never even sent me a card for my birthday or for Christmas either. I ceased to exist for him the day he went away. After the initial realisation and the terrible hurt at what he'd done, Gran said I turned into a thorough little monster! My mother ignored and either overlooked or excused my atrocious behaviour because she *knew*, and she understood, only too well that it was because of how much I hurt and how badly betrayed I felt. My mother was deeply hurt as well, he was the only man she'd ever loved, but she just had to get on with life, and she did the best she could by my two older brothers and me. She worked long hours in a big textile mill for little pay, then she'd come home to us and work on the farm some more. After it got too dark, or in wintertime when it was too cold to work outside, I remember hearing her sewing machine whirring hour after hour on the other side of my bedroom wall. She'd take in dressmaking, repairs and alterations, anything to earn a little bit of extra money for us, but even so, no matter how hard she tried, with three growing kids, the bills and the money she earned, well it never quite matched up. If it wasn't for Grandma and Grandpa helping out and taking us in, I don't know what would have become of us. But as Grandpa always said – when you love someone, you do whatever needs doing to get through, and when it's too hard to keep going, you grit your teeth, roll up your sleeves, and you work *twice* as hard and do it *twice* as good. That was my mother, right there. She showed everyone she wasn't some poor whimpering woman. She was a mother who needed to raise her kid's, and to raise them right. The town we lived in was such a small place, well you saw it, one where everyone knew whenever you sneezed. She thought no-one knew how often, or how hard she cried, all alone and locked in the bathroom, with her face pushed into a towel to muffle the sounds. But I heard her; I knew how badly she was hurting, because I was still hurting too. Never, never, did she let anyone know that while she made sure we all ate fairly well, she herself often stayed hungry, and she wouldn't take charity, oh no, not even from her own parents. When we did finally move into grandma's house it was so there'd be someone to look after us while she worked extra time. She told Grandma she wouldn't give them -the gossips- the satisfaction, we might not have had two brass coins to rub together, but Mama always maintained her dignity and her self-respect. Our personal hygiene, much to my brothers' loathing, was right up there at the top of her list, our home and our clothes were kept spotlessly clean. I don't suppose you've ever heard her favourite expression –hard soap and elbow grease is a marriage made in heaven? Well believe me, she scrubbed everything to within a skins thickness of its life! *Spotless* was the war cry around our house, as if it would bring her husband back. Do you know something Tyler? I didn't understand until long years later what she meant, but can still remember my mother warning me over and over again, to never give my trust too easily, that only amongst women, can your best, and most trusted girlfriend, be your greatest betrayer as well. That's how I found out my father had run off with her best friend, and Tyler, they'd been best friends since their first day at kindergarten too. So, suffering in silence and scrubbing the paint off the walls and varnish off the floors was her way of dealing with her pain. Eventually she did remarry but it was one of those out of the frying pan and into the fire sorts of things. Although she cared for him she wouldn't, or couldn't, allow herself to love him, but as luck would have it, it wasn't until *after* they were married that she found out he couldn't stand her kids, us! Oh joy, oh joy. But in spite of him and his penny-pinching ways, we all grew up and made good careers for ourselves. Both of my brothers are in good jobs that have great potential, and they've done really well - in spite of him. I say that because he wouldn't spare one single penny for our education, we all had to work our own way through college. I took a position as an assistant teacher at a special needs centre helping to co-ordinate lessons. I really enjoyed working with all of those so called -*handicapped*- children, so much so, that I redirected my teaching specialty from math's and English for middle school, to education of Special Needs Children, and, well it was my dream to open my own centre. Do you know Tyler, most of those kids are just *so smart*, and by that, I mean they're really, *really* intelligent kids. They have all the right beans, in all the right places up there, it's just the grinder that lets them down, or works a little differently. But by golly, they can really humble you *and* bring you back to earth with a thump. They show you every single day, and in so many ways, *exactly* what hard work *really* means!" Sara stopped, sudden tears sprang to her eyes when she thought about her favourite pupils, but she gave herself a little shake and carried on.

"Mama was always so proud that each one of her kids had made really good career choices, and that we were well on the way to making nice, financially comfortable, futures. Then her new husband got sick and died, and no one knew until his lawyer's contacted mum that he'd had a pretty hefty life insurance, *and* an enormous bank balance! which meant mum was finally free of all her financial commitments and had a *very* satisfying balance in her *own* shiny new bank account, enough and much more to allow for an early, carefree retirement. Thankfully we'd grown up and we were all well on the way to making our own lives successful. Her mirror told her that she'd aged well, and was still a very good-looking woman. Through it all, our father's desertion, a miserable marriage, and then becoming a widow, she's never lost her fabulous sense of humour, well, okay yes, I'll admit, it *was* dormant for a quite a while there, but she picked herself up again. She was still young enough to go out and have a good time, to enjoy herself and have some fun back in her life as a financially independent single woman. She thrived on being useful, and she thoroughly and genuinely enjoyed helping others. Actually, she'd hitched up the old horse trailer to carry back the supplies, she had long shopping lists from almost every farm in our little village. She'd driven into the main town with Gran and five friends to see a new movie after they'd placed the orders for everyone's provisions; she was reasonably sure that there was a good chance that at some point, with the way the weather was changing so fast, that the only road out might be flooded. Their plan was to see the movie while the warehouse filled their orders and packed the trailer, and then they'd head back to Shady Haven. But it all took too long, there had been another big storm further up the highway so they'd all been trapped in the town by rising flood waters. The water rose so quickly that it was impossible for them to get out and drive back home – especially as she was pulling that heavy old horse trailer. Then you came to help us, and the rest has sort of become our history, as well as being our new beginning, hasn't it?"

Just as I'd asked the question, we heard a really loud commotion coming from the direction of the caves. We both turned and sprinted back toward the quarters to find ourselves confronted by a sight, that well, it's one that *I* know for sure I'll *never* forget! It would seem that a couple of curious little go-bits had invaded the stores area. And oh, wow what a sight we saw! Mrs B and Mrs Armstrong were both trying to catch them; ah it looked hilarious! There they were, the two cooks had somehow managed to corner the animals, they were flapping their aprons and waving wet dishcloths around in the air –probably in an effort to frighten them- but *they'd also cornered themselves!* They weren't able move out to get some help, because if they did the go-bits would just run away again, so our poor ladies were every bit as trapped as those animals were. Mrs B didn't know what to do next, and Mrs Armstrong had tears of laughter running down her cheeks, and between giggles she was shouting at them "hey you! Yes you! You're our lunch, and *you* my hairy little friend" she pointed at one of the fat little animals, "*you* are cordially invited to be served up as dinner! Oh lordy, just look at you, you're so plump and juicy and, oh, I am just so heartily sick of eating rabbit."

 To begin with I thought there were only the two animals we could see in there, but Tyler –with his height advantage, counted seven! Because they're so quick, and can run up seemingly sheer walls, the only times we ever had go-bit meat has been when one of the men has managed to snare one, so this was a real treat alright. It's turned out that they *are* a quite small breed of goats, which will certainly solve quite a few dietary problems that might otherwise have arisen in the future as well, but *only* if we can manage to domesticate some of them, and to do that – well we have to catch some of the little blighters first! The goats, like our sheep, will give us milk (that will be much more plentiful and far more palatable than sheep's milk) plus yoghurt, cheese and meat, as well as leather and mohair! This was going to be *such* a huge bonus for everyone in the future, but right now we're all too busy laughing and we've gathered outside the kitchen shouting instructions and advising the women on how best to catch the little creatures! All the while we got a running commentary from young Lawrence who'd climbed up to a ledge on the wall to get a better look. Three of Tyler's men raced around looking for something they can make a temporary holding pen from so they can contain the animals, but whether we caught and penned them outright, or whether they eventually fell down from exhaustion didn't really matter too much at all, only one thing was an absolute certainty – those animals were going into a pen, and by hook or by crook, they were going into one *today*!

Nathan was the one to save the situation for us all, he managed to find some rope and make a lasso then the clever fellow systematically lassoed them, one-sneaky go-bit at a time, and dropped it into the pen that Fabs, Michael and Tyler had quickly put together using some canvas, rope, a huge cargo net, a dozen or more tent pegs and our now upside-down dining table. No one will have a problem with not having a table for a while, the important thing is – it's worked! We actually have some new animals that we'll start to tame and then breed from, what an absolutely terrific start to our Eden Day-One!

Everyone saw a completely different side of our cooks today, they've been laughing and joking around with everyone, for the first time in absolutely ages, but more importantly, they were both *genuinely* happy ladies this morning. They were also, so worn out from the morning's excitement and exertions that they couldn't function properly. Well, that meant that this morning's breakfast was going to be a bit of a help yourself affair, and made up of whatever we could find for ourselves in the kitchen or orchard. We had to balance our plates on our knees -due to the sudden, but temporary, repurposing of the dining table. Best of all though, Mrs B and Mrs Armstrong both had something to concentrate on, something that took their minds off their husbands' leaving, as well as the many revolting, cruel, and terribly hurtful words that they'd said before they left, (not to mention the big purple bruises they'd both received parting gifts) and thank goodness for that too, because they really *don't* cook anywhere near as well when they're angry or unhappy. All in all, it was turning out to be a perfect morning!

Little Anna looked really cute at breakfast time, Amelia had made an ingenious high chair for her by tying a small wooden box to a chair seat and putting her own small sleeping cushion on top, then she slipped a tee shirt over Anna's head *and* the back of the chair – making it into a harness! Amelia cut two holes for the little ones arms and sat beside her so she was able to help her with her breakfast and milk. The little scallywag surprised us all though, when between bites of corn cake and her cold scrambled egg, she leaned over to touch Amelia's cheek, and in her squeaky baby voice said very clearly – "you Annie mum-mum Meewi?" We'd all been taking care of her because, at a bit less than two years old we thought she wouldn't understand what had happened "Mum-mum gonned way" she said with her big blue eyes opened wide and holding her little hands out in front of her with fingers spread out like fat pink starfish. Then she wrapped her baby arms around Amelia's neck and looked up at her saying with a big smile "*Meewi* Annie mum-mum!" Amelia was so totally delighted, but the rest of us were shocked to our core. Out of the mouths of babes.... that *really* brought us all up short, *and* left us feeling more than a little ashamed of ourselves, mainly for being so relieved by the lack of tension and bad feelings, but not for one moment were we even appreciating the fact that the youngest ones would be feeling absolutely lost today because of the dramatic change our group had undergone in the last twenty four hours, being here without the other the kids and one or two of the more decent people from the Upper Valley group for the comfort and security they'd drawn from each other over these many months we were all together. The next thing we knew, young Rosie had started crying! She jumped down from the chair spilling her breakfast all over herself and then she raced across the grass heading toward the pond with Sienna and Nikki hot on her heels, at the same time young Shannon started to bawl! Michael was startled enough to say – "Jeez it's contagious!" But Shannon was really sobbing hard now. "W-what ab-bout m-me? I haven't g-got m-my m-mummy too! She for-g-gotted 'bout me. S-she said s-she'd be coming to g-get me, s-she *p-promised me* she would. Now s-she'll n-never come ffor m-me, she's left m-me too, just like my d-daddy did, I'm trouble n I'm a bad, b-bad boy." Big brawny Liam just dropped what he was eating and swept the little boy up into his arms and held him close, telling him that he was wrong, that his mother *did* love him, that she loved him more than anything in the whole world. The only reason she *didn't* come for him was because we all got lost in the storms. The big man walked away from the group with tears cascading down his face, still fiercely hugging and talking to the little boy, doing his very best to reassure him. Patrick looked up at me, his worried eyes brimming with tears, and in a voice filled with fear and tears he just said "Sara?" I squatted in front of him put my arms around him and smiled saying "hey, we're doing okay together aren't we Paddy?" Well do you know something - that was *the best*, squeezy, full of love, little boy cuddle anyone's ever had. I also got my very first soggy wet nose kiss on the ear this morning too. We all looked around at each other and shook our heads. I was thinking wow, what a mess *this* is. Here we are, living in caves, out in the middle of goodness only knows where, we've got hot showers and flushing toilets, yet we've somehow managed to overlook the very serious emotional needs of some extremely mixed up, confused, and very scared little kids, jeez, how did we ever get our priorities so wrong?

Jessica, looking every bit as awkward and confused as the rest of us felt, asked – "err, what just happened? Sheez, a minute ago they all seemed so, um, well, so *normal!*"

The morning had started perfectly before breakfast, next we had that really funny-wobbly patch with the go-bits, but after that, well jeez, breakfast turned out to be a real fiasco, and, by the looks of things the outlook for the afternoon's promising to be more of the same. However, I do firmly believe that destiny is a big part of life, and life has a funny way of dealing with people by giving them, not necessarily what they *want,* or even what they might have had *planned,* but they most definitely get what they *need.* Tyler asked me and some of the girls to take all the children over to the pool, "and maybe see if you can get Mrs Armstrong to fix up a picnic or something will you? I can't have any of those kids here when I'm talking about them, they're too darned intimidating. I'll most likely be calling some of you back as I need you alright? I think, no, no never mind... Let's play this one by ear Sara, if that's okay?"

Liam was the first person called to the *table*. An empty firewood crate had been dragged over and turned upside down. He approached Tyler and Mrs B looking like a lamb headed to the slaughter. "Liam, what was that all about this morning? I think we need to talk some, you and I, young Shannon touched on a really raw nerve in you, didn't he?" "Ahh jeez Sarge. Well, it's not something I'm real comfortable talking about, Sir." "Ah for Pete's sake man, you can cut out that military crap for starters Liam! We've been friends long enough, fought side by side, fallen down drunk together regularly enough, and trained and drilled until we can't think straight much too often to be *anything* other than completely straight with each other, don't you think?" "Well yeah, okay, I reckon so Tyler... yeah, you're right, listen man, hey look I'm sorry okay, and I'm sorry about this morning too but- well, it's just that, hell that little boy was, well he is *me* twenty years ago, and I guess it really got to me. Hey jeez, my reaction took *me* by surprise too ya know!? I thought I'd gotten past it all years ago, but apparently, well obviously it still stings. Anyway, seeing as we're talking about the subject, I have been wondering if I could, you know, um, sort of, well you know, maybe take the kid on, and kinda ahh you know, be his um, dad, his uncle, or his big brother or something. That is if no-one better comes forward for the job naturally. You know -I didn't want, well anyhow I never thought I um, you know, never wanted kids, but that little boy, wow, he kinda hit me right where it hurts, and I believe I can, well I probably understand what he needs, more'n some regular folks would." Tyler looked at his friend with a whole new respect, it's not often a man will *ask* to take on the role of single parent, especially to an emotionally troubled child, but this actually might just be a way to help fix *two* little boys, one of which is six feet four inches tall and weighs in at around two hundred and forty pounds of solid muscle, and the other is about twenty-five pounds -maybe, knee high and five or six years old! "Leave it with me for few hours and I'll see what can be worked out, that okay with you? Go on, go over to the sparring ring and work out for a while with Mike Bush or another one – oh hell take on *all* of the guys, let off some steam, it'll do you good, but please Liam, just don't break anyone will ya huh! Go on I'll see you soon." With that Liam went off to find himself a sparring partner, suddenly it was a terrific idea! Tyler went in search of a little boy. He didn't have to go far; he could hear the laughter. Shannon was with the other children and the girls over by the pond playing chasings or tips, some game where one runs and the others try and catch him/her. When Tyler found me I was leaning over with my elbows hanging across my knees panting; my hair had come loose from the plaits and was all over the place –not so very unusual for me. "Hey there lady! Can I talk to you for a minute or ten please? No, not here though, I want to talk about the little feller over there." While we wandered a little way away, I took the opportunity to re-braid and tie my hair back. Tyler told me about his conversation with Liam. "Well hey, that's great Tyler! I think they would make a *marvellous* team! Shannon was saying that Liam told him he knew exactly what it was like, and how much it hurt in your throat and down deep in your belly, to be left behind. So now, if Liam was telling *you* that he said *he* understands why *Shannon* is so upset, and hurt and angry, and Shannon was asking *me* if he could stay with *Liam*, like Patrick stays with me. You know what? They might actually be able to help each other get over their problems or hang ups, what do you think Master Gunnery Sergeant Wade Tyler?" And Tyler's reply? "I think I want to talk with Shannon, that's what *I* think – little miss smarty schoolmarm! I'll let you know how it goes Sara, I'll take it from here okay? Oh, and by the way, thanks."

Tyler and Shannon walked around until they found a good place to sit and chat. "Shannon, you *do* know what I want to talk to you about, don't you? About this morning because you were really upset and pretty angry too yeah, and sergeant Murphy told you he knew exactly how you felt?" The little boy looked really confused and asked "who's sergeant Murphy? Oh, d'you mean Liam? Yeah, he's real nice, he told me the exact same thing happened to him when he was ten, did *you* know that sir? Well, he said *his* mother was supposed to get him from the bus station at Christmas, only she never came, so he had to go into a home specially for unbrandended kids. He's real nice to me Mr. Tyler, an' you know how you was saying before that we can choose who we'd like to stay with? Well, if Liam says it's okay, and if I'm really, *really good,* and if I do all my garden chores and work real hard on my school work, and if I wash myself really good, do you think he'd mind having me around? I wouldn't make no trouble for him or nuffink I promise, and he'd be sort of, well he'd kinda be my dad or something, do you think he'd do that? I've never had a dad before" Tyler couldn't answer for a minute because he knew that if he opened his mouth, he'd just start bawling. This little boy wanted so badly to have someone of his own, and to *be* special to someone, so much so, that Tyler simply picked him up, said "I'll tell you what I'll do better than that" and carried him on his shoulders through the caves, all the way across to the sparring ring behind the trees. The man and boy stood watching Liam and Mike while they sparred, it wasn't too long before they took a break, and when they did Tyler called out to Liam to come over for a minute. Liam was towelling the sweat off when he saw Shannon up on his sergeants' shoulders. "Hey hiya Shannon! I see you couldn't catch a cab, so you had to hitch a ride on a donkey!" "Enough with the donkey stuff okay *sergeant*" said Tyler with mock severity. He lifted the boy back down to the ground and addressed both man and boy together. "Okay men, now the way I see it, it's like this, Sergeant Murphy, you need a nursemaid to look after you, and Shannon here, for some strange reason seems to like the look of you, yeah, goodness only knows why, it's got me beat too. But I think you two men should try to work something out together, what do you say?" Judging by the twin megawatt smiles it was already a done deal! So, Shannon swapped a donkey for an ass and rode off into the sunset –well maybe not quite sunset-but he *was* a very happy little boy. Tyler said "I'm heading back to the pond now because I've got some

serious business to attend to, are you two coming?" They looked askance at each other then their two heads nodded together. Tyler spoke over his shoulder as he walked away… "I'll see you over there then."
He was half way to the pond and I was running over to meet him, smiling like I was doing some crazy toothpaste commercial. "Guess what! Guess what! Rosie asked Jessica if she could live with her! And you'll *never guess* what Jess said, you'll never guess, not in a million years!" "Ummm" said Tyler thoughtfully rubbing his chin, "I bet she… I bet cried and said yes?" "Brute! Oh you! Who told you about it?" "Poor Sara!" He laughed, "You look like a pricked balloon!" Tyler did a quick calculation and said "Well that only leaves Lawrence doesn't it?" "Nope, you're too late, Corporal Sanchez stepped up to that plate while you were over with Liam and Shannon, it seems that those two sorted it all out between themselves; they didn't need anyone's help working it out either. Well Lawrence is what? Twelve or thirteen? … And Sanchez is one of about ten kids, so he should be able to manage okay." Tyler said, "I'll talk to him later on today. Right *now* though, I have some serious work to do young lady! Give me a kiss and I won't tell anyone you snore!" "I DO NOT SNORE!" I was scowling at him, so he said "Yeah, but they don't know that do they!" "Oooh, I was right about you all along Master Gunnery Sargent W. Tyler! You're a mean cruel porky… hahaha! No don't you dare! *Don't* tickle me STOP IT!! GET, go on, shoo get away from here, go and do some work!"
Tyler walked back to the dining area feeling like he'd won a million dollars with a tuppenny ticket. Once

there he immediately called our first New Eden Family Meeting. With the ~~good~~ fantastic news about the children having been placed with their chosen parent, everyone could relax and start helping them on their journey through the healing process. "Although it isn't an immediate problem, it *will* prove to be *very* important in the future. All our records, starting from the new beginning, must state very clearly that each of the children named, have been adopted, therefore they are unrelated by blood ties to any person in Eden at this time." There was a lot of discussion on this, along with many other, new, and diverse matters, things that would be of concern to the entire population of Eden in the years ahead. Some of the topics raised were put aside for the moment, as being important, though not requiring immediate attention, however those topics have been noted and will therefore be prepared, and ready to be listed at a future meeting.

Later on in the day, Mark produced quite a lengthy, and carefully detailed list of suggested changes, many of them would be requiring a full discussion and explanation before any could be implemented. He'd used the blank side of an unused page from the thick passenger manifest pad. Tyler was really surprised, he laughed and told Mark he'd missed his true calling when he joined the marines – he would have made an excellent secretary! However, the voting process couldn't be started immediately, actually it would have to wait several hours, because there were still loads of regular chores waiting to be done in the gardens and animal pens, and between catching and caging the go-bits in the kitchen, then the children having serious breakdowns at breakfast time, our schedules had been turned on their heads this morning anyway. Delaying the voting wasn't such a bad idea either because everyone would want time to get the details so they'd understand, and be absolutely certain of the issues they'd be voting on. So, after the chores were finished, the tools cleaned and returned to the correct place, everyone could concentrate on the next item of the day –voting for open and accurate record keeping- was able to receive their full attention. Many minds considered the seriousness of the underlying voting topic, understanding that while it wouldn't be important for the *current* population, it would certainly be important in the years to come. It also served to remind us that this place we have called Eden is now our home, our permanent home.

Certainly, each child and their new parent would be thought of as family… father and son, mother and daughter etc. however they all agreed that the records should and *must* show that while the bonds are strong, there are no actual or physical blood ties. It wasn't an issue now, but who knew what the future might hold? Tyler started reading from the list headed *New Families* handed to him by Staff Sergeant/ Secretary Mark Balas.

The inhabitants of New Eden, but more specifically the marines, were quite taken aback, though very pleasantly surprised, and *very* thankful for the many and varied changes in their Commanding Officer.

Tyler had, in the last few weeks transformed so totally and so completely, from being their meticulous and unbending CO, an officer who was notoriously severe, and equally unyielding -but always fair- in his judgments. Tyler was a man who'd been perceived as being devoid of anything resembling normal, human emotions, he'd been a demanding, and inflexible disciplinarian, a man who having set his standard, had neither smiled, nor permitted himself the luxury of relaxing, physically *or* mentally, for months on end, and his men knew only too well, that Tyler would accept nothing less from any man under his command. A few of his men were waiting for the hammer to drop... and hoped to God it didn't, because from such a rigidly disciplined, hard-nosed authoritarian, their CO had apparently changed in so many incredible, and pretty unbelievable ways. Make no mistake, he still expected them to maintain their customary high standards in all areas, and they knew to a man that there'd be hell to pay for anyone who cast the marines in anything less than a shining light. Somehow though he'd become a surprisingly gentle, a sensitive, considerate, and a truly caring man. This was a massive transformation from the man who *never* laughed, joked, or let his hair down at all, (apart from their occasional drunken sorties) he's now become a man who laughs and jokes around *all* the time, and he never seemed to stop smiling. "There's one helluva lot to be said for getting involved with a good woman!" commented Sanchez.

Tyler's eyes became quite moist as he read from the list Mark handed over to him....

"Mick Costa is our eldest member, and as from today he will be considered to be the Patriarch, or the grandfather, to our whole Eden family, by the way folks, if you'd like to, he *can* be addressed as

Grandpa. He has confided to me that he is deeply touched, and mighty delighted to accept this honorary roll. Mick has been a lonely man for many years and has been entirely without family as tragically he lost his wife and young family some thirty years ago in a motor vehicle accident, so he understands, actually, he knows only *too* well, and can empathize with *your* feelings, he understands, because he's lived with the pain of losing his own loved ones for far too many, as he described them, lonely and empty years." Mr Costa stood up and addressed the family. "I just don't have enough words to thank you, every one of you, for this incomparable honour. My life has, for thirty-one long years, been a never-ending chain of empty days, with nights and holidays to be gotten through, but *now*, well now, and with my immense gratitude to every one of you, I have possibly the most wonderful reasons to wake up in the mornings" he spoke quietly and with great humility, and I watched as a single tear trickled slowly down each of his weathered cheeks.

"Next is Millie Armstrong, one of our amazing cooks, she's of the same generation as Mick, and she also made the decision to stay here with us, forgoing all the many and varied delights of the outside world. Millie has, for twenty-six years performed her duty as hostess for her husband. His career as a diplomat had them traveling and living in Zones all over the world … because of this she says she was never blessed with making her own family. It has been suggested that she should be New Eden's Matriarch or Grandmother Figure (Grandma, Granny or Gran) and like Mick, she's absolutely delighted. Mrs Beatrice Beatty, is a wizard in any kitchen I imagine, she's the mother of seven, and a grandmother of sixteen, all of whom live in various outer Zones or overseas. If you've been wondering how she manages to put up such delicious meals every day, she spent six years as head chef at an exclusive boarding college for young gentlemen, and for the last ten years as the evening chef at a four-star restaurant in Van Langdon Dale. She tells me that she's simply a woman who loves to cook, that cooking, and creating fabulous recipes has always been her passion, therefore she is most wholeheartedly welcomed as our very experienced head chef, I don't believe a *simple cook* could possibly achieve the superb meals our own Mrs Beatty seems to find so effortless. Mrs B has also chosen to stay here, and desires nothing more than to put all the bad memories, and unpleasant emotions far behind her as well, so she's to be Ms B, Aunty Bea, or just Aunty, to all of us from now on." After another few minor points of business had been discussed, Grandpa started with talks centring on all of our newly formed couples. He has suggested that since we may never leave this wonderful valley, we should start by establishing some relationship formats for the future. "As we don't have all the mechanisms formerly required by law, we'll be able to adapt what we *do* have to create customs unique to Eden, and in a style that gives deeper meaning to a lifelong commitment." He paused to look around to see if anyone wanted to comment. "We have sixteen young, healthy people, right at this moment who seem to... well let's just say they find each other *rather attractive*" this incurred much giggling, blushing and embarrassed shuffling of feet "we also have *a Pastor*. Now, while in the outside world this might not be deemed the *ideal* state of affairs, it's what we have now, and what we will have moving onward into the foreseeable future. Also, as was discussed at last night's celebration, we have every possible skill required to, not merely survive here, we can really flourish *and* multiply!! Now, in the case of marriages, births and deaths, well it is absolutely crucial that they are recorded accurately, and lineages drawn for future generations, in the event we're to remain here in New Eden." He sat back down and looked around at the rapt attention on the faces of his young audience. "One thing that absolutely *must* be avoided - *at all costs* in the future, is inbreeding. But I'm getting too far ahead of what's important right now, although I am quite sure you can, as highly intelligent people, understand and appreciate my point. Another thing we *cannot,* and *must not encourage,* are any *indiscriminate liaisons* of a sexual nature, clean, clear bloodlines, will be *absolutely imperative* for our future generations, hahahah! I apologise folks, because there I go again getting way, way, ahead of myself! My apologies, I really intended to concentrate on what's important *today,* but my brain can overrule my mouth at times! Alright then, Dr Hank Dawson, also being a Pastor, will perform our marriage ceremonies, and all marriages, will be *as* binding, if not *more so,* as any other marriage, at any other time in history. Does that seem reasonable to all of you? Do you all understand *why,* and do you agree? Because *now* is the time to come forward and give us your opinion. We are making some of our laws here today, and they *will* have an effect on every one of you, sooner or later. We are trying to be as reasonable, and as uncomplicated as is possible, but unlike the lawmakers in our previous life, we actually *want* and we *need* your input as well."

I couldn't help but think to myself that Tyler had chosen well with Mr Costa, and he was, as always, trying to be totally fair and reasonable to everyone, in every possible situation. He's becoming such an amazing, even an awe-inspiring man.

Mr. Costa (Grandpa) continued with his very first communication to the residents of Eden...

"I have given this a great deal of thought in the time we've spent together, both here and in the first area, and I would like to take this opportunity, unless of course someone has an objection, to address all of the young, single, and marriageable members if I may?"

A common nod was all he required to continue.

"Here in New Eden, for our young people, it will be vital, that you are very careful when you choose a mate. While in the world outside, the divorce rate has risen over recent years to astronomical numbers, I think more couples were divorcing that being married! Therefore, I am suggesting to you all that divorce should be against our laws, *once a living child is produced.* The necessity for this law should be glaringly obvious to each of you, certainly without me having to spell it out. While our New Eden, even with all its wondrous natural beauty, and the almost endless bounty, it has one major, and insurmountable flaw. It lacks human numbers. This lack means Eden doesn't give any of you the luxury of having an infinite array, or an inexhaustible supply of eligible partners. We certainly don't want the next generations to be unknowingly reproducing with a brother, a sister, or a first cousin, right? Therefore, selective pairing is the only way to prevent such a distressing, and an unnecessarily complicated situation from arising for anyone right from the start. That being said, the young citizens of Eden will always have to choose a life companion very carefully, and to agree to be guided by the elders. It goes without saying that the elders haven't reached their advanced years without observing an awful lot, and learning a few things about love, lust and human nature along the way… those two emotions are often, far *too* often, confused.

Counselling and marriage guidance will be available to everyone, for the rest of your lives together. Am I being clear enough? Am I being understood? Please feel free, you can either speak to me now, or later on in private, if that's preferable to you, if you *don't* agree with any of these concepts, let us know, because around these parts, we're all *for* discussions and hearing the ideas of one another okay? You never know, you may ask about, or recommend something we haven't even thought about!" A soft ripple of laughter fluttered around the listeners.

There were nods and mumbled agreements from everyone there.

Anna turned her cheeky little face up to look at Amelia and gave her a great big smile and squeaked out gleefully "Meewi mum-mum!"

While Amelia and I took the toddlers, Tyler gathered up the children and took them down to the so far, half-finished playground that Liam and Rawlins had been building for them, to explain to them that since it was possible, even probable, that we might need to be living here in Eden, for a very, very long time, or at least until anyone could travel with complete safety outside of these walls, and not have to worry about being caught out by the storms. He explained –using language they could understand - that we have to develop our very own, brand-new community. "We've all had a few very rough days around here, haven't we? I honestly want all of you to know in here" he touched his heart "and above all, to understand in here" he tapped his head "that The Upper Valley people who decided to leave, left here because they didn't like being here anymore. But... and this is *so* important for you all to remember, no-one here *forced* them out or said they *had* to go, but as much as we tried, we couldn't stop them from leaving here either. Now do you all understand that?" Little heads nodded with wide eyed surprise that they were being spoken to, and treated like, they were real grown-ups. "In fact, I tried, I tried *really, really,* hard to get them to stay here, so we could start our village family all together, right here in this terrific place where we can all have great fun, but most important of all, Eden is our *safe place*. Even though I tried my best to get them to stay, for some crazy reason they thought it would be better for them, if they left and went back home. While we're talking about this, you all deserve to know the real truth; they'll never get back home again, because another storm came when they were too far away to turn around and run back inside again, they were blown away almost as soon as they left us. That's why we must *never, never, ever,* try to leave this place, we're safe here, we're together, and with all of you helping us, and with all of us helping you, it will grow to become a really special home. We are *one big family here,* some of you have lost the families you've grown up with, and so have we, and, well you should all know that everyone here wants you to be loved, every bit as much as you deserve to be, we're all your cousins, your aunts and your uncles now, and we really *do* understand how you feel, because every person here, every adult and every child, has lost *their* family too. A little birdy told me you have all chosen a wonderful and really special person to be your parent, or your friend, but I'd like you to know, and feel, that we're *all* one big very special family who'll live, work and play together too. We'll help you to get through any problems, any worries or sadness you might have, either now, or at *any* time at all – even when you're big like me! If you get sad, or angry, or unhappy, come and talk to us, any of us, because we will work things out together and help to make it better for you. There will be many, *many* times when we're going to be needing *your* help too!"

Tyler wanted the children to know they not only deserved to be, but were needed to be a big part of this new family, one that would help them to develop and grow up as healthy, strong and as confident as they were meant to be.

"Okay, does anyone have any questions?"

The next thing we knew Patrick was in mid-air launching himself furiously at Tyler, he was punching and kicking him saying "I want Sara for *MINE!*

Annie can have Amelia but Sara is *MY* special mummy" tears of anger and naked fear blurred his eyes and rolled down his cheeks in rivers "Now you *go way* and get your *own mummy Tyler!*" Tyler reached out and held the child, still kicking and screaming, at arm's length. He waited until Patrick seemed to have run out of steam a little bit. I swear, that man has become patience itself. He sat the squirming, still angry little boy on his knees, and held him there while he told him he didn't *want* Sara to be *his* mummy, no, not at all. But Patrick wasn't listening, instead he'd started drumming his heels against Tyler's shin bones and yelling "Sara mummy is *mine not yours, you go away*!" "Patrick! Ah come on Paddy, take it easy now son, no-one is trying to take you away from your Sara mummy at all!" He told the suddenly subdued little boy that he was a grown-up man now, he'd had his own very special mummy, so he didn't need another mummy now; but he *did* want Sara to be his wife. "Do you know what that means for *you* champ?" Tyler leaned down and whispered something into Patrick's ear, but Patrick refused to even *look* at Tyler, he kept his face down, determinedly focusing on the grass, he shook his head slowly, and then, as the meaning of what Tyler had whispered in his ear dawned on him, he quickly looked up at Tyler, his eyes were as big and as round as dinner plates in his sweet little red tearstained face, the next moment he was smiling and nodding so fast I thought his head would bobble right off his shoulders! "WOW! Hey everybody - I'm gonna have a mummy *and* a *daddy too!*" He jumped down from Tyler's knees, and streaked across the playground straight at me, yelling out at the top of his voice "hey, Sara! Sara! Sara! Did you know I'm gonna be getting a daddy *too*?" Tyler looked over at us and gave us one of his newly mastered big wide smiles.

All of a sudden, the happy time was shattered by a piercing, eardrum splitting three-part whistle, followed by loud, very urgent sounding shout from Rivers that snapped Tyler instantly onto high alert. I heard him yell something about Bush and Sanchez. But before I, or anyone else, could even blink, Tyler had, in a single motion, turned away from us and was flying across the wide expanse of ground and into the colonnade that connected the two valleys. His long muscular legs, were pumping like pistons, covering the distance like an Olympic Athlete; he grabbed hold of the rope ladder and swung himself up, climbing up hand over hand then expertly swung himself up onto the ledge. I wondered how he even managed to do that with his damaged hands – but that's my action-man Tyler. The echoes of their voices had barely died away when Tyler met them coming out into the sunlight carrying something. I'd followed Tyler, although at a somewhat reduced pace, and by the time I'd climbed the ladder, there were perhaps fifteen other people standing around up there as well. Bush was cradling the limp, and terribly bloodied body of Alisha, she was one of the youngest children who'd been taken out by the Upper Valley families. How, but who? *How* did she get back here? Was she still alive? Where was her mother? Her Father? My mind was galloping now, were there any others still alive out there? Where did they find her? Tyler turned to Rawlins and told him to "*go*, run and find Hank, get him over here, this child really needs a doctor *now!*" However, Hank was already there, he'd been heading to his room to have a rest when he heard all the commotion, and because it sounded urgent, he'd instinctively grabbed his medical bag and followed the voices; right now, that bag was open on the floor beside him and he was rummaging through it. Once he'd given her a quick examination, he asked that she be carried into a room that had good light – mine was the closest. Although she was in shock, Alisha was semi-awake and reacting to the pain wherever Hank touched her. The poor kid appeared to be pretty badly knocked about, there were deep wounds and nasty looking grazes covering her little body, and her hair was one big tangled mess, full of sticks, mud and a *lot* of dried blood as well. The poor little girl had one puffy black eye, and there was dried blood around her nose, her mouth, and fresh blood was smeared across her cheeks as well as her chin and poor little mouth, her lips were so badly swollen that her bottom lip had split wide open in the centre, she also had a long, very deep looking, jagged cut along her jawbone. She'd been wearing a light cotton shift when they left but that was gone now and goodness knows it wouldn't have afforded her any protection, but being naked had left her bare skin exposed to the icy cold night-time wind out in the passageway… Hank asked for everyone except Tyler, Bush and Ms Beatty to leave. I left too, but I decided to wait around the corner in case another pair of hands were needed. Ms B stuck her head out and saw me, "oh thank goodness you're still here Sara, I need to wash the child to get rid of all the dried blood and dirt so that

Hank can see what he's working with. Fetch the kettle of warm boiled water from the fireplace, oh and bring a small basin with plenty of clean cloths from the recycle box in the store room, then bring it all back here" I brought everything she'd asked for and –oh Sweet Mother of Mercy, that poor, poor little girl. Apart from all the dozens of cuts, bruises and scrapes I'd already seen, she had a stick, about as thick as an adult's index finger, deeply embedded into the muscle on back of her thigh. Tyler and Bush both came out together about half an hour or so later, and they were both looking pretty green and sick themselves. Mrs Armstrong made both men drink some lemon and barley tea and asked worriedly if young Alisha would be alright? Just as she was about to get an answer, Ms B and Hank came down to join us at the table, he said quietly that "she's sleeping now." Ms B told us that "Hank had removed a horrifically big piece of wood, and given her a shot, he'd cleaned out and stitched up the worst of her cuts and bandaged everything else. Hank was saying she'd been very fortunate, with it being so cold out there and getting soaked by rain, the blood flow had been restricted, so she does in fact look a lot worse than she actually is –well physically anyway, but mentally? well *that* I'm afraid, is going to be a whole different matter" Hank said to no-one in particular. "We won't know what happened until she wakes up, but even then, she might not remember, or, what's more likely, she'll remember but won't want to talk about it. The important thing is she's alive, and will stay that way, she's safe, and she's warm now, and for the moment that's what really matters most."

Tyler sent every man out to thoroughly search the whole entrance area to see if there were any other survivors, but as expected, they came back empty handed. It took two full days for Alisha to wake up, and another day and a half before she spoke a word to anyone about what had happened to her, or how she actually came to *be* in the first valley. Tyler and Hank sat with her and just kept a quiet, but unobtrusive conversation going on around her, they didn't speak directly *to* her at all. Hank said later "this worked mainly because she was fully aware of her surroundings, and if she *wanted* to, she *could* be part of the conversation, without needing to, or feeling pushed to actively participate. When *she* was good and ready, she would speak quite freely" which turned out to be exactly what she did do. Tyler related her story to us later, while she was sleeping again.

The group of marines were waiting very anxiously at the tables to hear the report on the child's condition. That was Hank's area of expertise, so Tyler left him there to make the necessary explanations, and to answer a dozen questions from the concerned men.

To Tyler's utter dismay, he saw that Bush was heading straight toward him across the compound, he looked around but knew there was no way he could avoid him. Tyler knew only too well from far too many past experiences to mention, that Bush could, and unfortunately would, talk your ears off about absolutely nothing at all. Whenever he opened his mouth, words just poured out. Since there was no way of escaping him, he'd just have to listen to whatever it was that the Private was bursting to say. Bush is just a goofy, big-hearted, good-natured farm boy. The man could barely read or write, but he was sure to find something strange, in fact he could be *guaranteed* to find something *truly amazing or mysterious* - in a boiled egg! What will it be *this time?* Tyler wondered.

Bush moved awkwardly, although that was certainly nothing new, Bush *always* moved awkwardly, the man was like a huge solid block of concrete in motion, and right at this moment he was lumbering up the stone steps two at a time, his mission - to intercept Tyler! Bush had started talking half way up. "Sarge, now I've been thinking…" Well now, that statement alone caught Tyler by surprise, simply because he knew for sure that Bush didn't waste an awful lot of time exercising his brain cells. "There's something peculiar about this place Sarge, I don't know ezacly what it is, but it's real mystifyin, you know all kindsa weird stuff's bin happenin ever since we got here don't cha? But I only'll talk about this newest mystifyin bit first, zat orright? Remember when alla them kids had them crazy tantrums at breakfast time in the morning today? Well, right smack bang then's when it started, do you unnerstan Boss, that if them kids didn't do the crazy stuff like what they done, then Murphy wouldn't a got hisself all hot under the collar over some little kid bawlin is eyes out - an *you* Sarge, well *you* wouldn'ta sent Rivers over to cool off with some sparring - then *Rivers* wouldn'ta got the stoopid urge to go aclimbin up that stoopid danged rock face over in area One and *I* wouldn'ta been drug away from my *food* to be his punchin bag or climbing buddy." Tyler couldn't take much more of this, so he asked Bush what was the *point* he was trying to make here. "Huh… the what? Oh, yeah, the *point*, well okay Sarge… the *point* I'm tryin to make here Sarge, is that if them kids done nuffin outta the ordinary like what happened that day today, this mornin, but just sat down all nice an' quiet-like, eatin' breakfast like they shoulda done - then that little girl could've been layin' out there for *weeks* or maybe *years even!* Me 'n Rivers never woulda bin out there in the first place to see her – well *I* wouldn't a bin over there and bin the one what was findin' her alive n all, that's for danged sure! *Now* can you see how the mystifyin's bin stretched out Sarge? This place is *spooky*, way, way too spooky, you've gotta admit boss, some pretty strange stuff happens around here. Like how come the *kid* gets saved but her folks is both goners, yeah reckon them folks' goners' fer sure eh? Can you tell me *that* Sarge? It's a *big mystery* Sarge *real spooky stuff.*" Tyler covered his weary, still painful smile, before turning a seriously thoughtful face to Bush – "You know what Bush, I can see what you mean now, and I totally agree. Now let me see…. Private Bush, how long have you been in the Marine Corps? Fourteen? Must be fifteen years by now, isn't it? Well then, it's obvious to me, that a man of your vast experience must surely realise the fates were all working together today. Heroes like yourself Bush, are made, I'm sure it was in your destiny to save that child's life." Tyler watched Bush's reaction to his words with barely concealed amusement, as the mans whole bearing changed. The word 'hero' had hit a bullseye, right on the intended target! Bush stood a little taller, his head and shoulders squared up a fraction straighter, his chest puffed out a little more, and his face glowed with pride, such words of high praise coming from his Commanding Officer! In an awed daze, he gave a sharp salute to his Sergeant, executed a perfect About Face and marched off, repeating those magical words to himself, *"I'm a Hero! It was my destiny to save her – I'm a Hero..."* Tyler stayed where he was, leaning against the stone wall just relaxing, and enjoying the suns warmth, wondering, -not for the first time either, how on *earth* did *that* man *ever* become a marine?

Tyler, picked six of his men, Rivers, Bush, Sanchez and Chung, along with McIntosh and Murphy, he thought it might be a good idea to put a scout team together to check over the first area daily, for a few more weeks, not that anyone really believed they were likely to ever find another living person out there, actually, it had been too long now, and far too many storms had passed through to hold out hope of more survivors, but it kept the men involved, and besides, it gave them something else to do besides sit around getting lazy. The rest of the marines were otherwise engaged in making furniture, or some other things Ms B said she'd find useful around the kitchen and dining area, so the men were trying to make some of her requested items using an assortment of recycled bits of plastic containers, wood and metal, using pure ingenuity for glue. In the meantime, while some of the marines were occupied in the search for any more possible survivors, and Ms B had a few working for her, the remainder had broken into three groups, some took care of the day-to-day jobs, another group was busy with figuring out the plan they'd need to get the family suites started and the third group was left organising a thousand different details to get Eden functioning smoothly. Tyler kept himself busy, and the men on their toes, by swinging back and forth between the groups.

Arrangements were made for the various couples seeking to form a permanent relationship, to receive guidance in many and varied forms. Katherine had been a professional masseuse and beauty therapist in her former life, so at Grandpa's suggestion she began working with Grandma to develop a Sensuality Program for the new couples. It would involve such things as blindfold touch, where they would use soft feathers, sharp grasses, pieces of soft silk material from the sewing kit, warm water and oil massage, to demonstrate how well, and how easily the sensory and sensual side of a relationship could be heightened, it also allowed couples to learn how to really satisfy, and pleasure their life partner. There are no theatres or other places of entertainment in Eden, so being close mentally, emotionally and romantically, as well as physically, and have the ability to keep each other stimulated would prevent boredom. The success of the program would be an essential part of every couple's marital wellbeing. A fulfilled and contented spouse is a happy and faithful spouse, said Grandpa. Grandma also initiated other life lessons like how to engage each other in everyday life, because when you are in such close proximity every minute of every day – conversation, and simply talking to each other, can be a serious casualty and while sex is wonderful, and exciting – it's not something you'll be doing over dinner.

The Elders acted as our councillors and held group sessions that discussed and dealt with things such as the best way to transition between what we had known previously, and this new way of life, debating the way we would be living now, (in Eden) and how to relate comfortably to each other in various ways, ways that truly mattered – with definite sensitivity afforded to the permanency of the future each couple would be sharing. While it's true that we certainly don't have the stresses placed on our relationships like – meeting, and seeking the approval of each other's parents, families and friends, or dealing with exes, or finding an apartment and furniture, picking out china patterns or securing a job with good bonuses and health insurance, or paying all the regular bills, and a mortgage, or even having to choose our mode of transportation. We most definitely *did* have other forms of stress and pressures, actually, in some ways what we have *now*, are even more significant burdens to carry, knowing that our choice of partner *cannot* be renegotiated later on in, say a few years' time, if we decided that we really didn't like each other anymore, or we're not interested in them anymore, now *that* is certainly *not* a light load to carry. Especially when you consider the lifestyles and modern societies, we've all grown up with and are so accustomed to. We have all acknowledged that growing up in what has, for a hundred or more years been a morally loose, throwaway society, has in no way prepared any of us for the absolute permanency and fidelity of an Eden marriage. These partnerships will be *the real deal*, an *actual* -till death do us part- vow in its most basic and non-negotiable form, and not the -until someone better comes along- ideal of our former society. Honestly, being part of a closed community, and making goo-goo eyes at someone else wouldn't work either. Preparation for a marriage in Eden does, it really does make you think hard - *really* hard, and you're forced to ask the big questions, not only about your prospective partner, but about *yourself* too.... *Can* I do this for life, *will* I be able to live with this person, sleep with this person, eat with this person, work alongside this person, *can I love this person every day –forever*? Do I *really* have the depth of feeling that right now I *think* I have? Will we be able to keep these feelings alive? And, what if I *am* wrong? *Will I be able to live with the consequences?* When you look at marriage in that way, there's *nothing* light hearted, frivolous, or temporary about any of our future relationships.

I suppose all these questions may have been pretty much the standard in a bygone era, but we're living in the twenty second century now and things are done very differently now! Well actually no, I may have to stand corrected on that particular detail. Things *were* very different – *right now* though, here in Eden things are almost back to what they used to be long ago, because we've gone backwards in time, way, way back, right back to a way of life that existed many long years before our time! Now we're back to living in the Stone Age – albeit with a modern twist. The newly selected Elders will be giving us younger ones the benefit of their own life experiences, and many of their own personal stories and observations too, however I personally believe that even they will have to remember, and take points from their history lessons.

Within the month following the Upper Valley exodus, our readjustment to a new way of life began to develop and was clearly taking shape. I think just about everybody was surprised that it didn't take very long for the new way, to become the accepted, normal, and natural way of living and doing things. Our beautiful Eden truly does feel like our home now. A good while back we'd stopped missing many of the things, we'd once considered to be the very basic must have, necessities of life and living.

One marine, who wasn't one of Tyler's original team, is a quiet, very sweet natured young man by the name of Zahan bin Zahan surprised even Tyler by demonstrating that he was quite a talented musician, he had in his kit bag, a set of exquisitely ornate hand carved pan pipes, a clarinet, and of all things, a set of bongo drums! Zahan had been hitching a ride from one base to another when he missed his connecting ride and ended up on the supply truck that had, in all the rush and confusion, mistakenly joined up with us…there's that thirteenth truck again. Anyway, he's offered to show anyone who might be interested, how to carve and make their own set of musical pipes, he also said he'd be delighted to teach anyone who wanted to learn how to play them correctly. Right now -he said- he'd already made the expanding frame and was waiting for the opportunity to select some fresh pig skins to stretch, in order to complete another, much larger set of drums, unless of course the skins were required to be made into something else - perhaps water carriers. This comment, aside from giving Ms B and Tyler a bit of a surprise because they'd never even thought of utilising the pig skins in any way at all, let alone to make buckets, but as chance would have it, it also provided the very shy Zahan, with the opportunity he'd been waiting for, to ask whether or not he might be permitted to fell one tree. I was quite startled for a moment when he quietly admitted he'd been –as he called it -putting the barrow before the beast- because his naturally deeply tanned complexion, deepened further, blushing to a glowing red with embarrassment... he continued, explaining himself at length, that while the groves in both the First Area, and Eden, held many beautiful specimens, and admittedly while Eden had some truly magnificent, and many varieties of very beneficial trees, none were what he required. Zahan said he'd been examining each individual tree that grew in the grove over in the First Area and he had carefully selected one particular specimen many weeks ago. The timber appears to be of the correct texture, and the trunk is large enough, providing sufficient wood for him to make a guitar, a new set of bongo drums, many different styles of flutes, and possibly even a violin, a lute or a mandolin, and in order to minimise wastage, he could carve many hair combs from scraps.

Everyone was feeling well fed, and lazy, so we remained seated around the dinner table while Zahan told us some hilariously funny stories about visitors to his ancient mountain top home. He said there are still a great many, incredibly vibrant, still strong and very healthy, although by *this* continent's standards, extremely elderly people in his grandfather's village, most of them were born, and had been living in that same village, high up in the mountains for longer than one hundred and ten years, and despite their great ages they continued to work their small plots of land, to milk and care for their own herds of goats or pigs. The village has nothing even approaching *modern*, there is no power or gas, no sanitation they don't even have running water! But to see, and to hear, these men, creating brilliant music, painting musical pictures and re-telling stories from many, many long years ago, on instruments that they themselves have crafted, is truly captivating. Apparently, as Zahan said, the hand-crafting of furniture, tools, and musical instruments is a skill that has faithfully been passed down from father to son for a great many generations in his village. He had found a suitable tree; now, and only *if* he was permitted, all he really needed were three things, the first was a little help from one of the toolmakers. No modern machinery is required for making the traditional pieces he had in mind, the designs for these instruments have been unchanged for longer than one thousand years and the tools required are made from the one thing both Eden and the village had in abundance... stone! The second requirement was patience, infinite patience, the third requirement was time, and we had all the time in the world.

Tyler readily gave permission for Zahan to have his tree, and then because Tyler couldn't tell the difference between an oak tree and an apple tree, he asked him what he'd meant earlier when he'd referred to the special benefits of many of the trees. "Sargent Tyler Sir," he said, "aside from the many unusual fruit trees, there are resin trees, Eucalyptus, Pine, Cinnamon and Turpentine trees growing in plenty. All very, *very,* useful trees to have growing here Sir, and the tree doesn't need to be damaged at all to reap their harvest." Once again Eden has revealed some more of her secrets and magic to us, for us to use.

Having completed our very intense sessions with the Elders, Tyler and I were the first to declare our intention to be married, Kristy and Mark made their own announcement the following day, we were all so excited to be the first ones who would -Tie the Knot. At first, I was so disappointed that there could be no announcement on the local news program, or any exciting parties to plan, there could be no engagement or wedding rings, no special wedding dress or photographs to capture our wonderful day, the caterers I'd dreamed of having for my wedding day were long gone now. Here in Eden, we have no special bridal vehicles or even a horse drawn carriage, and the unhappy realisation that there would be no parents, no family, or old friends other than the ones here in New Eden was, for me, extremely upsetting. I'd always taken it for granted that my mother and girlfriends would be helping me get dressed into my delicate white wedding dress and that my Gran would be there too, fussing over even the most minute little detail and making sure my veil didn't fall off - as hers had done on her own wedding day.

Kristy found me in a flood of tears by the waterfall, she'd come up here for exactly the same reason – to be alone with her disappointment. Together we went to talk to Ms B and she listened to us with motherly sympathy and such thorough understanding, because as she said, every woman deserves to be a beautiful bride, and you never forget even the smallest little detail of your wedding day. At her suggestion we called together all the young women and the men as well – not just the couples who were already engaged - because at different times we'd all be facing exactly the same emotions. Everyone sat together around the table and we talked our feelings through and opened up about what was in our hearts, and not surprisingly, we found that we all -brides *and* grooms- had pretty much the same thoughts, concerns and feelings. It not only gave us yet another strong bond, but also helped us to, each in our own way, to accept the future, our own futures, as it would have to be now. For those of us who were already couples, the many necessary changes we were about to make in our lives also became so much more clearly understood and more meaningful. The complete truth of, and the genuine reasons *for* a marriage, all the whys and the simple and straightforward, but necessary reasons, for absolute fidelity, became our focus. Many hours were spent in talks with the Elders, on every subject imaginable, along with even the most private and delicate issues. These conversations led to some surprising discoveries about ourselves, and the realisation that some of our own personal traits weren't perhaps quite as welcome as others, and that some hidden, or unrecognised sides of our nature may require a bit of further counselling until we could, in complete honesty say yes, yes *we are ready* and *we are able* to commit ourselves totally to the other person with a whole heart and without hesitation or reservations.

Our wedding day arrived. The previous night had, like every night since our arrival, been disturbed by more or less continuous storms, colossal amounts of electricity ripped through the heavens, putting on a fantastic display every time lightening struck the topmost edges of the rocky peaks, generating huge bursts of brilliant silver sparks that cascaded down like a waterfall of stars, the booming voice of the thunder bellowed, the mighty reverberations throbbed around the canyon walls, occasionally causing the ground under our feet to shudder and shake.   As it did with almost every storm now, my mind turned to the ones who had left, and I asked from my heart, that wherever they were, they be treated gently.

The morning of our wedding day dawned clear, clean, bright and beautifully fragrant.

Aunty Bea had been busily preparing for the first of the very special days ahead; she and Grandma had been unusually secretive over the past weeks. Now that I think back – they'd been behaving strangely even before we'd made our special announcements. They've been closing themselves away in their rooms, no sooner were the morning or evening chores finished, than they'd race off to their private quarters, pull the curtain across the entrance and stay there until early morning. I'd mistakenly put their odd behaviour down to their husbands and some long-term friends leaving Eden, but there's been a real air of mystery about them that none of us could figure out. Every time they saw one of us, they'd look at each other and a secret smile or a sly wink passed between them.

Our ceremony would begin mid-morning, it had to be organised that way to incorporate the wedding feast into our daily routine. The girls and I bathed and washed our hair, my hair had grown a lot longer since the evacuation and now reached well below my bottom! I was just about to zip up my freshly washed jeans when we were called over to Aunty Bea's private side chamber.

She told me she and Grandma had made something for our special day, and while Tyler and I would be the first, it would be for all of us to share. She turned her back to us and bent over, then as she stood up and turned to face us again, she pulled up from her sleeping place, a long kimono made from beautiful heavy, rich satin in the most delicate shade of palest olive green, and was made all the more beautiful, and so very, very, special because the two ladies had perfectly, and with superb skill, embroidered the garment with scenes taken from New Eden. There was the waterfall, worked in shades of blue, green, silver and gold silk thread across the back, and the beautiful fields of colourful flowers bloomed across both front panels, looking below the flowers you could clearly recognise the main chamber stitched in honey and gold silk thread on the bottom of the front crossover panel, there were also several birds and fish on the cuff of one sleeve and some sheep, pigs and even a pair of go-bits (the name stuck!) were embroidered onto the other sleeve. To complete the newly established ritual, she'd worked our names in black and gold silk thread along the sash. -Wade Tyler & Sara Johnson- She held up the splendid costume and told us that before each marriage; the names of the new couple would be added to the sash.

I hadn't seen Tyler since breakfast the day before. He, along with all of the other young men, had been sent to camp out in the first canyon, well away from the women, so we could both relax and prepare ourselves quietly and comfortably for our big event.

Aunt Bea helped me slip into the wedding kimono and then she gave me my wedding shoes, she had made a pair of simple dark green silk slippers embroidered with W&S and Grandma had woven a circlet of fresh flowers to wear in my hair, while I was with Aunt Bea getting ready, the girls had finished preparing a special marriage place for the ceremony with fresh sprays and garlands of flowers. When everything was ready, Pastor Hank sent Lawrence to sound the ceremonial bugle that would call the men back to the main chamber. The very first Tying Ceremony was ready to begin. Lawrence had been practicing to blow a three-note tune for two days, his first efforts sounded like a sick cow, but when the time came, he was terrific!

The main chamber had been swept as clean as it could possibly be, and the girls had decorated the area with beautiful wreaths of fresh flowers strewn everywhere and the young boys had carried in small but fragrant boughs taken from the pine trees, now the air was filled with their delicate perfume. The marines were looking very smart in their dress uniforms, their long hair tied back by a thin strip of leather. They marched in formation to escort the groom into the chamber. Oh, and didn't he look so very handsome in a short dark green satin kimono worn over a pair of loose black silk pants! The men's kimono had been embroidered with fishing and farming scenes from New Eden. Even though all the men were bare foot, Tyler wore a pair of dark green silk slippers embroidered with W&S. It quickly became apparent that Aunty Bea and Grandma had been working on these garments together for months, and not only since we made our announcement! Although they did say later that they really had to hurry to get all of the embroidery finished in time, they hadn't counted on there being marriages so soon, let alone so many so close together! Or as one of the marines jokingly commented – "we had a raging nuptial epidemic on our hands!"

Zahan, wove a delicate musical magic with his pan pipes, the gentle notes made a perfect accompaniment to these most beautiful moments.

Pastor Hank called each of us by name, and asked us to take our places before him, facing each other. A rope had been made using grasses harvested from the New Eden Pond, and woven into a fine rope about three feet long, the ceremony began when one end was offered to each of us to be held in our right hand. Next, he asked us for our promises to be spoken aloud to each other.

Tyler looked deep into my eyes and promised to endow me with his love, his companionship, his strength and his friendship, to be the provider for all my emotional wants and needs. He promised to be my shelter, and nourishment for my spirit, he said he hoped we would be blessed with children and he would love me, protect me and our family with his whole heart and body forever. Then he handed me his end of the rope to hold while he kept his finger in the centre of the loop. I, in turn promised to be a good wife, to be his companion and his friend, to care for the shelter he gave me, to be attentive to his needs both physical and emotional with love and devotion. I would welcome his children and I promised to be a good mother and teacher to them for the rest of my life. Then I passed my end of the rope through the loop, he took back his end and we pulled together to complete the knot in the rope. Pastor Hank took the rope then turned to the assembly of our friends. He held the knotted rope high and stated quite simply that he would like to present Wade Tyler and Sara Johnson-Tyler the first couple in New Eden to 'Tie the Knot' may we be blessed with many strong children to continue our community. I started laughing up at Tyler and he folded me in his arms and told me I was the most beautiful bride he'd ever seen, our kiss set the seal on our vows and we were welcomed by the whole Eden family. Grandpa pulled out his beat-up old mouth organ and began playing a lively jig, and Zahan joined in with his pipes. The children all joined hands and danced and cavorted around the new couple. Our laughter and singing bounced back to us from the high walls doubling the enjoyment for everyone. Aunty Bea and Grandma had not only surprised us with our wedding costumes, they had also excelled themselves with the variety of foods they had prepared for our special day. Although the feasting lasted only a short time, the food was as plentiful, as it was splendid. Aunty Bea had worked her magic once again. She had prepared spitted go-bit seasoned with aromatic herbs and served with fresh greens and sweetkins -a vegetable that is similar in taste and appearance to a blend of sweet potato and pumpkin, we ate braised rabbit with wild garlic and onions, and there was delicious grilled fish marinated in lymon juice. Among the many strange new vegetables and fruits, we'd also found another fruit that seemed to have a blend of two very distinct flavours, lemon and lime.

Our wedding cake was a delicious mango-coconut flavoured rice pudding that Grandma had made fresh that morning.

We've discovered to our absolute delight that a great many of the fruits and vegetables, as well as some of the newly discovered herbs and flowers, seem to have a combination of different flavours and scents in a single piece. The discovery of so many new, and very different herbs, vegetable and fruit varieties has been an amazing gift. Virtually every variety that grows so plentifully here were completely unknown to us before. For instance, there is a fruit that has the colour and outward appearance of a juicy red apple but it tastes and smells like a mix of garlic and strong onion! Those different blends and textures, give such an amazing variety of full, rich flavours and make for some very interesting and super tasty meals. Once the feasting was ended Tyler and I were led by grandpa to our new, much larger living area, where we would live together for always. Our new living suite consisted of four rooms, next to our bedroom was a smaller room also furnished with a nice new bed, a small square table and a stool, for our son Patrick. The marriage gift -built by Tyler's men- was a huge, incredibly comfortable bed. The frame was constructed using only the trunk and branches of one single tree (representing the unity, adaptability, and strength in marriage) and handsomely hand carved by Bush. The mattress base has been made using synthetic cargo rope (for extra strength) knotted and stretched through holes painstakingly drilled every three inches around the entire base frame, and then a strong double-plaited reed, intertwined with animal gut has been woven tightly through the cargo ropes, and topped with a thick mattress made of soft go-bit skins that were carefully cut to shape and stitched together to form a casing before being stuffed to almost bursting with a combination of clean sheep and go-bit wool, it was so soft and so comfortable – especially after we'd both been sleeping in hard canvas hammocks for so long. Our wedding knot hangs from a nail that's been driven into the rock and bent to form a hook above our entrance. Each new set of cave suites has a similar hook –just waiting…

Michael and Fabs had been out on a routine new-food finding mission, when they'd uncovered a small, dark green leafy shrub -the faint but obvious dark purple and yellow spots making it very distinct from the surrounding bushes- was growing thick and low to the ground against the wall, in the far corner of the natural gardens, the plant had been easily overlooked previously because it's growing behind another, much taller, group of flowering plants. At first glance, and because of the shape of the leaves, Fabs thought it looked a little like the mint his Nonna used to grow near the water tap in her garden when he was a little boy, this memory made him excited so he picked off a few leaves and started to chew them. However, his excitement soon turned to disappointment, but that wasn't all, there was something a bit worse still to come. The taste was similar to a very sweet aniseed, and not a bit like the mint flavour he was expecting at all. Michael said later that it was funny watching him at first, but after a few moments he began to get worried, because as soon as Fabs began chewing on the leaves it was obvious that his tongue, mouth, lips and throat had all gone completely numb and he'd started drooling uncontrollably! It was hard on Fabs for a little while, but it *has* given us another, *extremely* valuable and beneficial medical tool. When this amazing new herb is chewed, well, it acts exactly the same as a local anaesthetic! No one had *ever* seen our always cool, calm, and collected, Hank so wildly excited before! Once he'd been shown where to find the plant, he'd taken a whole big bunch of the herb and disappeared inside his work room, we didn't see him for days after that; he didn't even come out for meals. Aunty Bea took his food over to him. He was beyond ecstatic! He'd experimented and found that when the plant is oven dried and taken orally, in either a warm, or even a cold, tea-like brew, after about ten minutes it acts as a full, or general, anaesthetic. In other words, it induces complete unconsciousness. A mild dose will be effective for about thirty minutes (such as the few leaves that Fabs chewed) and depending on the different strengths that may be required, it can be mixed to last much longer. However, if it is freshly picked and then crushed using a mortar and pestle, it can be mashed into a paste and spread over a dressing that can be applied to any area of the body *or* used in the mouth, and it will render that area numb for many hours.

This herb really has been a major discovery, and one that Hank is very pleased (*and* very much relieved) to have this in his medical collection, because with this new gift, he can now manage any toothaches - including extractions if necessary, and for any occasional sprains etc. It will be invaluable too, for any wound that may need probing or stitching, the patient can be treated without having to endure any additional pain or suffering. The fear of performing an operation or a caesarean birth without pain relief has been the one thing that has made him lose many a night's sleep with worry, even more so since weddings have become a semi regular event.

Kristy and Mark had their own Tying of the Knot ceremony four days after Tyler and I had ours, then Suzy and Nicholas followed their example yesterday. Amelia and Fabs will also 'Tie the Knot' three days from now. My curiosity about his name has finally been satisfied. I had a sneaky peek when he entered his name and details into the record book, his name is actually Fabiano D'Angeliou. Now just this morning Reba and Michael have announced their own intentions to Tie. New Eden is really going to bloom, or should I say 'go boom'!

After each Tying of the Knot, the ceremonial costumes are carefully inspected for stains or marks and are spot cleaned immediately, if necessary, afterwards they are aired and refolded into a special box inside Aunty Bea's room where it patiently awaits the next Tying Ceremony.

Now we know that our community is not only going to survive, we're certain that it will really grow, and flourish. We all work closely together each and every day, for the benefit of all. Then; after our daily work is done, we have our very own paradise on earth to play in.

Every morning at daybreak while the rest of us are practicing our martial arts training, gymnastics, callisthenics, physical development, short sword sparring, spear throwing techniques, archery or meditation, Grandpa patiently goes about his self-appointed task. He is carving an elegant, thirty-six-inch-long wooden spear, following the arrow-head style of the hand on a traditional clock face, it's to fit into the centre of an immensely large, perfect circle, that he has painstakingly carved (and beautifully decorated) deep into the flat surface on the outside wall of the main chamber - the exquisite New Eden Calendar has three hundred and sixty-four days, plus one stand-alone day for Eden Day. That is equal to thirteen, twenty-eight-day months plus Eden Day, in our annual cycle. The months are also numbered, one to thirteen, instead of being named. We had to devise a system to record the passage of time. We didn't even know what old-time month or even what *year* it was, and we couldn't really begin to guess –even roughly- by the weather or season either, because inside these walls, well there seems to be only one real season – and that's 'pleasant' it's never too hot, nor does it ever get uncomfortably cool, and in any case 'old time' has no meaning in Eden. We have our calendar, and we have the time stones laid out to give us an approximate daily time, and that works very well for us, we don't *need* anything more than that, after all there's no Inter-Zone to catch…

From this point onward, every birth will be recorded and remembered once the cycle arrives at that point again. One old time year equates to one New Eden Cycle. This method is so much like everything else here in Eden, adapted to suit, simple, yet efficient.

Over the time we've been here, the storms have certainly lost nothing in either their frequency or ferocity, however, since we are never *directly* affected by them, they've gradually become a background noise. The only time we *do* actually stop what we're doing to listen, is when a storm sounds, or feels, significantly more powerful, apart from those times they're hardly even commented on anymore. Of course, there *are* numerous times every day when the rolling thunder interrupts classes or conversations, but like all such things – we've become accustomed to them and have adapted accordingly. I liken it to people who have lived by an Intra-Zone Line or a Government Operated Airfield – you just get used to those sounds.

Our lives are comfortable, we're settled and orderly, if an obstacle or challenge arises, we come together and discuss how it can best be overcome. Naturally, there are occasions where not everyone agrees, so by trial and error we have learned that the easiest and most positive solution is to put it to a vote, and the outcome of the vote is final, unless it's a draw, in that very rare event – we start over from the beginning but once an outcome *is* reached it is made law and as such, is incontestable. But life in Eden isn't about getting your own way, it's about getting along together.

Kristy and I are both expecting babies now, they will be the very first Edeners, the first natives of New Eden. I suspect Angie, Amelia, Xiao-Linh and Reba, either are, or very soon will be, expecting as well.
Hank is teaching us all, whether we're pregnant or not, special yoga exercises and breathing techniques, he has also offered to teach us self-hypnosis, he says it will allow us to cope so much better with the ordeal of childbirth. Every woman here has placed her confidence and her complete trust in Hank's abilities, he's proven many times over that he is a dedicated and generous man. Every person in Eden acknowledges the real gift he has for healing, it's his true calling. Hank's 'daughter' Alisha is almost as happy as all the other children these days, but yes, she does have some fearfully bad days when she won't leave her room, she won't eat nor speak, and there are still the occasional days when she just sits and sways, or cries silent tears. Although fortunately for her, as time passes those days are becoming fewer, their duration shorter and the episodes are farther apart, but like any good parent and child, they deal with the bad days as they come, together. Alisha is utterly devoted to Hank, she trusts him absolutely and loves him in a way that she was never able to love, or trust, her natural father. The child has never once asked about her parents, nor has she ever

referred to the way she was found, although Bush *has* become an extra special uncle, to her. To everyone's amazement Bush has turned out to be a man who's full of surprises too, he's proven himself to be very skilful when it comes to wood carving, he makes fabulous toys for her and the other children, and they're always made from wood, he mainly uses fallen tree branches, or offcuts for his craft, he's even made a cute little dolly pram and a tea set with miniature cups, a wonky teapot and wobbly plates to go with it. Bush's talent is really quite extraordinary, maybe the man can't read very well, but he made a fully functioning spinning wheel just by studying the *illustrations* in one of the children's old story books! Admittedly he did have quite a few false starts and he made *many, many* errors but in the end he crafted exactly what he saw! There's no denying that he had a bit of trouble figuring out how to get all the bits to fit together and work, but work - it most definitely does, and extremely well too because Grandma uses it all the time!

 The peace, the tranquillity and the beauty that is Eden, is a gentle reminder of all the ugliness, the senseless hatred and complete chaos we've left so far behind us. To see Grandma sitting comfortably in the sunshine on her favorite chair, spinning her go-bit or sheep's wool into a superfine thread, and Aunty Bea sitting right there beside her on her loom – yet another gift copied from a story book, and made by Bush - weaving the woollen thread into lengths of incredibly soft cloth. The Elder ladies have filled a number of storerooms with dozens of different lengths and widths of their hand-woven woollen fabric. They have recycled many pieces of discarded, or worn-out clothing, by cutting the less damaged pieces down, and then sewn them together like patchwork, and finally made into smaller, or different garments, although some fabrics are worn beyond saving, so they've become kitchen cloths! There is quite a large store of soft, cured lamb, rabbit and go-bit hides, and some biggish bales of go-bit wool and lambs wool packed away in the, now greatly expanded stores cave, to be ready whenever anything's needed. Seeing them over there sitting quietly, or looking around and smiling, or chattering away together, well it's a scene that tells the story of New Eden perfectly.

Goodness, so much has been happening here that I haven't given a single thought to this old journal for many cycles!
I am expecting our fourth child to be born in four more moons. The other children are all growing up so fast, Tyler takes our youngest daughter Allyana, our golden haired green eyed little minx of almost two complete cycles, wherever he goes – she enjoys nothing better than to ride up high on his shoulders where she can see everyone and everything. She's watching and learning all the time, yesterday she tried to climb into the go-bit pens and herd the animals as she'd seen the older children doing, but after a few jabs on her bottom from a pair of sharp horns, I don't think she'll be in such a hurry to be a shepherd now. We also have a son, Benji, who is our first born, he's very tall and has his father's dark good looks, and like his father, he's physically very strong,

he has also inherited his father's steely single-minded determination, fortunately though it's tempered with gentleness and generosity. Benji leads the younger children in their exercise program every morning before he goes to tend the lambs. Tyler and I have another daughter as well; Faith, she is also quite tall, with the long strong physique, and dark hair so like her father, but has my mother's dark brown eyes. Recently she was elected to be the captain of the girls' gymnastics team. Faith's always pushing herself towards physical perfection, in another life she's what we would have called an 'all-rounder' because even at a young age, apart from being a champion class gymnast, she sings like an angel, dances beautifully, swims like a fish and has the animals completely charmed to her ways; given the chance, they'll follow her everywhere she goes. Patrick has also grown so much, and enjoys nothing better than teaching the children martial arts and swordcraft. He's always alert to his younger brothers and sisters' welfare and often helps Tyler and the men with any and all work, from the gardens to the maintenance of Eden, he can, and will, happily turn his skilful hands to any form of work. I've found it's quite hard to remember that Paddy isn't our biological child, that there actually *was* a time when I didn't have him close by me.

Suzy and Nicholas have twin boys Jacob and Brad who at three cycles, are both complete joys to have around, and they toddle after Nicholas like he's a mother go-bit. Their gardening skills are … quite creative… they really and truly do need an awful lot of work though… They also have gorgeous daughter they've named Whitney, she's is tall and fair like her father, and quick witted, keen, and clever like her mother- oh, and she has a way with growing things that is almost magical, the gardeners love to have her with them whenever she's not attending to her other chores. Amelia and Fabs have a big strong son that they've named Brody, he's Benjie's main rival for the sparring championship, and they have the prettiest, sweetest, little girl too, her name is Bella, just like she is, all soft curly light golden-brown hair and big brown eyes. Reba and Michael have a new baby boy of two moon cycles; they have given him the name Adam, in keeping with his eldest sister Yvette, now *there* is a beautiful child! Evette was born seven cycles ago, she has red gold curls almost to her waist, a pair of intelligent bright green eyes and glowing honey-gold skin. Her gentle nature and her graceful movements have won her the hearts of every member of the Eden family. She cares for the newborn and sickly animals, with such tenderness and has an instinctive skill when it comes to healing. Their second daughter Angelique is also delightful, although she much prefers to spend her time with the boys, doing all 'boy' things, like climbing trees and chasing the animals. The only time we ever think about 'before Eden' is when a child is being named. There was a time early in my first pregnancy when we all got together and wrote down as many names as we could possibly think of, not only for our own children, but for the generations to follow – simply because one day it dawned on us that the future generations won't know *any* names other than ours, or whatever names we have had here. Therefore, at Grandma's suggestion we opened up a precious fresh note book, and each person tried to remember as many names as they could, gee there are a lot of names! With the input of every person in our big family, we filled the note book thirty lines deep by three columns across each of the one hundred pages! That is *nine thousand* names that we found! Although, from the original nineteen assorted racial origins Eden originally started with, we have only one race now, and that is the race of Eden. Every child born here is an Edener.

As with Evette and Adam, we did wonder –only very briefly however- if perhaps we should tell them the biblical story behind their famous names, *or* would we just let go of the past? We all, each and every one of us, believe in keeping this fresh start we've been given, as the beginning of our history. The old world as we knew it, with all the hatred, greed, racial tension, religious bigotry and cultural division, does not, and *cannot* exist here, and I seriously doubt that *anyone* here is a history professor, a qualified clinical psychologist, nor would be knowledgeable enough, or experienced enough, to teach such a highly volatile subject, and besides, there are so many different religions, and then there are also the many variations and different branches of each religion, so after we'd all given the matter a great deal of thought, and a few hours of discussion, it was a unanimous family decision that we should simply let the story begin here.

Once upon a time a terrible storm drove many people from their homes…

Kristy and Laksha are both very pregnant, Laksha is

preparing for her third child with Zahan, they have two boys already Deo and Sahil, so she would like a girl this time. Kristy's due to give birth any minute now too, poor Kristy, she slipped and fell heavily with her first child when she was almost into her sixth month, her baby boy lived only a few hours. The tragic loss was felt deeply by every person in Eden, and for a long time afterwards we thought Mark would surely lose his mind so devastating was his grief. Kristy shared her heart, and bared soul to him, and they managed to not only survive such a tragic loss and suffering, but as a consequence they grew so much closer, and their love became so much richer, deeper and stronger as a result. Hank has been working very closely with Kristy and Mark again, for the past few months they've been slowly working through not only the natural fear of losing this child too, but also shedding the last vestiges of their grief and bitterness, to a final and gracious acceptance, so that this precious child can be born into complete happiness, and be welcomed into the world without having to carry the burden of any residual torment that may otherwise have lingered from the first baby. The safe arrival of this miraculous little child will help to alleviate a great deal of heartache.

Grandpa, who I swear gets younger every day, is still working wonders in the gardens, although he isn't as physically involved these days. Under his guiding hands and incredible knowledge, our gardens have grown enormously in size too, they have been enlarged to cover more than seven acres now, and young Shannon who, at fifteen cycles, is almost as good at grafting and selecting plants, raising the seedlings, and bonding seeds as is Grandpa himself. In fact, it was Shannon who established our rice crop. We are continually amazed by the way good things just seem to happen for us. One morning Shannon was looking for a piece of string, and Aunty Bea told him to look through the recycling bags behind the kitchen, in an empty cloth bag he found a small amount -maybe a small spoonful of rice grains caught deep in the corners but instead of ignoring them and continuing his search for string, he forgot about the string and went off to the garden. Well, he placed those grains on a soaking wet rag and successfully germinated them, and from that tiny spoonful of grains a plentiful rice crop has developed.

Our Rosie is nearing eighteen cycles now, and is the guide for all of the younger children. Once a child reaches three cycles, Rosie teaches them which plants and flowers they can, or cannot touch, as well as demonstrating the reasons why, be it for their own safety, or whether touching them with still clumsy little fingers might damage the precious plant itself. They soon learn the important differences between our two separate areas. Some areas are good to play in, and there are areas they must avoid, once again, only for health or safety reasons.

She teaches them how to swim, and how to climb safely. However, the first, and most important lesson, is carefully woven into everything she teaches them, and that is the correct way in which to approach their elders. Rosie also reads to them from the treasured books that were carried into New Eden. Some of the stories are a little meaningless and have absolutely no connection with our new world, so in that instance the tales have been carefully adapted to reflect our lifestyle, others are funny stories about flower fairies (bees) and talking frogs, princes and princesses, but the story of the little Jungle Boy who was lost in the jungle as a baby and grew up learning from the animals and birds (only the ones we have in Eden though) is still a huge favourite, and the story of Goldilocks and the Three Bears (which have become go-bits) Rosie also teaches the children *how* to learn, she loves her work, and the children give her their love and their trust as a reward. Lawrence at twenty-one, apart from being totally besotted with Rosie, is the apprentice and constant companion to Hank; he is learning to identify sickness, and how best to care for an ailing person, something very uncommon here in Eden. Our gardens have also become our pharmacy; they generously supply us with everything we need, from simple herbal teas that soothe the rare fever, to plants that have antiseptic properties, or plants that will numb a specific area, or put you into a light sleep, or if necessary, render you completely unconscious. Lawrence also uses his medical training by adapting the things he learns from Hank, to tend to the animals and birds we have farmed. He can repair broken wings, or treat a wounded animal and even assist in a difficult birthing, every bit as well as any university-trained veterinarian or doctor. Hank is also dedicated to developing Lawrence's more sensitive and compassionate side, by training him to perform the formal marriage processes, counselling etc. and the simple graveside blessings a Pastor must have for his people. We don't worship in any formal way, and we have only one single rule that the whole community must live by.

That single rule has, quite literally, been deeply carved into stone. In reality it is carved in letters almost three feet high, directly beneath the Cycle Stone on the main wall of Eden. Our one rule is also our only real law, and that is "Respect" Respect, for all people, for all creatures and for all things. Without absolute and total respect, our community would have failed many cycles ago. There are no words like 'hate' or 'revenge' in new Eden; they have been removed from our vocabulary entirely, and the words 'fight' and 'war' are applicable only to our games and training. When I was a little girl, I can still remember that my mother had a poster on the wall which read "Children will learn what they live" and our children don't need to learn or even know about the many harsh or unpleasant things we've left behind us. Any expression of anger, which is so rare it's almost unheard of, or any undesirable emotions, are always dealt with quickly right at the source, and if there should be any lingering, or any negative feelings, these are counselled with understanding, love and gentleness.

Anna is growing up quickly now too, and at thirteen cycles she has become a really lovely young lady, she adores her little brothers and her new sister, Amelia and Fabs also have four boys Angelo, Brice, Carmichael and Damian, and a new baby daughter Elian. Anna has really blossomed since she started working in the kitchen, being taught the various culinary tricks and skills, by a seemingly ageless Aunty Bea. I, like everyone else in Eden, enjoy dropping by the kitchen to have a visit with Aunty Bea and Anna, I particularly enjoy listening to her sing while she prepares the food for us to enjoy.

There have been so many changes here in Eden that I really don't know where to begin. Not long after tying the knot with Tyler, I became pregnant and my body changed rapidly, unfortunately my only remaining clothing consisted of two pairs of threadbare jeans that had gradually become shorts, and three extremely holey tee shirts. With my growing belly I simply couldn't wear them anymore, it was the one and only time since we'd made our home here – that I have been brought to tears of despair. Katherine had stopped by to ask if I'd like to take a walk with her to the pool, but when she saw me with my hands on my tummy crying, she stopped and stood with her mouth open in complete shock – and worrying that perhaps something was wrong with the baby, she didn't think to ask *me* what was wrong, instead she turned and raced away to get Tyler instead! Poor Tyler ran in, ashen faced and thinking - the very worst I suppose, at least he did until he saw me standing there. Okay, well yes I accept that *maybe* I could *possibly* have presented a somewhat amusing sight; in my cut down jeans that would not go higher than my thighs, and my threadbare panties that had rolled down to sit under my belly, my favourite, much faded, and very holey Spacer Lee tee shirt, had rolled up and over my big round belly and stopped where it barely covered my swollen breasts; I knew my hair had escaped from the loose braid and was running wild, and perhaps my eyes *were* red and puffed up from crying. oh alright then, so my face *might* have been a bit stiff and

blotchy, and I just *know* my nose was bright red because I had to keep sniffling and wiping it with the back of my hand to stop it from running! Well do you know something…that big obnoxious beast just stood there, and laughed! He just laughed … and laughed… and laughed! He actually *laughed at me!!*… Well, that only made me cry all the harder. So, he tried making me feel better by picking me up and sitting me on his knees, he put his arms around me, and sounding genuinely concerned, he asked what was wrong. I explained between sniffles and sobs about not being able to go outside until after the baby was born because I had no clothes to cover me, he lowered his head and I really thought he was going to reassure me, to tell me I was beautiful, and that he loved me just the way I was - or something equally sweet. *But no* - The big brute just couldn't control himself. He threw his head back and *laughed* at me *again!* When he finally managed to regain control of himself, he wiped his eyes and turned to a thoroughly bewildered Katherine, and still half laughing half snorting, he asked her to go around and ask Aunt Bea if she would please come over. Aunty Bea, contrary to being put off by my plight, was well prepared - as she always is, in fact she told me she'd been waiting for this to happen to one of us. She'd already made me a couple of sarongs and shawls from the go-bit wool she'd woven. I must tell you, wearing a sarong is just *so amazing*. It's so comfortable and so soft, and really easy to wear *and* it adjusts to accommodate *any* size. And you can believe me when I tell you - I was becoming *any size* fast, *really fast.*
Throughout the next cycle, everyone started wearing

sarongs, simply because our old clothing had either become too large, too small, or the most common reason – it completely fell apart, and had been recycled into smaller items and placed in storage. Our new, and much larger, storage cave also holds many mementoes from our past. The men's military identification tags, all the travel documents, the military dress uniforms, belts, caps, dress shoes, and before being placed in storage, their long-range fire arms had been heavily lubricated with lard, as were their personal side arms, Laser guns, SMML's (Shoulder Mounted Missile Launcher's) each with their charger or power supply and Tasers. Actually, *all* weapons along with thousands and thousands of rounds of ammunition have been carefully preserved, and safely packed away- every item is individually identified. Any and all personal belongings of both Marines and civilians have been treated likewise with name, rank, home base, old addresses, and any watches, rings, earrings and other jewellery belonging to the members, along with a special book containing the full name, gender, age, previous address (if known), medical history and family details identifying not only the founding family, but also the other evacuees from the Upper Valley, and the nineteen persons who perished on the way here. All the requisite information, and the circumstances whereby they met their fates, is all meticulously detailed. Tyler's passenger manifests containing the necessary information have all been carefully stored, packed away and locked securely into a wooden chest. They will be there if ever they are required. Personally, I sincerely hope they never again see the light of day. The men have kept their army knives and their boots (or what's left of them) out because about every fourth new moon a group, usually led by Tyler, make a short daytime expedition into the out lands to check the surrounding area, mainly to see whether or not mother earth is beginning to recover yet. Men really are the strangest creatures you know; they'll make a serious competition out of absolutely anything – or nothing at all. These days whenever they leave Eden, they manage to incorporate a challenge. Each man has to scale the walls and abseil down to the ground, the first one to reach the ground and safely stow his gear wins fifty points for his team. Soon after the Upper Valley people left, the gate that had concealed the entry point to/from the outlands was changed and permanently closed off by a rather ingenious screen. We've been told that on the outside it looks exactly like a continuation of the stone wall, although it's actually a gate that's eight-foot-high and made from heavy, thick planks made from hardwood that Bush painstakingly carved, weathered and stained with wood-ash and rock dust mixed with fat and rubbed into the wood, to blend in with both the contour and the colour of the stone walls. The gate is checked for damage or discolouration every time the men venture outside.

There is a lot of talk going on now amongst the men's teams and surprisingly enough, the women's teams too, about holding an Eden Games. The proposed competitions will be tests of both strength and endurance, every contest will be adapted to make them suitable for the younger teams to compete safely as well, so everyone is training hard. Apart from using the sparring ring, the he only time the men really leave the new area is to alternate between ponds. When the fish pond needs to rest and allow the baby fish to mature, they fish from the first area pond for some months or longer if it's deemed necessary. The only other time they venture over is when they to go the very far side of the first area to collect the fine white clay, so Reba and Amelia can make whatever new bowls, jugs, cups, platters or plates are needed to replace the ones that break occasionally.

Reba and Michaels cheeky sons, Sanchez and Raul, enjoy nothing more than to cover themselves in wet clay and run around while it dries, the sight of them often frightens Colleens little boy Bailey and sends him running to his father for protection. Davy just sweeps him up onto the safety of his shoulders, and from up there, the suddenly very brave Bailey, laughs and pokes his tongue out at his tormentors. Boys, no matter where, when, or how old they are, boys will always be boys.

New Eden has, I'm both proud and happy to say, become a true and fully functioning community now, it's become our real home, where real people are able to live, love, work, play, grow up and grow old in. The Elders often tell us that they are enjoying their twilight years so much more than they could possibly ever have anticipated. Indeed, most of them had -in the old world- lived in terrible fear of becoming old, and being all alone, or worse, feeling useless and being forgotten. Ha, well there's no chance of that here! As I was saying, the men *do* leave New Eden from time to time to see what –if anything –has improved in the outlands. But personally, I think they go out simply because they *can*. We women think it's just a *man* thing that they feel the need to do. Although it appears that nothing out there *has* changed, or improved, at all. The storms seem to have lessened a little in frequency although their ferocity doesn't seem to have abated all that much over the last few years, or maybe it only seems that way because we don't really take much notice of them anymore. Although one thing that *hasn't* changed, Tyler and the other men have never, in all their forays to the top of the caves or over the tops of the canyon walls, sighted any other living thing outside of the canyons. There *is* one thing I *would really like to see* for myself though; Tyler and the others tell us that looking down from the top of the walls, Eden is quite undetectable, they've all said it's actually invisible. It must be some strange optical phenomenon or else a trick of the light that renders the brightly coloured gardens, and the acres and acres of beautiful green grass covering the canyon floors, a misty dull and lifeless grey which actually means our paradise is undetectable from the air, but apart from experiencing that, I have absolutely no desire whatsoever, to venture anywhere even *near* the outlands ever again. Tyler says there are still no insects, animals or birds, because there are no trees, no flowers or grasses, to act as homes for them and for them feed off, we're told that it's still as hot as a blast furnace out there and the same ocean of sticky brown mud that despite the incredible heat, never seems to completely dry out and is the same as when we arrived. Whereas *inside* our beautiful, peaceful haven, there are all sorts of small animals (although, we never did find that horse!) and we have a staggering array of birdlife, birds that none of us have ever seen before. We have an enormous flock of chickens, there are so many woolly sheep, a hundred or more long haired go-bits, innumerable rabbits and dozens of pigs, and between the two ponds -while admittedly the fish aren't enormous or challenging - the supply of fish is, as a rule, usually quite plentiful. No-one knows what our future will hold in the long term, although Grandpa, Grandma and their councillors have planned and prepared future high councils for every contingency. They have spent far too many hours to count, planning and setting out instructions for a safe procreation program should we, at some point in the future, suffer a serious imbalance of the sexes. Those instructions have been sealed and are kept locked away with the passenger manifests. As we are now, and for the next few generations at least, it won't be necessary to put any such program into effect.

Within New Eden there is one essential law, once again drawn from *Respect* that everyone learns from infancy. The law concerns antagonism, in *any* form toward another person, either verbally, physically, or emotionally; no cruelty or violence either toward, or involving, another living creature will be tolerated. Any time there is an altercation, the aggressor is encouraged to discuss the reasons that led to such a confrontation, and if further counselling is necessary, then it takes as long as it takes, until the emotional balance has been restored. The penalty for continued non-compliance is expulsion from our community. Ultimately, it's a death sentence. The Council of Elders have never been called upon to enforce the law, but the law is there, and everyone is aware of it.

Our rule of life, is our way of life- and is lived from the youngest child, to the eldest adult; *Respect* for *all* living things. With the passing of each cycle our community becomes calmer and ever more dedicated to Eden, and to each other. We are all completely aware that there is, in all likelihood, no chance of a sustainable life for us outside of Eden, and without us, much of Eden would also die. I honestly don't remember the last time I heard a reminiscence of 'before we came'. Our lives are lived very simply, but they're lived fully. All of the babies are growing so fast, they learn everything from, and live close to, the earth. Their games and education all revolve around family, each other and their own special place in this dream land we live in. Within Eden there is almost no sickness, apart from the very rare, or infrequent injury. But coughs, colds, influenza, and childhood diseases just don't exist here. I used to wonder why, but I've come to the conclusion that we are all just too healthy now, our food is very basic, but it's fresh, untainted by chemical interference and is plentiful, we all have plenty of rest and exercise, plus there are no drugs, alcohol, cigarettes or pollution here in Eden. One might say there is simply no room for germs.

Every single day after the group yoga and meditation session, all males, and children from the age of four cycles practice gymnastics, callisthenics, wrestling and various forms of unarmed martial arts training, spear throwing, archery and/or rock wall climbing, to keep their bodies strong and supple, and their minds and reflexes sharp. Although injuries are never intentional, and avoided wherever possible - they are not feared. The mantra is -Practice Prevents Pain- There are now seriously competitive games held twice each cycle in the First Area. They involve of games of skill – equivalent to a combination of old-time croquet and golf. There are also games of precision, the competitions for archery, spear throwing, bow and arrow, and darts are strongly contested. Swimming and diving are both challenging and are contested very enthusiastically as well.

There are also some, let's just say, more *sedate*, competitions for the women. There's the Culinary Delights sector, where there are contests for the most imaginative dish, the most enjoyable dessert or the tastiest relish. But as these delicacies are all judged by the men - who undoubtedly thoroughly enjoy being judges, and regardless of who wins, the men are definitely the ultimate winners. All the women work together to develop new recipes for the pleasure of the men and children. Since they both take inspiration from the native plants, Carol and Luke have teamed up, working closely together they share ideas and have found some quite unusual ways to use these strange flowering plants, Luke has developed an amazing array of herbal beverages, relishes, sauces and chutneys, he has a gift for blending and he's developing various herbal remedies and salves, which are very useful, especially for delicate baby skin. Luke's also developed many of the amazing flavourings the cooks use every day now, but regardless of his many successes he always works closely with, and takes instruction or advice, from Hank. Carol's keen to develop a fragrance that she hopes will one day be suitable for humans. So far, she says the only admirers of her efforts are the pigs! Although I must say, our pigs seem to take great pleasure in the malodourous concoctions she's produced so far. It's to be hoped that once she and Ricardo Tie the Knot next month, she'll be able to concentrate on her work once again.

All children -both boys and girls- once they've reached their fourth cycle, commence rock climbing, at that age they are considered old enough to be able to understand and follow instructions properly, without running off to play elsewhere, they are also free from that age to take part in any artistic challenges. These challenges are really wonderful, they don't prevent anyone of age, or stage of pregnancy or feeding, from participating either – you may think these challenges sound simple, actually they're anything *but* simple and a child can only be given assistance until they reach their eighth cycle. In these competitions, the difficulties arise from each competitor having to find the materials and create their own, coloured stains; the paper each person uses has to be hand made from recycled materials, as do the brushes. Hank and Luke are busily trying to develop a new glue from tree sap or resin; so that we can glue or bond the rabbit hairs to a smooth wooden handle, so far we've been trying to tie or bind them onto the wood, which has proven to be a complete and utter waste of time, as they invariably fall out immediately. However Laksha did make a passable paintbrush by vigorously chewing on a green twig, the result was a feathery end that was much better suited to painting than a small pile of rabbit hair and an empty stick! Apart from the painting and sketching section of the art competitions, there are also pottery designs, wood and bone carving, there's also the weaving, this incorporates improved use of colour, design and uses. Then we have the true test of patience and ability... the pottery making challenge. Here again, all the materials must be collected by the competitor, he or she must collect sufficient quantities of the correct type, selected from the seven different varieties of clay available for their planned potting. The required material must firstly be located, then be collected and carried from the First Area, through the caves to Eden, and the clay must be kept moist enough to prevent it from drying out, but not so wet that it dissolves and becomes useless. With the weaving, months of planning is involved as all the reeds or grasses have to be gathered, dried, treated and colour stained in advance by the competitor as well, and let me tell you *that* isn't always as easy as it may sound either. The first difficulty to overcome is that the best and longest water reeds are found about nine or ten feet below the surface of the water - and although we *do* have breathing reeds of a sufficient length for diving and staying down, the gathering is still quite a difficult challenge in itself, moreover we must always keep in mind that we are harvesting the food that the fish prefer to eat, so collection has to be strictly controlled, and then there are the tuft grasses, these are the grasses that are also well-suited to weaving, however, these also happen to be the go-bits favoured fodder, therefore finding grasses of a suitable quantity, *length and quality* is practically impossible. Oh, and don't forget the go-bits themselves either, they'll butt and bite to protect their food! So, one of the most difficult parts of collecting the grasses is working out how to outwit those crafty little go-bits, and that can be a real challenge all on its own… and very funny to watch! Kristy has no serious competitors –not yet anyway- so she always wins the art contests; she has drawn and painted stunning, truly outstanding murals on the walls in the central chamber and right throughout the entire colonnade of caves that join the two areas together. She's told our story in picture form, depicting the numerous trials challenges we've been confronted with and overcome, she's shown our simple daily routine, the life of the community. Within her own cave suite Kristy has covered almost the entire surface area of walls *and* ceilings with sketches and striking portraits of Mark in his various guises, her much admired man, the serious marine, beloved husband, lover, and fieldworker. There are life-size charcoal sketches of him looking very handsome in his formal dress uniform, and with the portrait she's drawn of him in his ceremonial kimono and pants she has captured his softer, more romantic side, she's even drawn large as life portraits of him training in the arena; I particularly like the one where she has sketched him walking out of the pool with a huge happy grin on his face and with water dripping from his hair and body just after he'd won the diving competition; there is also an exceptional but honestly heartbreaking, almost life size drawing of him down on his knees, on the day he was preparing to return their precious baby to the gardens. Somehow, while suffering her own shattering heartbreak and misery she's captured all the unbearable pain, the anguish and the yearning, that only one who understands and shares that pain, could possibly depict. I'm not the only one who has an emotional reaction, each and every time I see it, I've often wondered how they can live with such a constant reminder of their lost baby. I did ask Kristy about it once, and she said "this is the only thing we have of our son, and it gives us strength." We know the truth of that statement because they've proven their strength, their tight bond, and their absolute and utter devotion to each other, time and again.

Reba has won every single pottery contest that has ever been held. The fact that she's the *only* real potter we have doesn't deter anyone else from having a good try either. Although in fact, I'm thinking Rivers *might* just be giving her some really strong competition this time. Reba's just such a great person though, because she'll gladly teach you, just as she has taught Rivers. She'll guide you, and show you how and where to select the best clay to use for your chosen project, she'll even show you the best way to carry and store it correctly, and then she'll start you off, right from the very beginning and carefully explain to you all the neat tricks and different techniques she's learned and adapted over the many years she's been potting. She particularly enjoys showing us how to use each one of the seven different potter's wheels that Bush has made for her. Whoever is learning, or perhaps just standing around watching -as long as you stay well out of throwing, or spatter, range –you'll have a really good laugh. Consequently, even though our competitions may *sound* really easy, the difficulty factor is most certainly there. Eden is, thankfully, strong on talent, and fortunately, exceptionally feeble when it comes to selfishness, jealousy or greed.

The marine's training is one of the major bonds that have held these men and women together, to never give up, even in the face of seemingly insurmountable difficulties. Nothing, not one single thing has been really easy for us, and it certainly hasn't been a stress-free time for anyone during the transition from the twenty second century where every device and comfort is right at your fingertips, to going all the way backwards as we have, to living in an updated version of the Stone Age. Naturally there have been countless trials, tears and tribulations on so many different levels, but our strength comes from not merely surviving, our real strength is in surmounting our differences, overcoming our difficulties, and working through our troubles. This communal strength we've found and worked so hard to develop and maintain, allows us to live in complete harmony with each other, and with Eden. Our children are the ones who are really reaping the many benefits and the rewards of our recently acquired second chance lifestyle. We instil respect and strength, both physical and emotional, in each of them, and they know they can always rely on us, and will always support their fellow companions in their own lifelong stroll through Eden.

Oh goodness! Anna has just called me; she says that Kristy is calling for me, and Mark wants me there to assist her, it's time for them to deliver their babe!

Goodbye my friend – whoever you are. I hope you're reading this diary right here in New Eden many, many cycles from now, and that our community has continued to grow and thrive. I will have just enough space on this page to tell you his or her name! Kristy and Mark are overjoyed to announce the safe and serene arrival of their big healthy son Lance. We all hope he grows as straight and strong as his namesake.

II

NEW EDEN CONTINUES

The grandmother of my grandmother is known to us as - to give her, her correct and well-deserved title – The Most Revered Elder Sara.

Elder Sara was one of the courageous Founding Family.
One of the family members who were not born within New Eden's walls, but who came to this protected place as a young, untied woman. She was but one, in a large assembly of people who were in desperate search of sanctuary, seeking to escape the indescribably treacherous storms that were, in their time, cutting a swathe throughout the Outlands. The fearsome storms of their time were decimating and razing everything that lay in their path.
The lands beyond the security and protection of our walls are known to us only as the Outlands, a perilous place where there is nothing certain except extreme danger and certain death. The Founding Family came upon this haven of peace and tranquillity that we, their many descendants, know only as New Eden. Eden is our sanctuary, our home.

Ten cycles past, my own grandmother fortuitously discovered an extremely old collection of three journals, the second of these journals bore this thrilling inscription –
This Journal belongs to: Sara Anastasia Johnson who has this day, with immense joy, Tied the Knot with Wade Gabriel Tyler.
Most Revered Elder Sara's personal journals had rested, high upon a very shallow rock shelf, where they had remained well concealed, inside one of the,

now generally disused, cave rooms within the first chamber. We, her descendants, have had no knowledge as to the existence of these journals, consequently the precious, very significant words they contain have been well preserved having remained unseen and untouched by human hands, and therefore become thickly covered in dust over many, many, cycles of time. Upon further examination of the topmost ledges of the chamber, a further two Journals belonging to her were also revealed, each in identical condition to the first. The bindings are no longer soft nor are they supple due to their great age, and the spines of the fine leather coverings, have dried and cracked over time, although unlike the spines, the page cover of each journal still retains the original colours of deep pink, pale mauve and rich purple.

This wonderful discovery generated tremendous excitement for everyone in New Eden.

Grandmother was, very reluctantly, granted permission by our present Ruling Elders, who asserted that they must first examine the contents of the three journals closely before they could permit my grandmother access to read them herself.

However, once the elders had satisfied themselves that there was nothing in any way disturbing or seditious contained within the pages, grandmother was permitted to share the content of the journals with the rest of Most Revered Elder Sara's descendants, our present community.

We, the children of Eden, are honoured to be the descendants of those immensely brave Founding Family Members.

Through the many hundreds of closely written pages of her journals, there have been innumerable, incredible things discovered, or re-discovered, about our home.

Stories and word pictures –that have been faithfully passed down over a great many life cycles, have been – through the gift of her delightful words- most generously repainted, redrawn, and now reinvigorated. The long-familiar story lines that we, each and every person, know by heart, though never tire of hearing, are now made so much clearer. Not merely in their context, but also for the great significance to those of us who came after.

These historical Journals have given everything we have ever known, everything we have ever learned, along with everything we firmly believed we understood about those magnificent people, a new, more wide-ranging definition, a fresh and extraordinary clarity. Old stories, that have been told and re-told for numerous cycles, have become new, and truly alive again for us, although *now* those stories glow with considerably fresher, and so much brighter colours and emotions, for each and every member of New Eden's family to enjoy. Along with a significantly deeper appreciation, a clearer understanding, compassion and humbleness, for the incalculable sacrifices, the hardships and ordeals, that the Founding Family were, by so many unforeseen circumstances, compelled to endure, so that we, their many descendants might have every chance to live.

Through the gift of words on these pages knowledge of our forebears has been greatly increased, we have learned many, previously unmentioned details of events regarding the many trials, the great fears and confusions that belonged to the Founding Family. Many painful incidents belonging to those beginning years were absent, or left unspoken to their children, or their children's children, therefore much of the significant history, and details pertinent to many of their ordeals, were omitted from stories passed down generation to generation. That being so, much has been missing from the totality of their life stories for the ensuing generations of the families' members. Which has, subsequently led to our own lack of true understanding and appreciation.

From the Establishment of Eden, to this present day, there are exquisite wall drawings in many of the rooms that accommodated the Founding Family and throughout the Great Colonnade that connects the two areas of New Eden and Eden, they remain as clearly drawn and as fresh today, as on the first day the charcoal and stains were applied to these smooth stone walls.

From the time when I was a small child my own favourite amongst these many fine drawings, is of a man who is strong in both his physical form, and his fine facial features. This man has been portrayed down on his knees with his arms reaching out and his hands filled with fresh earth as though he is beseeching or pleading with someone. His tears appear to flow freely, running down his tortured face as he stares into the eyes, or perhaps into the heart, of the artist.

I have always felt I could brush away his tears, so lifelike does he look.

From the readings, we now understand that he is gazing into the eyes of his woman, he is despairing and his grief is devastating to witness as he kneels upon the earth bed of his dead newborn infant son. With this newfound knowledge, no one can help but share his pain. For his pain is real, the raw emotion emanating from his eyes, touches me deeply; it reaches down to me from the wall and takes a hold of my heart, and brings tears to my own eyes.

From the moment my grandmother read to us the story of the great loss of the first child born in Eden, my heart reaches out all the more to the Most Revered Elder Kristy, and the Most Revered Elder Mark.

Throughout the caves, the many likenesses of themselves, their numerous children and the likeness of every Founding Family Member are beautifully, and carefully drawn in charcoal. The sometimes sad, but always remarkable illustrations, cover every available surface of their now long disused quarters.

Their personal history has been displayed in many, many scenes, portrayals that illustrate so many special moments, or activities of their youth, and they are continued on throughout the rooms that belonged to their children, to record their life events, from their youthful arrival and continuing through to their revered old age.

They are drawn so skilfully, showing many different situations with their seven children and their many grandchildren. These drawings stand as a testament to their enduring life commitment to each other, and to their own family, as well as to the greater family of New Eden.

We, the descendents of those fine people are enabled, now that we are aware of the complete truth, to hold them up as being yet another true example for ourselves, the succeeding generations, to emulate.

From the written words, and somewhat crudely drawn images in Sara's journals, our home, while it has changed quite considerably in some ways, it remains much the same in appearance as it had been when the time of her passing came, and she was laid to her rest, to forever become as one with her beloved gardens.

Most Revered Elder Sara has written about the storms of her time at great length, and though we do occasionally have storm activity, we have never suffered through anything comparable to the frightful experiences our forebears endured so bravely. It is true that the storms, have at no time – in all of the one hundred and eighty-nine cycles that our families have lived within the sheltering walls of New Eden – adversely affected our home. However, they do continue to deliver to us their many gifts, as they have done since the time of the Founding Family.

The waterfalls continuously provide us with their gifts of beautiful rainbows that delight our eyes and lift our spirits; the clean, clear water regularly supplements our dinner tables with their appetising plants and delicately fleshed fish. Although, and perhaps the greatest and most significant transformation today, is in the fields, the fields have been extensively redeveloped and are undoubtedly significantly more than doubled in area now. From the descriptions set down in her journals, we now have many more diverse crops growing, compared to the basic fare of her time. The enormous variety and many variations of plants are ongoing living gifts, from The Most Revered Elder Shannon, who arrived here as a young orphaned child himself. Throughout his long lifetime he worked tirelessly, cross-pollinating and cross germinating seeds, grafting fruits and flowers, to produce ever greater assortments in the plentiful crops we still delight in today, a great many cycles of time after his passing and being laid to his well-deserved rest in the gardens.

As with the gardens, there are a great many additional gifts from the Founding Family that are still in use today.

We have the great windmill designed and constructed by Revered Elder Bush, and the maze of watering canals that were designed and hand crafted by the Most Revered Elders Tyler, Manuel, and Zahan. The windmill is maintained constantly, allowing it to continue pumping water throughout the entire area of the gardens, the water flows through deep narrow channels painstakingly chiselled into the stone floors of the caves supplying water not only to the main gardens of Eden but the water also travels through the colonnade, out into the gardens of New Eden also. A channel was made within the same system to divert water into the solar heating storage units for the water that is used in the now much larger kitchen and the bathing rooms.

The Founding Family had large shining sealed containers to hold the water, however, over time those containers became damaged and inefficient, so the engineers of my grandfather's time were obliged to remove them, replacing them with numerous wide interconnecting semi shallow canals that had to be carved and shaped from the bare rock. As the containers were an enclosed unit and the canals are open, we have thick pottery covers to maintain the purity of the water and to retain the water's heat.

We also use recovered water from both the kitchen and bathing rooms, for the latrine services that have, incredibly enough, never failed in all the cycles of time they have been in use.

Each of these things are the enduring gifts left by the Founding Family, for the comfort, the convenience, the health and wellbeing of every person who has followed.

The herds of go-bits, sheep, and pigs have greatly increased in numbers, as have the rabbits and the egg giving birds.

Since the cycle of my own grandmother's birth, the go-bit and sheep herds, along with a great many of the mature pigs, have been moved across the canyon into the First Area grasslands; where they are cared for by the younger, untied males of our community.

The reason for their removal is easily explained. As the herds of animals grew in numbers, they also created a variety of unpleasant predicaments for everyone, largely because whenever the animals could, they would escape the confines of their corrals, and run through our living areas causing much damage and destruction. It did not take long for their unwelcome practices to become a regular occurrence! It was always so much fun for the children to watch the men attempting to recapture and return them to the holding pens again. Well, *frequently* and *many times*, eventually became one time too many... the escaped animals would upset the beehives as they ran free, and the wonderful honey would be lost to the soil; therefore, the beekeepers protests and the cooks' complaints to the High Council were addressed. A grouping of very large, considerably stronger enclosures for the go-bit, sheep and pigs and a number of escape proof rabbit enclosures – one for females, one for males and smaller mating hutches were constructed almost immediately and the troublesome animals were relocated to the First Area permanently.

Our cave system has –once again due to necessity - been opened up greatly since the early entries were made in the Most Revered Elder Sara's journals, a short time after her arrival in Eden, when there were only seventy-three lives dependent upon the sheltering caves and the native fruits of New Eden. We now number one hundred and thirty lives with six more ready to arrive, although sadly for our entire family, we will soon lose our much loved and revered Elders, Tara, Rachel and Manix, to their resting places in the gardens.

It has been Elder Tara who has supported, and assisted, my mother in her efforts to produce a more robust writing product, so that she too can leave behind a legacy of the many stories and wonderful recollections she herself has to be handed down, to add the thread of her own great life time, that it may be passed along for many future generations of children who will be born to Eden.

Elder Tara has lived for ninety and six cycles; her life stories are wonderful to hear. I remember as a small child, feeling very privileged to hear her speak of her life, and of the remembrances she held of those who had gone before her. She told us such wonderful stories of the first people to arrive here, fearful and homeless. (The journals hold tales of which even Elder Tara has no knowledge!) She told stories of the terrible trouble that developed between the two differing groups, Upper Valley members and the marines (who had saved the lives of those unappreciative people) and the other refugees. She told us that the discontented ones were given a choice – they could leave the safety and security of Eden, and take the risk of losing everything, including their lives, in the Outlands, *or* they could make the mental, physical, and emotional adjustments necessary for them to stay on and become productive members of the developing community. They decided however, to their ultimate peril, to leave New Eden.

Not one of those people were ever seen or heard from again – it is believed that they were taken by a storm almost immediately, or within a very few moments of leaving. Although, we have stories of two girl children, one of whom was only a small infant, whose mother brought her back inside and the girl child was delivered into the waiting arms of Most Revered Elders Tyler and Sara, and thereby saved from sharing the same dire fate undoubtedly suffered almost immediately by her parents, and their companions.

This story is told to the young children, so that they too, may learn that selfishness, and disharmony, will only lead you in one direction - to your *own* peril.

The journals also tell of another small girl child who was found abandoned, injured, and ailing. She was rescued by the very heroic Private First Class Bush, she was saved and taken in to be raised as a daughter by Most Revered Elder Hank, the first medic of New Eden.

Although the storms have not entirely left us, they have become greatly less disturbing to the outside world. Our present Elders tell many awe-inspiring stories of very formidable storms occurring as frequently as twenty-five, and sometimes even twice that number might occur between sunrise and sunrise. At the time of my own writing however, there will be one or perhaps two storms in one whole moon life, but then another moon life might pass without the sky above ever darkening to a true storm. I must add that the storms we experience now, in our time, hold very little by way of comparison to the terrifying ordeals described by the Founding Family. The storms we experience now, these many cycles later, are most certainly a great deal less severe, with almost no audible wind and very often there will be copious quantities of rain falling, with little or no lightning, and only small rumbles of thunder. However as in the days of the Founding Family, the song of the waterfall tells us there is still water falling outside these secure walls.

Throughout every cycle we see birds, strange outlandish birds, these colourless creatures are very different to the brightly feathered birds of Eden and quite unknown to the Elders, or to the farmers of New Eden, nor do these birds appear in any of the many representations in the great colonnade.

We also see peculiar birds that fly so high that they appear only as small points of darkness moving very swiftly high above us, these birds leave a long white tail behind them as they pass over our heads, and sometimes we can even hear their whistling call, my friend says they may be searching for a mate.

My brother tells me that the forbidden outside world has now become covered with green grass and plants. Although he says, in all the secret forays he has made to the outside, no living creatures, other than the strange whistling birds, have ever been seen.

My brother, and some of the other untied males, have asked the Revered Elders for permission to walk the Outlands, as did the Most Revered Original Elders - Tyler, Michael, Nicholas, Fabs and Mark, in order to go in search for others of our kind.

Still to this day they have been denied permission outright.

In the deep stillness of night however, I have heard my brother and his friends conversing in whispers, they talk of venturing out on their own, even if it must be without the Elder's permission. They are saying it is time to see what there is, or whether there actually *is* anything, to be discovered on the other side of the wall. My brother and his friends often speculate as to whether perhaps there may be other communities similar to our own to be found, communities who might possibly have among their numbers other women with whom they may be tied. The young males are becoming quite concerned that they may never have the opportunity to tie, as the breeding selection in New Eden is now all but exhausted, ever since the establishment of Eden there has always been a preponderance of male children born, and the Tying-Clean opportunity will come to an end with this generation. There are now insufficient numbers of unrelated females, from which the young men are able to select a life mate.

Without new bloodlines from which to breed, our beloved New Eden will eventually wither and die.

My heart holds great trepidation for my brother when he speaks in this manner; he knows only too well that if caught, the elders *will* expel him, along with all who might follow him. The Elders will banish them forever, from their families, and from the protective walls of our valley and caves. Such an expulsion would have such far-reaching effects on New Eden. If these young males are forced to leave the family group, there will be many areas where their absence will be felt, not only in the inability to continue our family lines, their numerous skills also, are unable to be replaced or replicated, the fields and the gardens would suffer greatly, some, from among his friends are inordinately gifted when it comes to growing plants in the gardens, and others are the finest animal handlers and breeders. However, my greatest fear is that they may well perish outside, die alone, uncared for, and unable to be returned to the gardens. The High Council has agreed that the time has come to activate the plan set down in writing many cycles past by Most Revered Elders should a serious imbalance arise. At that meeting it was divulged that should there be a lack of male sires or females then it fell to the current High Council to personally rectify the imbalance. The solution would be corrected by sacrificing the specified number of untied males, or females essential to restore balance. However, when the High Councillors grasped that they *personally* would be required to slaughter their own much cherished grandsons, the order was unanimously rejected. As a result, the subject and the meeting were dismissed.

My grandmother has whispered to me that The Revered Elder Women have been making preparations, they are secretly organising themselves to be involved in something serious, a thing so momentous, and something so utterly improper for *any* woman of Eden. Never before, not once, and with certainty not since the beginning time when the first women came to Eden... the Revered Elder Women, have now finalised their preparations to *interfere in Men's Business.*
Their proposal is to bring together a complete assembly of the Elder's, one that will engage a panel of both Men *and women,* in an effort to, not only convince the Revered Elder males of the urgency, and the dire need, to seek out females with fresh bloodlines to produce the next generation, but also endeavour to convince some among the younger male elders to accompany, and give guidance, to the younger males - if so permitted.

The Elder Males (they say) *must* be made to understand that it is not simply a fanciful whim of the young seeking an adventure, it has now become so much more urgent than merely necessary, it has now become *imperative* that we venture beyond the walls of Eden, to actually go outside, to move through the unknown Outlands, it has, they're saying, become of the very essence to our continuance. Therefore, the need to seek out others of our kind has become crucial. However, we can only wait for the High Council, and hope that true wisdom guides their decision.

At last, the time is come!
Every man and woman above fifteen cycles have been gifted a journal. Each journal has been beautifully bound with embossed pigskin, the leaves of the journals have been painstakingly prepared of fine, scraped go-bit skin on which to set down our own individual life story, to describe daily life, to express ourselves to those who will come after us. We will now have the ability to tell stories of the children and families, to relate their experiences and achievements, to each set down their own thoughts, their own imaginings, and to convey also, their fears and desires.
I have great hope that these journals will, in the fullness of time, also be passed to future generations of Edener's. However, that future reader may well never be born if the Elder Women are denied their appeal. As we now have these three wonderful and remarkable journals of many, many, cycles past, relating to us stories of how the Founding Family

overcame a multitude of seemingly insurmountable obstacles, by using their collective ingenuity, and tenacity, until they could finally, and fully appreciate, the results of their many cycles of backbreaking work, the many hardships, the daily trials and errors, of exploring new and different techniques to do even the most ordinary things until they achieved success, coping with cycles of uncertainty, the fear that they would never be found, coupled with the fear that they *would* be discovered and therefore be forced to leave - so too, will our descendants have our own lives on which to contemplate, and to reflect upon the many modifications, and successes. It appears to us that all the things the First Family struggled so hard to provide were not only for themselves, we now understand the Most Revered Founding Family left Eden ready and cared for, to be enjoyed by their loved and longed for descendants.

Over the cycles, many things in New Eden have changed, some greatly, others have been adapted to suit a larger community, but the majority of our most important life rituals have remained unchanged, or are closely similar.

I give as an example, the one thing closest to every young person's heart - and that is to be tied with another for life, for the procreation of children, and for the approbation always afforded to a breeding couple.

The exquisite Ceremonial Tying robes are still in use, although now with the passage of time they have become quite fragile, and are therefore only used when leading members of Eden are being inducted into official roles. I give as an example, being elected as members to the supreme council. In truth, the original robes are only worn very briefly, every two cycles.

In their place we now have other, equally beautiful robes, that have been woven from the finest white go-bit wool, and are coloured with the roots, juices and skins of vegetables, fruits and flowers, they have been made, and decorated, in a similar fashion for us to wear for our own Tying Ceremonies, and the names of each couple are still embroidered onto the sash. There are a multitude of such sashes filled with the names of life partners, and all the sashes are packed up together with the ceremonial robes and the special pair of tying slippers worn only for the duration of the ceremony.

Every young woman dreams of the day when her father announces that she is ready to be tied. Once the couple are selected, together they begin the customary preparations with the Elders. The girl's father will proudly go out to select the pond reeds he will use to make the ceremonial Tying Rope, the rope that will one day hang proudly outside the cave rooms he himself will select for her. Once that is done he will then enlist the assistance of his woman and together they will commence working on the furnishings. We each dream of the time when our mother will begin collecting the skins, feathers and wool to make the sleeping pad, coverings and dressings for the new sleeping cave, and for the chambers her daughter will share with her life mate.

The daily routines of working the land, and harvesting food for the community's needs, remain relatively unchanged. With the education for our young children, in all the many and varied areas of New Eden's life requirements, one thing remains completely unchanged. We work together companionably, for the health, and the wellbeing of each other.

Requirements such as fishing, farming, art, crafting, archery, potting, cooking, spinning, and the weaving of both spun thread and grasses, knitting and sewing, the choosing of various skins, and the preparation of them -a certain quality is used for making new journals and their bindings for educational needs, another lesser quality is used for clothing, and the rougher, or less than perfect skins are used to make the headrests and sleeping pad cases. Then there is the crafting of various sizes of the writing quills, and the preparation and production of writing stains along with the many different implements used for gardening, construction and carpentry. The making of these important items continues to be a large part of our ongoing education and occupation. This is our life.

From the first day a child born, they are massaged twice daily with rich oils, this is done to stimulate both their brain and muscle function. Once the babe begins to crawl and walk, they are taught - through play - how to exercise appropriately, and in doing so they are able to strengthen their core muscles and to develop natural strength, agility and fitness.

By implementing these methods, we also teach a young child the best way to avoid the likelihood of injury wherever possible, and perhaps the most difficult, although a very necessary lesson in exercise, is, if you do fall, how to land properly in order to minimise injury and avoid breaking a bone.

From the age of four cycles, boys and girls begin training quite differently, while they continue to work side by side in the gardens and fields, it is at this time when their life lessons take on different aspects of each task.

The practice of yoga effectively begins from birth, and then, as each girl attains eight cycles, she begins the second level of yoga which includes deep meditation, to instil patience, and to develop good posture. At this age yoga instruction also supports preparing her for the coming of womanhood. Subsequently, as she develops further, she is given very precise and detailed instructions - ones that were specifically developed by, and have been handed down very accurately, from the first yoga master - guiding her through the techniques for controlling the birthing of her children when her time comes.

Boys are also given instruction, although in quite different, but again, very specific areas, while for them, yoga is not only designed to strengthen their bodies and to keep them flexible, there are exercises and meditations to strengthen and develop their focus and control of their own mind. At ten cycles all males begin a different form of training, particular exercises and meditations have been designed to assist them in containing certain physiological and psychological urges that are a quite normal and natural part of a young un-tied man's personal life.

The crop farming, and the animal nurturing areas of our education, continue to be particularly important for the prolongation of Eden, our whole life long.

From the age of four cycles, all children commence working in the children's garden, where they start with the most basic methods of weeding, preparing the garden beds and planting out seedlings, once they've learned that, and as their knowledge and their skills improve, they are guided through more detailed methods of selecting seedlings for planting, and how best to care for that particular plant. Having gained confidence, and a little experience, they move along to the all-important identifying and sorting the dried seed or bulbs saved from a previous harvest. From that point on, or as soon as they have proven to have a sufficient grasp of the various stages of a plant's life, they are able to progress to the next important stage - they move into the secondary area of the main gardens proper. Understanding the different cutting or gathering methods required by our various crops, also the purpose served by each different method is of utmost importance. Because each crop we grow is distinctive, the young gardeners are encouraged to have patience, to care and to respect the many wonders of nature. Their ability will only come from watching, listening and doing. Knowing the importance of observation and of timing, by practical hands-on experience and employing the correct methods and the tools necessary for each different crop. Some children seem to pick it all up very quickly, while others are slower to gain confidence, there are however, never any time limits or restrictions in Eden, therefore each child is permitted to learn at their own individual pace. We've often found that the longer it takes a child to fully grasp the concepts and significances, the better he, or she, enjoys working with the gardens.

Prodigious importance is also placed on animal husbandry, as our lives depend on the health and wellbeing of our herds. From quite a young age, Eden's children are carefully coached in the best, and most effective, ways of feeding the very young animals, and how to handle the very different young go-bits, lambs and piglets – without being bitten! The children are instructed and shown as often as is necessary the most suitable way of bathing and grooming each individual animal, and above all else, to maintain the animals' comfort and health at all times. Every child is taught the most practical method of milking a sheep, or go-bit. Each and every one of these lessons takes much time and endless humour - not to mention unlimited patience, if the child is to learn properly.

Over many cycles we have established that if a child is able to find real pleasure in a certain task, then he, or she, will perform that duty both gladly, and extremely well.

As a child grows from baby days into early childhood, there will be a very select few from amongst varying age groups, who are nominated as possibly being suitable to begin training for key positions in Council Orders, such as medics for the animals, medics or nurses for the aged and infirm. Only those most suited to a specific Office will be successful, and the remainder will return to their previous groupings and progress through their own regular training schedules. Other candidates are destined to be the educators for the future. These children will one day be responsible for teaching reading, writing, and mathematics, or perhaps they will be trained as the physical education and fitness instructors for the next generation.

Educators, and Instructors in particular, are expected to achieve considerably higher standards, as well as being prepared to set substantially higher goals for themselves in order to be suitably knowledgeable, well organised and resourceful when the time comes for them to take responsibility for the safety and well-being of their teams. For another Council Order, yoga - a candidate must definitely show superior ability if they're ready to be trained to become the next yoga instructors. Yoga Instructor is an incredibly demanding position for anyone to strive for – let alone to attain, and only a person who is naturally gifted, and one who has total commitment, will be suited to this office, it may take ten or more cycles before a suitable candidate is finally chosen. Apart from those offices already mentioned, we also have to select, and train, our future apothecaries, these people are given instruction over several cycles and particularly close guidance in the method of growing, developing, and blending specific medicinal herbs, along with various methods required to distil and purify remedies to the very exacting standards required for therapeutic and recreational uses. With all the many important training programs we have, the most important of all of them is perhaps the only one where it's the job itself, and not the council or elders who chooses the candidates – and that is our cooks – the candidate is drawn to the kitchen and will enjoy nothing more than being creative. From the very first, we know that meal preparation and cooking for the family is a calling that won't be denied. The Founding Family cooks taught us that nourishing those you hold dear with the foods grown and cultivated by shared efforts, is considered the greatest and most satisfying of all offices.

There will also be one lone Notary of Eden chosen from each generation, he, or she, is trained to keep precise, reliable records of the community, the Tying's, births, injuries, illnesses, and deaths along with any rare changes or amendments to the all-important High Council's laws. If there is ever the event of an accusation, a record of the charge, the names of the Claimant and the Defendant, together with the names of the members of High Council in attendance, the decision and the judgement must be recorded in full detail. However, since the many unfounded accusations levelled against the Founders that lead to the voluntary departure of the Upper Valley people to this day, there has never been another accusation put forth, and therefore no judgement, to be recorded.

The position of Pastor has always been a difficult choice, and a challenging role to fill. When a Pastor is chosen, it is a lifetime position, and the current Pastor often chooses his or her own successor, Ultimately, there can be only one person from each generation chosen who demonstrates the emotional resilience, compassion, and who possesses the *courage*, the humility and the *intelligence* essential to perform the duties. The chosen one *must* possess a respectful nature, although having a generous nature is also vitally important, the chosen one will require natural patience and an innate calm in order to guide those who are in need. The Pastor is called upon to guide and assist the parents and families who suffer the loss of a baby, or who may be experiencing some difficulty with a child, or for children who may be having complications with their peers or parents. Our Pastor must be able to guide and counsel couples who may have developed doubts concerning the choice of their life partner, and the Pastor must have the moral capacity to give them complete and unbiased support at such times. There is also the extremely rare, but not completely unknown occurrence - of a mentally or emotionally troubled one within our family. Admittedly, this mainly only ever occurs in our most senior members. Our Pastor also performs the ceremonies for Tying, for naming children, and Garden Committal Ceremonies, although perhaps *the most* difficult and demanding duty of all, is to be the sole confidant to the High Councillors. Hearing all, and knowing all, while being unable to share that burden with anyone. Even though it *is* perhaps the greatest honour, it is also one which places the greatest burden upon the mind.

The roll of Pastor, as well as being the most demanding, and certainly the most challenging position of all for which to train, is also the most respected. That is not to say that those who *aren't* chosen, who *don't* qualify at the end of the lengthy trial period to receive instruction to higher office, are in any way disappointed or are left with a reduced sense of self-worth - in reality they seem to feel that *they* are the more fortunate ones!

Each and every member of our community knows, and fully appreciates his or her own value within the community; each person is well aware that there is no single occupation that we can live without, and still maintain our family, or our harmonious life balance.

Each position is considered equally worthy of approval, no matter how outwardly important or simple it may seem, *none* can be dispensed with. Over the many cycles, from the time our community was first established, Eden has evolved into a smooth-running apparatus, however, if one single part fails, or is neglected, then the whole system will break down, if ever that were permitted to happen, our entire community would suffer, it may even collapse.

To illustrate my meaning more clearly, I shall commence by using the yard cleaner as a prime example; if the animal yards are not kept clean of mud, food scraps, and manure, then the animals living area will become tainted, and as a result the animals will eventually have problems with their hooves and in time become ill, and a sickly animal will not produce good milk, nor can it be harvested for food, although in some cases the wool, skins and intestines would still able to be collected and used, the meat however, will be wasted.

If the water carrier, were not to perform his or her duties efficiently, then the seedlings would suffer, and perhaps, if that situation were to be left unaddressed for some days, the plants could wither and die, therefore once again, our food supply would be much depleted. If the medic or the nurses do not perform their duties in an appropriate or timely manner, individuals will suffer needlessly, if the physical trainers are less than vigilant, senseless accidents and serious injuries would become commonplace, or if the flint taken from the top of the walls is not cut, or should the straw be left unprotected from the elements it would begin to rot, therefore our cooking fires would remain cold, consequently no food could be cooked, and every person in Eden would suffer. If the councillors do not enforce the Law of Respect, then the whole foundation of our society would falter, and may over time, possibly even crumble.

Therefore, there is no single occupation in Eden, whether it be large or small, that our people are able to forgo and still be able to maintain the balance so successfully.

Each and every person in Eden is equally valuable, and is equally valued. We carry that knowledge within ourselves, and we perform our duties accordingly.

Our spinners and weavers are constantly endeavouring to find new ways to vary the threads, in order to improve upon the strengths and varieties of the cloth; our skinners seek alternative ways to preserve the go-bit and sheep hides intended for clothing, and to simplify the method employed currently for making writing materials. The skins of the pigs are used mainly for making strong book coverings and buckets or bags to carry water, or for making strong carriers in which to move fresh clay or else cut into wide strips and woven into large baskets used to transfer the harvests from one area to another, only on very rare occasions they are required to make new drums.

As our farmers continue to develop new crops, our cooks take great delight in finding innovative ways in which to use the produce they are given, they are frequently – but by no means are they always - successful.

But the pigs never complain. Every family member from the youngest child, to the eldest member, strives to make the best uses of our many gifts. These gifts are shared, and always given whole-heartedly. Just as the sunlight warms us, and the moonlight shines upon us and guides our footsteps by night, with no thought or need of reward.

Oh, this news is so exciting! a message runner is going to all the different work groupings to inform everyone that there will be a meeting of the Most Revered High Council, one that will include *each and every Elder* to be held tonight after the evening meal. In addition, all family members above fifteen cycles are required to attend the meeting. All the younger children will be cared for in the playground. Or is it terrifying?

 My chest has tightened quite suddenly, my breathing has become difficult and my heart is filled to bursting with great unease, not for my brother only, but also for his friends.

Many of the others who are working with me in this section of the garden are acutely aware of the restlessness that is scarcely being contained in my brother and some of the other young males, it is almost as though their skin has become unreasonably tight on their bodies and they're constantly trying to wriggle free of it.

We talk amongst ourselves in low voices as we work, there is much speculating as to the possible reason behind tonight's unexpected meeting.

Many of us are anxious that the young men's outland exploration plans have somehow been exposed, and should that be true, then perhaps there will be many young males expelled as a result. My head is faint and my stomach is churning.

My dear friend Celina, who has now passed sixteen cycles, wisely says we should keep whatever information or knowledge we may *think* we have, or suspect, close to our hearts, but far from our lips, for fear of being overheard, she says also, that there is nothing to be gained by tormenting ourselves with the unknowable, instead, we should sing some planting songs together to unburden our minds and lighten our moods.

Caleb had just started singing the third verse of Our planting Song, his rich deep voice awaiting Tallulah's high sweet notes to join in, when we were approached by a junior member of council. Immediately everyone's eyes were turned to the ground, as though he might be able to read the truth in our minds through our eyes if we were to look directly at him.

However, he was simply informing us that the time of the meeting has been brought forward, and would now be taking place *before* the evening meal is taken, rather than afterwards as we'd been informed previously, he also advised that we would do well to make haste if we are intending to freshen ourselves beforehand.

He gave the whole group a questioning look; he must have wondered why we all suddenly appeared to be so relieved!

As one, we collected our tools, cleaned them, and returned them to the storage area before making our way over to the bathhouse to clean ourselves before the meeting.

I turned at the sound of my name being called, and watched as my brother Jacob and his friend Lucas came running toward me with enormous smiles lighting up their strong sun browned faces, the soft unruly curls that always seem to escape their braids and bleached almost white by the sun, bounce around their shoulders and down their backs. Lucas jumped high up into the air laughing, as he gave a victory punch to the sky, then started chanting. "We did it! Cara, we did it! The High Council has decided to let some of us walk out from Eden into the Outlands, and search for others of our kind! Tell no one, until the Councillors have informed the rest of the community." His triumphant smile was as bright as the noonday sun. "Soon Cara; soon, *if* I am chosen, I will walk confidently upon the Outlands; we will make a pathway, and it will lead us on to great adventure!"

My brother ran as though he possessed the wings of a bird, instead of human feet.

I continued making my way over to the bathhouse to freshen myself, and to change into a clean sarong for the meeting.

I saw Caleb walking toward me and quickly changed my direction, I did not want him to look into my eyes because he would know immediately that my thoughts were unsettled, and I did not want him to commence asking questions of me that I could not answer without breaking my promise to Jacob. I was confused by my feelings, and yet, I was also confused by my confusion. I was genuinely delighted and also greatly relieved, that my brother had found no trouble with the Council of Elders, and that they had perhaps agreed to allow him this escapade. I was also tremendously relieved that he was not, as my heart and mind had feared, to be expelled from Eden. His talking about walking the Outlands as did our grandsires was one thing, having it become a reality, filled me with profound anxiety for him.

I was deeply disturbed by the knowledge that he was truly going to venture outside, out and into those unknown lands that lay far beyond Eden. Who could know what adverse conditions awaited them? What if they met the same fate as the Upper Valley people, when they chose certain death over staying within the high safe walls of our home? What if they *did* find others like ourselves, and chose not to return? Or worse, what if they were *not permitted* to return?

I decided it would be best for me to heed Celina's advice, and become informed of the Councils Plans, before I troubled my mind further.

I was among the last to arrive at the meeting of the High Council, so I slipped quietly into a place saved for me by my cousin Sofia, and we concentrated on the words Elder Thomas had to say.

Elder Thomas commenced his speech without his customary lengthy preamble, his deep voice rumbled like thunder over our heads.

"We of the High Council, have this day made the momentous decision that the time has arrived to venture outside, and trek far beyond the safety of New Eden's protective walls, and endeavour to establish whether or not there are others of our kind to be found somewhere in the forbidden Outlands. If such a people do exist, they are certainly far beyond the safety and security of our known boundaries.

Moreover, while the present Council has the utmost respect for the instructions set down by the Most Revered First Elders many cycles ago, and we are able to recognise the wisdom of decisions made at that time, which were, to remain secluded and safe, here within our walls, however those fundamental reasons for this rule no longer apply. The tremendously destructive storms they so courageously endured are of many cycles past, in addition, as we are all aware, the storm activity, and severity of those storms, have, over time, abated significantly, leading this Council to believe that a small group comprising of six New Eden males, should be able to conduct a search for others of our kind in the Outlands with reasonable safety."

Someone from the front rows stated that for the High Council to go against all the Founding Family warnings, there must surely be an exceptional reason for this expedition to be considered, let alone arranged? Elder Thomas resumed speaking, and he clearly explained The High Councils reasoning.

"For some cycles now, Council has been concerned that our male population far exceeds that of our female population, and while The Most Revered Elders have, in their wisdom, left us written instructions as to how the imbalance might be reversed, we of the present High Council, have decided that the methods laid out in the instructions are somewhat… extreme. Therefore, a small task force will be sent out as reconnaissance party." A loud rumble of conversation, and of questions directed at the High Councillors erupted, but Elder Thomas, his face reddened with annoyance, held up his large hands demanding silence.

"These men will collect any, and all, relevant information in relation to any others of our kind that they may encounter. The chosen males will be permitted two complete moon cycles in which to accomplish this task and to return to us with their findings. In the unlikely event that they *do*, actually encounter another community such as ours, they are to act as observers only; no contracts or agreements are to be entered into until this High Council has carefully examined that female population, for both their physical, and their mental suitability, with a view to Tying with our pure, untainted Eden bloodlines. Until such time as any feasible inter tribal meetings are held, and amicable agreements can be arrived at, on both sides, there can be no approval given for *any* male of Eden blood, to Tie. In the event a male of Eden should take it upon himself to Tie with an outsider, and doing so without High Council approval, then that male will be considered lost to us for all time, his name will be expunged from all records, he will, in factual terms, cease to exist. The reconnaissance team will be provided with sufficient food, water, and all necessary accoutrements, including their skinning knives, spears, bows and sufficient arrows with which to protect themselves, should they find themselves confronted by some hitherto unknown danger, they will carry their personal weaponry also for the purpose of hunting for fresh meat – *if* any be might found, or be made accessible to them." Once again Elder Thomas paused to give his words time to be absorbed.

"Should there be any present among you, the people of Eden, who have *any* objection to this arrangement, then you are required to stand now and state those reasons."

People in the front turned around to see if anyone behind them had stood to voice an objection, although not one person in the whole community raised a hand or voiced any disapproval to this historical decision. We, as a family, recognised how vitally important this venture would be for our beloved Eden's continued survival.

"Very well, as you are all in agreement with this course of action, the men concerned will now be advised. These men will each be given clear instructions concerning their conduct, as well as being given the necessary supplies from the store cave within the hour, each man should be prepared to depart Eden at first light tomorrow morning. Go now, return to your recreational activities and we will reassemble at the evening meal."

Jacob and I joined up with another group and we wandered across to our designated dining area; I listened to the excited young males talking about who they thought should be part of the expedition to the Outlands. They all readily agreed that Cain should be one of them, and most agreed that Simon would be a good man in a tight place, and Theo who could climb just about anything and was able to put his spear precisely where he wanted it to go intuitively, certainly without thought or plan.

Peter was the best man with a bow, and William could kill, clean and cook birds, rabbits or herd animals better than any of the others, along with Jacob, who apart from excelling in physical combat and being as one with all forms of weaponry, he had the ability to draw whatever he saw or construct a map of where they'd been and portray accurately anything else that they saw or found. If, in the very unlikely event that a female was allowed to be part of the expedition, everyone agreed it should be Allyana, as she is regarded by many as being vastly superior, to even the best of the young males. When it came to all schools of weaponry, she has mastered every weapon in the armoury to the point where no one, female *or* male, dared to challenge her. Her speed, agility and accuracy, with her endurance and strength are in many ways beyond credibility, if she had been born a male, she would certainly be counted among the chosen few. However, the choice has been made by the Elders, and we will all know who has been chosen very soon now, because I see that the Revered Elders have moved to seat themselves at the main table.

Councillor Elias stood up and addressed himself directly to the male population of Eden, he said that while there were many who desired to be counted as a part of the expedition, and there are a great many others who are equally qualified. Consequently, the final selection made by the High Council has not been arrived at without some degree of difficulty.

The choice has been made, therefore, unless there is a valid reason for one of the chosen *not* to be included, the party would be made up of two senior men whose combat skills, judgment, athletic ability, strength and endurance, could be relied upon, as well as four young men – who have also been chosen for their close combat and weaponry skills, their dexterity, athletic abilities, speed and certain other essential talents, in the event that strength and physical endurance may, at some point prove to be crucial for survival.

The names were to be announced immediately and the chosen ones were then asked to stand, and convey their willingness to participate, or, to offer their refusal, as their name was called; Senior Freeman, Senior Alder, Cain, Theo, Jacob and Marshall. Each man stood in response to his name, all wore beaming smiles as they stood to attention, proudly waiting for whatever was to come next.

"Do you accept the challenge that the people of Eden have placed before you?" There were shouts of "Yes Lord High Councillor I do accept the challenge put before me Lord High Councillor!" Each of the chosen men stood with their right forearm placed across their chests, right fist to left shoulder.

In this manner the salute was given.

"You are all required to attend a conference with the High Council, the meeting will take place immediately after this meal has been taken."

Jacob was so ecstatic he could barely contain himself. His dream - the dream he'd been having since he was a small boy, listening to his father and the older men when they sat around the fires late into the night, telling, and retelling the stories of the Founding Family, of their heroic struggles and how they overcame a great many adversities and dire perils. These tales recounted how, fearing for their lives, and rapidly approaching desperation, with all resources dangerously depleted, they had stumbled upon this remarkable, although nameless, and hitherto untouched place.

A place that was completely unknown to any of them, as it did not appear on any of the intricately detailed military maps they had had in their possession. It was, in truth, the safe haven they craved, this perfect place, that they gave the name - Eden.

Jacob, his eyes sparkling brightly with excitement, could scarcely control his exhilaration. No longer would he feel the urge to perch atop the walls for hour after hour baking his skin in the scorching sun, looking to the outlands, and imagining himself walking there, forging a path that would lead him to high adventure - because his dream, his vision, was about to become reality! He would walk openly and bravely, outside these beloved walls and he, along with his companions and Elders, would find an unknown, but often dreamed of, pathway through the wilderness, in anticipation of finding where others of our kind might walk also.

Jacob's father, Murphy, followed his son into his sleeping place, and offered him words of both praise and caution.

He confessed to his son for the first time that he too, had held similar dreams in his youth, but the need was not upon them at that time, therefore the High Council was unyielding in their refusal to decide in their favour. In fact, he was most fortunate *not* to have been expelled altogether.

Travel safely my son, walk in the footsteps of your grandsires, should you be confronted by unexpected danger, remember your great grandsire Liam, for he was amongst the bravest of the brave, and his courage lives, and flows strong in your blood.

Jacob really thought he was too excited to sleep, but before he knew it the first light of dawn was lighting up the entrance of his cave room. His mother Ravenna had packed a second sarong, and the exquisite ankle length hooded cape she'd had made, using only the softest go-bit hides and lined with soft rabbit pelts, (he only ever used it when there was an animal due to give birth, it was for his night shepherd duty) his allocated weapons, and his food supplies, in accordance with the Council advisors' instructions. A pigskin pack stood ready and waiting for him by the main entrance. While her son had slept, Ravenna had made three pairs of strong leather straps and attached them to the back of his supply pack, a long set that he could put his arms through as she had seen others do, so his pack would hang from his shoulders instead of having to carry it in his hands, another set to hold his bow had been attached to one side and another set securing a full quiver of arrows, thereby firmly securing them to the opposite side of his pack and leaving his hands free, his pigskin water pouch had been filled with fresh water and now hung from the centre.

Jacob looked around him; at the only home he had ever known, and realised he was both exhilarated, and faintly uneasy, about what the days to come might bring.

His proud father, his beloved mother, sister, and his five younger brothers stepped aside, allowing him to pass.

Jacob stopped and looked into the loving eyes of his father, gratefully accepting his warm embrace, he then turned to wrap his adored mother, who he knew cherished him above all else in this life in his arms, and then he turned to the children, and told them excitedly that he would make them proud of him when he returned with great news, and perhaps even news of a new family member for Eden!

"Have a care, Jacob! The Elder's orders were very precise on that point, you are to *observe only* my son!" Admonished his father. His mother also started to cry out a warning, suddenly fearful for her firstborn child. However, Murphy held up a hand for silence and Ravenna immediately complied.

"*My son*, among the first ever to be granted a leave of absence from Eden with approval of the entire High Council." There was uninhibited pride and deep emotion in Murphy's voice.

"Come now my son, we must make our way to the main cave and join together with the others; you don't want to be left behind, do you?"

With those words barely out of his father's mouth, Jacob raced across the grass to the main chamber where most of the community had already gathered to bid a history making farewell, and wish good fortune and safe return to the six men.
The habitually long winded Most Revered Elders, spoke only briefly to the assembled group of men, and after imparting a few, very short words of wisdom, they too raised their hands in a salute, as they bid them success, good fortune, safe journey, and a speedy return. Andrei, another young man who had hoped to be among the chosen for the expedition ran to Cain and whispered loudly – don't forget to look for a woman for me!

Senior Freeman – is a very tall, *very* fine-looking, well-muscled man of mature cycles, he has a smooth, unblemished deep caramel complexion, his dark wavy hair is tied back neatly in the customary long thick plait that falls well below his hips to his thighs, he has intelligent, almost black, slightly almond shaped eyes, eyes that even when relaxed and smiling, habitually took in every detail of his surroundings - led the other five men out through the colonnade of caves and into the first area, known as New Eden, where all the men who had followed stood around calling out advice and cautions. The small band of explorers turned one last time to look around at their friends and families, who, with a loud chorus of safe return, burst into song as they all waved good-bye to the small group of intrepid explorers.

The six men walked in single file through the narrow passageway chattering away like children, until they reached the still well-hidden entrance in the rock face. It took the strength of all six men to move the three heavy tree trunks that have secured the hidden gateway for many years. Senior Freeman turned to Jacob and said quietly, well young man, as you have been out here many times past, which direction would you suggest is the one to lead us to our destiny?

Jacob and Cain both paled suddenly, they turned and looked at each other in complete astonishment, wondering *how, how* he could *possibly* know anything about their secret forays beyond the walls. Jacob looked back at the two Senior men, and simply pointed in a southeasterly direction, and stuttered to Senior Freeman, "I – we –that is, I, well, I didn't know anyone knew." Once again, the senior spoke quietly. "Jacob, *nothing* moves in Eden that goes unnoticed by the council, you are not the first to explore the immediate area of the Outland's son, in my own youth your father Murphy and I did exactly the same things as you boys have done, and for exactly the same reasons, therefore I understand only too well that strong pull to adventure, it's a hunger born within us and cannot be denied, and there's a special excitement from doing something prohibited isn't there? Our natural curiosity, combined with caution and a lack of self-restraint in some areas, flows as intensely through us, as it did our grand sires." He looked from one young face to the other before speaking again. "Men such as us, are not easy being kept behind our walls permanently. Where one man always sees Eden as a paradise, another man may – at times - feel caged, like a go-bit in a pen. Remember our history, and those Upper Valley people who felt imprisoned, and left? That feeling of being locked in cost them their lives, however, we six are all very different men, living in different times. From this moment forward" – he placed his hand inclusively on Alder's broad, muscular shoulder- "we are no longer your seniors, we are -as our revered ancestors would have said - comrades in arms, equal in all things, sharing all burdens, all hardships, and all discoveries, equally. From now on we are Freeman and Alder. Now let's move out."

The two older men were totally different in appearance. Alder, although equally as tall as Freeman, was of heavier build, and as fair skinned, light haired, and blue eyed as Freeman was dark. It would be a very unwise man indeed who would trifle with either of them. The four boys were younger versions of these two, all were tall, with outstanding good looks, all were long limbed, with agile, well-muscled bodies that each carried with the easy, graceful movements, of well-trained warriors.

The men walked in companionable semi silence for many hours, their long strides eating up the miles, while their eyes were constantly being drawn to something new or different.

For these men, none of whom had ever ventured such a distance beyond the walls of their home before, the contrast between this hot, hostile outer land, and the lush beauty of Eden, was incredible. Out here the only things to see were low rolling grasslands, the coarse grass was scattered here and there with spikey bushes that grew low to the ground, and the scenery was the same in every direction for as far as their eyes could see.

How different this grass was! The Outland grass was sharp, prickly and filled with tiny black burrs that stuck to their short sarongs, and to the hairs on their arms and legs, causing their exposed limbs to become red and irritated. Alder called for a stop around midday, with every intention of refreshing themselves by taking a little food and water, as well as to give their shoulders some respite from the weight of their packs.

However, as soon as they sat down, they were besieged by small flying pests. Never had they seen anything resembling these tiny creatures before, they were like miniscule birds that rose up from the grass like a fine black cloud, and flew into their eyes, up their noses, and into their mouths and buzzed around their ears.

As if those creatures weren't bad enough, there were also tiny little orange and black things with six legs that crawled up from the ground, and were running up their legs and even under their sarongs, crawling over *every* part of their bodies, and inflicting upon them a most unpleasant stinging, burning sensation, that rapidly became an excruciating itching red swelling, and to their complete dismay, the men soon discovered that the more they scratched, the bigger, and itchier, those swellings became. Freeman spoke first, he was – like them - busily brushing and slapping at the little offenders. "Shoulder your packs and run!" And run they did. Laughing at themselves and the strange spectacle they must present. They were still running when Marshall, who was way out in front of the rest of the group, turned back and reported that he could see water ahead.

The group continued running toward the water with every intention of diving straight into the welcome coolness, but instead, coming to a complete stop when Alder called for caution.

Each man, with his short throwing spear in hand, stood four body lengths from the man beside him around the edge of the water, searching for anything that might represent a physical threat to them. They approached the water cautiously, not knowing if there were any dangers from fish, or whether perhaps some other biting or stinging creatures were hiding below the surface patiently waiting for them. However, the tranquil water appeared to be clean, cool, and very inviting, so they gladly dropped their packs to the ground, untied their sarongs and throwing caution to the winds they ran, totally naked, launching themselves head first into the water and began splashing about like children. They swam and splashed in the crystal-clear waters of the pool only long enough to cool off.

After their very refreshing swim, and having eaten a little of their rations, they were feeling adequately rested, so they refilled their water skins, and were ready to resume their mission.

As they continued their trek across the grasslands, Marshall was watching the sky slowly changing colours, from the brilliant blue they'd seen all day long, to a strange orange and then a purple colour, their daylight was dimming rapidly into nighttime.

Freeman and Alder stopped and crouched down to scrutinise the ground, they were looking for more of those same nasty little biting things they'd had the misfortune to encounter earlier, and finding nothing troubling, Alder called out for the boys to halt, telling them it was a good place to break for the night. A simple meal of smoked go-bit meat, fruit, and water, was sufficient to appease their hunger. Once they'd eaten; they each rolled up in their hooded cloaks and folded a fine woollen blanket from their pack under their heads and slept completely undisturbed until the first rays of watery sunlight touched their faces. A new day was upon them. Marshal woke up, feeling a bit confused at first, but when he remembered where he was, and why, smiled broadly and stretched as he watched the dew glistening on the long grass stems near his face.

The men ate sparingly, consuming only fruit for the first meal of the day, and after performing some basic exercises for half an hour to loosen up their muscles, they were eager to resume their journey once again.

And so, they continued on, following the routine of walking, eating, and sleeping. For thirteen more, long, steaming hot, disappointing days they walked. While their eyes continuously scanned every inch of their surroundings for dangers, for others of their kind, or threats, but as for there being any sign of other human beings, or even a place where human occupation might have been possible, there was nothing. The grass grew taller but aside from that

very minor detail the scenery around them had changed little. Far in the distance they could see something shimmering, Cain thought it was another, much larger, pool of water, but Theo said it was much too high to be water. Freeman suggested they wait until they could see what it was before they'd decide what to do. Their long strides continued to eat up the miles and the shimmering they'd thought might be water had disappeared a good while ago. "HALT!" Alder called out; he held up his hand for complete silence. "Can you hear that? What *is* that sound?"
There was loud whoosh-whooshing noise, very faint at first, but rapidly becoming much louder. Each man stood perfectly still, with only his eyes darting around to try and locate the origin of the strange outland noise.
Jacob felt a peculiar shaking sensation deep in the pit of his stomach. It was the first time in his life he'd ever felt dread.

Cain saw it first. A huge ugly, black featherless bird, rose up slowly from a gulley. This strange creature was like nothing they'd ever seen before. This bird had an enormous, bulbous head, with one huge eye, and directly behind the head was a long thin tail, they could see that this bird had no wings, but it *did* have the strangest spinning feathers on its head and on its tail, and it gave off a strong wind, so strong that it caused them to stumble backwards in alarm. The long grass was being beaten flat beneath the strange powerful bird.
The men of Eden huddled together in horror, laying flat on the ground as the bird, paused directly above

them, just hanging there watching them. It swayed gently, moving from side-to-side until it hovered only a few feet above the ground, and directly in front of them.

Instinctively they jumped up and tried to run back to the safety of Eden, but even as they ran, they knew it was a hopeless exercise. Eden was too many sunrises away, and this bird could easily dive on them and devour them in seconds.

Astonishingly, the bird started speaking, although they could not understand the words it spoke, as the creatures head feathers were making too much noise. Freeman called for extreme caution, while Marshall pulled open his pack to offer the bird some dried go-bit meat, hoping that it would simply eat it and fly away again. However, far from taking the offering and departing, the giant bird lowered itself slowly down the few remaining feet that had separated it from the earth, and came to rest gently on the ground. The spinning feathers on top of its head began to slow down, with a loud whoop, whoop, whoop, until they too gradually came to a silent stop. The monstrous bird just sat there staring silently, with sunlight glittering blindingly off that single big eyeball, it simply stayed there, not blinking, not moving, just staring straight at them.

Bravely, Marshall took one single, tremendously cautious step closer to the bird, holding the dried meat out in front of him with a shaking hand. All the other men were desperately trying to see its mouth; whispering quietly, Alder said surely it must be underneath the eye, "look under the eye Marshall," he hissed, "can you see it?"

However, before Marshall could reply, one side of the birds' head opened up, and a strange-looking green creature, stepped out.

As one, the men dropped to the ground, wrapping their arms around their heads for protection. They were absolutely petrified, having no knowledge as to what this awful creature was, or what it could, or would do to them, *or* what was to become of them now.

"Silence men, remain silent and perhaps it will tire and leave us alone."

They heard the scraping sound as the other side of the head was opened up too, and allowed another green creature to step out and slowly walk towards them. These creatures were armed with peculiarly crafted long, unwieldly looking spears. They couldn't possibly be throwing spears, because they appeared to be too bulky and awkward, besides that there was no pointed spike on the end, these were the strangest looking spears that Freeman had ever seen, because instead of coming to a point the spear end appeared to be a hollow tube, similar to the breathing tubes they used whenever they gathered reeds from the pond. He thought they resembled the blow guns he'd used as a child only these were much, much bigger, far too big to be an effective blow gun. His attention was once again taken up with the strange creatures as they slowly moved closer and closer. All Cain could see from his position on the ground was part of a long green leg that ended with a black hoof.

By this time the men were visibly shaking with revulsion; the first two creatures were soon joined by four more, they were speaking to each other in a strange language, although there were a few words sprinkled here and there that the men of Eden thought they recognised, but weren't able to comprehend. Jacob lifted his head up from under his arms, and his eyes looked straight at the coldest, most aggressive, fearsome looking bulbous green head belonging to one of the creatures. It was ugly in the most extreme sense, having an overly large round, green and black head, two enormous shiny black eyes, a small nose, a small mouth, and a black chin. Jacob cautiously looked around at the other creatures, and found them to be almost identical. Gathering all his courage, Jacob stood upright and attempted to speak, but his throat was so dry that his voice failed him. Cain had felt Jacob move, and followed his lead, and in one synchronised motion Freeman, Alder, Theo, and Marshall all followed suit. The six men of Eden were standing shoulder to shoulder, as brothers, facing this unexpected and unspeakable danger as a single unit.

Suddenly there were repeated, brief flashes of brilliant lightning coming from somewhere directly behind the larger group of creatures, although these flashes were so much brighter than lightning that sometimes struck the topmost edge of their valley walls; this strange lightning caused the men to back away fearfully and shield their eyes.

The next thing the men knew, the creatures had taken full advantage of their sudden blindness to force them back to the ground face down, from there their arms were secured firmly together behind their backs. There were many more flashes of lightning, although the flashes were moving closer to them now too, and it sounded intolerably like these creatures were laughing at them! Cain drew on all his courage and spoke. He strained his neck to look up at the first creature and asked it what it was, and what did it want of them?

At the same time Freeman found his voice and said- "We are men of Eden; we have come through The Outlands in search of others of our kind." In mid conversation all talk and laughter ceased immediately, meanwhile the now silent creatures all turned in unison, to face Freeman. The men of Eden were roughly dragged to their feet, and motioned to stand still. What took place next was, without doubt, the most nauseatingly outrageous thing any of the men had ever witnessed, and as one they wanted to vomit – the creature actually detached a part of its own head, and dropped it to the ground! The creature's next action was equally disturbing for the men, when it *removed its outer eyes*, and dropped them carelessly into the hard outer shell of the head. Following on from that revolting spectacle, the creature spoke into a small box on the back of its claw. The men were forced to stand there, with their hands strapped tightly behind their backs, guaranteeing there was no way for them to gain access their weapons, consequently they were compelled to watch and study the strange actions of these gruesome creatures carefully, especially those numerous individuals with the long, strange looking spears, the men of Eden couldn't help wondering what would happen to them next. Would they be killed? Would they ever see their home again? Alder, speaking very softly, asked if Freeman could hear another, different sound, it seemed to be getting louder.

Just as he spoke, a huge green *thing* rolled into view coming across the grass and straight toward them, making a fierce, deep angry growling sound that suddenly stopped when the beast came to rest nearby. More and more of the green creatures tumbled from the beasts' belly and began running toward them, brandishing their spears, shouting loudly, but unintelligibly, while they quickly and completely surrounded the bound and helpless men of Eden.

One very dark creature that appeared to be a great deal larger than the others, and was obviously their leader, walked, empty handed, toward the six men and stopped, just short of a spear's length in front of them. There were more dazzling flashes of lightning emanating from a very small brown creature that appeared to be hiding behind the leader. The lead creature having previously removed both its own outer head and eyes, stood in front of the men. With the outer head and eyes removed, the creature's inner head -even though its skin was striped dark green and black, it closely resembled a human. It spoke slowly and clearly, using words not unlike their own language.

"Who are you men, and where have you come from?" Freeman looked directly into the creature's empty black eyes, and replied just as slowly; "We are men of

Eden, we have travelled through The Outlands in search of others of our kind who would be willing to return and tie with us." Freeman thought it apropos to add: "You are the first living creatures we have seen in fourteen sunrises."

As he spoke the sky overhead blackened, thunder roared, and lightening flashed. AN OUTLAND STORM! To be caught beyond reach of the safety of the walls in such a storm meant only one thing to the men of Eden. Certain death. The men dropped to the ground in abject terror, as a heavy deluge of freezing cold water fell from the skies, wetting their bodies and clothing, before soaking into the earth around them, like heavy spray when the waterfall was in spate – however, these strange creatures seemed not to notice the storm at all.

Three more beasts rolled up behind the bird disgorging many, many, more spear wielding creatures that circled around and came up behind the men from Eden and began prodding them with their blunt spears, forcing them to stand upright once more, when the men did not react, the creatures began poking and pushing them more forcefully, shoving them forward in the direction of the now snarling beast.

Alder, as with the other men of Eden, quaked with fear as they were pushed and prodded, forced to crawl on hands and knees into the empty belly of the beast and once inside made to squat down on their haunches while more and more of the foul-smelling green, creatures crawled in and sat around them with their spears ready should any of the men of Eden attempt to move.

The angry beast growled loudly as it was forced to move, lumbering back the way it had come across the grasslands.

At one point when the men had attempted to speak, they were poked sharply in the back by a spear-carrying creature, so they had to endure not only the terrible stink of the creatures, but also the beast's foul breath, the bouncing around, and the terrifying growling of the furious beast, in silence.

In about the same length of time it takes to kill, clean, and skin a go-bit had passed, the jolting movement ceased, and the beast rested for a second time. The belly of the beast was opened up and they were forcibly dragged out into the darkness by green creatures and made to stand in silence surrounded by more spear wielding creatures.

Their leader reappeared, and before Alder could ask why their packs had been taken the men were moved out -once again at spear point. With their hands still bound tightly behind their backs, the six men of Eden were pushed and prodded through the cold and damp darkness, this time into an enormous brilliantly white cave with many entrances and strange rooms. Cain and Marshall stood rooted to the spot as they looked around them in awe. Somehow these creatures, as crude as they were, they had managed to smooth the walls until they were perfectly straight – it must have taken years, but the men still preferred their own, more welcoming cave rooms in Eden. These creatures had by some means the men couldn't begin to imagine, also captured sunlight and now, in the dark of night, it was shining brightly from many places in the roof of the white cavern.

Everything in this cave made strange noises, sounds they'd never heard before; whirring, clicking, or beeping sounds came at them from every possible direction and surface. Inside this large cavern there were yet more, a great many more of the green creatures, however these creatures were more ordinary in appearance in as much as they had no outer heads or outer eyes, so they must be of a different or a lesser breed, because these creatures wore no facial design and they carried only hopelessly small spears.

Inside this cave there were also women, many women, women of all ages, sizes and shapes. However, and to his extreme disappointment, Jacob saw none he would ever be willing to tie with. He glanced over at an equally disappointed looking Marshall, and shook his head in silent agreement. As they stood waiting, an older women spoke to the leading green creature – who didn't seem to be listening. 'Corporal, they have arrived and are already waiting for you in room Z-223. Corporal? Corporal! *Room Z-223 NOW!'*

Seeing so many women in one place had momentarily distracted the men from the predicament they had found themselves in, so much so that when the Corporal suddenly came to a halt outside another cave access, it went quite unnoticed by the men of Eden and they all stumbled into him!

A solid white privacy shield opened to reveal a man, much like themselves in height and appearance although he was dressed from head to toe in very fine white robes.

At this point the men of Eden were separated, each man was taken into an unconnected cave room. Once inside, and the privacy shield had been secured, Jacob's sarong was forcibly removed, leaving him to stand completely naked, in the centre of the freezing cold room.

Another, quite different white robed male entered the room and handed Jacob a strange looking garment, indicating that he should cover himself with it, before directing him to sit on a chair. Jacob tied the rough garment around his waist, then sat and waited, uncertain about whatever might happen next.

The waiting also seemed to be an eternity for Cain as he sat alone and shivering – from fear and uncertainty, as much as from the freezing cold air blowing through an invisible unplugged hole somewhere in the roof above him.

What has happened to the others, he wondered? Were they, like him, naked, alone, and left waiting in a cold cave? Or, were they still together? He had no way of knowing.

Even though he could read the words written on walls all around him with ease, he could make no sense of them at all - No Admittance – Staff Only – No Exit - Fire Door - Nurses Station – Resuscitation Cart – Emergency Treatment Room - he could not figure out what many of the words meant, and the words he *did* understand, like, nurse, fire, cart, no, and only, these words had no connection with the accompanying words as he understood them.

Sitting immobile and wasting valuable time was beginning to frustrate him, so he stood and walked over to the entrance and opened the privacy screen, seeing no one about, he walked out into the long white tunnel, where a green creature saw him and immediately raised a spear, aiming at Cain's head and waving it menacingly.

Unbeknown to Jacob or Cain, waiting in an identical cave just a little further down the long white tunnel, Marshall too, was in terrible distress. A group of the white robed men were touching him, prodding and feeling his private places, they were doing things to him that as an untied male, shamed and humiliated him. A tall male, dressed entirely in white robes, squeezed his arm and leg muscles, and then a small, fat male, also dressed in white robes, pinched and twisted the skin on his face and ears. Both white robed males were working together; they probed his body with various cold hard instruments, as well as using their long bony fingers, fingers that were covered in a very strange, bright yellow skin. His eyes were searched with blinding pinpoints of light, and a long probe was pushed into his ears, after that, a wide band was placed around his arm, and as it tightened it squeezed his flesh alarmingly, the band tightened until he thought his arm would surely break. Next, and to his great indignation, the taller male pulled, prodded, cupped, and poked around his genitals! He was forced, by two green creatures, to bend almost double, and another probe was pushed deep into his anus. Marshall let out a roar of outraged disgust, however the two green creatures holding him were joined by two more of their kind and working together they just exerted more force to hold him still. When the gross indignity finally ended, the young man was released before being pushed down onto a cold hard chair.

Before Marshall had a chance to object, a creature grabbed his arm while the tall white robed male had stuck a short thorn into his elbow and took out his blood, at the same time as this was being done, his long plait was grabbed from behind and yanked down hard, his head snapped back and his mouth was forced open. The small fat male put his sickening, nasty tasting yellow fingers inside, searching for something, he probed around inside his cheeks, under his tongue, around his gums and the inside of his lips, next he carefully inspected each of his teeth with a shiny tool and then used the bright pinpoint light to look up his nose! But those yellow fingers never rested, they carried on relentlessly, squeezing and feeling his tongue, twisting and pulling at every tooth in his mouth before he was made to stand inside a clear grey box that showed his bones clearly against the wall...

After that series of indignities, Marshall was made to stand on a small square box that had spinning numbers. He thought they were finally finished with their shaming of him, but no, following that round of degradation, the tall white robed male pushed him hard up against a vertical line of numbers on the wall and kicked repeatedly at his ankles until the backs of his heels were pressed hard up against the wall, as soon as the white robe was satisfied with his subjects position, he proceeded to slide a disc down the row of numbers before pressing it firmly to the top of his head. All the while these shameful, and to Marshall's mind, quite senseless things, were being done to him, the lad had heard only a few grunts, however, not one single word passed between the two white robed males. The taller, and apparently superior of the two white robed men, gestured for Marshall to once again return to the chair, while he made his words on a book.

This gave Marshall an idea; he walked over to the man, looked him straight in the eye, and gently removed the pen from his hand and wrote: Marshall Tyler 20 cycles, untied man of New Eden - in a clear and beautifully crafted old-fashioned script. The tall white robed male's head snapped up leaving his mouth hanging open, just staring up at his subject wordlessly. He gestured to the small fat male to follow him and they both ran from the room! Marshall, thinking he'd unintentionally committed a disrespectful act, and wanting to apologise, ran after him calling loudly – White Robes! White Robes! I intended no disrespect... The other five men of New Eden, on hearing Marshall's worried voice, also ran from their separate rooms and joined in the chase.

From somewhere a honking alert horn sounded and the sunlights in the roof started flashing. The next minute green creatures started arriving in droves, pouring into the long white tunnel from every possible access point, they seemed to fill all the available space in the tunnel. Quickly positioning themselves in front of, alongside and behind, successfully surrounding the men of Eden, and every single green creature had their spear held shoulder high, the unspoken message was perfectly clear. Stop

where you are - or you die. The men of Eden knew, and understood, these warning signs only too well from their own war games, as a result they stood quite still, with their hands behind their backs, their feet apart and at ease, because unlike their war games back home – these creatures *would* kill on command and without hesitation. They maintained that position until the tall white robed male forcibly made his way through the throng of green figures and spoke directly to Marshall. "Where did you learn to write? Are you able to understand me when I speak to you?" Freeman stepped in front of Marshall, and spoke quietly, calmly and clearly.
"I am Senior Freeman McIntosh; I am the team leader and the person responsible for this expedition through The Outlands from our home in New Eden." Every creature there, stopped moving and held their breath. More, many more, white robed males forced their way through the, now very attentive throngs of green creatures. One white robed man in particular, who himself had the proud bearing of a senior, and was therefore automatically given due respect, asked Freeman and his group to follow him. As he turned around, he shouted at no one in particular "and turn that goddam thing off!" the loud hooting noise and flashing sunlights stopped almost immediately. The senior white robe turned and beckoned to another, less impressive white robed male to join him. He led them through the swarms of green creatures that were quickly moving aside and pressing themselves hard up against both sides of the long, almost painfully brilliant white tunnel, creating a pathway just barely wide enough for the group to pass in

single file and enter into a side chamber. Once inside and the privacy shield fastened, the most senior white robed male asked them to "please be seated" and motioned for the other white robed male to seat himself also.

He then proceeded to do the strangest thing! He picked up a short, thick black stick from the table; he placed it next to his ear and after a few heartbeats started talking to it! After a brief interval he replaced the stick on the table and stood up. "Mr McIntosh, I am Doctor Vernon Gatemen, I am also a Full Colonel in the Andeseine Army, and this" he gestured to the other white robe "is my esteemed colleague Doctor Elijah Helot, also a Full Colonel in the Andeseine army."
This Gateman person's voice was very harsh, and his clipped words have a tendency to to imply a definite threat.
"You Sir, *and* your men, are a complete mystery to us. Will you please tell us a little about yourselves? Can you start by telling us *where* you've come from?" he paused long enough to look at each man in turn.
"Will you explain -because we're also very interested in exactly *how* you six men have managed to completely elude not only our *supposedly* elite border guards, but your group has, by some, *as yet*, unknown means, evaded every security device and every very costly, piece of surveillance equipment as well!"

With each *request* he struck the table with the flat palm of his hand, in addition, along with each round of questioning his phrasing changed subtly from, will you? To – you will! A slight, but nevertheless disturbing deviation that was not unnoticed by the six men of Eden.

"You will tell us *how* you managed to *survive* in the restricted zone.

You will tell us *exactly* how you've come through more than *six hundred miles* of rough, hostile terrain, without benefit of aircraft *or* land vehicles, you have no protective clothing, no boots, and you carried only minimal supplies of rations, there was nothing apart from some dried meat and water. And yet, you have all remained, quite inexplicably, in perfect health. I want to, no, it's absolutely *essential* for me *to know how that's possible.*"

His emphasis now lay heavily on the, '*You Will*' it had become a definite command now, and almost – but not quite yet – a threat. It soon became apparent that there were to be no more *requests*.

"You *will* tell me *exactly how* you achieved this quite incredible feat, and I *demand* a truthful answer, simply because *it is not humanly possible!*"

He was shouting now. "You are clearly *not* Andeseine, so *which* colony have you come from? *Who,* are you *spying* for, *who* do you report to, and *how* do you make your reports? Since we have been unable to detect any communicative devices in, on, or about your person or your packs."

As he spoke, he glared menacingly at each of the men in turn.

"What are your ranks?" Bang! Down went his hand.

"*Who* is your commanding officer?" Bang! Again, he slammed his hand down on the desk. Bang!

"*What* is the purpose of your mission?" Bang!

"To which *force* do you belong?" Bang!

"Where are your uniforms?" Bang!

"You *do* realise that you are in total violation of far too many rules of engagement to count, do you not?" Bang!

"I'm positive that you *do* realise that you could be imprisoned under war crimes legislation, for the rest of your miserable lives - with *no* chance of parole." Bang!

He wiped away a froth of spittle that had gathered at the corners of his mouth. As he stared down at the calm, impassive faces of the men seated before him, he was becoming increasingly baffled.

They obviously understood his words, yet they showed no emotion at all. None whatsoever, there was not as much as the flicker of an eye, or a twitch of the lip, from any of them.

There was neither fear, nor arrogance, apparent in any of them, he was trying to identify the unfamiliar expression on their faces, however the only word that came to mind was *innocence.* That's what he saw in them; yes, that was most certainly it, innocence. It was also *not* possible *or* acceptable.

Innocence certainly wasn't something he came across every day, he could not in fact, remember the last time he *had* seen it in *any* grown man's face.

He had to get to the bottom of this. He did not like being confused, and these men had him totally mystified. Their military baring belied that innocence, and yet... and yet... what if... no, that was completely impossible.

At that moment there was a loud banging on the privacy shield, a creature entered the room holding something that looked like a journal book, he handed it to the white robe, and then raising his hand to his head the creature clicked his heels together, turned and exited the cave room, securing the privacy screen behind him.

The men looked at each other, each of them wondering *when* they would be invited to speak, and also wondering how they could possibly answer the white robes questions, when he gave them no opportunity, nor invitation, to do so. He told them they would have to give him answers, however up to this point, there had been no invitation extended to respond.

"Well gentlemen, I have here the results of your health checks, and for the ravages your bodies *must* have sustained out there, you are all in extraordinarily good condition, that being so, there is no reason for your de briefing to be delayed a single moment longer." The white robe shuffled through some pages before he seemed to come to a decision. "If you will follow the sergeant here, he will take you along to our Major Delaney."

A green clad creature stood in the doorway, and Jacob counted seven more of them each with their spears raised in readiness, waiting outside in the long white tunnel.

The men of Eden remained seated, looking expectantly at doctor Gateman, waiting to be invited to speak, to give him the responses he demanded - but instead of inviting them to speak, the doctor turned to the waiting creatures and growled tersely – "get them out of here."

Without reason or warning the room filled with irrational unnecessary shouting, much loud stamping of booted feet and great confusion.

The men of Eden were grabbed tightly from behind by both arms, and held firmly by a green creature on each side who yanked them roughly from their chairs, and force-marched them out of the cave and into the long white tunnel where were spears pointed menacingly in their direction from every side.

Alder spoke quietly to Freeman, asking him what they should do. "If we are not invited to speak soon, I will be forced to violate our law, I will be forced by circumstance to put Respect aside, momentarily. I will be obliged by these most difficult and extraordinary situations, to speak out of turn."

The thought of breaking Eden's most fundamental law for *any* reason, caused the men great moral discomfort, but the alternative was to be trapped here in The Outlands. Being detained so far from family and community, was for them, an indescribable torment.

"Silence you two! No talking allowed!" Growled out one of the lead creatures menacingly. "Just keep quiet and follow me."

Therefore, that's exactly what they did, for the next one hundred and sixty paces.

Until the creature leading the way stopped outside another privacy shield.

"Wait here, *do not move*, and *do not speak*," instructed the green clad creature. The leader knocked on the privacy shield, and after another moment or two a different, though equally rough voice, bade them enter.

The men were unceremoniously shoved inside with a force that was completely unnecessary.

Looking around them, they found themselves in a green walled cave, high above their heads two rows of eight brilliant sunlights shone down from the smooth white roof, there were also eight seats, six chairs had been placed along the front of a long table with the other two situated behind it, and facing the six. There was a not very tall, but very heavily built, brutish looking man, with a very red, very unhealthy-looking face waiting inside. This male belonged to a different breed altogether, he obviously wasn't a white robe, as he was attired in foul-smelling soiled and unkempt dark blue robes, so he wasn't of the greens either – but whatever he was, he remained standing behind the table staring up at them with cold hard grey eyes.

By way of a greeting, he shouted for them to come forward and sit down.

The men followed the simple instruction in silence, and as soon as they were seated, the blue robed man immediately started shouting and gesturing wildly at them, while the slapping of his hands on the table kept time with his bellowed demands. He continued shouting loudly that every word spoken in this room was being recorded.

Irrational anger and illogical rage were evident in every line of his face, and all too apparent in the way he carried his bulky, very awkward body.

The men of Eden had no idea what they could possibly have done to warrant such appalling wrath, but whatever it was, Alder had had quite enough. He'd had more than enough of these people, with their disrespect and completely unjustifiable insolence to himself and to Freeman, after all, they were both Seniors, and to be disrespected at all was insult enough, but to be so blatantly disrespected in front of the impressionable younger men, such behaviour brought too much humiliation for them to tolerate, and he intended to at least attempt to reason with this irate blue robe.

With his eyes forcibly downcast as a sign of respect, a respect that he most certainly *did not* feel, Alder controlled his own anger as he stood up, and spoke. Keeping his tone even he began. "Sir, pray tell us what it is we have done to you, and to your people also, that has brought forth such fearsome antagonism, and aggressive hostility in your behaviour?" He paused, giving opportunity for the blue robe to respond, when a response was not forthcoming he continued. "We are but passive and simple farmers, we are a people who are unaccustomed to your ways, and unacquainted with your edicts; please sir; will you do us the honour of sanctioning us to share dialogue with you, as Senior to Senior? Moreover, let there be no unseemly acrimony, nor rancour, between us. Up to this point in time we have not been invited to communicate openly. Your medics have asked a great many questions of us, the senior white robe also, has asked of us numerous questions, as you yourself have only mere moments past, asked an abundance of questions of us also. However, no one has, as yet, granted us the right of reply. You stand over us, your attempt at intimidation is as crude as it is transparent, you demand of us the answers to a multitude of questions, yet you treat us with such intolerable disrespect by withholding both the right, and the *time*, in which to articulate an appropriate response. I ask you sir, in all humility, what answers do you require of us?" A brief silence met with no response, so he continued.

"We cannot speak without your sanction to do so, and certainly it is impossible to respond when no opportunity to do so has, thus far, been forthcoming."

The major was flabbergasted by the completely unexpected reply; he was confused by the man's strange, antiquated phraseology, as well as by his unfamiliar accent, and the precise, overly formal manner of language he used.

The men calmly observed the blue robes increasingly agitated demeanour, as he strode across the floor; he pulled the open the privacy shield, using unnecessary force, and roared at one of the green creatures, barking an order for him to bring the two doctors to him *immediately*.

The men sat patiently and waited in the now empty cave, talking quietly amongst themselves, totally unaware that their every movement, and every word, was being recorded from all possible angles, by both concealed cameras and hidden microphones, neither of which the men of Eden knew anything about.

Their conversation however was quite innocuous, simply that of people concerned for their families should their return to Eden be delayed by this tremendously unfortunate interlude.

Cain and Theo voiced their dismay at this waste of valuable time. "What if there won't be sufficient time remaining? If this interruption to the mission is to be prolonged indefinitely it will mean we'd be unable to find suitable women for the young men of Eden to breed with." Jacob had only been half listening, because he'd been carefully repeating and examining every word the blue robe had said to them in his mind and now he put it to the group that these people not only spoke falsely, but they did so in an open, and shameless manner. Not understanding Jacob's reasoning, Alder asked for him to explain his theory more thoroughly.

"Have this blue robes' very own words not exposed him as communicating to us complete and outright falsehoods!? When first we were brought into this cave, were we not, by his own utterances, informed that every word spoken within this place was being recorded? Is that not factual?" Each man agreed it was indeed an accurate account of his words. "Where then I ask, *where is* this taker of records?"

He made a show of looking around the small room.

"No person in this room do I perceive, with the exception of men of Eden, although, and with certainty, there is none other present with the means of recording our speech!"

Moments later the privacy shield burst open and the blue robe strode in, followed by the two white robes. This time however, they were accompanied by another three people who were each attired entirely in close fitting white robes.

The newcomers, two women and one man, walked over and took in every aspect of the decidedly unusual group of people sitting calmly, and quietly at ease, in front of them.

The first thing they noticed was that all six subjects were impressively tall. The group consisted of two, ruggedly handsome men of early middle years, and four adolescent males, all of whom were very muscular, and physically well proportioned, each man had strong white teeth and clear, very tanned skin above their long beards, and all six of them wore their hair in an extraordinarily long, very thick braid that hung down their backs, most reaching far below their hips, each man also wore a thin plaited leather strip tied around his forehead, their strong, long fingered hands were resting lightly on their knees.

The men of Eden immediately stood and bowed their heads respectfully as the women entered, both Freeman and Alder walked around to the other side of table to hold out chairs for the ladies to be seated.

This action caused a slight stir amongst the other males present, and a bright, delightfully appreciative smile from the women.

The briefest of introductions took place and the men were informed that now they 'could really get down to business,' as they returned to their seats.

However, that bit of information left the men of Eden well and truly confused, and this time it was Freeman who felt compelled to speak out.

"Sirs, and ladies, please be assured we have not come to this place to conduct business! Nor do we have business, of *any* nature, to be offering to you! We are, as we have stated very clearly on more than one occasion, naught but simple crop farmers. We are also breed egg giving birds, rabbits, lambs, pigs and go-bits. Our people have no need to buy, nor do we have need to sell, although we *have* learned of this, very strange concept in our schooling, however, as I have indicated here, there is no need of it, as Eden provides in plenty for all her children."

It was the white robes' turn to look utterly confused now, until one of the ladies stood and introduced herself, as Doctor Sámi Kayla, resident psychiatrist, "Sir, I am afraid you have misunderstood the Major, the term 'down to business' is merely a somewhat crude turn of phrase, it means quite simply that we can begin to talk."

Alder asked her – respectfully – "why then was the blue robe not straightforward in stating; 'the time has arrived for social discourse?' If we are to communicate with effect, then we must engage in a collective social dissertation. As men who hold senior status…"   "STOP IT! ENOUGH! ENOUGH OF THIS CRAZY TALK D'YOU HEAR ME!" Roared the blue robe, he was standing and leaning over the table now, snorting noisily through his bushy nostrils and pounding the tabletop repeatedly with his fists.

Oh, how these people *infuriated* him! He was accustomed to, and expected nothing less, than immediate and *total* compliance whenever he spoke.

His face had turned a dangerously dark shade of red, and thick white spittle flew out from his tight lips as he spoke.

He looked slowly around the table; he saw five pairs of eyes looking at him with alarm, and six pairs of eyes that all too clearly, revealed complete and utter contempt and revulsion.

Doctor Kayla rose gracefully from her seat once more and began speaking in a measured level voice;

"Gentlemen please, please, let's not begin badly, shall we?" Even though she was looking at the men, it was clear to everyone seated around the table that she was speaking to the angry, obese blue robe.

"Freeman, oh, pardon me, may I call you Freeman?" He bowed his head graciously to indicate acceptance. Once again, she was taken aback by the remarkably handsome features, and the Olde Worlde charming manners of these fascinating men, sitting there, as he was, in a simple blue hospital shift, with his stately, yet genteel bearing, he might well have been wearing a well tailored suit of the finest silk.

"Freeman, you have stated here" – she indicated the journal – "that you are simple farmers, and that you have travelled, on foot, with bare feet at that, for fourteen days, from a place you called Eden, is that correct?" Once again Freeman inclined his head graciously toward her, all the while maintaining direct eye contact.

"Please Freeman, you must speak up and answer these questions clearly." "Yes madam, we *are* simple farmers from Eden, which is a march taking in fourteen- and one-half sunrises, from our borderland, to the place where we were forcibly detained."

"Freeman, exactly where *is* Eden? It does not appear on any of our survey maps, and Freeman, before you answer the question, I feel it only fair to tell you that our maps are taken from satellite images, so they are pin point accurate, therefore what you have just said to me, to us, is quite impossible, this place you call Eden, most certainly *cannot be* within a fourteen day walk of where you and your group were found. Freeman the *nearest* settlement is more like a *four-*

month hike from here, and all of it, even if it *were* accessible on foot, the only possible way would be by crossing extremely treacherous terrain, if the extreme daytime heat didn't kill you, the freezing overnight temperatures would, because your body simply cannot adjust."

With those words the blue robe rose to his full, but less than impressive height, and shouted angrily across the table on which he slapped down hard with both palms. "I *demand* to be told the truth! Or else you will all suffer the full consequence that this army reserves for liars, and more especially, *for foreign spies!*"

Alder rose from his chair with great dignity, and turned to address the white robed woman; "I personally assure you madam, of the veracity of our statements. Speaking falsely, as is being suggested by this blue robe, would do a grave disservice to both parties present, plus, if we were to communicate falsely we, as seniors, would be exhibiting the poorest of examples to our younger members, for which under our law, the consequence is dire, in the extreme."

Once again, the blue robe roared; "What the hell is he *saying*? Speak properly man so that we can at least understand you!" At that moment a shrill noise sounded twice from a black stick vibrating on the table, causing the men to shove their chairs backward, and stand up in alarm. Immediately the armed guards turned their weapons on them. The blue robe spoke to the stick, nodding his head, and making grunting sounds, then said. "Is that so Sir… I understand Sir…yes Sir…immediately Sir!"

He returned the stick to the table, and then ordered the guards to lower their weapons and leave the room. He then turned and indicated the group of white robes should join him in the tunnel for a moment.

The men of Eden were once again left alone in the cold, all-white cave to talk quietly amongst themselves.

Alder and Freeman were fast losing the inner battle to keep their utter mortification and anger under control, anyone who knew them would have already noticed the thick veins pulsating in their necks and temples - it was certainly *not* a good sign. Freeman, speaking louder than was the custom, said; "that blue robe is naught but a posturing dim-witted fool, he is heaping insult upon mistreatment. Not one basic act of decency has been afforded us since we were so violently detained, we have been forcibly dragged here, thrown inside a foul beast, bound both hand and foot like a go-bit ready for the cooking fire. They have heaped maltreatment and appalling insults upon our persons with their medics' tools, we have been abused and erroneously accused of wrongful actions - actions of which we have no knowledge! However, we have been offered neither food nor drink, nor have there been any physical comforts provided to us for our use. The absence of fundamental decency *or* basic courtesy from these people is not only offensive, it is entirely inexcusable, and it is overwhelmingly ignorant behaviour on their part. Although in hindsight that offers a great deal by way of explaining the blue robes appalling behaviour"

Now once again, they'd been left alone in this cold cave, totally bare except for the table and chairs, wasting more of their valuable, but very limited time, when rightfully, they should be far removed from this place and continuing their search for suitable mates.
Freeman rose from his chair and walked to the privacy shield, he turned the handle as he had seen the others do, however it would not open, so he copied the rhythmic banging he had observed the blue robe making, although as before, there was no response.
He had just returned to his seat when the privacy shield opened, and a large group of the green clad creatures entered.
The blue robe was with them, and as he handed each man of Eden into the custody of two of the faceless creatures, he growled out. "These soldiers will take you to your temporary quarters, where you will find everything necessary for your stay with us, food, drink, clothing and some reading materials, telescreen, music etcetera are all provided. I will be seeing you again a little later, after you have had a chance to rest." He turned to the line of green creatures and snarled "Just get them out of my sight. *NOW!* GO!"
With that, each man was taken –none too gently- by two creatures, a further one hundred and nine paces to two huge silver doors that marked the end of the long white tunnel. The new tunnel divided three ways and the group were turned into another area

where many numbered privacy shields opened off yet another long white tunnel there were a great many sunlights shining from that roof also.

The creatures called a halt outside an open privacy shield, and with unnecessary force, pushed Theo inside before pulling the shield closed, the men of Eden were quickly moved along to the next numbered privacy shield, the actions were repeated five more times. Alder noted that beside each numbered door there was another door next to it displaying the same number but with a letter of the alphabet as well.

Theo looked around him in complete dismay; he was all alone in this cold white place. White walls, white floor, there was a thick white cloth covering a too soft –he surmised it to be a sleeping place, there were rough white robes, and an assortment of strange cloth garments he didn't recognise at all, against a wall stood a smooth white table and two heavy white chairs that had only one central support which was set deep into the floor, he discovered however that even though he was unable to move the chair, the seat turned completely around! There were also some square black things in the wall that he had never seen before. There was another white privacy shield directly across from the first, and looking up he discovered there were three disappointingly dark sunlight's set into the white roof and two, high square openings that allowed limited daylight into the cave, however they were carved too high to see outside.

He walked to the second privacy shield and turned the handle, it opened onto a stark white bathing room, complete with what he really hoped was a latrine! To his immense relief it was. After a little trial and some startling errors, Theo eventually managed to work out all the knobs and buttons in the bathing room, they were very different to those at home, but not so much so that with a little trial and error he couldn't work out their purpose.

Once he had relieved himself, like any young, healthy, intelligent young man, he investigated his new surroundings.

The sleeping place was uncomfortably soft, he preferred his nice firm pallet at home. The journals that lay on the small table were of a strange, yet he had to admit, a very fine material indeed, even though reading any of them presented him with quite a challenge.

The depictions were all alien to him, he didn't understand what he was looking at, and as for the words, they made little, or no sense to him either, even though the alphabet was the same as the one he had been taught to read as a child. He put the journals aside to look at later. He decided he'd feel much better after he'd had a shower and washed his hair. He wished he still had his satchel because his clean sarong, his comb and his cloak were all inside it. He had no way to comb his hair, or get rid of the rough cloth garment they'd forced upon him now.

It actually took him more time to work out how to operate the shower, than it had taken to investigate his quarters! Although, there was one incredibly exciting feature in the cave, it was right next to the sleeping place!

A large mirror had been set into the wall. He had only ever seen a very small one before, a broken and very badly speckled mirror that belonged to the Founding Family, was kept safely locked away in the main chamber with all the other artefacts belonging to the Founding Family, but touching it was strictly forbidden, only once in his life had he seen himself reflected in it. Usually, the reflection in pond water showed him what he looked like.

However, *this* mirror was simply magnificent. He could see his entire person, head to toe, reflected very clearly! It amused him to pull faces, to smooth his fine beard, to check his mouth and teeth, to investigate various body parts, and to look up his nose! It was also amusing to see how fast he could turn around and 'catch' himself!

The doctors seated on the other side of the two-way mirror had absolutely no idea what to make of these people. They all agreed however that, on one hand they are, by today's standards, exceptionally primitive. "It's patently obvious that they don't have, or even understand the importance of proper clothing, their only garment is a simple homespun woollen cloth worn tied around their hips, and although they are a very beautiful garment, their goat and rabbit skin cloaks are hand sewn, and animal gut has been used for thread, it's also evident they've never worn any form of underclothing, trousers, shirts or shoes; they seem to know absolutely nothing of even the most basic objects of modern civilisation either.

Yet, on the *other* hand, they are all, extremely articulate, each one of them is highly intelligent, and they are most definitely educated, albeit a very rudimentary level of education, they can all read, write, add and subtract, multiply and divide, quickly and accurately. They've given me the impression they come from a very structured, although - if they *are* what they say they are – an extremely primitive culture, however, to add even further to the confusion, they are to a great extent, highly refined gentlemen!"

"They are decidedly civilised, although their etiquette and their manner of speaking are both out-of-date, by about two hundred years or more, as is their beautifully crafted but most definitely old script, handwriting."

"Nothing, but nothing, about these men is adding up! How can there be a well-mannered, highly respectful and educated man, walking around in nothing but a homespun loincloth and animal skins? The only way to describe them is that they seem to have been caught in a time warp!"

"Clearly, none of them have ever cut their hair or shaved their facial hair, not one of them has even given the razor a second glance, so it's obvious they don't know what it's used for. The first thing each man did was to relieve himself, shower, and wash his hair, although, while none of them touched the soap, they were very thorough with their washing, so their personal hygiene is obviously of great importance to them."

"What about all the antics in front of the mirrors? Bizarre, it's all just too peculiar. We have ourselves a mystery on our hands here gentleman, a real live mystery. Times six."

Although the good doctor was honest enough to admit to herself that she was greatly intrigued by them.

An onlooker may well have observed that she was captivated by them, even more so, by one in particular!

In her notes the doctor suggested continued observation of each man individually. She hoped that she would come to learn more about them in due course, after she had viewed, and had had a good chance to study all of the video and voice recordings, from their interactions as a group, and also their solitary behaviour, much more closely.

Meanwhile, and unbeknown to the men, they continued to be observed closely.

They were all given food and drink; however, as instructed, each man was to be left completely alone, to see exactly how he reacted to this apparently new environment.

While her initial written comments and notes were taken by messenger to the Base Commander in the afternoon, and that should have been an end to her working day, Dr Kayla continued her observations long into the night.

A substantial meal was taken to each man in his room and placed on the table along with the suitable condiments, cutlery, and glassware.

The meals consisted of meat, vegetables, rice and pasta; there was a bowl filled with jelly and ice cream, and another bowl of assorted fruits for dessert, along with a slice of either chocolate cake or cheese cake, there was also a small platter of various cheeses and crackers, and a pot of tea or coffee, all men were given a carafe of water.

Some of the meals were served cold; others had cold tea or coffee.

Each room was equipped with a small microwave oven for their convenience; however, it soon became very evident to Doctor Kayla that they had no idea it was there, let alone what it was meant to be used for. Likewise, the telescreen, not a single man took any notice of the TS or of any of the other electrical appliances available to them. Jacob had, after a while, managed to open the microwave oven door but found only an empty box, next he tried to open the *door* of the telescreen, but gave up after he couldn't find an opening. She made a note in the margin, while they don't actively avoid these appliances, it's quite apparent that they simply don't know what they are. Just as mysterious, and every bit as interesting to the doctor, was the fact that they didn't seem to understand the lighting system either, when it became too dark to see any longer, they simply pulled the covers off the beds onto the floor, laid down and went to sleep!

Where have these people *been*? *Where* or *what*, is their Eden? Can it really exist at all? She'd pondered these questions many times over in the last few hours, and was determined to find the answers.

The doctor was, by this time, truly and deeply fascinated by her new subjects; she couldn't wait to review the rest of the recordings now. Even though the video surveillance for the whole division was supposed to be cut off once the men were asleep, Dr. Kayla decided to keep recording – just in case they were trying to fool her. If they were though, then they were all exceptional actors.

The Commander was supposed to be informed of any changes made to the routine, but the hour was late, too late to inform him now, and besides, he'd told her he would be off base for the night, and she didn't think it was an important enough change to disturb him.

In the small silent hours after midnight, Freeman was roughly dragged from his sleep by four burly green clad creatures and taken back to the largest - but now vacant - interview room, where they had been taken the previous morning.

The soldiers were completely oblivious to the fact that the concealed camera surveillance was still operational or that both the audio and video had started recording as soon as the door was opened.

Once again Freeman was stripped of his clothing and left standing totally naked and made to stand at attention.

The Major came striding in and dismissed the soldiers.

"Freeman" - he bellowed – "I am going to ask you some questions. You *will* talk to me, and you *will* answer each and every one of my questions again. Only *this time you will answer truthfully.*"

"Interrogation will begin *NOW*."

"Who are you?"

"I am Freeman McIntosh.'

"Where do you come from?"

"Eden is my home."

"Where is this, *Eden*?"

"Fourteen- and one-half sunrises long march from the place where you detained us."

"WRONG! That is the *wrong* answer sir! There is NOTHING within a sixteen -WEEK march from here. Armed border guards are PAID; and they are paid very good currency to make sure *nothing* comes *or goes* within the Classified Zone."

"Alright, let me see, I think we'll try something else here, let me call it a new approach to get to the truth."

From behind his back, he pulled a long metal tipped riding crop that had been attached to his belt, and he slashed it down hard and sharp across Freemen's bare shoulders. Pain seared through Freeman's back, though he gave no outward sign of it, but he mentally braced himself for another strike.

"Now, let's try that question again." The major was really disturbed by the big man's lack of reaction. "Where IS this Eden you speak of?"

Freeman replied exactly as before, his voice calm and steady. "Fourteen-and-one-half sunrises long march from the place where you detained me."

Again, the whip flashed out, only this time it struck Freeman across the cheek, laying the flesh open in a long thin bloody line. The Major raised his whip preparing to strike Freeman a third time.

Both the Major's frustrations, and his intention, were clearly reflected in his eyes, and Freeman's reaction was fast, very, very, fast indeed. Before the Major could act or open his mouth to taunt him again Freeman's arms flashed out with lightning speed, he flipped the Major flat onto his back on the floor, effectively trapping his whip arm beneath him. Freeman dropped down and pushed his knee into the Majors chest. Hard. Once again Freeman's hand snaked out, this time seeking a specific point between the Majors neck and shoulder; the magic spot, to which he applied some serious pressure resulting in the temporary, exceedingly painful, but complete paralysis of his assailant. Freeman stood up and calmly raised his right foot to rest it on the Major's heaving chest.

The Major was forced to lie there, sweating heavily, in considerable pain and totally immobilized; he was certainly in no position to argue or attempt any further damage tonight.

Freeman stood over him, and as quietly spoken, and respectful as always, said; "Major, I have repeatedly answered each of your questions fully and truthfully; I am Freeman McIntosh, 35 cycles, a respected senior in my community, I am a farmer, I am also a tied man, and I am father to five sons and two daughters. I was ordered by the High Council to lead this expedition into The Outlands in the hope of finding suitable women for our young men with whom to tie for the safe and the healthy continuance of our community. We must have fresh bloodlines from which to breed the next generation. We have no other option available to us, or we will be breaking the Most Revered First Elders rules. Now Major, I require some answers from *you.*"

Freeman removed his foot, squatted down and stared into the eyes of the hostile Major.

"What is *so* significant about The Outlands, that you would so brutalise innocent men simply because they walked there? You keep repeating that it is impossible for anyone to traverse six hundred miles in fourteen-and-one-half sunrises undetected; now I want you to tell me why, and who or what, *is* a Six Hundred Miles? Also, what is a Weeks? Also please provide a valid reason as to *why* you think it is so impossible."

Freeman heard a rustling noise behind him, he turned, poised ready to defend himself once more, he saw only the same group of green clad creatures who had dragged him into that place standing and staring, open-mouthed, at the sight of the stricken Major, who still lay sprawled flat on his back on the floor, sweating profusely and unable to move.

Freeman turned to them and barked out an order of his own, with the unmistakable authority of a high-ranking officer.

"Return me to my quarters, immediately, and then see to the Major, he's not permanently incapacitated. Giving a crooked smile, Freeman added -he is merely - resting."

The following morning the men of Eden were once again reunited. This time however, they were taken outside into the fresh air and sunlight, for a fifteen-minute walk after breakfast.

The men all agreed that this strange food was not at all to their taste, and did not sit well in the stomach. Ten minutes into their exercise time the sky clouded over and they all raced for cover. They were ushered back inside, and taken to the same large interview room as the previous day; the same room Freeman had been taken to in the early hours of the morning.

The doctors met outside to discuss all they'd learned from the previous day's recordings, the recorded verbal exchanges, along with any information they'd collected from, or regarding, each man individually. Dr. Kayla had not, at this point, had enough time to review the recordings made after midnight – she planned to watch and listen to them later in the day.
The first thing Dr Kayla noticed was Freeman's wounded shoulder and cheek; she immediately gave an order that he be taken to the infirmary where the wounds could be treated. While that was being done, she would expect a full and detailed explanation as to exactly *where* and *how* he had acquired such injuries.
She then turned her attention to the other men, noting Cain's flushed face and glazed expression, she decided to examine each man. Immediately following their examinations, she ordered a full set of New Zone vaccinations for each man, Freeman, she said, would be examined and fully vaccinated while he was in the infirmary.
"According to our test results these men have, inadequate to *non-existent*, immunity or resistance to *any* disease, they are certainly *not* immune to any contact with the average person on this base, because we all carry easily transmissible infections and contagion to which we ourselves are immune, however, for one reason or another, none of these men have developed any such natural immunities."
Doctor Kayla gave them a few minutes to digest this information before she continued.
"This condition alone indicates that they are telling the truth. As implausible as their story sounds to *us* – it may very well be true, that they live, and have lived

for generations, in an unknown and entirely isolated community."

She was addressing herself to the collection of medical personnel who were busily entering this vital new information into their reports.

The men were escorted back to their quarters, with orders to rest for the remainder of the day.

By this time the whole section was abuzz with the news of the Majors' sudden incapacitation, and the story of how he came by his injury, was spreading throughout the base like a wildfire.

The confrontation with the Major also created tremendous interest for the doctors, who found it hard to believe that the same, courteous, quietly spoken, genteel Freeman had so effortlessly overpowered the battle-hardened Major.

Over the next week the men were allowed to rest, and recover from the vaccinations they'd received, and Doctor Kayla showed the medical team the unauthorised recordings she'd removed from all the machines.

"There is more, *so much more* to these men than we are seeing," said Doctor Raoul Voss, as he leaned against the wall thoughtfully stroking his short, meticulously trimmed beard.

Doctor Gateman had an idea.

"What if we were to allow these men interact with a few of the soldiers, maybe they'd speak more freely to them do you think?"

The doctors began passing ideas, suggestions, and arguments, back and forth for another half hour before coming back to Doctor Gateman's suggestion, and finally all were in agreement, although, it was decided that instead of putting the men amongst the *enlisted* men and women, instead, the *soldiers* would be medical personnel wearing enlisted men's uniforms and have a mini recording device in their pockets, that way the more important questions could be asked, and they would have the responses recorded. Thus, negating the argument of word of mouth, of context, or perhaps even confusion, should any legal situation arise. While quite unorthodox, the idea definitely had merit, great merit in fact.

 Doctor Gateman went into the interview room alone and sat directly opposite Cain, however he addressed all the men, they spoke of generalities, 'how are you sleeping? Are you getting enough food to eat? Is there any food you would prefer for meals? How would you like to meet some of the soldiers here? I could arrange it if you would like to, it might make a pleasant change for you to make some new friends while you're here.'

Alder spoke up for the first time; he agreed that "It would be good for the boys to have other young people with whom they could communicate and share social speech."

It was so easily done. Within the hour eight *soldiers* were ushered into the interview room, followed by one of the catering crew pushing a large trolley filled with a wide variety of foods, fruits and beverages, for the men to share.

The men of Eden, after experiencing the first round of unpleasant stomach problems, due to the unaccustomed, overly rich foods, wisely sampled only the fruits, although Marshall *did* manage to cause quite a stir when he tried to eat an unpeeled banana! The conversations were a bit awkward for the first few minutes, until one young *soldier* introduced himself as Bobby-Dean, he told them he was enlisted as a mechanic, but his real interest was in farming – the doctors felt this would give the strangers some sense of connection, and they were absolutely correct. The men of Eden, being completely without guile, joined in and the conversations started flowing immediately.

Introductions were made and the stories began to flow, easily and very naturally. Jacob told the *soldiers* of the beauty of their gardens and the ancient water collection system they used. Cain described their methods of go-bit breeding, and to prevent wastage, how every part of the animal was used, and Theo, not to be outdone, told his new companions about the fishing and the many colours of the fish they had. Marshall sat and listened in on the various conversations going on around him. The questions and answers soon had him feeling terribly homesick. One of the *soldiers* asked about their home and how far away it was, it sounds like you have yourselves a real paradise there! The farms around this zone are nothing like you're describing, our farms are all real hard work, and no play for anyone, ever - because they have Zone quotas to fill every season.

Marshall began to speak to the group about the Founding Family. He told them how they too had been military marine men. He went on to tell how they had been sent to rescue a small community and instead of a simple pick up and deliver to another area, they had been forced to seek shelter from the storms that were destroying the countryside in every direction, thus leaving them nowhere to safely relocate the people they had rescued. That is how they had discovered New Eden many, many, many cycles of time past.

The men spoke longingly of their lives in Eden, and of how much they wanted to return now, with, *or without*, any suitable women.

That remark was picked up by another of the *soldiers* and his questions led to them telling of the dire shortage of suitable partners to tie with, and of the reasons why. "Bloodlines, he explained, can only be tied cleanly, and we have almost exhausted our available mating selection. If we don't find new women for breeding, we will all grow old and return to the gardens."

"If that happens, who will return the last person to their earthly bed with their due respect?"

As Marshall spoke, the whole group fell silent, to listen to him. The sincerity, the utter simplicity and vulnerability of this young man was as incredible to them, as it was incomprehensible.

They were more accustomed to the tough, macho heroics, and the -I don't care attitudes- of the Army personnel as a whole.

As the *soldiers* listened to, and observed, each of the men in turn, they were taken by surprise with the sudden and unexpected melancholy that overtook their cheerfulness, their longing to return to their Eden was expressed so very clearly, and with such simplicity and honesty. It could be seen quite clearly in the unconscious drooping of their broad shoulders, in the way their eyes glistened momentarily, and by the profound sadness that came over their handsome faces.

Trying to lift the mood again, a *soldier* asked if by chance they knew any of the first people's names.

Jacob laughed, and said *everyone* in Eden knows the names of the first people *and* each of their descendants!

Cain said excitedly, we have their uniforms, their boots, and identification tags, we even have one of the military hats along with a great many other artefacts that belonged to them; all are kept in a large wooden chest in the first chambers. Unfortunately, the question regarding the location of the '*castle* of chambers' was left unasked, because at that moment a messenger arrived with orders to return the men to their quarters, the doctors were waiting for them.

Each of the doctors had studied all of the video and audio recordings made when the men were together, and whilst they were alone in their quarters.

Although the recordings taken of the men when they were together were of great interest, it was the surveillance videos of the men alone in their rooms that received the greatest attention, especially amongst the female doctors and nursing staff…

One such glorious physical specimen was a genuine rarity, so to have two mature males, with the physiques that a healthy twenty-year-old would be jealous of, was just amazing, but to have *four*, remarkably good looking twenty-year-old's, each with simply magnificent, unblemished, muscular, and perfectly beautiful bodies, was completely unheard of in this day and age.

Apart from the rapidly healing bruise and wounds on Freeman's face and shoulder, there was not a mark or a blemish to mar any of their perfect bodies. The heavy muscle development in their necks, chests and shoulders, their upper arms, thighs and calves, spoke of years of dedicated, rigorous exercise. Their slender waists and well-defined abdominal muscles, their taut, high rounded buttocks, clear skin and thick, healthy hair were all evidence of a healthy lifestyle. Even their hands were beautiful, long strong fingers neat, clean fingernails and they all possessed a complete set of strong, perfectly straight white teeth, not a single cavity between them either. They have none of the oral disease so prevalent in young adults today, and there's no indications of dental work ever having been performed in the past, nor is it necessary now. The impeccable condition of both physical, and oral health, indicated a balanced diet high in protein and fibre rich fresh, pesticide and chemical free produce, equally obvious is that fats, starches, salt and sugars don't feature in their diet at all. Yet there was no vanity in any of the men at all. Typically, a man with such a body would strut around and flaunt himself, however these men appear to be completely unaware of their striking looks and extraordinary bodies.

Doctor Kilmer, the leading medical expert for the investigation team, continued to hold onto the opinion he shared with the Major, that these men were spies. Spies who had been sent here from a rival nation, to gather information on the strengths and possibly report any weaknesses of Base WX93. He was absolutely convinced that WX93 was being set up for an attack on a very large-scale.

The doctors continued to debate amongst themselves for a while, before Doctor Kayla spoke up saying that she "did not, for one minute share that opinion, and it would be a very difficult, if not a completely impossible task, to convince her that these men were *anything* other than what they have declared themselves to be. I believe in science Doctor Kilmer and the result of every medical test, the recordings, and the meetings, *confirm* their words. Besides, they just don't seem to know *how* to lie!"

She had spent more than half the night searching through the archive records. She had extended her search back as far as one hundred and ninety-seven years. All the way in fact, to the beginning of the 'Planetary Weather Transformation' that every civilised man woman and child knows took place then.

"In my research, I *did* in fact find a reference to not one, but many hundreds of thousands of missing Military personnel, the exact figures of the peoples lost have never been published, but I kept narrowing my search, Zone by Zone, until I found that several Marine Bases *were* operating Relocation Teams, across the zones many hundreds of thousands of civilians had been evacuated and relocated."

"This present Military Protectorate Base is sited on what used to be, way back then, a Southern and a South Eastern state or as they called them back then, a Zone, roughly an area of four thousand square miles. Along with so many others, both of those states were totally destroyed by the rogue storm activity.

Whatsmore; I discovered that there were no survivors. However, due to the fact that every bit and byte of military information entered into *any* computerised system back then was *also* immediately transmitted to the Presidents Military staffers and stored inside super computers deep within the underground city, and retrieved again decades later when the weather finally stabilised, so I was able to do a search and find- even amongst the many hundreds and hundreds of thousands of lost civilians and military personnel - with the names of all the missing marines, as well as the refugees listed on their passenger manifests, are an exact match for the names these men have given to us as being the Founding Family of their Eden! Even the names of the civilians that were reportedly lost in transit, are a perfect match for the names these people have given to our bogus soldiers today! So, what do you all make of that?"

"Yes, yes, yes. That's all well and good and very interesting Doktor Kayla, but do tell me please; do you think that you are the *ONLY* person in this world to be able to access those records? Do you, eh, really? Of *COURSE,* the names *MATCH woman! They were meant too!* These men, they have been *exceptionally* well coached in a farfetched and totally implausible story, but one that we are *supposed* to believe *doctor* ... that's what spies *DO*, they *LIE*. Tell me, *why* did they come to *this* particular area Kayla? Why did they *not* suddenly arrive in Area 16, or 29, or even Area 35? I'll tell you *why*, because *this* is the only area that could possibly tie in with their preposterous *supposed* history, the very *same* history contained within the records *you* so painstakingly wasted your time *discovering!*" He strode up and down the room with his hands shoved deep into the pockets of his lab coat.

"They are spies, and nothing you can say, or do, or find, will convince *me* otherwise."

The bitter and unveiled contempt for his much younger colleague dripped from his words.

Dr Zander spoke up and said: "Well Herr Kilmer, let's be very accurate here, those men *did not actually come* to WX93 under their own steam now did they? No, they *were actually forcibly detained.* They were bound hand and foot, and *illegally transported* sixty miles east of the pick-up point, under armed guard in the back of a blacked-out vehicle to this base. Therefore, if they *are* spies as *you* seem *so determined* to prove, they do not know their present location, and that being true means they have no worthwhile information to report do they? You are arrogant and bull-headed Kilmer, and if I were you I'd be very careful about the accusations I make, because these things have a way of returning to discredit you."

While Dr Kayla was shocked by Dr Zander's almost hostile words, she was pleased too – but they didn't progress her case any further.

The meeting lasted another quarter hour before the doctors returned to their regular duties. Dr Kayla walked quietly through the corridors wracking her brain for a way she would be able to prove to Kilmer once and for all time, that these men really *were* the genuine descendants. Everything Kilmer had said *could* be true, all his assumptions *were* plausible, but something deep within her said he was wrong, so very, very, wrong.

It would be up to her and her alone now, to prove it.

Dr Kayla's mind just kept on ticking through all the information she'd gathered so far, because she was confident that there *had to be a way* to prove her theory one way or another, she'd overlooked something, some detail was eluding her, something small, but definitely vital, and she knew that she had to find whatever detail it was that she'd missed, and she had to find it very soon.

Besides, she would eat her stethoscope before she'd allow herself to be bested by Dr Kilmer, the small minded, pompous ass that he is!

It was later on in the day, while she was with another patient, and only half listening to the poor girls' tale of woe about her youngest brother needing a kidney transplant, and how, when they were all tested, none of his siblings was a match. When the truth finally came out it stunned the whole family, it seemed that her mother had had many affairs because she couldn't get pregnant with her husband and that meant that her brothers and sisters were not actually her fathers' children at all – that's when the solution Sami was looking for came to her with a jolt. It had been staring her in the face the whole time! Hot damn, old fashioned DNA testing! It's been around for well over two hundred or so years and *all* military personnel have been recorded since its inception! That was it! Their own DNA would either prove, *or disprove*, their story. Tonight, she would visit each man and take a cheek swab and blood sample, and ask for some of the family history that they all seem to be so very proud of. Each man's knowledge of their complete family lineage going right back to those *supposed* Founding Family Members, would put the icing on the cake –so to speak.

She knew too, that *if,* in the unlikely event she was proven to be *wrong,* she'd be needing some hot sauce on her stethoscope *and* she'd be hard pressed to ever find another job, Kilmer would see to that, and take great satisfaction in doing so too; in fact, she'd be lucky to get a job in a junior military school as a nurse, handing out bandages. But if she was *right,* and she firmly believed she *was,* then *she'd* be the one put up for a promotion, and Dr Kilmer's job, would in fact, be the one in dire jeopardy. Waiting had never been her strong suit, but she had been told that the men were being shown the latest range of hand-to-hand combat weapons, along with the newly arrived lightweight shoulder mounted missile launchers, cavity grenades, and anything else the major might think would impress them, and more especially, the people he was so convinced they were spying for. He will no doubt show them the comprehensive on base arsenal. Probably so that as *spies* they could report back to their superiors as to the imprudence of trying to attack such a well prepared and heavily fortified post.

Fools, these men are all such utter fools, all arrogance, and ego, with little to no actual active brain function.

Be that as it may, she still had a lengthy list of other patients to attend to right now; "it's only eleven hundred hours, so it's going to be a very long day today," she mumbled as she walked back towards her consulting room.

The men were, at that very moment, being shown a vast array of weaponry that were well organised, displayed and easily accessible to the soldiers should the base come under attack.
Freeman and Alder were each being given instructions on how to handle several of the new weapons. The Officer in charge of the arsenal, who was acting as their guide/instructor was truly amazed and extremely impressed by their target accuracy. As soon as they had the feel and the weight of a weapon balanced, and had gauged the signature recoil of each firearm, both men hit the targets *bulls-eye* time and again. The average time for a *career soldier* to have the weight/recoil down and committed to memory was around three full sessions. These men weren't supposed to *be* military personnel at all, and yet they'd mastered every piece in the very diverse range of weapons within five rounds, only a matter of seconds, and where a soldier always had to familiarise himself again with each weapon to recoup his accuracy, the men of Eden required no such practice, in fact they could switch between each and every unit without hesitation *and* give 100% accuracy each time.

While the Elders were being shown the extensive range of hand guns, machine pistols both short and long range, and the Armory's pride, the latest state-of-the-art laser rifles, the younger men were being guided through another wide selection of weaponry.

Among the many different weapons on display were a collection of hand-to-hand combat weapons and gear, along with various different models of plum sized hand grenades. These weapons were standard issue to each and every soldier – or so the younger men were informed.

Actually the men were greatly impressed and very interested in the *fiery hole diggers* as a possible farming tool, because one single plum grenade could break up solid ground or rock in the time it takes to blink your eyes instead of digging for many days! The instructor informed them that "they could clean out a whole platoon with just three well placed grenades, and it'd only take a few seconds."

"What's a platoon?" Cain asked, "is it a weed or a fallen tree? How would it be cleaned out at other times?"

The startled instructor started to answer him, but then thought better of it, instead, he shook his head and made words in his book then he led them over to a table covered with assorted handguns all set out in neatly in long rows. The boys were given instructions on how to load the various pistols and the accompanying spare clips, after they'd practiced and understood the stacking of the bullets into the clip as they'd been shown, they – like the older men hit the *bulls-eye* time after time. The instructor was extremely impressed, and even considered asking to have them in his own squad…

Next, the instructor set up a paper Man target and told the boys to "aim for the head, heart, shoulder, or knee, depending on whether you wanted to make a kill shot, or to immobilize your opponent, so as to keep him alive for interrogation."

"KILL another MAN? But why? *Why* would you ever even contemplate taking the life of another man? A sickly, or a gravely injured animal yes, *that* I can understand, to prevent it from suffering unnecessarily, but what could *possibly* motivate one person to take the life of, or to injure another person *intentionally*?" Asked an astounded Marshall, and the other boys, who were all equally, not only repulsed, but also bewildered by the very idea of deliberately doing harm to another, nodded their agreement. "It is against our law to take a human life; no one in Eden has *ever* died at the hands of another. Our law of Respect forbids it under *any* circumstance. We require no knowledge of such things as this sir!" He said as he dropped the weapon back onto the table as though it had bitten him; the others had already put down the offensive objects, turned, and walked away.

The instructor was so totally confused by this outcome, he'd been told to assess their competency and familiarity with each weapon, so far, they'd not appeared to know a single thing about any of even the most basic hardware, and yet they were all first-class sharpshooters and marksmen. And *since when* did a soldier *ever* question the killing or maiming of an enemy? So, the only thing the instructor could do was to report his findings, as confusing and as contradictory as they were, to his superior officer immediately.

Freeman and Alder were as equally disgusted and mortified as were the younger men, when they were informed of the weapons intended use and purpose.

They had also dropped the guns onto the tables like hot potatoes! Both Freeman and Alder strode purposefully across the hard packed earth of the yard, to where the young men had gathered outside an area classified as -The Firing Range- and saw to their dismay that the young ones had also been treated with the same abysmal level of disrespect.

"Greetings to you Cain, Jacob, Marshall, Theo," (each greeting was given and received with a slight nod of the head) "our greetings we give also to you Freeman, Alder" responded the boys in unison. I can see by your expressions we have all been subjected in the same repugnant presentation, let us purify our hearts and minds with some sweet and cleansing Eden song."
The suggestion almost brought the young men to tears of gratitude, they were so confused by the extreme contrast in morality between the two very different cultures of Eden, and Andesine. A cleansing and re-grounding was exactly what they craved right now. Alder led off, then they joined in, one by one, giving voice to the different animals, the birds, the waterfall and people, in a song of New Eden. Far across the compound the office workers and nursing staff heard the deep basso profundo of Alder, followed by the lighter, true baritone of Freeman, and then as the younger, lighter voices began to harmonise, they created magical vocal images. When the men of Eden closed their eyes they could see the long fall of water that created a gentle breeze and set the grasses swaying, the waterfall sang to all who listened, colourful birds called to their mates across

sweet, fragrant meadows and grasslands, in their minds they could hear the young shepherds crooning and calling to their flocks.

Enlisted men and women gathered in groups outside the main building leaving their workstations unattended to hear the magical song more clearly.

All too soon the song was terminated by the sharp report of a gunshot roaring up into the sky.

The major stood before them with his legs spread wide, his thick fingered hands, their knuckles showing white under the skin were now shoved down onto his hips; there was an ugly, derisive sneer on his pugnacious face. "Just what do we have here eh? The Andesine boys choir perhaps? Or is it just you ladies having a nice little sing-a-long after your tea party?" He laughed heartily at his own tasteless joke before he barked out "Now get yourselves back to the quarters assigned to you, you damned sissies."

He executed a perfect parade ground about face and stalked off, leaving the men of Eden watching his rapid, rather ungainly departure.

"He is not a happy man at all; there is no lightness or sunshine in him, only senseless hostility and futile rage fills his belly, it consumes him and isolates him from all who might otherwise care for him. I feel a great sadness for the major, I sense that he does not like, or accept himself, and because of this, his isolation is of long standing, and completely self-inflicted, therefore even with a great deal of love and counselling, such a condition cannot be easily, nor quickly rectified."

Following the Major's order, each man dutifully returned to his assigned quarters, where he bathed and waited for – well, they didn't actually know *what* they were waiting for now, but rigorous exercise had always been used to calm and centre the people of Eden, and so this is how they intended to pass their time while confined.

As it turned out however, their waiting was short lived. Dr Kayla called in to each man's room and spoke with them individually. She asked each man in turn if he would object to her plan of finding out, and proving beyond any possible doubt, that they were, who they said they were, and promising to call on each of them after working hours.

"Please, say nothing of this to anyone, I'm afraid that if you do I will be stopped, and you may all well suffer as a consequence." While Dr Kayla was speaking to the last member of the Eden team, an orderly was knocking on the door of the first member, their presence was required at once, they were to return to The Firing Range where they would be met by a new instructor.

As the men approached their destination, Freeman stopped and turned to address his men, "We are all well aware that we are being tested, I am certain that the major will attempt to inflict upon one, or all of us, severe physical harm, he wishes to impose upon us debilitating pain, and he will keep trying to affect that outcome in any way he possibly can, be it physically, emotionally, or mentally, we may all be assured that he will do his utmost to achieve that end. We however, have the advantage of knowing that his sick and troubled mind is working against us. We men of Eden are superior in our mental strength, as well as our physical assets; he will not hesitate to damage us, he will use whatever force he considers necessary in an effort to undermine our courage without hesitation. He believes that we can be undermined as surely as fast flowing water will undermine a boulder. But do you remember what happens when a stick is placed in the water? The power of the water is diverted so much that it loses its power! Therefore, *we* must become the sticks diverting his water course. I fear that he is obsessed, so he will not stop. Therefore, it is up to us to put an end to this, *we must*, regardless of how distasteful it is for us personally, we must break *him* first, and since he has chosen to take this path with us, he has left us no recourse." There were nods of agreement all round.

They hadn't counted on the dogs.

None of them had ever seen or even *heard* of a dog, in all their lives.
The men were so totally unprepared for the almost overwhelming ferocity that awaited them.
Two massive, snarling, slathering mastiff's stood glaring at them, their lips curled back exposing bared, fearsomely long, razor sharp white teeth, the dogs were pulling on short choker leashes and barely being held in place beside their straining handlers, while the major strode back and forth, his favourite riding crop striking the thick leather of his knee-high boots with every step. This deliberate tactic was intended to

further agitate the savage dogs, who were by this time, starting to foam at the mouth, both animals becoming crazed and eager to hunt down their victims, so much so that their handlers were actually struggling to restrain their animals.

Freeman whispered to his men; "remember The Most Revered Elders left in their teachings a section on mental torment? Well men, *this* is what I believe to be -Posturing or Intimidation- such childish games from a man fully grown is disrespectful in the extreme. Cain, you are the calmer of animals, you know what we will need to do, guide us. The major however, should be thoroughly shamed and made to shovel go-bit droppings for a month – by hand!" They all shared a small laugh at the major's expense while they approached the gathering, the major held up his hand and ordered them to stay right where they were, which was about four hundred and fifty yards from him, his men and the dogs were another fifteen paces further behind him.

Freeman's little pep talk had achieved its purpose, and the men were now ready for anything the major could deliver.

"Unleash those hounds!" The handlers were unsure as to what the major wanted them to do, but an order was an order. Pharaoh and Cleo were the two biggest, most valuable, most highly trained, and without doubt, the most ferocious dogs in this, or any other facility. No expense had been spared in their breeding or for their training; literally millions of Andesine Thaels have been spent on them. Between them they could rip a full-grown bull apart and leave it living, no-one knew what damage they could inflict on a human, but the handlers felt quite sure they were about to find out, and that mental image was sickening in the extreme.

"Order them to attack!" On hearing the Major's yell for the dogs to attack – and acting on sheer instinct, Cain hissed quickly to the men; "Circle sit, backs out, all sing harmony with me, *drop, now!*" Immediately the Beasts had been given the Command to Attack they streaked across the field toward the men, the hot sun shone down on their sleek black and gold fur making it gleam like burnished brass on black enamel. With their legs stretched to maximum extension and necks straining, their ears were pricked forward and fully alert to their surroundings they made no sound except for the rapid scratching of their sharp claws as they dug into the hard dry ground in order to gain better traction for their long attacking strides. The only evidence of their silent passing was in the tiny puffs of powdery grey dust raised by their pounding paws.

The two beasts skidded to a halt at the unprecedented sight and sound; for in all their highly specialised training, they were well accustomed to chasing down a *running* target, and mauling a well-padded body until the shredded padding littered the ground around their 'victim' or until their handler called them off.

However, these targets were not running, they weren't even moving; leaving the confused dogs to circle their would-be quarry and whine in uncertainty.

Both dogs had been thrown into confusion by this sudden and unparalleled change of tactics. So, they laid down side-by-side panting. Nothing in their training had prepared them for a passive resistance, and the low melodious tune coming from the men had blunted their blood lust.

The major, along with the heavily armed soldiers stood absolutely transfixed and incredulous at the astonishing, completely incredible, totally unbelievable sight before them. When the major snapped himself out of his nightmare, he ranted, and he screamed filthy obscenities at the bewildered, embarrassed, but somewhat relieved, handlers.

"These are your man killers? *These* are the animals you *guaranteed* could bring down a wild bull in a full charge" JUST LOOK AT THEM! *LOOK-AT-THEM! They're useless, they're less than useless*!" Every word brought a heavy spray of spittle with it.

"I've seen pet rabbits with more guts than those, those, *things* GO! Get them out of here *NOW, before I shoot the useless mongrels myself*" he bellowed at them "and while you're taking these pussies to the kennels, send down number one and two teams, tell them to be prepared for some serious hand-to-hand. Oh, and tell them to bring their favourite weapons. ANYTHING THEY LIKE." The major knew that the men of Eden had seen all the weaponry available to the soldiers and expected them to show panic, or hopefully, some fear – however all his anticipations had fallen flat when the six men gave no indication that they'd even heard his words, let alone shown that longed for expression - terror.

"Do we tell them to bring a selection of weapons for these men as well major?" A contemptuous look was his only answer. With the dogs gone and no harm done to them, the men stood and started walking toward the major. "STOP! STOP right there, do not move, do not even breathe hard, just get yourselves ready for a little bit of contact sport with my personal, hand selected, Elite Teams! Oh, and be assured, *these* teams aren't anything like those playful little puppy dogs either, *these* men WILL bite! And make no mistake *these men* WILL relish the taste of you.

And just so you know, this clash will be recorded – just so I can enjoy it over and over again like a good bedtime story. I love happy endings."

The major sauntered off chuckling to himself over his own sick little witticism.

The men of Eden heard the off-key singsong chanting, a few seconds before the fifteen strong team of well trained, hard-core, professional Andesine military combatants came into view.

The Majors teamsters laughed loudly amongst themselves when all they saw were two middle-aged men and four adolescent boys with long hair squatting on their heels with their arms hanging loosely across their knees. To all outward appearances they seemed totally relaxed, just waiting. They heard one soldier call out "You are NOT going to like THIS little lesson boys" The whole group tried to look as hard and as mean and menacing as possible, as they slow jogged toward them.

Each soldier was wearing full combat dress, and his face smeared with black and green camouflage paint, they were also well armed with several of their personal favourite combat weapons. One of the soldiers yelled out across the dusty yard.

"Lesson one is about to begin, get ready to learn about some very *real pain* now boys, or with all that hair, are you really *men* at all? Well? What's it to be?" The soldiers looked almost pityingly over at their targets as they came to a noisy stop a few yards away from them. They saw six men who were clearly unarmed, with bare feet and almost naked, their only clothing being a short woollen loincloth. The leader of the soldiers turned and said laughingly to his comrades "man oh man, this is going to be *the* quickest and *easiest* thousand Taels we've ever made!"

Theo smiled and speaking quietly to himself as if by way of reply "yes, *we* are quite ready, but are *you*? You can by no means know *who* will be the students or who will be the ones *teaching you* what might perhaps be the most critical lesson of your life!" Alder said simply "Remember our training, separate mind from pain and get the job done, there is no Eden award this time, but perhaps after this new *lesson* we can go home."

The soldiers started coming closer; their footfalls becoming increasingly heavy and more deliberate, their chant had become a deep rhythmic growl – intimidation tactics again – how very immature these people are.

The men of Eden now rose to their feet and began a chant of their own, one that had been written by the Most Revered Elder Mark to lead the teams into mock war games. Games where limbs were sometimes broken, due mainly, to the lack of attention or appropriate training practice, and on even rarer occasions, severe injuries had been sustained. How could these soldiers possibly know that the men of Eden have always been well versed in what the military called guerrilla warfare, or that unarmed, hand-to-hand combat was their specialty? As they raised themselves to a standing position the men almost felt pity for these soldiers, because they were only attempting to execute the orders of their warped major and follow his ill-conceived instructions.

Well now, and with thanks to the conceited arrogance of that same major, Freeman and his team were about to execute their own brand of business. Alder spoke only one word, although it was posed as a question. "Clean?" to which Freeman replied "If they perform with honour then yes, most certainly. However, my every instinct tells me these paid warriors are totally bereft of decency, therefore we will do whatever is expedient, but we must allow them to make the first contact."

The fifteen soldiers came to a showy stop, each soldier drew himself up to his full height (even wearing heavy boots, the tallest was still a good three inches shorter than the men of Eden) and stood ramrod straight, to less skilled men they might have appeared threatening, very threatening indeed. A mere arm's length was all that was separating the soldiers from the men of Eden, who stood their ground quite impassively. Neither by their facial expressions, nor by their casual, even relaxed stance, did they give any warning of the blood bath *they* knew was about to ensue.

From the pathway that led down to the combatants there came excited shouts and the sound of a great many running feet, the soldiers had told anyone who was free, to "Come out and see *them weirdo farm boy's* get taught the lesson of a lifetime, come on down, you really don't want to miss this, it's going to be a lesson they'll sure never forget, and that'll only happen *if* they live to talk about it!"
The soldiers began circling again, woohah-ing softly while building the chant louder and louder, pumping themselves up while to all appearances the men of Eden remained quite relaxed and totally unprepared for the next move.

The wait wasn't a long one. Fifteen Elite Fighting Corps soldiers, all highly trained, well-armed, dressed and booted for close range armed combat - against six unarmed farmers in loincloths, incredibly poor odds - for the soldiers if they'd but known it! The soldiers had a prearranged signal, a simple cough and the mêlée commenced!

From the sidelines all the spectators could see were arms, legs, bodies, heads, and feet flying in all directions, within seconds the Eden team had lowered the odds significantly, without sustaining a single telling blow to themselves. The seven soldiers they'd already dispatched were definitely in need of immediate, and in a few cases, acute, medical attention. To that end one spectator excitedly ran back to the main building. Another few moments passed, and three more soldiers became casualties, that left only five of the Majors fifteen battle hardened soldiers still standing, even if they *were* bleeding from various orifices, and numerous open wounds, where their *favourite weapon* had suddenly and most unexpectedly become a deadly adversary, without ever leaving their own hands…

The crowd started calling out for the Major to come back and put a stop to the bloodbath, because it was *his* squad that was being given a real thrashing!

The Major came lumbering back to the field again as though all the devils of hell were chasing him, and much to his horror he arrived just in time to see the last of his *elite squad* crumple bloodied and defeated at his feet.

The men of Eden bowed and thanked the mainly unconscious soldiers for their brave efforts, and their very *edifying lesson. They* also congratulated the teamsters on their fine performances; they then nodded courteously to the major who was left staring at the carnage with his mouth hanging open, and made their way back towards the main building, being passed by a fleet of ambulances with sirens blaring on the way.

Even though the Men of Eden were covered from head to toe in blood, none belonged to them, they had come through the contest completely unscathed, except for Cain who'd stepped down heavily on a stone, resulting in a bruised heel.

However, in spite of their victory the Men of Eden received a less than kindly reception on their arrival back at the main building. Because news of the Elite Squad's thorough trouncing, plus the fact that the odds of nearly three to one had been more than stacked in the militaries favour, had preceded them.

They heard snippets of various conversations, things like; "I heard they're *supposed* to be farmers, but I've *never* seen no farmer kick the livin crap outta anyone, leastways not like they just done!" And, "I've just lost a whole damn month's pay!" Then another "If those guys are hick farmers, I'm a girl cadet!" Or, "It was *fifteen* of us, against *six* of them, how in hell's name did they DO it *and* still come out walking?" Yet another group was heard to say. "They might talk kinda funny, but they sure gave them cocky bastards a real whuppin, I reckon it's one *they* won't be forgetting for a long, *long* time neither!" And another laughed as he remarked that "That idiot major's going to have some real hard explaining to do this time…it's about time he got back some-o what he's always so danged quick to dish out!"

Dr Kayla, heard voices raised in excitement, delight, and sheer outrage right outside her office. She stepped out, interested to find out the reason for such an uncommon and loud disturbance. Immediately upon seeing what was causing such a stir in the normally silent building, she hurried along the short corridor to meet the men and escort them safely through the throng of people who'd gathered in the foyer.

She was both shocked and horrified by their appearance, they were blood spattered and looking wild. While she walked them back into her office, she was trying to assess any injuries that they may have received.

Once she'd closed the door, and sat them down; she continued questioning them as to their wellbeing. "Have you any injuries? Any cuts, bruises, sprains, or pulled muscles?"

Freeman answered in the negative for all of them.

"I give you my absolute assurance good doctor, we are well accustomed to such physical application, since all children of Eden are taught self-defence from an early age, equally as a competitive sport and as a form of regular daily exercise. We do not however, condone the use of violence for the purpose of sheer brutality - which goes against everything we believe in. In this instance we were forced into a position where avoidance would be called cowardice and therefore not possible. Please understand this; we can, and we will, always defend ourselves, or each other, no matter the opposing numbers. Had we been a cowardly or a weak-minded people, we would never have survived. Any of our children – male or female - above ten cycles would have achieved exactly the same result as we ourselves did today."

These men amazed, astounded, and thoroughly delighted Dr Kayla, on so many different levels.

As medical subjects they were unique, on a human level they offered an insight into a completely different world, one she had come to realise, that she craved to experience for herself, perhaps even to be a part of, and the more she saw of these six men, the more she wanted to see them.

Alder was of particular interest to her.

"Do you remember our conversation this morning? Well, would you or your men have any objection to me bringing my assistant with me, to help speed things along?" Alder smiled at her ladylike discomfort, and placing his hand gently upon her shoulder, he assured her it would be entirely acceptable.

To her surprise and delight Dr Kayla felt a real fizz of excitement travel all the way from her shoulder and continued tingling its way down her spine at his ever so gentle, touch.

The actual gathering of the specimens and testing took only minutes with each subject, but the actual lab work and then waiting for the results to be correlated would take all night.

The first pale rays of dawn peeked through the laboratory blinds to find Dr Kayla, still waiting for the antiquated GDRS (Gorgon Data Retrieval Supercomputer) to do the magic. Once she'd completed the last entry the evening before, she'd swung her chair around, and hit the blinking *ready* switch on the coffee machine, and poured out the first of the twelve cups of fragrant black coffee that would sustain her throughout her, self imposed, nightlong shift.

Twelve hours later she was stretching her arms over her head pulling some kinks out of her neck as Dr Kilmer walked through the doors, heading to his own alcove at the rear of the Lab, not even bothering to notice her, which suited her just fine. She didn't want to have to explain herself to anyone this morning –not yet anyway.

She stirred creaming powder into the last cup of coffee a few moments before Gorgon began spitting out the information she'd been waiting for. MATCH FOUND-MATCH FOUND- six times that beautiful pile of silicon chips repeated itself, then she did something very uncharacteristic and *very* unbecoming for a young woman of her professional standing... she leaned across and kissed the old machine! There were only three little words running in circles around her buzzing brain and bringing a self-satisfied smile to her lovely lips. 'I knew it! I knew it! I knew it!' Her rapid footsteps took her into the commander's office where she told his secretary that she was here on a matter of absolute and utmost urgency, and that he would want to be appraised of her findings immediately.

She just hoped that it was true! Dr Kayla was invited to take a seat, but after sitting at her desk for so many hours she was impatient to see the commander - she paced back and forth instead.

"The commander will see you now Doctor."
"Sámi! It's always good to see you, but what brings you here so early in the morning?" Sámi didn't reply to his question, instead she placed the computer readouts in front of him and said "This report changes a lot of things, although I think that maybe it will actually change *everything* Sir. What was merely conjecture on my part yesterday, is irrefutable *fact* today - and I would like to have your permission to be in full control of whatever further tests, or treatments, these men are given. The Major has some

real issues with these men, he has repeatedly
mistreated, abused and…"

"Yes, yes, Doctor" he said as he glanced up at her,
"the Major's *issues*, as you so politely call them, are
being dealt with as we speak. He was removed from
his quarters and taken to the stockade last night, soon
after I was made aware of the fiasco he caused on the
lower range actually. As of this minute I have fifteen,
fifteen mind you, of my absolute best, my most
trusted, totally irreplaceable, elite soldiers... out of
action and confined to sick bay, and *eleven* of those
men will be unfit for *any* kind of duty for some
months to come, with broken bones a torn kidney and
what-have you. And that's not the end of it; I was also
informed this morning of something so *much worse* – it
appears that we now have two completely *worthless
and useless* Andesine War Hounds! All the currency
that's been spent on a never before seen scale, the
extensive, actually it was a worldwide search to locate
a superior male and female to be a breeding pair,
specialist veterinarians hired to ensure impeccable
breeding, *unlimited* currency has been spent on those
hounds, not to mention their wretched specialised
diets, imported foods, and I shudder to even *think*
how much was spent on their training, and now,
thanks to that useless spawn of a moron major, every
single Tael of it has been lost, I might just as well have
flushed it all down a drain!

That major is in way over his imbecilic head, he's in
deep, *the deepest*, trouble; even if I have to lock him in
a storm cellar myself, he will never give another order
in this lifetime. In fact, he'll be lucky to see daylight
again if I have *any* say in the matter, and I sincerely

hope I do! Now go, take a bit of time to rest, because by the look of you, I dare say this" -he indicated the report- "took you all night to get through. Right now, though, I will need to give your report my complete attention, go on Dr Kayla, go to the commissary, and get yourself some breakfast; I'll see you back here in my office, in one hour."

There was nothing else she could do, but to obey his order.

In the commissary she ordered a plate of reconstituted ham and powdered eggs with a side order of toast, and more coffee, then she wandered over to sit at a table by the window. The view wasn't anything exciting; it wasn't even a view really, well not unless you think of a view as being dry, hard packed earth topped with grey dust, and ringed by twenty-foot-high electrified fences, sectioned and topped off with razor wire...

As she sliced her ham into exact bite sized pieces, and moved the rubbery scrambled eggs onto a slice of toast, she wondered for the hundredth time what the outcome for Alder and the other men would be.

In her mind she went over every image she'd seen on the video surveillance tapes. The way in which these men moved, was so unlike any regular guy, soldier or civilian that she could name, most men who looked like them would strut around like peacocks, others would slouch over as if they've been given a good gut punch and never recovered, then there were others who marched to the beat of an invisible band. No, these men of Eden were in a league of their own, they moved with such a loose-limbed grace and, yes dammit, they moved with poise. There was like a calm and quiet field surrounding them, one that followed them wherever they went. Their exceptional bodies, their remarkable good looks, their genteel behaviour, even their antiquated speech, and old-fashioned mannerisms had her perplexed, and much of the time, more than a little flustered! The good doctor had enjoyed quite a pleasant, if somewhat erotic flight of fantasy while she was waiting for the test results last night, the mere memory of it made her blush!

"Well, well, well, that's some nice dream you're dreaming there doc!"
The waitress had come over to clear away her empty dishes. "I haven't seen such a dreamy smile around here since forever" Oh good grief! She didn't remember eating a single bite. She glanced up at the clock on the wall and decided she had just enough time to go to the locker-room and clean up before she met with the commander again.
"Oh dear, maybe I should have come in here *first*" she said to herself when she saw the tired dishevelled woman with dark circles under her eyes that the brilliantly illuminated mirror reflected back at her, "oh goodness, today's just getting better and better..."
She looked like she'd been up all night. Well, she *had* been of course, but she felt that she shouldn't *look* as though she had! She had a quick wash and dragged a comb through her long red-gold hair, re-braided it, then wound the long heavy plait around her head and re-secured it with her hairpins. There wasn't much she could do about the bluish marks under her

green eyes or her crushed uniform though. Oh wait, I think I might ... and yes, she did indeed have a clean white coat in her locker.

By the time she stood outside the commander's office door for the second time that morning, she looked, and felt, a whole lot better.

One hour he'd said, so she was right on time.

Waiting…waiting. One and a half - two hours, and *still* she was kept waiting. She just hoped that the Commander was studying the report, and not having a nervous breakdown!

She paced back and forth across the small foyer, with her jittery, caffeine driven hands pushed deep into her pockets in a futile effort to keep them still, Dr Kayla couldn't help wondering what could possibly be taking him so long, and hoping above all else that he hadn't called Kilmer up to his office to review her report. Surely, he wouldn't do that to her – or would he?

The secretary asked her if there was anything she could get for her.

"Yes private, there's plenty, but getting me in to see the Commander would be a really fantastic start." She said - only half joking. Dr Kayla had just resumed her seat for the umpteenth time when the door opened and the Commander finally called her in. She gave up a silent 'Thank You' when she saw he was alone. The Commander sat down heavily behind his desk, there was no greeting, no preamble, and no gentle lead in, just a series of irritated questions. "You took the samples personally? You checked all of the data in here yourself? There can be no possible mistake? You *are* absolutely certain I suppose? Of course you are you wouldn't be sitting here if you weren't.

You *do* realise don't you Dr Kayla, that these" (he said, shaking the bundle of papers at her) "have proven beyond *any* possible question *or* doubt that these men *are* definitely the direct descendents of marines that originally came from bases that were once called Ford Ludlow, Portland Esker and Byron Ridge, marines who vanished without a trace along with two hundred and *forty-nine million* other people across the local zones in the weather disaster of ONE HUNDRED AND NINETY NINE YEARS AGO..."

"Ah, well sir that would have to be a very definite - yes- sir. The records clearly state..." she didn't get a chance to finish because he wasn't listening, he just kept rambling on.

"Why now? Why me? Why did they have to come *here*? Why, why? Those men have caused nothing but one disaster after another since they were brought in" groaned the suddenly weary looking Commander in exasperation – and throwing the reports down so hard that they missed the desk completely and fluttered to the floor - as he tried to understand this, the latest of so many senseless misfortunes, one that he felt had been sent above all, to plague him. "That goddam Major started this chain reaction by bringing them here!"

Dr Kayla, with her hands splayed out, leaned over the Commanders desk, was totally oblivious to the horrified look he gave her- as she launched into a truly mind boggling collection of names, dates, ranks, qualifications, explanations, abilities, talk of DNA, blood groups, total lack of antibodies, lineages, direct descendants, pure bloodlines, physiques, pure foods, natural medicines, she rattled on and on, and on, with a truly bewildering quantity of facts and figures. The Commander was pushing his fingers through his thinning hair causing much of it to stand on end like a cactus bush!

The woman's turned into a damned machine! This was the only other coherent thought that passed through the Commander's mind -besides his future retirement pension – or perhaps more accurately, the very likely *loss* of it.

The Commander was scared to interrupt her, but he was equally fearful that she'd never stop long enough to draw a breath!

"Yes Doctor, but...excuse me...Doctor Kayla. Excuse.... *Doctor Kayla will you please, S-T-O-P talking!*"

Finally hearing him, Dr Kayla stopped speaking abruptly, in mid word – much to the Commander's obvious relief.

"Oh, thank you, - look here, I have absolutely *no* idea whatsoever about the um, scientific side of all this, - he waved his hand over the scattered computer printouts - but I think I might have the general idea of all you're trying to tell me.

In a few *simple* words, and please, feel free to correct me if I'm wrong. I *think* you mean that this is a significant medical, and historical find, and it's also one that is going to cost this Area, *my area* HUNDREDS of *BILLIONS* of Andesine Taels – tell me Doctor, am I right? Am I close?"

The good doctor had the grace to blush for the second time that morning, and say, "Well sir, yes sir, but there's more, so much more we could learn from

these men, for medical and scientific purposes you understand, and I would very much like to be the one who does the finding, if I may Sir."
The Commander stood and stretched, then pushed his long bony fingers through his now bristly, thin silver hair making it stand up in even more comical little points all around his head. He tried to stifle a yawn (wondering the whole time, what on earth he'd done to deserve all this, and *how* he could get out of it with his rank *and* his very substantial pension, still intact).

His next very unpleasant, and extremely sobering thought, was that he might have to go through all this, this – whatever it all was that Dr Kayla had just said – *again* with Dr Kilmer, and given that *he* would be heavily on the defensive now, simply because he'd only been interested in proving in any way he possibly could, that the men *were* spies, oh, and he'd also be resentful of the fact that she'd spent hours of her own, her personal, *unpaid time*, because had been so enthusiastic about their story, that she'd gone ahead with the testing - *and* that the final outcome has resulted in a history making discovery, well that will not only take Dr Kayla a high step above him, but *she* would be the celebrated one and it would be *her* name, not his, going down in history... while he'd not only come out looking stupid and unreasonable, but he'd also be left looking thoroughly unprofessional, and *that alone* would be sufficient to make him feel obliged to do at *least* double the amounts of testing and *that* meant he would –as their Commanding Officer– he would be forced to sit through double the number of meetings and incomprehensible reports...

While the Commander was grasping at short straws in an attempt to buy himself some valuable time, time he desperately needed if he was going to manage to wriggle out of, and distance himself from the dire consequences. He had an idea...

"I'll tell you what Dr Kayla, you may not only be a *part* of the Top-Secret team to do the testing, investigating or whatever, of these men, but *you* will be solely responsible for choosing a complete team of whatever professionals you might require, *and* I will expect you and you alone, to lead them. You will be responsible, and you will report, *only* to me. They will all sign a confidentiality clause, ah, and um, oh yes; NO papers are to be published – not just yet anyway. I am going to raise your security clearance to level One Red, equal to my own clearance, and I'll also be authorising a new Dino-Mayte computer to be delivered directly to your office within the hour, you are to keep it *on your person* at *all* times, *you*, and *you alone* will have the password. NO information – none at all -concerning your group will leave your possession, unless I say so. *Is that absolutely clear Doctor?"*

"Oh Sir, yes Sir, everything will be brought directly to you, and you will decide what will be done with the statistics, and important scientific data we gather." (She laughed inwardly as she watched him grimace) "But Sir, if I may I be so bold as to ask if I can take them back to their home again? It would only be to gather further intelligence obviously; we must learn *how* they've lived and survived and so on, for so long, *and* all without ever having been discovered *or* located by satellite. That information would look so much better in your reports as well sir. What I mean is that if you were to have a complete and comprehensive coverage from all possible angles. Of course, Sir, if you'd prefer, or if you'd like things to be wrapped up more quickly, Doctor Kilmer and I could work in conjunction" (By his thoroughly horrified and confused expression she knew for certain, that he'd give her *whatever* she asked for now) "And Sir, we'll need air transport and provisions, and then there'll be all the supplies, the medical testing equipment..." As she spoke Kayla's brain switched into overdrive and picked up the thread of the tenuous plan that had begun formulating sometime in the long mind-numbing hours she'd spent waiting for the test results the previous night. An idea that she'd hoped would develop enough to *become* a real plan. The Commanders eyes had begun to glaze over...

"Yes, yes, I'll authorize everything, anything, whatever personnel and supplies, *and* whatever you want - it's going to be your choice of transportation. Doctor Kayla, you just do whatever you think is necessary. For my part, I need you to guarantee that there will be a spectacularly impressive outcome for this command post. Then, and only then, Dr Kayla, will you report back to me. No one else! Certainly *not* to Kilmer, you keep that man as far away from your research as – look, just keep him right away from it, do you understand me? And remember Dr Kayla, *none* not a single one of the other doctors, not even one single lab technician, is *in any way* to be further involved in this -not in any way -at all, ever, do you hear me? Report your findings to me, just me, and only me, and *always* in my private office. My eyes only, remember that Doctor. My secretary will be advised to give you full access or authorisations for whatever you need, whenever you need it." The commander sat with his fingers flexing nervously as he spoke.

"I'm counting on your absolute discretion Dr Kayla. If you can accomplish this mission successfully, and *only if*, there will be a permanent, and a *very* significant, promotion for you." Kayla could accept his commands and the restrictions he imposed easily, simply because the testing was finished and a satisfactory outcome had been achieved - there *was* nothing further to be tested!

Dr Kayla was practically walking on air all the way back to the hospital wing. She'd done it! Somehow, she wasn't quite sure *how*, but she'd done it! The idea that had begun quietly germinating, way, way, deep in the back of her mind last night after she'd submitted the first sample for DNA testing, had become an almost fully developed plan now, thanks to her nervous, greedy Commander. Her biggest hurdle had just been overcome, and she hadn't even had to lie! Oh, how she loved this Commander –he's just *so* ineffectual in his position, and oh-so-very-protective of his big fat pension!

Okay, first things first now Sámi.

She would require a complete staff of doctors comprising of, a dentist, paediatrician, and a general surgeon, nurses with some unique talents, optician (must note: all with their full equipment and kits) and at least two, hopefully three, capable helicopter pilots, all in all she would be looking at a twenty to thirty strong team. All must be young and healthy, all female, and all willing to take a one-way journey back to the past. Am I *totally crazy* to think I can *actually* pull this off? Well, I suppose I won't have to wait very long to find out, she thought as she prepared yet another pot of coffee.

Half an hour later there was a quiet knock on her office door, an orderly stood there with a small unmarked, unidentified parcel addressed to her; it turned out to be the most recent model pocket computer. She was so excited to have this tiny new gizmo (it was less than half the size of the palm of her small hand) and all that went with it.

Dr Kayla inserted the infinity power chip and booted up her ever so tiny, but oh so powerful computer. Once she'd activated both the remote projector screen, keyboard and the printer, she entered a *very* secure password for her newly acquired top level clearance and began digging into the Strictly Classified, Private and Confidential files of all the female personnel attached to the base.

She commenced her search by entering the necessary medical qualifications, photographs, the statistics of age, and most importantly, those with no family ties to hinder them, (or make a fuss when they disappeared), sexual preference - after all, they'd be no good for the purpose at hand at all, if they didn't like men, and any ongoing health requirements.

Finally, after re-checking that all the vital data parameters she'd entered were correct, she was able to let the computer begin the initial work of sifting through hundreds and hundreds of personnel files for her. Meanwhile she locked her office door, and then she settled back more comfortably in her chair, put her feet up and took a much-needed nap.

The sound of the alarm pulled her out of a surprisingly sound and dreamless sleep.

Turning back to her desk she saw a satisfyingly large, neat stack of paper in her printer tray. That stack of paper represented all the information she would require to move on to the next step. There were over ninety names on the list, and she only needed twenty-three, maybe twenty-four, young women, so if her plan was to get off the ground, she had to start the interviews, actually she needed to begin immediately.

After a quick run through the records each with an accompanying photograph. Within the first hour she'd rejected a half dozen candidates who, she knew from personal experience, to be troublesome, and another two dozen or so because they didn't fit the general criteria set down by the men of New Eden themselves.

She also couldn't select anyone who was not a physically perfect specimen, no one who had implants of any kind, who required regular medication of *any* kind, no one who wore spectacles or contact lenses, nor could she choose anyone who wore dentures, or had problem teeth.

With that initial task completed she e-messaged the secretary of the personnel office with the names of the female staffers she would require to be interviewed. It seemed to her an eternity that her finger hovered over the holographic keyboard before she took a deep breath and touched on SEND.

Dr Kayla took another deep breath, smiled, and thought to herself - And so it begins!

Sámi returned to her normal rounds, taking particular care today, to really *look* at the people who came to her for help with their many and varied problems, she was really taken aback when she realised that she didn't feel guilty, not even the tiniest twinge of guilt at the thought of walking away from every single one of her patients, *or* her responsibilities.

Eighteen months ago, when she had been promoted to her present position, she would have been completely aghast by the mere *thought* of giving anything less than 110% of her total attention and compassion!

Ah yes, but then again, eighteen months ago, she hadn't met Alder.

For the next nine days her small office was a beehive of industry. However, by mid-afternoon Friday, she had chosen her team of twenty-three young women. She herself counted as number twenty-four.

Most of the women were between the ages of eighteen and twenty, but none were older than twenty-one, (except for herself, Sami was nearing twenty-three) they were all very healthy and extremely fit, most were more than reasonably attractive, however, and most importantly for her purpose, for one reason or another they had no family ties.

To her total incredulity she'd learned just how many women -and she supposed it would be the same for the men- actually joined the armed forces to get a surrogate family. The realisation saddened her a little too, but if everything went according to her plan, and if the men were speaking accurately, and not just figuratively, which was highly unlikely, they would, very soon, all have more family than they'd ever dreamed possible.

The next items on her list were equipment, and the all-important medical supplies; obtaining sufficient vaccinations and having them suitably stored, and be ready to use prior to leaving, was *the* absolute, number one priority. If everything else went wrong, the vaccinations had to have priority. The main reason being, she and her crew were carrying within themselves, enough contagion to seriously infect – if not kill - every living person in the mysterious Eden.
Clothing wouldn't be an issue, but for cover each woman would pack five changes of clothing, all personal effects, and the non-essentials would all be left behind, as would money and property. The main objective of the plan was to avoid putting up any red flags.
The next requirement on her long list were three long-range helicopters, not so much for the distance as for the space necessary for machines, cargo and personnel they'd be carrying, complete with an ample fuel supply, sufficient for the nonexistent return journey. She double checked and re-checked her lists and inventory, looking for any holes or possible flaws, but mercifully finding none.

Keep it simple Sámi, had become her personal buzz phrase; chuckling to herself she leaned back and laced her fingers behind her head, then closing her eyes, she savoured the moment before standing up patting the tiny lump inside her secure hidden zip pocket, before quietly closing, and locking the office door behind her. She'd even gone so far as to pencil in her patient list for the week she returned, if her appointment diary was blank, then awkward questions would certainly be raised.

No red flags Sámi, she repeated to herself once again. No red flags.

"Oh...but Freeman...please, *please* trust me, it *will* work! I *know* it will! I have planned everything down to - *and including* - the smallest detail. All of these women, every single one of them, are strong and healthy, they have no family and no romantic ties, so no-one will come looking for them; naturally, they understand it's not a holiday camp, they know that it's a one-way trip, and, and this is most important for everyone concerned, they all *want* to go.

We can bring the new blood to your people; *we can* keep Eden alive for another hundred years, maybe even two or three hundred years, just as your forefathers planned, *please* Freeman, *please*, let us at least *try,* won't you? If you think we can't do it, then we'll all leave again, it's that simple."

Freeman stood quietly, looking thoughtfully down at the tiny figure of Dr Kayla standing in front of him and hearing again the words of warning from the High Council –do not bring any woman without their express approval.

"Okay then" Dr Kayla said trying a different approach "please, just listen to me for a moment here, why don't you talk to your men and put it to a vote; I, we, will abide by the decision, I can't be any fairer than that now can I?"

The next hour seemed like a month to her as she waited for Freeman and the men to arrive at their decision, so much rested on the outcome, for her, for them, for Eden, and in no small way, for her volunteers too, because after all is said and done, it will be *their* futures in the balance as well!

Freeman and Alder came striding down the long corridor toward her, their handsome faces were completely devoid of expression, giving her no hint as to the result of their vote. They continued on down the corridor until they stopped and stood quite still, looking down at her.

Freeman said the decision had been voted upon, therefore he was now permitted and had been endorsed to speak on behalf of the men.

"We are very appreciative of your prodigious disquiet where our welfare, and also our wellbeing is concerned, equally for your determination to achieve the continuation of Eden; therefore, we each accept your offer with profound pleasure and immeasurable humility. We are most grateful to you, and also to the superb young women you have selected to accompany you to Eden."

She stood absolutely still, transfixed, unable for a few heartbeats to believe her own ears. She suddenly found herself wanting to hug them, to jump up and down on the spot and do a victory dance. Woo-hoo! Yes! Yes! Yes! Woo-hoo! Yes! Yes! Yes!

But instead, she looked at each of the men and said quietly "the honour is ours; we won't let you down. Please, may we return to the others? We must complete organising ourselves as quickly as possible, time is of the essence now."

The room was positively alive with excitement, the boys had been told that their mission was now to be considered complete, successful and almost at an end. They were going home, home to their beloved Eden, just when they'd thought all was lost to them, this most wondrous of conclusions had been attained for them. "The rest of the planning is in the doctor's very capable hands, she will articulate to us at what time we are to be standing by to leave, however, you must comprehend one important detail. Dr Kayla has informed me that we shall be leaving for Eden in a big bird." He allowed time for that to sink in before continuing.

"The doctor has also communicated to me that the exact distance that we travelled in fourteen days long march, will take only a small part of one day travelling in the stomach of the big bird. Go now - return to your quarters where you will take food and rest - speak of this no more."

An exhausted Dr Kayla promised herself that she really would get some sleep - soon - but for the next few hours at least it was necessary to finalise the remaining formalities. She had to get all the travel papers signed and processed. Oh, and she mustn't forget to repack the big bundles of vegetable seeds, the assortment of grains, and the hydroponic fruit trees or the boxes of dry yeast into strong travel containers. She wanted them to be a special surprise for Alder, oh, *and* the people of Eden of course; she must them packed up right now, and label those cases with *Caution: Delicate Medical Equipment* labels whereas the other *genuine* equipment boxes were labelled slightly differently. Once that was taken care of, well, then she needed to really get a hustle on and get on with a thousand other things. Only then could everything be made ready for first light tomorrow. Sleeping would just have to wait a little longer... She couldn't afford any delays, or to allow the Commander enough time to either have second thoughts *or* to read the pilot resumes too closely, or to think about, or question, that the service crew were all very young, and all female, *or* to give anyone else time to ask her any difficult questions. Thank goodness the Commander had sent Kilmer away on leave for two whole weeks. Oh, what *I* could do with two weeks of free time right now – although given the way I'm feeling right now I'd most probably spend the time sleeping, she thought as she stifled another tired yawn...

The full group of service personnel would meet before sunrise at 0530 hours on the Heli-pad.

The two distinctly different codes of medical equipment would be loaded first; they would need to be weight shared between the three aircraft to balance evenly, and to cope with it all. The men of Eden would all be travelling together, along with the doctor and the pilot in the first aircraft, with their fair share of the cargo. The other two helicopters would be assigned an all-female crew, comprising of medical and engineering personnel...

Then eleven more women, including the pilot, would board each of the other two craft.

At Doctor Kayla's insistence, they must be ready to leave no later than 0630 hours and that would time their departure to be exactly when the rising sun flooded the Heli-pad with blinding light. The necessary flight documents and supply release forms had already been signed and stamped. Each of the aircraft's instruments had been carefully checked, their twin tanks fuelled to capacity, and the shipment had already been loaded and secured by strong cargo nets to prevent any shifting or movement in flight.

Finally, the assigned passengers would be signed off and on board by 0626 hours.

The doctor had spoken to the men the night before and explained to them about the very high noise levels they would experience, she also assured them that they had nothing to fear, nor did their families, nor did the good people of Eden have anything to fear. Doctor Kayla explained to them, fully and carefully, that once the helicopters had performed their transport duty, all three machines would be destroyed, but in such a way that they would be easily found by a search party who would assume that the men of Eden, along with military personnel, had all perished in the crash and were forever lost to the world. With that presumption firmly in mind no one would ever come looking again.

Dr. Kayla knew with certainty that the Commander would be more than willing, euphoric even, to let the whole problematical matter disappear - along with all the paperwork and documentation- everything, in any way relevant or significant to these men, would simply vanish...as though none of it had ever existed.

That way he wouldn't have to answer to the President – oh, and let's not forget that his precious, all-important pension, would finally be safe and well secured! He only had to find a way to explain away the major's indiscretions, the hounds, and the hospitalised soldiers... well as the Camp Commander he would lay all the blame squarely on the major's doorstep they would become his problem entirely, and as he'd been confined to a psychiatric ward for the criminally insane, who was going to believe any of his crazed chatter about cavemen!
What could possibly be better than a happy outcome for everyone?

The view from the helicopter at sunrise, was magical, simply spectacular; at one point Cain and Marshall, far from being afraid, leaned out a little too far in their excitement and had to be pulled back inside! The young pilots were great; all three young women had only passed their first basic flying test two weeks ago, and now here they were flying a mercy mission! Strictly speaking they weren't supposed to fly without a qualified pilot sitting beside them yet, but Dr. Kayla knew that they'd each passed in the top four of their respective classes. There would be no necessity for aerobatic skills or fancy flying on this trip so she was quietly confident that their ability to take off, fly in a straight line, and land again, would be more than adequate. Their comparative inexperience would only add the necessary layer of authenticity to her planned *disaster* There may be a few questions raised initially, however with no families around to be asking awkward questions, or seeking compensation, Kayla knew there would be no serious follow up investigation and so the whole 'tragic matter' would just go away quietly.

They flew around for a little while giving the men a bit of a thrill ride, and to give the watchtower time to lose interest in their flight. Dr. Kayla's pilots knew there were first timer students flying this morning, so the control tower would, without doubt, be overwhelmed as it always was on 'novice flight' mornings.

Later, a little after mid-morning, the men began searching the ground below for New Eden, they asked how low the birds could fly without falling, because they couldn't recognise anything from up here. The young pilots were more than happy to oblige by dropping down as low as they dared and within minutes Freeman shouted "THERE IT IS!!" The crew was at a loss as to what he was seeing; all the women could see was a long barren rocky outcrop that went on for long grey miles, with no visible life or colour whatsoever!

"Down! Down! Go down now!" The pilots flew in closer to the rock face and gently came to a rest on the ground. Freeman, Alder and the younger men jumped out and started running toward the rock wall, they stopped, looked all along the rocky outcrop in both directions, and then started pointing and running back to the aircraft. "That way! We have to go one half day's walk that way! It is there that we will find the opening."

Doctor Kayla looked at the immensely high, totally unremarkable, drab, grey rock wall and felt positively sick. She turned and said to Alder "Did we do all that preparation, come all this way - for this, this big ugly rocky nothingness?"

At first, he looked distressed, even hurt and confused by her words and by the sharp tone of her voice, then his handsome face broke into a magnificent grin of pure happiness "Ah, but good sweet doctor, do not look at this! This is but the shell, the perfection is only to be found once you have reached inside the shell."

The doctor remembered his first experience with shellfish, he was so unsure when he looked at it, and his look of dismay when he'd tried to bite into it – she had told him the perfection was inside the shell! She was thrilled and deeply touched that he remembered. He smiled down at her as though he'd heard her thoughts – "Yes Sámi Kayla; I remember, as I remember every word that has passed your lips, every touch of your gentle hands, since the day of our first meeting."

Something very pleasant went tzzzing...deep in Sámi Kayla's belly.

They flew for another few miles around the forbidding pale blue-grey stone wall, and on a whim the lead pilot, who was immediately joined by the other two - flew over the top of the outcrop to see if she could land somewhere, but all that could be seen was rock, rock, and more rock, certainly nothing resembling the promised paradise on earth!

Something else was strange about it too, and then she realised what was missing, there was no colour down there, in fact she couldn't even *see* the ground, even though they were flying quite low, she was thinking 'that's just weird surely, we should see something, *anything.*' All of a sudden, the electronic gadgetry on the consoles started blinking and alarms sent out shrill warnings; every instrument in the cockpit was going haywire!

In unison, the pilots swung away and headed back over the top of the wall.

Oh, please let there be something good down there. The other pilots and their crews were becoming a bit panicky and really doubtful now too, looking at each other with puzzled and confused expressions.

"Now, here! Now… go down now! Go down here, now!" Alder called out, pointing excitedly at the ground and shouting to be heard above the noise of the rotor blades. His instructions were followed, and moments later they came to a soft landing almost exactly at the opening, although it was quite invisible to the untrained eye. The men jumped down and ran along the rock face laughing like little children at a fun park then suddenly they just, disappeared! They were there running and laughing, and then, and then, they weren't there at all!

The women had gathered together around the aircraft, and from the muted conversations she managed to overhear, Doctor Kayla knew they were – like herself - all far less than impressed with this *paradise* and wondering how they were going to get themselves out of this. For her part Doctor Kayla thought if this Eden *wasn't* actually the paradise they'd been led to believe, and so far it was really looking that way, then they might have no choice but to go with what she's told the Commander, return the men home, gather information, and return to the base. They'd spent over half an hour walking back and forth along the impenetrable wall in the exhausting, sweltering heat, trying to find where the men had simply vanished to…when just as suddenly the six men reappeared, followed by many more young men in sarongs.

Here were more, many more, exquisitely beautiful, longhaired, bearded, tall and, tanned, broad shouldered, lean hipped, muscular men in loincloths.

Oh…. Wow!

This was the one, the *only* single thought shared by the young women. The sight sent their hearts racing, and more than one thought she'd better slow down a bit before she fainted!

The girl's mouths started watering, and the doubters felt that if these young men were any indication of what lay beyond the ugly stone walls, well there was a good chance that perhaps the promised paradise might not be lost to them after all!

"Greetings to you Senior Freeman and Senior Alder, Cain, Marshall, Theo and Jacob, our hearts are lightened once again, now that our eyes see you are safely returned to us. We have partially cleared the entrance in preparation for your return, although we had not anticipated your homecoming so soon, nor could we, in any way have anticipated your return in such a manner, nor that you would have such company!"

"Harmon has returned to Eden to announce your safe and welcome return with many, many young women! There will be a feasting and a celebration this night such as there has never before been held in all our history. I bid welcome to all the newcomers, welcome to our home, now come! Come, stay with me, I will lead you safely through the caves and to a salutation such as we have never seen!"

"Oh, my, God! I'll sure stay with *you* darling!"

Exclaimed Georgette, she was laughing nervously.

"Did I just see what I think I just saw?"

Was Antonia's whispered question. "Oh my, oh my, oh my! This is going to be a feast all right. I thought *these* men were gorgeous, but, oh, wow, *all* these men are simply mag-ni-fi-cent!"

The women giggled and laughed, surprised by their own nervousness as they followed the unbelievably handsome young man through the narrow entrance.

"Hey girls, don't for goodness sakes, put on any weight or we'll never get back out through here again!!!"

The young man stopped dead in his tracks, and turned to the women, his handsome face had become a mask of tragedy.

"You – you are not staying? If you do not have the intention of becoming women of Eden we must proceed no further." He looked as though he was ready to burst into tears!

At that moment Alder came loping up to the young man and said something to him about our manner of speech not being clean –as yet– "it is not as you imagine Lieth, these women have agreed to come and tie with our young men, to become one with the community, be not fearful nor downcast I beg of you. Continue now, continue on to Eden!"

The women didn't know where to look first, there was so much to see, there was a strange fragrance wafting through the colonnade, not unpleasant by any means, actually it was a sweet smell reminding them of, of, something they couldn't readily give a name to, but they agreed it was very pleasant. The honey-coloured stone was cool to the touch, and much smoother than was to be expected. The caves themselves were simply stunning, there were fantastically large, beautiful portraits and drawings of many people, men, women and children of all ages, all depicted doing different everyday things, it was almost like walking through the family photo album.

Then without any notice or warning from Freeman or Alder, they walked through a truly beautiful archway and heard excited cheering and loud laughter coming in through a solid wall of glowing golden sunlight ahead of them.
"This is the entranceway," said Alder. The sunlight had blinded them all, temporarily forcing them to stand quite still, but the beautiful young Leith kept urging them to, "come, come follow me, come, we are arrived in Eden! All who see you count you as family from this moment onward; you will carry us into our future."

When their eyes had adjusted to the light, they saw hundreds of people, people of all ages standing there before them on a lower level - in the most fantastically stunning garden any of the women had ever seen; it was like something taken from a movie set!

Such strong, healthy-looking people, and the girls saw that every single person from the oldest to the smallest child, was clothed in the same simple, delicately coloured sarongs. The whole of Eden community had gathered together in a large group, and they were standing in the midst of magnificent flower filled gardens, tall exotic plants of outrageous, never before seen colours, and trees filled with brightly coloured birds. It was hard to say which was the most colourful, the flowers, or the birds!

A waterfall in full flow could be heard, but was not yet visible, and judging from the deep-water sounds coming from it, it promised to be as large and as beautiful as Alder had assured her it would be. "Oh wow, will you look at all that grass!" called one of the young women. The grass was the most perfect shade of deep jade green.

The light down here inside the canyon was quite peaceful, it was extraordinary, so unlike the brutal flesh burning, eyeball scorching sunlight they'd experienced on the other side, out there it was really intense, enough to cause some serious physical discomfort; on the other side of the walls, it was a cruel and blistering sun. However, once they were safely inside the high protective walls that sheltered Eden, the sunlight became more of a subdued light that was still plenty bright enough, but in here it was

tamed, it was gentle, and so soft, nothing anywhere near as sweltering or intense as it had been only feet away. More than one of the newcomers started to cry with happiness, or relief, or perhaps a bit of both – while a few were a little apprehensive, but still prepared to start a whole new life here.
The doctor came through the entranceway with Freeman on one side and Alder on the other.

Freeman called for the Most Revered Elders to greet all the newcomers – "But in particular my fellow Edener's it gives me the *ultimate honour* to introduce you to Doctor Sámi Kayla. She alone, is responsible for our safe return. She alone, is responsible for bringing to you these young women, the women who will bring continuation to our beloved Eden!
Sámi Kayla is in all truth, the embodiment of the true spirit of Eden. Her singular courage and her tremendous fortitude have been unknown to us since the first and Most Revered Founding Elders!"

The silence that followed his announcement was profound and lasted about ten heartbeats. Then a single voice, singing high and heartbreakingly sweet about a 'bird that would one day return to the nest to care for its young' was joined by another and another, different voices picked up the tune until every throat had joined in the achingly sweet melodious song.
Alder turned and spoke to the doctor; "you are awarded a great tribute. Come Sámi Kayla; please, grant me the honour of leading you down now, to take your rightful place amongst us."

As soon as her feet touched the ground, many hands reached out to touch her, gentle caressing touches that conveyed their gratitude as nothing else, and no words ever could.

Sámi Kayla felt for perhaps the first time in her life, that she had done the right thing for the right reason. Any shadow of doubt that may have been lurking in her subconscious, rapidly and permanently, vanished.

The young women were led through a maze of naturally formed corridors, the walls around them were the same soft honey colour as the grand colonnade, they were shown where they might cleanse and refresh themselves, in preparation for the evening's celebration feast.

Their first evening passed in a blur of impressions, it seemed fantastic to be living in caves, and yet to have fully functioning bathrooms, albeit they were older than any Andesine antiques. They found themselves emotionally and wholeheartedly welcomed by so many into these very primitive, yet oh so perfect, surroundings.

Long trestle tables were laden with a mouth-watering array of delicious foods, none of which the young women had ever seen or tasted before. The meals were eaten gracefully, yet without cutlery and served up on simple unglazed earthenware platters, plain pottery pitchers and cups held exotic juices that were both pleasant to taste and cleansing on the pallet.

Men, women and children of all ages came over to welcome them and to offer them small gifts, there were previously unknown flowers that were richly vibrant in colour yet delicately perfumed, or sweet fruits such as they'd never seen before. Their welcome to Eden was as sincere and heart-warming as it was uncomplicated.

When the feasting had finally exhausted itself, the new women of Eden were shown into their temporary sleeping rooms. Elder Rita apologised profusely for not being fully prepared for them as their arrival today had been most unexpected. Although for tonight she was sure, they would all be quite comfortable, as long as they felt no discomfort sharing a room.

"She obviously doesn't know about army dormitories! The twenty to thirty bunk beds to a military barracks!" called one young woman

"Hey! Hey! Girls come in here!" Nisha called out to the other women. "Come and see these drawings, they're absolutely stunning!" The women poked their heads around into the empty cave room where Nisha had a tallow lamp held high to show off her find. They were all looking at the portrait of Mark coming out of the pond dripping wet. "I don't know who he is girls, but I hope he's one of the single ones 'cause he's gorgeous! Oh, look, here he is again! I wonder what happened he's got handfuls of dirt, poor thing he's crying, he looks heartbroken. Ah wow, look this place is full of him look over there!"

"Oh, I get it now, he must be one of the first marines, one of the ones who found this place, see there, and look at the funny old-fashioned uniform!"

"Oh jeez, will you look at that! He's even been drawn up on the roof!" The women admired all the many drawings and marvelled that they'd remained untouched for well over a century, and maybe, if the man's uniform was anything to go by, even much longer than that. Back home these drawings wouldn't have survived a single day – some idiot would have spoiled them with crude additions!

New sarongs of the softest go-bit wool had been placed on their freshly made, sweet smelling grass and wool mattresses, and clean bed covers of soft supple hide and loose spun lambs' wool waited, ready to keep them warm.

Once the girls had seen their *accommodations*, and had felt and touched and giggled, or ooh'ed and ahh 'ed over all the softness of the fresh coverings and garments, they were shown a different, more direct route from the sleeping place, down to where they could shower and relieve themselves, they were also shown how to get across to the kitchen where they could find refreshments should they become hungry or thirsty in the night. After guiding the girls on their tour Elder Rita bid them goodnight, and walked serenely over to her own suite of caves, she was so glad that this long, and exceedingly emotional day, had finally come to a close.

Once they were alone, as all women will, they sat around and discussed their first impressions of their new home.

Sometime later Doctor Kayla poked her head through the opening into the overcrowded room and reminded them that "Tomorrow will be here soon girls, I suggest you take the nice lady's advice and find yourself a bed, and get a good night's sleep because we've got a very busy day ahead of us tomorrow."

Early the next morning, long before the sun had reached the breakfast marker stone, the men stood gathered around the helicopters, wondering what to make of the strange aircraft. They were all eagerly waiting to unload them.

The newcomers were trying to get over to the entranceway to direct and assist with the unloading but found themselves surrounded by the many curious ladies of Eden, touching their hair, fingering their strange and unlovely military clothing, and laughing at their heavy leather boots! While all the laughter and chatter were going on Sámi slipped out to find Alder. All the equipment she'd brought here would be less than useless! Without really knowing why – and completely against all logic, and the evidence that she herself had gathered to the contrary - she'd assumed (wrongly) that Eden had a power plant! Although in this instance her plan would actually work out even better than she originally thought.

Once again, she found herself calling on Alder and explaining that as they didn't have - sunlight in the roof as they'd had at the base all the equipment she'd brought with them would be useless here. "However," she instructed, "the boxes labelled *Medical Equipment* with the green and purple stickers *must* be offloaded and taken inside, the remainder however will be jettisoned along with the aircraft, that way it would look like the inexperienced pilots had unfortunately crashed and burned with all personnel and cargo lost. I had planned on just burning the aircraft, but with the equipment still inside it will be totally believable, that's why I wanted long range craft - for the big fuel tanks, the extra fuel will burn fiercely hot, hot enough to melt the metal and in reality, it would even reduce all the bones to ash. If anything *is* found it will only be melted aircraft metal, and maybe some stray buttons from our uniforms, mixed with the twisted or melted remains of the equipment. I'll have the girls fly them a few miles further down away from the wall and far away from the entry..." Alder held up his very graceful, long fingered hands to silence her... "No Sámi Kayla, it would be better if your helicopters gave the appearance of having crashed into the walls would it not? That way they will not look for you here. It is written in the book of our great grand sire, The Most Revered Elder Wade Tyler, that the best place to hide something is in plain sight, is that not still true? Our entranceway can be blocked with dead bushes many man lengths deep; it will discourage even the most zealous of searchers, and" he said with a cheeky grin "as you yourself can bear witness, there is nothing of beauty to be seen from above."

True to his word Alder had fifteen of the strong young men attach sturdy ropes made from thick strips of raw pigskin plaited together with animal gut and tough grasses, to the aircrafts landing skis and they used sheer muscle power to drag the helicopters right up to the base of the rock wall and tangle them together as best they could. The blast from the exploding fuel would complete the scenario.

Once they'd stripped the aircraft of anything that might be useful like ropes, cargo netting, seats, and had taken a few souvenirs, the helicopters were prepared by soaking everything, including the surrounding earth and splashing fuel -as far up the wall as three men standing on each other's shoulders could reach. The pungent smelling aviation fuel was then ignited by using a simple but effectively placed detonating device in the form of a bow and arrow shooting a flaming rag soaked in animal fat.

There were three enormous *WHOOSH* and *KRUMPH* followed by an incredibly powerful shockwave of hot air from the exploding fuel tanks as they each detonated in turn, knocking a few of the men who were standing about one hundred paces away, flat on their backsides. The effect was spectacular, and the machines burned fiercely hot and furiously for more than half a day, thick plumes of black smoke rose high up into the clear blue sky, coating the high walls with black soot that gave off an appalling stench. Eventually the fire burned itself out, and by the following morning the aircraft had been reduced to nothing more than a large, still smoking mass of grotesquely twisted, melted metal.

A wide arc around the *crash site* was burnt and blackened, and the walls of Eden were stained black forevermore.

True to their word, the young men sealed the entrance using many layers of large rocks and debris - taken from the huge stockpiles of rocks left over from the various tunnels and excavation sites. The barricade was built high enough and deep enough to discourage even the most ardent of searchers.

The real commotion started two weeks later, when four small search and rescue helicopters flew a standard grid pattern for 200 x 200 air miles in every direction, increasing the search areas by 100-mile increments after the women failed to return at the designated time.

The search craft flew over the crash site where the burned-out wreckage was located and reported. Harmon, Leith, Jacob, Cain, and Theo sat high up on the wall, well hidden from view, watching the actions and movements of the search party on the ground below.

However, the Search and Rescue Team, after examining the wreckage and determining that judging by the amount of melted metal all personnel and the medical equipment on board had been destroyed by the explosion and ensuing inferno.

The report stated: After finding no trace of survivors anywhere in the vicinity, it must be assumed that all twenty-four members of the medical and engineering teams, along with the Team Leader Dr.S.Kayla and six unidentified male civilians on-board, had all been killed on impact and the subsequent blaze had incinerated the bodies.

The Report also contained a footnote that the terrain within the Exclusion Zone was still between forty-seven and fifty-three degrees Celsius, unbearably hot and unable to support anything but the crudest plant and insect life.

After photographing and recording footage of the crash site, the barely recognisable burned-out hulks of what used to be helicopters, and collecting various samples of debris for the inquest, they returned to base.

The Commanders report stated that the inexperienced pilots had been flying too low and had obviously mistaken the rock wall for a fog bank; as a result, they crashed and burned leaving no survivors. A brief memorial service was held for the Fallen Comrades, and once that had been concluded normal routines returned to the base.

No report was filed; indeed, none was ever prepared in regard to the illegal detention of six men of Eden, nor of their claims of being the direct descendants of a Missing Marine Rescue Unit from the WWWP era.

The Major was transferred to a military prison hospital for the criminally insane, and his papers were marked 'Never to Be Released' he was subsequently forgotten about. Dr Kilmer was transferred to a base closer to his own hometown as were the fifteen members of the Elite Squad. Many other key members received unexpected transfers to far flung bases across the forty-one zones – thus effectively breaking the gossip and curiosity chain. The Commander was an extremely relieved, and exceedingly smug man once all those nasty loose ends had been tied up nicely, and he knew his pension was safe and secure once again. He intended for it to stay that way.

III

NEW LIFE IN EDEN BEGINS

The women awoke in their new surroundings to the sweet, soft and melodious sound of song floating up from the groups of women working below. The words were a little indistinct due to the echoing nature of the caves, but the sentiment was as clear as crystal to each and every one of the new arrivals. 'Welcome, welcome to your new home' it was simply beautiful and incredibly heart-warming for these young women who for whatever reasons, had been without a caring family for a very long time.

They climbed a little stiffly from their bedding and stretched languidly. "Morning all, what time is it? I feel like I've slept for a dozen years!"

A lovely young native of New Eden, by the name of Keelee, met up with Sámi and they went from room to room waking up the women, informing them that as soon as they were ready, they could join together again down in the eating area. Sámi kept reminding the various groups, "there are lots of things we have to get done today ladies. Don't forget our first responsibility is to take care of these people by protecting them against ourselves."

The first few days after the newcomers' arrival were quite traumatic for the people of Eden, with the necessity for the vaccinations explained they *did* understand, but even so, *understanding* and *liking*, are two very different things. There were a few sore arms, some headaches and one or two cases of nausea, but within the week Eden had returned to its normal tranquil routine of work, exercise, play, song and family time. There were no dramatic casualties, no fuss, and no hurt feelings, instead, there was a deep gratitude that the young doctor had had the foresight to protect them. What a lovely way to begin the rest of their new lives together.

The women adjusted to their new surroundings with surprising ease and enthusiasm. They did encounter some temporary issues - like getting used to wearing only a single garment and going without their customary underwear, and neither cosmetics or jewellery were either justified nor necessary.

None of their Outland equipment was kept either, their jewellery, watches, radios, communicators, cameras and any other gadgets were given the same treatment as the founding members worldly goods. That is to say their personal possessions were carefully packed up and locked away, along with their comprehensive personal details as far as they knew them, for the benefit of future generations. They experienced no real sense of loss, because once inside Eden's walls the women found that all signals to radios and communication devices were blocked, their watches had stopped working, and camera batteries had drained in a matter of minutes, so nothing worked anyway.

However, their emotional transition, in regard to going many hundreds and hundreds of years *backwards* in time, almost to the Stone Age, was in fact a whole lot easier, and so much smoother than anyone, least of all the young women themselves, could ever have anticipated.

The strict exercise regime, aside from the rock climbing, archery, and spear throwing, which were a bit of a novelty at first but they eagerly took as a challenge, however, the unarmed combat, gymnastics, short sword dexterity and callisthenics, were, for the most part, all very familiar to the new women, and their overall stamina and fitness levels were almost, but not quite, equal to the natives of Eden. All, that is, with the notable exception of Sámi Kayla, she fell abysmally short in every aspect of physical exercise, and was equally as hopeless in any form of warfare training, however her saving grace was yoga, it was her passion, and she far surpassed even the senior instructors not inconsiderable talents.

The Elder womenfolk took the newcomers under the shelter of their very loving wings, and they conferred with them over many things that were definitely *women only* matters. Some things were never, not ever, spoken about, or even referred to, in front of *any* male, of any age, at *any* time.

When their moon cycle came around, it was easily dealt with within the woman's domain. It was during their many, many hours of talking and getting to know, and to understand each other, that the newcomers realised just how much catching up they had to do socially.

For the first few months their yoga, meditation and self-hypnosis classes, were actually quite intense, but very necessary, if they were to be prepared in time for nature to take her course. It was fortunate however that most of the ,young women had studied either yoga, or undertaken a similar form of exercise and meditation while they were either in a junior military school, or once they'd joined the services.

The wise Elders had placed the women into small groups of no more than three and each group was given a native helper, this assured that their transition, and their learning the ways of Eden would be as pleasant as it would be easy. The young women found the gentle melodious songs, were used not only as a form of entertainment, but also as a therapeutic tool to aid, calm and heal. Many new friendships blossomed and cemented firmly between the two groups of women in those first months, and within the first half of the cycle it was difficult to tell the difference between natives of Eden, and newcomers. For their part, the newcomers, experienced true freedom for the first time in their lives, each chose to remain in the grouping arrangement of the first night until such time as other arrangements were made.

By the completion of the first half cycle, the Female Elders had become quite knowledgeable about their new charges, and of an evening they would sit around like so many old aunts, and watch the interaction between the young men and women.

Various 'matchings' or 'pairings' were discussed and either actively encouraged, or set in motion. The Elders tried as much as they could to bring together temperaments that would compliment each other, not only for the immediate future, but also in anticipation for the long years ahead. These wise elders knew very well that the newly discovered passions of a freshly Tied couple had their place in youth, though when the blood cooled, and the children grew, their basic friendship, trust and respect for each other would be relied upon carry them through and into their twilight years. The absolute rule of 'Once tied, Forever tied' unless a life partner was returned to the garden in death, was made absolutely clear to the newcomers, very early on.

In the first days, the law of Respect was given to the newcomers and they all agreed that it really is the only law that any civilisation needs, because it encompasses absolutely every facet of life.

The first genuine, and in some cases, it was a major hurdle that the women faced, was their casual, crude or lazy manner of speech. Learning to use Eden's very structured and antiquated form of language was a real challenge, especially as a few of the younger women were prone to use coarse or rough language. Elder Ruth, a very wise and kindly woman of perhaps eighty cycles, devised a very simple tactic to 'assist' these young ladies in overcoming their undesirable speech habits. The young woman concerned was invited to explain to a child exactly what the actual meaning of a word was whenever she used an undesirable word or phrase, and as the *factual* meaning of a word, and the *context* in which it was used -differed greatly... well, let's just say the young women were encouraged to think carefully before they spoke. Elder Latika was overheard to say – "Indeed thought before speech is a very desirable trait in all persons."

While all of these things were going on, there was the other area of their day-to-day life happening too. Within days of their arrival, the newcomers began working in the gardens, working side by side with native children, and in so doing they discovered that the feel of the raw earth, the planting, nurturing and growing the food that you yourself will eat and will share with your family is tremendously satisfying, or sitting by the water and fishing to supplement the supper table, they discovered that each new task was an enriching and a deeply fulfilling experience. Within that first half cycle they each felt that they truly belonged here. Each newcomer had memorised, and could now recognise and correctly name, each person within the community, however they all wondered if they'd ever master the lineages!

Courtships began slowly, once the young women had overcome their initial drooling and bravado, an unfamiliar shyness and a lack of self-confidence set in; however, those awkward feelings were short lived once they started to get to know the lovely natives of Eden as individuals, as genuine people with greatly differing, but always gentle personalities, not simply as beautiful beings to be ogled.

One couple that are definitely ready to Tie are Natasha and Leroy, they haven't taken their eyes off each other since she walked out into the sunlight on the first day! Leroy was captivated by her tiny, perfect body crowned by a cap of short curly golden hair and he was spellbound by her lively green eyes. Natasha, being blinded by the sunlight, took the hand that he held out to assist her down the stairs, when she looked up to thank him, she saw a young man who set her pulses racing! Leroy's tall, tanned, well built and almost too beautiful to look at with his waist length black hair and even blacker, long lashed eyes, however it was his kind and gentle nature that truly captured her heart.

Sámi and Alder are also ready to approach the Revered Elders now and request a special Tying ceremony, because although Alder has already been tied, it was many years ago when he was a young man, sadly his partner died shortly after childbirth, and he had willingly remained a single man –until now. Moreover, as he had no wife or children at the age of thirty-five, he wanted to begin a new life with Sámi Kayla. Sami laughed at his use of her full name, she had even gone as far as calling him Alder John Tyler for days at a time, but he could find no fault with that form of address either –it was his name after all! The women were really enjoying the quaint mode of courtship that was practiced here; no touching, no intimacy, no seclusion and *absolutely* no kissing! Wherever a young couple went they were most definitely assured of company. Privacy was only permitted to Tied couples, and trying to really get to know someone in their modern sense, was quite a challenge for them, and made all the more so by the elders wanting a full account of everyone's movements. To the great surprise of many of the newcomers, the fact that there had never been a child born to an untied female was virtually unbelievable, and that there had never been a quick, or a forced, tying either, that there were, and had never been, any secret affairs going on, was equally surprising. Until one remembered the ever-present company! Even the concept of a hurried, a super-quick or a forced Tying, was mystifying to the Edeners. All these beautiful women, and the gorgeous young men, walking around is simple sarongs, and swimming naked in mixed groups - just thinking about it was enough to raise your temperature and set your pulse into overdrive. Once again Elder Ruth came to the rescue with the rationale for their absolute fidelity.

"Since our community is born, raised and schooled together, you must also be mindful that we eat, sleep, play, swim and grow together, every moment from birth to the time we are once again called to become as one with the gardens, each person knows all there is to know about each, and every other Edener, so there is no interest of a carnal nature, until we, the High Council suggest it is time for this man, and that woman, whom we consider sufficiently well suited, to undergo sensual instruction together to help them see each other, not only as a neighbour and childhood friend, but as a possible life partner. Although as for the sanctified act - *that* is very strictly reserved for tied couples only – the instructors will not permit it under any circumstance. At all times the final decision whether to Tie, or not to Tie, rests entirely with the individual couple... We of the High Council always abide by their wishes."

"What about falling in love Elder Ruth? Don't two people ever fall helplessly in love here?"

Love? Love? This Love you speak of is a perplexing concept for the children of Eden; we have no real understanding of it. In the journals of our Most Revered Elder Sara, she tells of the great and enduring love of many of our Most Revered Elders, I give you the example of our Most Revered Elders Kristy and Mark, she writes of their love and devotion often, and there are almost innumerable drawings of them and their children and grandchildren throughout the colonnade – and my, weren't they a handsome couple too! Have you noticed the similarities in the features here in Eden? If you look closely, you can see who sired each of these people from the colonnade drawings, beautiful, hmm beautiful, although for all of their descendents today, it has become a word without substance, a word of unknown value if you will. Is there an understanding of it in your previous time and place? We have vast knowledge of a great many things that grow or live, or fly, or swim, but this word love, is simply an old-time word to us, and so it is unused." "Elder Ruth, from what I've known, I think you would understand true love as being the ultimate form of respect between a man and a woman, and what a parent feels for their child."

Elder Ruth went quiet for a moment as though she was trying to recall something.

"Ahh yes," Elder Ruth picked up the thread of her thoughts again, "In the Most Revered Elder Sara's journals, she wrote that she loved Tyler with her whole heart and soul. The whereabouts of a heart we know well, but where is a soul? Is that something of which you have knowledge?" "It's something I know nothing about, in my previous life I have not heard that word, to my knowledge it has never been used but oh, Mother Ruth...the things I could tell you about love! About being in love! It's the most wonderfully amazing feeling! If you would like, one day when you have time, we can speak about Love in some of its many, and glorious forms. OH! OH! I do beg your pardon; I should say Elder Ruth shouldn't I!" Giggled Nicky. Elder Ruth looked through her gentle watery blue eyes at the young woman who was almost an exact replica of herself as she once was, her hair, once so dark and gleaming in the sunlight, was now the purest silver white, and her body, once so strong, so straight and tall, was now bent with age, and as she held her hands out before her, she recalled the beautiful long straight fingers she once had, not these shaking wrinkled old hands that were hers today. The old woman's' eyes glazed over with that far away look; she seemed to be looking backwards through time. The dear old lady was becoming a little more muddled each day now. Whenever she looked at Nicky she was seeing instead, a much younger version of herself, often recalling her own carefree youth, mistakenly thinking Nicky's own delicate features were so similar to hers also, the same blue-black hair, and wistfully remembering the sharp sighted deep blue eyes she once had, but then she would remember that Nicky is a whole living breathing other person from another place, and not the ghost of her own youth. Ruth smiled and said aloud, to no one in particular "and she's so vibrant! In fact, she's everything I once was myself!" She turned her gaze once again and said "Do you know Nicky; I do believe I took pleasure from you calling me Mother Ruth! It was...satisfying, yes definitely satisfying. You may address me as Mother Ruth if you would so wish. Yes, being your mother is most satisfying." The darling woman's mind wandered off again along one of its many pleasant corridors, leaving her students sitting quietly on a nice warm rock step and talking quietly amongst themselves, until her mind wandered back to where they were waiting patiently for her to continue with their instruction.

There was no hurry, that is the true beauty of Eden, life happens when it's ready, and never because some clock on a wall says it's time.

 Therefore, the day's weeks and months marched on, merging gently one into another. Many young couples formed, and some even found the enigmatic love, but even they found that they couldn't explain the feeling adequately either! Others settled down quietly, content to become friends, with definite visions of their shared future.

The young men, once so fearful of remaining untied for life, were spoiled for choice now that the women were established and fast becoming true assets to their new community.

Alder and Sámi Kayla were Tied in an especially touching ceremony, and moved into their own, newly developed suite of caves above the kitchen, where they were the first to see the morning sun, and where the afternoon sunlight warmed their caves in the evenings. Very soon Alder had to carve wider steps for his precious Sámi; being heavily pregnant she found it difficult to see where she was placing her feet!

The Eden games had some hot new contestants this cycle, and they were surprisingly good! The fiery maned Ashleigh was the first newcomer to win the archery contest, making her betrothed, Cain, a very delighted man indeed. Claire showed off with her gold medal winning diving prowess and promised to teach the younger ones her skills. Dejong and Jacob have formally requested a Tying ceremony as well,

His mother Ravenna is simply overjoyed that her son is so very happy and looking toward settling down, he says he's had more than enough adventure now, and that he never wants to set foot in the Outlands ever again.

Sámi and Alder are the joyful parents of triplets! They have two daughters and a son, Faith, Bella and Lachlan. Motherhood came as naturally as breathing to Sámi, and Alder, who was always a very attentive husband has become a wonderful, devoted father, who is now never seen without at least one, and most often all three of his children in tow!

Sámi tried, she really did, she tried incredibly hard, but in the end, she failed miserably at her attempts at pottery, however she has found that her placid nature and her medical knowledge is such a huge bonus to her new home, because the only medical understanding they had, had been passed down by word of mouth and was hundreds of years out of date! Nevertheless, in the eyes of every Edener, Sámi Kayla-Tyler could do no wrong. She had single handily saved their home, and secured their future for many generations to come. Sámi didn't need to do anything else – because in the eyes of each and every Edener - she was perfect.

However, with all the new crops growing from her gifts of a profuse assortment of many different seeds, and a great deal of input from all the newcomers, she did introduce many new, and delicious dishes to the tables. Bread, cakes and fruity pancakes were the first choices made from the wheat flour, and then she introduced them to pasta! Although she was quite aware that some of the new, and much heavier foods couldn't be on the menu regularly, the cooks were delighted to find that pasta, like rice, could be dried and stored to be cooked on another day.

The First area has been reopened, and redeveloped for regular use and sectioned off, the animals have been moved to the lower section near the closed entrance, the sports arena holds centre stage now that new fields have been planted with the wheat, barley, maize and corn, there is also a small, but very pretty orchard growing peach, plum and apple trees, grown from the hydroponic gift plants, they also introduced tomatoes, potatoes and beans, all brought in with Sámi Kayla and the newcomers.

There has been much talk among the men of continuing with the tunnel through the far rock wall that leads into the next area, it will take almost another full cycle to complete, however with the population growing so rapidly now, more space would be a blessing for everyone, and then there was the ever-growing population to feed, so new gardens...

Looking out over the top of the canyon walls there is still nothing much to see, except a vast wasteland of stunted coarse grass. No birds or animals can survive the heat out there, it's as though nature is determined to keep Eden her own secret, her beautiful, her perfect secret, hidden away from the ugliness of the civilised world.

The peaceful village of Eden and its three hundred and eleven inhabitants has remained, by choice, virtually unchanged in its wholesome simplicity for four hundred and twenty-eight cycles, whereas the world so far beyond their boundaries continues to make bad choices, and dramatic changes almost hourly, often out of selfishness or desperation, and those changes are seldom for the betterment, or for the benefit, of all mankind.

I suspect that mankind is still waiting for the elusive miracle.

I also suspect that mankind as a whole, is very unhappy with life, with the criminal activities, the constant wars, the infinite numbers of their young breeding men and women going off to war, fighting and dying senselessly, when the answer the whole world is searching for is simple, perhaps far too simple for them to recognise. The world beyond The Outlands really needs to learn and to understand the only cure that will save and heal their world is to teach…